Monogamy

I Found My Heart in San Francisco
San Francisco
Book Thirteen

Susan X Meagher

Monogamy

I Found My Heart In San Francisco: Book Thirteen

© 2012 BY SUSAN X MEAGHER

ISBN (10) 09832758-5-8
ISBN (13) 978-0-9832758-5-5

THIS TRADE PAPERBACK ORIGINAL IS PUBLISHED BY BRISK PRESS, BRIELLE, NJ 08730

FIRST PRINTING: October 2012

By Susan X Meagher

Novels
Arbor Vitae
All That Matters
Cherry Grove
Girl Meets Girl
The Lies That Bind
The Legacy
Doublecrossed
Smooth Sailing
How To Wrangle a Woman
Almost Heaven

Serial Novel
I Found My Heart In San Francisco
Awakenings
Beginnings
Coalescence
Disclosures
Entwined
Fidelity
Getaway
Honesty
Intentions
Journeys
Karma
Lifeline
Monogamy

Anthologies
Undercover Tales
Outsiders

To purchase these books go to
www.briskpress.com

Dedication

To Jamie and Ryan's patient, faithful fans. Without your
avid interest, they'd just be talking to themselves.

Chapter One

The first faint hint of dawn crept into the slightly chilled room, and with it, a bright blue eye cracked open, shifting around to orient the fuzzy mind of the owner. The eye closed; having recognized the approaching dawn, its task was complete.

The tall, lean woman was lying on her left side, and a substantial weight was pressed heavily against her back. Her right leg was drawn up towards her chest, and another leg was plastered to her own, mirroring her pose. She could feel skin, and a tuft of springy curls tickled her ass when she twitched it slightly, so she knew she was bare from the waist down.

A warm hand gently held her breast, and her heart beat against the soft skin of her lover's palm.

Her ears got into the game then, picking up the slow, steady sound of Jamie's breathing. Judging by the volume, she guessed that they shared a pillow, one of her partner's favorite morning habits.

Then her nose performed its duties, and her mouth twitched into a slow smile when she filled her lungs with the lingering musk of their lovemaking. *That was clearly not a dream.* A sense of relief mingled with pride filled her, and she let the pleasure from that discovery linger for a few moments.

Only one sense remained, and for unassailable proof of the previous evening's activities, she held her hand under her nose, then licked the tips of her fingers, grinning broadly when she tasted the unmistakable essence of her partner. "Nice," she purred, not even realizing she'd said the word aloud.

"What's nice?" a soft, raspy voice whispered into her ear.

"Waking up like this. Feeling so close to you...feeling so well loved... having you hold me like this. It's incredibly nice." She shifted out of Jamie's hold and lay on her back, snaking an arm around her partner. "Thank you."

Jamie placed a kiss on her chest, then nuzzled her slightly cold nose against warm skin. "You're welcome. The pleasure was equally mine."

"I guess that's true, isn't it?" Ryan dipped her head and gently kissed the pink lips, tasting herself on her partner. "You had me in every way imaginable."

"Not true. I've concocted lots more ways in my little head to have you."

"I eagerly anticipate being on the receiving end of that quest."

There was a slight pause, then Jamie hesitantly asked, "Really?"

"Really." Ryan hugged her tightly. "You helped me break through my fears last night, sweetheart. I think we're gonna be fine."

"Hey, now," Jamie began, soothingly stroking her partner's belly as she spoke. "Don't push yourself too hard. If we have trouble again, or if you need to go slow or change anything that we do, it's okay with me…"

Mid-statement, a pair of warm lips cut off her words. After kissing her thoroughly, Ryan said, "I don't need to go slow. We've got a lot of time to make up for." She hugged her again. "This is like falling off a horse. The best cure for your fears is to get on her back and ride her."

"With pleasure." Pulling Ryan's arm from around her neck, Jamie rolled her over and sat astride her ass, hips thrusting lasciviously. "I'll ride you all day."

"You've gotta love a woman who takes you literally," Ryan purred, not caring if her riding lesson made her miss an entire day of school.

🐴

Jamie only had time for a quick ride, and, much to Ryan's amazement, she scampered out of bed just minutes after her usual wake-up time. Ryan wasn't usually so completely enervated by early morning lovemaking, but Jamie had managed to rock her world thoroughly, and before she knew it she was out like a light.

Waking at seven, Ryan stretched and rolled around the bed like a big cat, twitching her body into a multitude of contortions to get the kinks out. *My God, Jamie nearly loved me senseless. Ooo, but what a way to go.* She linked her fingers and stretched her arms straight up over her head. *I'd love to wake up exactly this way every day for the rest of my life.* She lay quietly for a few minutes, the thought of having Jamie right by her side for all of her days making her hum with pleasure. *Every day for the rest of my life.*

Suddenly, she sat up in bed, thoroughly bedazzled. *What in the hell are we waiting for? We talk about having a commitment ceremony—of publicly declaring how we feel about each other—why haven't we done it? Good, God, we almost died during the carjacking—and if that taught me anything, it taught me that every day is precious. I want to—I need to—show Jamie how precious she is to me. I want to marry her in front of everyone we know—and to give her a ring that she can look at every day for the rest of her life and know that I love her with all my heart. I can't waste another minute!*

🐴

Minutes after she had made her decision, Ryan paced in front of a buff-colored telephone, which rested on a small, wooden table near the front door of her home. She had been pacing for quite a few minutes, and was no closer to picking up the phone and dialing than she had been when she had begun.

There was no good reason to use the land line. She rarely touched it, and they only kept it because it was bundled with their Internet service. But making such an important call seemed to require a secure line that wouldn't drop at an inopportune moment.

Still, she dallied. *This is silly*, she reminded herself. *There's nothing to be nervous about. You're only being polite, and you know it. His opinion means little at this point.* Her mouth curled into a smirk as she looked down at her roiling stomach and said aloud, "Hear that? The brain is telling you to calm down. Don't you realize the brain is in control around here?"

Okay, now I'm talking to individual body parts. Not a good sign...

Decisively, she picked up the phone and dialed the long series of digits. "Senator Evans' office, this is Margaret Aimes. May I help you?"

"Hi, this is Ryan O'Flaherty. I'd like to speak to Senator Evans if he's available."

"Ryan O'Flaherty," the woman repeated, pleasing Ryan by getting the pronunciation correct. "I'll see if he's available, Ms. O'Flaherty."

She waited just a moment before his voice came on the line, sounding slightly agitated. "Ryan? Is anything wrong?"

"No, not at all, Jim," she said, acknowledging to herself that a call from her was a pretty rare occurrence. "I have a couple of things to ask you, if now's a good time."

"Yes, it's fine. What's on your mind?"

Avoiding the more difficult issue, she chose the easy one. "I wanted to make sure you're still planning on coming to Jamie's birthday party. I'm trying to get a final count."

"Of course I am. That uhm...does bring up one issue, though, so I'm glad you called. I uhm...know you'll tell me the truth."

"Sure. What is it?"

"I was going to bring Kayla with me. Do you think that will present a problem?"

"Kayla, huh?" She let the question rumble around in her mind for a moment.

"Catherine claims that she doesn't mind if I start to see her again," he said, obviously trying to convince her.

"Jim, I don't have an opinion about who you date. I'm only trying to consider how it will affect Jamie. I know you don't want to make her uncomfortable on her birthday."

"Of course not, that's why I asked."

She spent a moment thinking of the dynamics of the group that would be at the party, and she answered him as honestly as she could. "I can't imagine that it won't make Catherine uncomfortable, no matter what she says. If Catherine is uncomfortable, that might make Jamie uncomfortable, too. But, she claims that she wants you both to move on—so I imagine she'll do her best to get over her discomfort."

He sighed and said, "That's what I thought."

"Let's be honest. Jamie would prefer that you and Catherine were still together, but since that can't be, she's actively trying to get used to the fact that you're both free now."

"I'll call Catherine and ask her directly," he said. "I wouldn't press this, but I'm in kind of a bind here. Kayla's going to be with me for some meetings on Thursday and Friday, and I don't want to exclude her from the party if I don't have to."

"Well, I'm sure Catherine would appreciate the 'heads up,' if nothing else."

"Right." Letting out a breath, he asked, "What else did you want to talk about?"

Her mouth was suddenly very dry, and she wished she'd brought a glass of water into the living room. Clearing her throat, she forced herself to say, "Circumstances didn't allow me to do this in April of last year, even though I wish that I could have."

"Go on," he said warily.

"As you know, we've had a rough month. One thing the carjacking reinforced for me was the fact that life can be short, and it's best not to put off doing the things that are important to you."

"Yes…?"

"One thing that we've been putting off is having a formal commitment ceremony to celebrate our union. We both very much want to do this, and have from the beginning, but we'd agreed to hold off until everyone we loved was willing to celebrate with us." She took in a breath and added, "Up until now, you were the only hold-out. But, it seems that things have been going well between us for a while now, and I hope that you'll agree to not only come to the ceremony, but to participate in it."

Silence came from Jim's end of the phone line, but Ryan let it go on, knowing that it would take him a while to get used to the idea. "Why didn't Jamie call to ask me?"

"She doesn't know I'm planning this. I want to give her a ring for her birthday, but I don't want to even bring up the topic if you're unwilling to attend. We're only going to do this once, and I know she'll always regret it if you don't share this with her."

Ryan could hear him exhale sharply, and heard a slight squeaking as he probably rocked in his desk chair. "You'd wait until I was ready to do this?" he asked quietly.

"That's the only reason we didn't do it originally. Ideally, we would have had a ceremony before we moved in together, but that wasn't possible."

"I suppose not." He was quiet for a minute and finally asked, "Did you predict I'd be so opposed to your relationship?"

She paused for a moment and tried to recall how she'd felt before they spoke to Jim and Catherine about their love. "No, I didn't. I actually thought Catherine would have the harder time with it. So did Jamie," she added quietly. "She was sure you'd be behind her."

"She's always given me too much credit," he muttered. With his voice at normal volume, he said, "I'll be there for her this time."

"That's great to hear, Jim. Jamie will be very pleased." A moment passed, and she added, "I'm pleased, too. Having both of our families there will mean a lot to both of us."

"Uhm…forgive my being dense, but this feels like you're asking for my daughter's hand in marriage. Given all of the recent tumult about gay marriage in California, I know that's not possible."

Ryan gritted her teeth slightly, her anger over the statewide ballot proposition prohibiting gay marriage very much on her mind. "No, not technically," she said. "We're going to ask your father to perform the ceremony, of course, so it has religious significance, but it has no legal import."

"I see," he mused. "But you're not an Episcopalian. Will the ceremony satisfy your needs?"

She chuckled mildly and said, "There will be a long wait before my church comes out of the Dark Ages to acknowledge same-sex relationships. Besides, I don't think God belongs to any particular denomination. To be honest, what matters are the vows we've already made to each other—it doesn't matter who blesses us if we don't honor those."

He was quiet for a moment, and she realized he might think her comments were aimed directly at him. "Ahh…that's what I thought. Well, I'm sure it will mean a great deal to you both, even without the state's recognition."

"It will. We pledged our love to each other before we…moved in together," she said, deciding not to mention that it was actually right before they made love for the first time. "This is an occasion to repeat those vows in front of our families and friends. It's a lot more formal and a lot more public, but the meaning is the same."

"I see. Now, you say you're going to do this for Jamie's birthday, correct?"

"Yes, that's right."

"Good. I won't say a thing when I talk to her."

"Thanks, Jim. I really appreciate that you're being supportive of something that I know you don't approve of."

"I approve of my daughter—and her choices," he said quietly. "I've come to learn that being supportive of her is sometimes difficult…but always rewarding. Besides," he added, laughing softly, "you're pretty easy to like."

"I suppose I have my charms," she said, joining him in the laugh.

Less than an hour later, Jim picked up his private office line to hear his daughter's cheerful voice on the other end. "Hi, Daddy. Have you got a few minutes?"

"Sure, Jamie," he said absently as he made a note to mark his place in a document he was reviewing. "Funny that you should call today. I just talked to Ryan." The words were out of his mouth before he realized what he was saying.

"Pardon?" she asked. "Why did Ryan call?"

"Oh! Well, she wanted to make sure I was still planning on coming to your party," he explained, hoping she'd buy it.

"Odd…the O'Flahertys never care how many people show up. Oh, well. I hope your answer was yes."

"I wouldn't miss it for the world. Now, why did you call? Same reason?"

"No, I want to bring up a subject that might be a little difficult for you to come to terms with, Dad, but it's something that's important to me."

"Okay, what is it?"

She let out an audible breath. "Ryan and I both want to have a celebration of our commitment to each other, and I'd love to have your approval."

Good Lord! These two really do belong together! They even think alike! "Yes, go on, Jamie," he said, feeling grateful that Ryan had prepared him already.

"We've wanted to do this ever since we became a couple, but…well, things didn't quite work out that way."

"That's putting it mildly."

"Yes, well, I was playing golf this morning, and something hit me, Daddy. None of us knows how long we're going to have on earth, so it seems wasteful to delay doing the things that mean the most to us. Nothing is more important to me than showing everyone the place Ryan holds in my heart," she said quietly, her voice catching with emotion. "We wanted to do this earlier, but it was obvious that you wouldn't have participated then. I want you to be a part of our ceremony. It would make me very, very happy. But whether or not you're able to support us—we need to make our plans. I can't wait any longer to do something this important."

"I'll be there, Jamie," he said, the emotion welling up inside of him. "You can count on me."

"Really?" she asked with a voice that reminded him of when she was a small child. "You're okay with this?"

"I think it's a wonderful thing, and I'm touched that you gave me some time to come around. I know how hard that must have been for you," he added, his voice heavy with regret over his actions.

"I wish you were here right now. I'd give you the biggest hug you've ever had!"

Leaning back in his chair and gazing at the ceiling with unseeing eyes, he let the warmth and love that filled her voice wash over him. "Not many children would be able to forgive the things I've done. I'm eternally grateful that you're an extraordinary woman, Jamie. I mean that in every sense of the word."

🐉

Standing right outside of the locker room at Levine-Fricke Field, Ryan adjusted her baseball cap to keep the sun from her eyes and called Catherine. "Hi, there," she said, long past the point of having to identify herself even when she called on Catherine's home line which didn't have caller ID.

"Hi, Ryan. How goes it?"

"Good. Very good, as a matter of fact. But I have a favor to ask."

"Anything in my power, Ryan. All you need do is ask."

"Okay." She sucked in a breath. "I'd like to borrow your daughter for, oh… I'd say, the rest of her life. Is that okay?"

Catherine's amused chuckle soothed the slight bit of anxiety that had been building up in Ryan all afternoon. "You want to know if Jamie can come over to play for seventy or eighty years?"

"Well, that's a fairly modest goal. I'm hoping to squeeze an even hundred out of her. She's got very good genes."

"I can't think of anyone I'd rather entrust her to, Ryan. But now that that's been established, can you tell me what you're getting at?"

She laughed softly and said, "I think it's about time we made honest women out of each other. I'd like to have our long-delayed commitment ceremony, if you approve, of course."

"Oh, Ryan," she sighed, "of course I approve! I'm wholeheartedly in favor of it." She paused for a moment and asked, "If you don't mind sharing, could I ask why you've decided to do this now?"

Ryan cleared her throat, not having prepared herself for the question. She surprised herself by speaking straight from her heart. "Because I love her so much it makes me ache," she said softly. "She's the most important person in my life, and I want my creator and everyone I know to hear me pledge my life to her."

Catherine was quiet for a moment, then asked, "Do you speak like that to her?"

"I do," Ryan said, just a little embarrassed about being so open. "I try to tell her every day how much I love her."

"She's a lucky woman. And so are you. She loves you with all of her heart, Ryan."

"I know. And as much as you try to avoid taking credit, part of her ability to love comes from you, and I'm very thankful to you for giving her that."

"We weren't always the best parents, but we both tried to show her that we loved her—even though I know she didn't always feel what I tried to convey."

"More got in than you realize," Ryan said.

"I hope so. You know I support you both completely. The question remains about Jim though, doesn't it?"

"Surprisingly not," Ryan said, the bright tone of her voice telegraphing her news. "I spoke to him earlier today, and he's agreed not only to come, but to participate. He was very gracious, Catherine," she insisted, still surprised, but very pleased.

"Well, I give you credit for having the nerve to ask, and I give him credit for the progress he's made. This is very good news."

"I certainly think so. Now all I have to do is buy Jamie a ring as special as she is, and I'm good to go."

"You should know there's no such thing," she teased. "But I might be able to lead you to a place that can help you to come close. What's a good time for you?"

"How about Thursday morning? I've got a few hours then."

"That would be great. Call me on Thursday morning and we'll arrange to meet."

🐉

"Charlie? It's Ryan," she said as she reached the last key player.

"Well, hello, Ryan. To what do I owe the honor?"

"How would you feel about blessing Jamie and my commitment to each other?"

"I'd feel great about it, Ryan! Just great!" *Are these two sharing a brain? I haven't been off the phone for ten minutes from Jamie asking me the same question. And she used practically the same words!*

🐉

Jamie had to rush, but she managed to arrive at Levine-Fricke Field in time to watch the last half hour of her partner's first softball practice. She was a little surprised to see Jennie standing over on the grassy shoulder of the field, playfully tossing a ball with Ashley, Ryan's volleyball teammate. Both of them waved at Jamie, and Jennie came running over, giving her an enthusiastic hug. "Ashley's gonna go over my homework with me while we watch practice," she gushed.

"That's great, Jen," Jamie said. She walked the girl back to Ashley and shared a hug with the freshman. "How does Heather feel about starting a new sport?"

"Good, I think. She's a little nervous, since she doesn't know many people." She grinned at Jamie and said, "I think having Ryan here made all the difference."

Jamie patted her on the back and said, "I think having Heather play pushed Ryan over the edge, too."

Ashley blinked at her and her mouth gaped open. "Really? I...uhm... really?"

"Yeah," Jamie said, smiling brightly, reminding herself that the freshmen from the volleyball team considered Ryan to be slightly god-like. "She wanted to have a friend on the team. She likes Heather...and you, of course."

Ashley beamed a luminous grin at her. "Ryan's the best. She and Jordan made this the best year I've ever had playing volleyball. I know she's gonna have the same kind of impact here."

"I sure hope so," Jamie said, her worry evident. "She sure didn't make much of an impact on the basketball team."

"I don't know what that coach's problem was," Ashley said, shaking her head. "Ryan could have lifted that team into the top three in the PAC-10."

Jamie nodded. "It was a complicated team, and I'm really glad she's off of it."

Ashley shot a look at her young friend and said, "We'd better start looking at your schoolwork, Jen. It's starting to get dark."

Jamie looked at her watch. "Those are some nasty looking storm clouds. It's only four thirty. It shouldn't be nearly this dark yet."

Smiling, Ashley said, "Good thing the bleachers are wood, huh?" She and Jennie went up into the stands to have some quiet time, but Jamie stayed close to the field, wanting to closely observe her partner. She noted that most of the players were wearing sweats, and a few had on jackets over their sweats. Yet, there was Ryan, wearing only a pair of navy blue Lycra shorts, with a small Cal bear near the hem of one leg, and a bright gold T-shirt with "Cal Softball" imprinted on the chest.

Looking around, Jamie spent a moment checking out the other players. She recognized Heather, of course, and she remembered Michelle, the woman that Ryan had worked out with, but no one else looked familiar. Her perusal led her to decide that these women looked more like average women than either the volleyball or the basketball players. They were mostly average height and weight, and even though they looked fit, their bodies didn't scream "jock." Ryan was, of course, the exception, and stood out on many fronts.

Ryan was the tallest woman on the field, topping Heather by a few inches, and most of the other woman by a lot. Jamie noted that one woman looked to be less than five feet tall, and when Ryan stood next to her, the top of her head didn't quite reach Ryan's breasts. *I like her view, but I wouldn't like having to stand on a step stool to kiss my sweetie.*

As the minutes passed, the wind picked up until it was blowing fiercely. Jamie had thought she was dressed warmly enough, but after a few minutes of sitting still she was chilled to the bone. *Ryan's in shorts and a T-shirt? I wonder if I'd embarrass her if I took off my jacket and made her put it on?* She entertained the idea for only a second, recognizing that Ryan would rather freeze than be embarrassed in front of her teammates. *Besides, she's probably not even cold,* she reasoned. *She hasn't stood still once since I've been here.*

A light drizzle began to fall, and Jamie climbed the stands to join her friends. "I'm taking off. How about you two?"

"I have my bike," Jennie said. "I don't mind riding in the rain." Jamie gave her an assessing look and immediately removed her Gore-Tex jacket and handed it to over. "Put this on, Jen. You'll freeze to death once your sweatshirt gets wet."

"I'm really oka…" she started to say, but Jamie tapped her on the head and said, "Humor me."

"I'm gonna wait for Heather," Ashley said. "They'll stop soon."

"Okay, guys. Tell Ryan I'll see her at home, okay? Tell her not to rush."

"Later, Jamie," Jennie waved. "See you tomorrow?"

"Maybe," Jamie said, unwilling to commit until she got a look at the weather. "I'll see you at some point in the next few days. We've gotta keep our girls motivated, huh?"

"Right," Ashley said. "They don't have much of a rooting section."

Jamie looked around at the completely empty stands and said, "Maybe it'll fill up a little when the games start, huh?"

"Couldn't help it," Ashley said as Jamie waved goodbye. She carefully climbed down the now-slick stands, feeling colder by the minute as she got wetter and wetter. She ran as fast as she could, darting into buildings whenever possible, finally arriving at the student store, where she purchased a rain jacket in a woman's extra-large, knowing that Ryan could always use a spare.

When Ryan came home an hour and a half later, Jamie walked into the living room as soon as she heard the door close. She stood with her arms crossed; a scowl on her face, watching the rain drip from Ryan's thoroughly drenched body. She had on a pair of jeans and a hooded sweatshirt, both of which were utterly sodden.

"Did it look like rain when you left the house?" Jamie asked, narrowing her eyes dangerously—slapping the wooden spoon she held in one hand against the palm of the other.

"Mmm…not really," Ryan said, stretching the truth to dangerous limits.

"It looked like rain when I left this morning," she said, the spoon cracking sharply as she continued to whap it against her hand. "Did it clear up on just this side of Berkeley?"

"Uhm…no?" Ryan's blue lips twitched into a guilty smile.

"Good answer. I'll go a little easier on you for not lying." She came up behind her partner and said, "Take off your pants and your sweatshirt. I don't want you dripping all over the wooden floor."

Ryan kicked off her shoes, which squished audibly as she did so. Next came the jeans, which she had more than a little trouble peeling off, due to their water content. The sweatshirt was easy, and she breathed a sigh of relief as the wet, heavy garment hit the floor. "Cold," she said needlessly, her hands chafing her bright pink arms as she hopped back and forth from one foot to the other.

"I want you to go upstairs and get into the shower. Stay there until you're warm," Jamie ordered. "Dinner's ready, but it can wait until you've warmed up."

"You're so sweet to me," Ryan cooed as she bent over to press her ice-cold lips to her partner's. "Trying your best to keep me nice and warm."

"Oh, I'm not done," Jamie said. "I'm gonna heat up another part of you, right now." She cracked her partner across the buttocks with the spoon, laughing evilly as Ryan's hands shot to her butt to protect it.

Even her large hands couldn't protect everything, and Jamie got in a few more sharp slaps. Clearly realizing she was allowing herself to be vulnerable by remaining in place, Ryan took off, running for the stairs with Jamie right on her heels slapping at her wet bikinis as she gave chase. They made such a ruckus that Mia popped her head out of her room as they came thundering down the hall. She stood in her doorway, arms crossed over her chest, smirking widely. "I always knew there was a dominatrix in there waiting to get out."

"Help me, Mia!" Ryan cried, running behind their roommate and trying to use her as a shield.

"Jamie," her old friend soothed, "violence isn't the answer. Come on…give me the spoon."

Jamie gave her partner a narrowed glance, but complied. Ryan gave Mia a hug for being such a good protector, but her chilled skin made the smaller woman squawk. "Jesus! Have you been in the freezer?"

"She's trying to catch pneumonia," Jamie complained. "She practiced in a T-shirt and shorts, then came home in the driving rain in a sweatshirt and jeans." A further narrowing of her gaze accompanied the rest of her comment. "It's not like you don't have proper rain gear. We bought it for you after the last such incident."

"I have to take it somewhere to get the bullet hole sewed up," Ryan said.

Turning to the miscreant, Mia shook her head and said, "I think you can afford a new jacket. That's a ridiculous excuse." She gave her another swat, snapping the spoon much harder than Jamie had. "Get in the shower and warm up, or there's more where that came from."

"What is it with you Hillsborough girls?" Ryan cried as she covered her stinging butt with her hands and ran into the bath. "Bunch of sadists," she grumbled as the door closed on the laughing friends.

"What ever are you going to do with her?" Mia asked, smiling sympathetically at her friend.

"Everyone on that field had on sweats today...but not my Buffy. She thinks it's a sign of weakness to stay warm and dry."

Mia shook her head. "My Jordy has the jock gene, but she doesn't have the 'I'm tougher than you' gene. You have my sympathies."

"Please don't say that it's a gene. Then she might pass it down to our kids."

"Tough break, babe," Mia said. "I think you'll have a bunch of kids just like her. You'd better stock up on wooden spoons, 'cause you're gonna break a few on those cute little O'Flaherty asses."

Jamie went into the bathroom while Ryan was still in the shower. The room was steamy, and she could tell by the way her partner moved that she was nice and warm now. Ryan turned around and placed her butt up against the glass door, showing Jamie the bright pink stripes that crisscrossed her cheeks. "You do good work," she said, a wry tone to her voice. "You can take my Granny's place as the enforcer in the family when she can't carry the load any longer."

Jamie winced when she considered that Ryan might not see the humor in being spanked, even though she'd meant it as a joke. As Ryan turned off the water, Jamie handed her a towel, and then took another and rubbed her back briskly. Kissing her warm, damp skin, she said, "I apologize for hitting you. I was only teasing, but it probably didn't seem like that to you. It was particularly insensitive of me to make a joke of spanking you. I don't want to bring back bad memories."

"It's okay," Ryan said, giving her a big smile. "I don't mind when you do it. As a matter of fact, it's kinda…kinda hot."

Letting her hand drift lower, Jamie smiled back and said, "Oh, you're hot, all right. You're positively sizzling back here." Her hand caressed the warm skin, gingerly touching the fading pink stripes. "Does it hurt?"

"No. It marked up more because of my wet underwear. Wet skin makes it smart a lot more. It just tingles a little now. If you haven't spanked anyone before, you don't realize how hard to do it."

"I've never spanked anyone before, and I won't do it again," Jamie said. She gave her partner a sexy grin and added, "Unless you ask me to, of course."

"We'll see. I'm not sure I want to go there."

"No rush to decide. We have time."

"I'm as hungry as a wolf," Ryan said. "Can we eat?"

"Go put on your warm clothes. I want some form of fleece on every square inch."

"Yes, Mom," Ryan said as she gave Jamie a playful tap on the butt. She smiled as she added a kiss. "You might like a little swat once in a while, too. Tingling in that area can be a good thing."

"No thanks," Jamie said firmly, shaking her head. "I don't have a butt fetish like you do."

Ryan started to object, but realized that she did have more than a casual interest in both her own, and other's butts, so she shrugged her shoulders and went to follow orders.

After thoroughly encasing herself in fleece, Ryan joined her partner and Mia at the dinner table. "How's your ass?" Mia asked, giving her a leer.

"Excellent," Ryan purred, dropping her voice an octave and intentionally trying to be provocative. "How's yours?"

"You'd better watch it, buddy. If she spanks you like that for getting wet, imagine what she'd do to you if you checked out my butt."

"The mind reels," Ryan said, her eyes round with imagined fear.

"Knock it off you two. I wanna hear all about Ryan's first day." Jamie turned to smile at her partner and asked, "Were the other girls nice to you?"

"Yes," Ryan said, a playful grin on her face. "I'm glad I hung around for a while. I found out that they've already got a nickname for me."

"Ooo…let me guess," Mia said.

"You won't get this one," Ryan said. "They've been calling me Notorious R.O.F. because I was in the paper so much. It seems that Coach Roberts informed them that I might join the team, and their interest in my celebrity was piqued."

"I loved Notorious B.I.G.," Mia sighed. "Biggie came correct."

Ryan smiled at her, always amused when Mia spoke of her deep love of rap and hip-hop music. The art form had always eluded Ryan, but she assumed that was because she hadn't gotten in on the ground floor. She had developed her musical tastes from her much older cousin and her mother's old records, which were still stored in boxes in her closet, and had never had an interest in exploring the developing genre when she was young. Mia was a true fan, though, and she knew most of the performers and could imitate some of her favorites to near-perfection.

"I want a rap nickname," Jamie said, grinning.

"You've already got a porn name all picked out if you ever shed your good girl image," Ryan reminded her. "Isn't that enough?"

"Tell! Tell!" Mia begged as Jamie jumped up and tried to muzzle Ryan with her hand.

After being spanked, Ryan was in no mood to go easy on her partner, and she grasped both of Jamie's hands while she choked out, "Cinna Bunz! Her name's Cinna Bunz, 'cause they're so sweet and tasty!"

Mia laughed long and hard at that one, as much at the outraged look on Jamie's face as the nickname. "That's awesome, Ryan. Just awesome."

"Well deserved," Ryan insisted as she grabbed a handful of the sweet cheeks and gave them a squeeze.

"Ryan's is Randy Libido," Jamie revealed, joining in the laughter.

"I want one," Mia pouted.

"You've gotta have Jordan pick it out for you," Jamie said. "It doesn't work if you self-name. It's an honorific."

"I'll get on it tonight," Mia said. "It's my turn to call her, so I can keep her on the phone as long as I like."

"Your portion of the phone bill was obscene last month," Jamie reminded her. "Your dad's gonna wonder what's going on with you."

"Nah…he never seems to care what the bills are. He just hates it when I spend a lot on clothes and stuff."

"Okay," Jamie warned, "but you'd better have a good excuse if he asks why you have a three hundred dollar bill—all to Colorado Springs."

"One more indication of why you're not a good liar," Mia insisted. "All of the naturals lie best when it's extemporaneous." Mia looked at Ryan and sighed as she said, "She'll never be good at it."

"My loss," Ryan said, patting Mia on the hand sympathetically.

"So, sweet cheeks," Jamie said when Mia got up to clear the table, "tell me how you feel about your new team."

Ryan sighed and stretched a bit, getting some of the kinks out of her shoulders. "I like softball. It has a different energy from the other sports I play. It's kinda slow, and the action is sporadic, but you have to be mentally ready, and your reflexes have to be really sharp."

"I know yours are," Jamie said, smiling sweetly.

"Yes, well," Ryan sniffed, tossing her dark hair over her shoulder. "I think softball is the perfect sport for me right now. I'm still toast emotionally, as you might have noticed, and it feels good to join a team that's already established. I'm not the only senior…they went to the College World Series last year, so they've got a strong nucleus…they're not looking for me to make a big contribution. I can relax and enjoy myself."

"I didn't know that they were that good. I must have been otherwise occupied last spring. I don't remember a thing that happened around campus."

"It's all a blur to me, too," Ryan said. "I only remember trying to find out where a certain blonde was at every possible moment, and keeping my lips on her when I caught her."

"Same problem," Jamie said, as though just having the memory hit her. "Only my fixation was for a gorgeous black-haired beauty with the most incredible blue eyes in the known world."

Ryan leaned across the table, closing those incredible blue eyes as she drew near. They kissed softly for a few moments, just long enough to start a slow fire burning in each of them. "Nice," she sighed as she sat back down in her chair. She placed her elbows on the table and set her chin upon her hands, gazing at Jamie with her best lovesick expression.

"Do you think your team will be as good this year?"

"Mmm-hmm. I think so. We have our starting pitcher back, and as you know, softball is mostly about pitching. I watched Heather warm up for a while, too, and she has a gun. She'll be the third pitcher, from what I can tell. That'll give her a nice opportunity to get comfortable without having too much pressure put on her."

"That sounds perfect. I didn't even ask, but what position will you play?"

"Well, the first baseman is good, and is the best hitter on the team, but she's not real agile. I'll probably be a defensive replacement for her in tight games. I can also help out in the outfield wherever they might need me. I can play second and third, too, but those positions are locked up by seniors, and I don't expect to get any time there, unless there's an injury. Looking at the team critically, I'd say I'm probably the first call off the bench."

"Must be some team."

"Yeah…they're good," Ryan said. "I'll be happy just to be a part of it. It would be a thrill to get to go to the World Series."

"I know you'll do everything you can to get there. You're indefatigable."

"I'm gonna try not to be so indefatigable," Ryan said her, smiling wryly. "I learned something important playing basketball."

"What's that?"

"I learned that winning isn't the most important thing." She smiled as she said, "Most people learn that before they're twenty-four, but I'm a little slow."

"Yeah, that's how I think of you. Slow and plodding."

"What I mean is that if the basketball team had been undefeated, I still would have hated it. The chemistry sucked, and I hated being the one who everyone looked to when we were behind. That's not teamwork. As far as I can tell, that won't happen here. I wanna be one of the guys. That's what I'm comfortable with."

"That's how it is with you and the boys, isn't it?"

"Yeah. They're bigger and stronger, but my speed and my quickness help equalize us. I never dominate when I'm playing a game with the boys. I like that. Now, lord knows I like the limelight. I love to show off. But I don't like to have to. Do you see what I mean?"

"Yeah, I think so," Jamie said, thoughtfully. "It puts a lot of pressure on you, doesn't it?"

"It does. But more than that, I don't want to be where I'm not wanted. I don't want to try to force my personality onto a group of people who don't want it. That's another thing I learned this winter. I learned that I couldn't change a team that didn't want to be changed."

"When did you realize that they didn't want you?"

Ryan chewed at her lower lip for a moment, trying to be honest with herself. "Before I started practice. I knew Coach Hayes was gonna be difficult, and I knew that Lynette was giving me fair warning." She looked at Jamie with a sheepish grin and said, "I thought I could change them."

"It must have been hard when you realized that you couldn't."

"It was a bit of a blow to my ego. That had never happened before," she said, smiling gently at her partner. "Usually, I'd go onto a team that wasn't very good and make an immediate impact. Within a few games I'd be the leader, and eventually, we'd start playing as a team." She looked at Jamie and said, "It'd always worked before, and I guess I couldn't imagine that it wouldn't work this time. I was a casualty of my hubris."

"That's one way to look at it. Another is to acknowledge that something that had always worked didn't work this time. As a scientist, that should be something that you expect to happen every once in a while, shouldn't it?"

"I suppose so," Ryan said. "But I want you to know that I did learn something else this winter. I learned that it's the relationships that matter... not the box score."

"That's true in most areas of life." Jamie said as she moved to her and climbed into Ryan's lap, straddling her. She bent her head and kissed her thoroughly, smiling to herself as she felt her partner respond enthusiastically.

They were about to head for the bedroom when Mia emerged, dishes washed and put away. "Gosh, look what you two are doing. How rare."

"It's not what it looks like," Jamie murmured, her lips not more than an inch from Ryan's. "We're working on our relationship."

"Hmm…" Mia mused thoughtfully. "Jordan and I call that foreplay… but the nomenclature isn't important. Have at it, girls. I'll give Jordy your regards."

"Hey," Ryan called out as Mia started to climb the stairs. "I've got a tournament in Las Vegas in a couple of weeks. See if Jordan is able to fly out and meet us."

"Cool! I've never been to Las Vegas."

"That makes two of us," Ryan said.

"Neither have I," Jamie chimed in, stunning the other two.

"Well, that's a first," Ryan said. "I thought you'd been to every place large enough for a zip code. This sounds like the makings of an adventure."

Chapter Two

"Good morning," Jamie said as she entered Mia's room on Tuesday morning.

"Hi. Toss me those jeans, will you?"

Jamie took the jeans from the bed and threw them to her. "Wanna play golf with me this afternoon?"

While wriggling into her pants, Mia gave her a puzzled look, "Don't you have your teammates to play with?"

"Yeah, I do, and they'll be there, but I want you to help me figure something out. Besides, I haven't had a chance to talk to you in any depth since we've both been back. I miss you."

"We do some of our best talking while riding around a golf course," Mia said, smiling. "Yeah, I guess I can do it. I only have one afternoon class today. Will I have to skip it?"

"Well, we play at one..."

"No problem. Where are we playing and what do you want me to help you figure out?"

"We play at Tilden. Be home by twelve thirty and I'll drive. Our goal is to figure out if one of my teammates is hitting on me."

"Ooh, this I'm good at! Is she a hottie?"

"Uhm...she's actually pretty cute, but I'm not in the market for a replacement. Ryan's all I want or need."

"Yeah," Mia said, running her fingers through her curls to provide some order, "I think Ryan's enough for any woman." Mia started to gather her books, saying, "I was thinking about her last night after I spoke with Jordy. Having Ryan as a girlfriend is really a full-time job. She's a weird kind of high-maintenance girl. You don't think of her as high-maintenance, since she doesn't spend a lot of time on her hair or makeup, and she's always ready to go—but she gets into so damned much trouble that you have to keep an eye on her all the time."

"That's my Buffy," Jamie agreed, smiling broadly. "But I love every little trouble-attracting part of her."

The other girls all chose to walk, leaving Jamie to rent an electric cart so she and Mia could dish while they drove. "Well, what do you think so far?" Jamie asked, after they'd teed off on one.

"She's cute—definitely cute—at least, I think she is," Mia said. "Could she wear that visor any lower on her face?"

"She likes to concentrate. And I'm not seeking opinions on her attractiveness, I want to know if you think she's gay—and if you think she's sending vibes my way."

"Oh, lord! Of course she's gay! Are you blind?"

Jamie looked at the determined young woman again, trying to see her through Mia's eyes. No matter how hard she tried, Juliet didn't look one bit gayer to Jamie than any of the other players. "I don't see it. I honestly don't."

"How can you not? She oozes lesbianism." Mia gave her a puzzled look, cocking her head while she wrinkled her nose.

"What's the key? What do you look for?"

"I can't believe I have to tell you these things, James, I mean, you're a full-fledged member of the club."

"Well, I don't have gaydar—for women, at least. I can almost always pick out gay men, though."

"Now, there's an unhelpful skill," Mia said, patting her hand.

"Come on…you have to be able to give me some clues. How do you tell?"

Mia sighed, then looked at Juliet critically. "Okay, here's one. When we went to check in, the guy at the starter's window was totally cute. And he was flirting his ass off with every single woman who was standing there. Every one of the women acknowledged him in some way. Those little freshmen blushed, the juniors acted like they didn't notice he was flirting, and you were your usual friendly, but not flirty self. You gave him the 'I'll be nice to you so you don't give me a bad tee time, but don't get your hopes up, buddy' look that you're so good at."

Jamie's mouth gaped open in surprise. "I do that?"

"Yep. Constantly. You've been doing it since I met you, almost eight years ago."

"Go figure…I didn't realize I did that."

"Well, you do. Now, Juliet…she acted as if there was a robot at the window. She didn't acknowledge him as even a human—much less a man. That's gay. Way gay."

"Maybe she has a boyfriend. Maybe she doesn't like to encourage men to flirt with her."

"Nope. Not buying it. When you're attuned to men—you're always attuned to them. You don't turn it on and off. The juniors acted like they had boyfriends and they were telling the guy nonverbally that they weren't interested because they were taken." Tilting her head in question, she asked, "Do they?"

"Yep. Every one of them."

"Ha! Told ya! I'm great at this."

"Maybe she isn't into anyone. She's so focused. Maybe she's asexual."

"Mmm…maybe, but asexual women don't put their sunglasses on so they can check out your ass when you put your spikes on."

"She did not!"

"She did so," Mia said, laughing heartily. "She waited until you stuck your foot up on your bumper, then she hurriedly put her glasses on, and turned her head so it didn't look like she was facing your way. But she was," she said, giggling fiendishly. "I moved over so I could see her eyes behind her glasses, and they were definitely on your sweet little ass." She elbowed her friend in the ribs and said, "Your butt looks adorable in those pants, by the way. Can I borrow 'em?"

"Oh, lord!" Jamie dropped her head and let it rest on the steering wheel. "I don't want Juliet checking me out. It makes me uncomfortable."

"Why?" Mia looked totally perplexed, her face scrunched up in question.

"Because I'm married!"

"So? She's just looking. You don't have to let her touch. It's a compliment," she said, shrugging her shoulders. "I love it when people check me out. Hell, we're only gonna be young and hot for a few years. Enjoy it while you can."

"You and I are wired differently. Besides, I know it would bother Ryan, and I don't want to get her riled up right now. She's got enough people on her hit list."

"She doesn't seem like the jealous type to me," Mia said. "She's so full of confidence it's sickening."

"Mmm…not so much now. The carjacking has changed her. She was so jealous of one of the golf pros down in Pebble Beach that she nearly threw a tantrum when I played golf with him."

"Ryan? Ryan did that?"

"Yeah. My sweet Ryan did that. I don't blame her, and I really do understand, but it was still hard. She felt so broken that she started to doubt who she was. It deeply affected her self-esteem."

"Uhm…I don't wanna pry, but you two looked pretty normal after dinner last night. Is everything…working again?"

"Yeah." Jamie nodded as she blushed slightly. "We've been making very slow, but steady progress, and I thought it might take us another month or so to be open again. But we worked through some tough things on Sunday night, and Ryan really pushed herself. I don't wanna jinx anything, but I think we're gonna be fine. I was so moved…" She shook her head and shrugged her shoulders. "She touches my soul when we make love, and she touched it all over again on Sunday night. I was so overwhelmed that I decided that I have to marry her," she said, smiling shyly. "I just have to."

Mia threw her arms around her friend and whispered, "I'm so happy for you, James; I knew you'd get it back. You guys have too good a relationship to let the sex fade away."

"Thanks. I even called my father and asked if he'd participate in our ceremony. To my amazement, he not only said yes—he was supportive."

"That's great! So—when are you going to ask your maid of honor if she's busy?"

Jamie wrapped an arm around her friend and kissed her cheek. "I don't know when we're going to have the ceremony—probably early this summer. Can you make it?"

"I think I can squeeze you in. As long as you don't have it during the Olympics, I'm there."

"Well, we obviously haven't discussed the details yet, but if my hunch is correct, Jordan's gonna be an integral part of the ceremony."

"So, Ryan doesn't know yet?"

"Nope. I've got to get a big, flashy, engagement ring for her," Jamie said, smiling brightly. "This is probably my one and only chance to get some diamonds on that lovely left hand—so I'm gonna take full advantage."

"You are so gonna take me with you when you go shopping. I wanna go to one of those snooty places where they bring you champagne and caviar while you shop."

"I'll definitely take you with me. We're gonna have to negotiate on the champagne and caviar, though. You know that I love a bargain as much as I love champagne—and those ritzy places are waaaaay overpriced."

❧

Both Jamie and Mia were playing well, and having the cart allowed them to sneak ahead to the green on most holes, giving them time to sit and chat while Juliet and Lauren caught up. "I opened my big mouth at practice this morning, and suggested we have a party at our house this Saturday night," Jamie said, looking glum.

"Oh, James, don't make a big deal out of this. If Ryan sees Juliet staring at you, she'll loosen a few of her teeth and it'll all be settled."

"You act like this is a joke, but it's not. Ryan's usually so placid and peaceful, but lately her temper can get away from her. I know she's feeling a lot better, but I still worry about her."

"Can I come to the party, or do I have to make myself scarce?"

"Of course you can come. I don't know why you'd want to, to be honest, but you're certainly welcome."

"Why wouldn't I want to come?"

"Well, this isn't the most interesting group of people I've ever met," Jamie said, shrugging. "The athletes that Ryan's played with have been outgoing and fun-loving for the most part, but this group isn't like that at all. I think the fact that many of them have dreams of playing in the LPGA has made them a lot more serious about the game than is wise. Juliet in particular acts like she's merely marking time until she can play professionally. She doesn't seem to be enjoying college at all—and that just seems a shame."

"Well, maybe you can have a wild party and loosen them all up. Wanna make Jell-O shots?" she asked, her eyes lighting up.

"Mmm…I don't know if that's a good idea. Some of the girls are just eighteen."

"You're not their mom, James. Come on, loosen up a little. Part of the fun of being in college is getting drunk. Everybody knows that."

"We'll see. The question remains why you want to come. Don't you have more interesting things to do on a Saturday night?"

"No," she said, shaking her head. "It's no fun doing things without Jordy. I doubt that I'll hang out much at your party, but I don't want to leave the house if I don't have to."

Jamie patted her leg. "I hate to see you so down."

"It's hard," she said, looking like she was on the verge of tears. "I had no idea how hard it would be to be this far away from her." She wrapped her arms around her knees and leaned over, hugging herself. "She gave my life a focus—a direction." Looking at Jamie, she cocked her head and asked, "Do you know what I mean?"

"Yes, of course I do, but it's only for a few more months. Still, I hate to see you having so little fun during your last semester. I'd love to see some spark back in those big, brown eyes."

"That's where you're wrong, James," Mia said, her voice sounding flat and lifeless. "It's gonna be a lot longer than a few months if Jordan fulfills her dream."

"Huh?"

"When she signed on for the team, it was with the intent of staying with them until she was cut. She hopes to play in Athens in 2004."

"You're…you're kidding!"

"Do I look like I'm kidding?" Mia asked, looking anything but. "She says that it takes a long time to make a team gel, and that playing together over a period of years is the only way to do that."

"Oh, Mia…" Jamie said, patting her leg in sympathy.

"She's willing to quit after Sydney—but I know that's not what she wants to do. She'd only do that if I want her to, and that puts a tremendous burden on my shoulders. Jesus! I don't want her to resent me for convincing her to abandon her dream before she's ready. But I also don't want to live in Colorado Springs for the next four years—working at some crap job while she's off playing volleyball all around the world."

"You could go with her when she travels."

"On what? She'll make around thirty thousand, and she's got to pay for her own housing and meals. That doesn't leave much money to be buying me plane tickets for everywhere on earth."

"But what about her modeling money?" Jamie asked. "I know she has to make a good buck for that."

"She does, but she's trying to put that money aside to pay for graduate school. She wants to get a master's degree when she's done playing, and she doesn't want to be saddled with a lot of student loans."

"You two are very creative people," Jamie said. "I know you can figure this out. Heck, you could go to grad school in Colorado, and that would keep you busy while Jordan was playing. Then you'd have the credentials to get a good job and support her while she was in grad school. You've got to put your minds to it, honey."

"Yeah…I guess. It just seems like there are so many barriers. It depresses the hell out of me."

"I understand. If I didn't have Ryan nearby, I'd go bonkers."

"Who knew being in love with such a wonderful woman could suck so bad?" Mia asked, getting out of the cart and grumbling to herself as she walked to the next tee.

🐎

Mia's sour mood didn't last long, and when Jamie walked back to the cart after her tee shot on nine she couldn't help but see the smirk that her friend was trying to hide. "What's funny?"

"Nothing…nothing at all."

"Come on. I know that look, and I know that I'm the butt of the joke. Spill it."

"Well, butt is the operative word," Mia said, trying to look innocent.

"Mia…out with it!"

"Okay," she said, still trying not to laugh. "Did you know that you wiggled your butt right before you swing?"

"I do not!"

"Yeah, you do. You always have. It's part of your swing—no big deal. But I've been watching Juliet try to get into position to watch you without anyone else see her do it. That time she almost broke her neck when she backed into the ball washer." Mia was smiling brightly, but Jamie's expression did not match hers.

"Damn it! I'm gonna have to have a talk with her. I refuse to let her gawk at me."

"What can you say?" Mia asked, still chuckling. "She's very subtle about it, James. She'll know I ratted her out."

Scowling, Jamie crossed her arms over her chest. "I'll have to wait until I catch her."

⁂

After the round, the pair went to a nearby coffee bar to warm up. The afternoon had grown chilly, and there was a definite hint of rain in the air. "Well, that was an all-time sucko round," Jamie said, looking at her scorecard. "I had a thirty-five going out and a fifty coming in." She looked up at her friend and said, "Of course, trying to swing without wiggling my butt might have contributed to my stellar play." Rapping Mia over the head with the card, she said, "Thanks for totally messing up my swing, pal. I never knew that my butt was the key to my success."

"Why do you think this bothers you so much? She's not being aggressive or anything. She thinks you're cute. Why is that so awful?"

Jamie sighed and rested her head on the table, mumbling into the wood. "I don't know. I just can't stand the thought of someone looking at me without my permission."

Laughing, Mia said, "James! You've had the majority of the press corps taking your picture for over a month, and you got through that without much trouble."

"That didn't bother me as much because those weren't people in my life—if that makes any sense. Juliet is a teammate. She's someone who I wanted to get closer to, to bond with. I don't want to feel like an object with someone that I let inside my circle of friends." She shook her head and sat up, running her hands through her hair. "I don't know. I don't have a lot of patience lately. I'm not sleeping well again, and it's pretty darned easy to piss me off."

Reaching across the table, Mia slipped her fingers through Jamie's and held her hand. "Tell me why you're not sleeping well."

"Oh, it's the usual," Jamie said, giving Mia a resigned shrug. "I have a couple of good days, then I have a few nights in a row where I have nightmares. They scare me, and make me afraid to go back to sleep."

"Are the nightmares about the…"

"Yeah, they're about the carjacking in some variation. Last night was a new one, though. In this one, we were in the boat with the paramedics and I was struggling to regain consciousness. I finally focused on Ryan, and saw that she was crying hysterically. When she saw I was awake, she looked at me with an expression I'll never forget and said, "We lost Caitlin."

"Oh, God, James! What a horrible dream!"

"The worst part was that I was the one who'd lost her. I'd been holding her, and she'd slipped out of my arms. It was all my fault," Jamie whispered, as tears started to run down her cheeks.

Mia scooted her chair around and wrapped her friend in a hug. "Shh…it's okay, baby. Caitlin's fine. You saved her."

"I know," Jamie sniffed. "But at night, my imagination goes wild. I've been through every variation possible. Some nights I die and I feel my soul hovering over my body while Ryan beats on my chest to make me breathe again. That one is so horrible," she whispered. "Seeing the pain on her face breaks my heart—and I want to come back so badly—but I can't. I feel myself slipping into an unfathomable darkness, and my last thought is that I'll never see my Ryan again."

"Oh, James, that's so horrible," Mia said, tightening her hug.

"It's even worse when she dies," Jamie murmured, her voice choked with tears. "She's died every way possible in my nightmares. She's gotten caught on the submerged car; one of the carjackers fights with her and knocks her out and she drowns; she's fallen off the car—and I see her land and split her head open. Oh, and I had a doozy where each of us was killed—in a dark alley, execution style—and I was last. I got to watch both Ryan and Caitie die."

"You poor, poor thing," Mia soothed, rocking Jamie in her arms. "I didn't know it was still so bad for you."

Jamie sat up, trying to regain her composure. "It comes and goes. Ryan's doing pretty well this week. When I wake up, she's usually sound asleep. It's like one of us gets worse when the other one gets better." Wiping her eyes with a napkin, she said, "Anna says this will pass, but it's awful while I'm in the middle of it."

"Have you told Ryan that you're having nightmares again?"

"No. She's just starting to get some of her equilibrium back, and having her worrying about me won't help a bit. It also won't stop me from having nightmares," she said glumly.

Mia reached out and touched Jamie's chin, lifting it so she could see her eyes. "Am I your best friend?"

"Yes, of course you are."

"Then let me act like it. The next time you have a bad nightmare, I want you to come wake me up. I haven't been through what you and Ryan have,

James—I'm not all stressed and wrung out like you two are. I have the capacity, and I'd like to help you get through this. Knowing you're not alone and knowing that you can talk to someone might help."

Jamie gazed into Mia's eyes for a moment, seeing that her friend was very serious about her offer. "All right," she said, nodding her head. "That might help. Lying there in bed and feeling so alone makes it a lot worse. Talking to someone who's not running on empty emotionally would really be helpful." Hugging her friend soundly, Jamie said, "Thanks."

"Don't mention it, James. We're all in this together, babe."

Jamie woke at her normal time on Wednesday, and automatically reached out to cuddle for a few minutes before she had to get up. But her cuddle partner was notably absent, and Ryan's side of the bed was cold. Jamie sat up and switched on the bedside light, squinting against the brightness. There, atop Ryan's pillow, was a pithy note.

5:30—went riding. Love you, R

Well, given that it's just after six and still dark out, she'd better be using her headlamp. Damn, if it's not one thing to worry about with her, it's another.

Taking the quickest shower of her life, Jamie got dressed and drove around the streets of their neighborhood, finally finding Ryan about four blocks from their house. She didn't chase her down, since it was nearly time for golf practice, but she had to reassure herself that Ryan was all right. *Well, this is going to be fun. I'll get to lie in bed and worry about her, then have to track her down before I can go to practice. No coffee, no breakfast…I should be in great spirits today. Shit! I may as well do the damned ride with her!*

That afternoon, Jamie sat in Anna's office, her mood having grown darker over the course of the day. "I know that I can't make Ryan give up her plans to participate in the AIDS Ride, but I'm spending so much of my energy worrying about her! I know that's why my nightmares are back."

"I take it you've told Ryan this?" Anna asked.

Jamie shook her head. "No, I haven't." She sat quietly for a moment, then looked at the therapist and said, "One of the reasons we have a good relationship is because I give Ryan the freedom she needs. The problem is that she needs a lot of freedom—and when it comes to something like this—her needs and my needs can't both be satisfied."

"So…does that mean that your needs have to be ignored?"

"No," Jamie said a little tentatively. "Not…ignored. But this is an either/ or situation. Either Ryan trains as much as she can so she can do the ride properly, or she cuts back and risks injuring herself."

"There's another option, Jamie, and I think it should be on the table as well."

"Yeah? What's that?"

"You can let Ryan know how much you're worried about her, and try to find an alternative to her doing the ride."

Jamie's head was shaking before Anna finished her sentence. "She knows I don't think it's wise for her to do this. But it's truly important to her."

"And she's important to you. Given what you've told me about Ryan, I can't imagine she'd intentionally participate in something that was causing you a lot of distress. I have a feeling that you haven't made clear to her how much this is worrying you."

"No, you're right," she said softly. "I haven't let her know that." She shook her head again and asked, "Is being in a relationship ever easy?"

"Yes," Anna said, smiling. "And when you're feeling better, you'll get your perspective back and remember how easy it sometimes is." Anna's eyes crinkled up as her smile grew. "You have to realize that you've chosen a woman who will always challenge your patience."

"You don't think this is a phase, huh?" Jamie asked, a smirk forming.

"No, Ryan sounds like the type who will always be a handful. But, I have a feeling that's one of the attributes that appeals to you. You don't seem like the kind of woman who would be satisfied with a predictable, stodgy partner."

"Stodgy and Ryan don't belong in the same sentence," Jamie admitted, a smile finally beginning to form.

After her session, Jamie went over to the softball stadium and hunkered down in the warmest, least windy corner. Ashley arrived about an hour later, and came over to sit. "I just stopped by on my way home," the freshman said. "It's too cold for me!"

"It's awful out," Jamie agreed, her body shivering.

"Why don't you go home?? They sure aren't doing anything very interesting."

"Yeah, I probably will," Jamie said. "I'll leave in a few."

"Okay." Ashley got up and said, "I'll see you when it warms up a bit. Don't freeze!"

As Jamie watched her go, she rolled her eyes as she considered what she was doing. *You can't keep her in your sight every minute. Sitting here in the cold to keep an eye on her is stupid. You know darned well that she's going to go ride that damned bike for an hour after practice, and you can't follow her around in the car. You've got to let go!*

After returning from her pre-dawn bike ride the next morning, Ryan reached her mother-in-law. "I've got three hours available from eleven to two," she said. "Is that enough time to go to the best jewelry store you know?"

"Hmm…no, that won't do, since it's in Rome," Catherine drawled. "But that's ample time to go to the best jeweler in the Bay Area."

"Great. Should I come pick you up?"

"No, it's in the city, dear. I'll meet you. Now, let me in on what you're planning to buy. Are you looking for matching bands?"

Ryan smiled broadly, even though Catherine couldn't see her. "Oh, no. Jamie will want to continue to wear my mother's wedding band. I want to buy her an engagement ring, Catherine. A ring special enough that Jamie will proudly wear it forever."

"Oh, Ryan," Catherine chided. "If it came from you, Jamie would be pleased to wear a ring from a Cracker Jack box."

"Maybe, but it's important to me that she have something really nice."

"Then, I'm your woman," Catherine said. "Really nice is my specialty."

Mia was up for a shopping trip as well, and the three of them arrived at Catherine's jeweler of choice just after eleven. "Mrs. Evans," the elegantly dressed man murmured as they were admitted to the small store located on the upper floor of a building near Union Square. "It's wonderful to see you again," he said, giving her a wink to show that he remembered to be discreet, careful not to mention that Catherine and Jamie had an appointment for the following Monday to purchase Ryan's ring.

"Thank you, Jeffrey," Catherine said. "This is Ryan O'Flaherty," she said, "and our friend, Mia Christopher."

"Pleased to meet you," he said to each woman.

"Ryan is in the market to purchase a ring for my daughter, Jeffrey." Ryan raised an eyebrow at the relaxed way that Catherine announced this fact, but she was very pleased by it.

"Marvelous," he said, acting like he was very used to women buying women engagement rings. "We have every style and size stone that you could wish for. Would you like to begin by looking at some diamonds?"

"I think so," Ryan said. She turned to her companions and asked, "Jamie's a diamond kinda girl, isn't she?"

Catherine and Mia shared a look, then both of them said, "Or an emerald."

"Really?" Ryan asked. "We've never discussed this, so I have no idea what would appeal to her."

"Well, she and I talked about it until I was ready to gag her," Mia said. "When she and Jack were getting serious, we went to every jewelry store in town; and she always gravitated towards the emeralds."

"Hmm…but she didn't wear an emerald when she was engaged," Ryan mused. "She wore Jack's grandmother's diamond ring."

"Yeah, and she was perfectly happy with it," Mia said. "It didn't bother her one bit that it was a dated style, with a tiny diamond. She was touched that it meant so much to Jack, and that he wanted to share it with her."

"What do you think, Catherine? Would Jamie prefer an emerald? That is," she scowled slightly, "if I can afford one."

"I don't want to influence you too much," Catherine said. "I meant it when I said that Jamie would love anything that you gave her." She gazed at her daughter-in-law for a long moment and decided, "If I had to make the choice, though, I'd choose an emerald. She's spoken of emeralds as her favorite stones ever since she was a young girl." Smiling at Ryan, she added, "Besides, diamonds are fairly traditional. And neither of you seems too bound by tradition."

Jeffrey caught Ryan's eye and said, "Let me go to my safe and bring out a selection of diamonds and emeralds. Seeing the stones might help you decide between the two."

As he left, Catherine said, "Don't let the cost influence you, Ryan. You're only going to buy a stone like this once in your life. I'm sure Jamie wouldn't want the price to even cross your mind."

Ryan cleared her throat. "I'm not using our money." At Catherine's raised eyebrow she extracted a small, blue, dog-eared document and said, "All of the money I have in the world is in this bank account. This represents the savings that I've been accumulating since I started to baby-sit when I was thirteen."

Catherine looked from the bankbook back to Ryan's sober face, urging her to go on.

"I won't spend more than I need to, of course, but I'd like to use this all to buy Jamie something very special."

"Oh, Ryan! Jamie wouldn't want you to do that. I'm sure of it."

"It's what I want to do, Catherine. Really," she insisted, the determined look in her eyes emphasizing her point. "I want to make a statement with this gift—I want to show Jamie that I'm giving up all of my worldly goods to commit myself to her. I'm not sure why this means so much to me, but I want to see her wearing the evidence of everything I had when we started out—for the rest of her life."

Catherine slid her arms around her, repeating an oft-expressed feeling. "I'm so glad that she found you, Ryan. You are such a gift."

"I don't give my heart away easily, and Jamie deserves everything that I have to give."

A very discreet clearing of his throat announced that Jeffrey had returned, and before Ryan could make her way back to the counter, Mia was eagerly sorting through his selections.

The threesome used all of their allotted time, but by one thirty, Ryan was completely satisfied. Catherine and Mia agreed with her selections wholeheartedly, and after measuring Mia's ring finger—which was exactly the same size as Jamie's—they departed the small shop.

"When will you give her the ring?" Catherine asked.

"On her birthday." Catherine's eyes involuntarily widened, and Ryan raised an eyebrow and asked, "That's not a good day?"

Mia broke in, "Jack broke up with her on her birthday last year. Why don't you do it on Valentine's Day instead?"

"Isn't that a little cliché?"

"No! I think Jamie would prefer it," Catherine said, both she and Mia nodding in unison.

"She'll love it," Mia said once again. "We've talked about this, and it's what she'd want." When Ryan continued to look doubtful, Mia said, "Trust me—it's a girl thing."

"Oh! Okay, then," she said, as they walked to the elevator lobby. "I don't know where I was when they were handing out the girl lessons, but I seem to have missed every one of 'em."

"You were probably at softball practice," Mia teased, getting a pinch in the side for her suggestion.

Chapter Three

On Friday night, Ryan dragged into the house at six fifteen, tossed her bicycle helmet onto the front table, and called out, "I'm home, babe." Idly looking through the mail, she barely noticed when Jamie came up behind her and wrapped her in a hug.

"How's my sweaty girl? Ready for dinner?"

"Yeah, I guess." Ryan turned around and gave her partner a proper hug. "Let me go get out of these wet clothes, okay?"

"Sure, honey." She pulled back and gazed at Ryan for a moment. "You okay?"

"Yeah, sure. Glad it's Friday, though. It's been an extraordinarily long week. I guess it's gonna take me some time to get used to practicing every day."

"That's probably it," Jamie said, patting her lightly. "Go take a quick shower. You'll feel better."

"'Kay."

Ryan started up the stairs, and Jamie could just see the fatigue in her body. *Of course, you might be tired because you're up before dawn riding your bike for two hours every morning, and another hour after softball…but I'm not going to say 'I told you so.'*

Over dinner, Jamie put on her brightest smile and asked, "So, how do you think your first week of practice went?"

"All right," Ryan said, nodding while she chewed thoughtfully. "I really do like the other girls, and the coach is pretty cool. The assistants are nice, too. I think it's gonna work out. I just have to shake this lethargy." She gave Jamie a very perturbed look and said, "I'm not bouncing back the way I normally do. Maybe I should start taking some supplements, or something."

"Want me to call the doctor for you, and ask what she recommends?"

Ryan shrugged. "Whatever. I can do it if you don't."

"Hey,"Jamie reached out and covered her partner's hand, "what's bothering you? I know something is."

Putting down her fork, Ryan pushed her plate away and leaned over, resting her chin on her stacked fists. "I'm not having fun."

"Why, honey? Isn't softball like you remembered it?"

Staring across the table, Ryan muttered, "Not softball."

"Huh? What is it, then?"

"Riding."

She said it like a curse, and Jamie got up from her chair and pulled her partner upright. Drawing Ryan's head against her, she stroked her back and said, "Tell me. Tell me why it's not fun."

"It's only work this time," she said, her voice muffled by Jamie's sweater. "No camaraderie, no teamwork, no—getting pleasure from helping people— like you—reach a goal."

Jamie pulled back and looked into her eyes, seeing the deep sadness that lurked within the blue depths. Screwing up her nerve, she made the proposal that she'd been working on all week. "I have an idea I've been kicking around."

"Yeah? What's that?"

"Why don't we consider volunteering this year? You've always said that the volunteers are the most vital contributors. Why don't we see what it's like to be on that team for a change?"

Ryan was quiet for a minute, while her hands nervously played with her silverware. "I don't know," she muttered. "I meant it when I said the volunteers were important. But I'm not sure I could stand to drive people around in one of those little vans all day. I'd feel all cooped up."

Jamie smiled at her, and said, "How would you feel about it if you could still be on a bike; you could still be outdoors; you and I could be together; and you didn't have to train?"

Ryan crossed her arms and gave her partner her most dubious look. "This I've gotta hear."

"I've been talking to the people at the Ride office to see what I could do as a volunteer," Jamie said, surprising her partner completely. "Mostly because there's no way I'm going to let you share a tent with some stranger."

"So possessive," Ryan said, reaching out to tweak her partner's nose.

"Damned right. Anyway, one thing that we could do together is motorcycle support," she said, waiting for Ryan to respond.

"Motorcycle support?" she asked slowly.

"Yep. I thought it would be fun. We'd be able to interact with a lot of people—heck, we'd be chatting all day."

Ryan looked skeptical. "Where would you get a bike?"

"I found a place that rents 'em. I think I'll rent a Harley Sportster. It's much more my size." She blinked her eyes at her partner and said, "Soooo... someone's Fatboy is still available for use."

Ryan shook her head slowly, letting all of the information digest. "I don't know, honey. I mean, motorcycle support is very important, and the people who do it seem to love it—but I don't think it's my style."

Jamie's heart sank, knowing that Ryan wasn't likely to budge from her first impression. Sighing, she asked, "What is your style, baby? What would make you happy?"

"I need time to think," Ryan said. "Give me a little quiet time, okay?"

"Sure. Uhm...there's not much to do to clean up from dinner. Why don't you go upstairs and take a bath or something."

"All right. I'll go chill for a bit."

Jamie did the dishes in a leisurely fashion, and just as she was finishing, Mia came in. There was a decent amount of food left over, so she sat at the table while Mia had dinner, and they chatted about their respective days.

Nearly an hour had passed, but Ryan hadn't reappeared, so Jamie went upstairs to check on her. There was no sign of her in the bath, so Jamie poked her head into Ryan's bedroom, slightly surprised to find her sitting on the floor, in a yoga pose—looking like she was meditating. Sneaking out quietly, she went into their room and worked at her computer for a long while. It was nearly bedtime when Ryan came in and lay down on the bed, her head down at the foot so she was closer to Jamie. "Well, I think I sorted out what about the ride means the most to me."

Swiveling around in her chair, Jamie gave her partner her full attention. "Tell me."

"It's always been a multi-step process for me. The training—meeting new people—sleeping with new people," she added, chuckling a little. "All of that was a lot of fun, and made me feel part of the whole. The months leading up to the ride let me share my excitement with a lot of people, and that really meant something to me."

"And that's why not being able to lead training rides has been so disappointing for you."

"Yeah...that's exactly it."

"Well, maybe there's some way we can figure out..."

"No," Ryan said, holding up a hand. "It dawned on me tonight that as much as I enjoyed all of that—it's not why the ride has so much meaning for me. The bottom line is that all of the other things were nice incidentals. What mattered the most was the quiet time I had every day—to think and reflect about Michael. Those few hours each day seemed like a culmination of several months of work that I dedicated to him. It was a way to keep him close to my heart."

"I understand," Jamie said, quietly. "Really, I do, baby."

Ryan nodded. "I knew you would—once I figured it out for myself. So, I'm gonna have to do the work the hard way this time—because those hours during the ride mean more to me than the pain I'm gonna have to go through to get there." She didn't look terribly happy, but the look on her face was one of resolution, and Jamie knew that Ryan would stick to her path—now that she was clear about the goal.

With some trepidation, Jamie got up and lay next to her partner, pulling Ryan's head to her chest. As she stroked the soft, dark hair, she offered the suggestion that had occurred to her as Ryan was speaking. "Let me be sure I understand, okay?"

"Sure."

"You're willing to give up all of the fun parts just to have a couple of hours of quiet time a day during the ride?"

"Yeah, I am. Being out there in nature, making my body do something that's difficult lets me concentrate in a way that I'm not usually able to do. Those few stolen hours mean too much to let them go."

"How about this?" Jamie asked. "I agree completely that you need to spend time honoring your cousin's memory. I know how easy it is to let things like that slip by when your life is as busy as yours is. I get that, Ryan—I do."

"Thank you. That means a lot."

"But this year, with all that you have going on—I worry about you, sweetheart; and if there's any way to fulfill your needs without stressing you more, I want you to consider it."

"I know you worry about me, but I can take care of myself. Really—I can."

Looking into her big, blue eyes, Jamie steeled her courage and told the whole truth. "I can't stop worrying. I've tried to—I swear that I have. I've talked to Anna, I've prayed over it, I've talked to my mom—but I can't stop worrying."

"Hey," Ryan soothed, shifting to wrap her arms around her partner. "I didn't know it was bothering you this much."

"It is. I lie in bed in the morning worrying about you riding in the dark. And my stomach's a nervous wreck when you ride after practice; there's so much traffic around here, honey. It makes me crazy!"

Ryan was quiet for a minute, her hand softly stroking her partner's hair. "Then I'll quit. This is important to me—but it's not important enough to cause you pain. I've given you enough to worry about for a lifetime."

Jamie lifted her head and gazed at Ryan for a long time. "You love me very much, don't you."

"I do," Ryan whispered. "I love you more than I ever knew was possible. You're my life."

Kissing her tenderly, Jamie rolled her partner onto her back and stared at her for a minute. "You're mine, too. So, let's figure out a way for both of us to get our needs met."

"Sounds like you've got something brewing up in that active, little brain," Ryan said, smiling up at her partner.

"I think I do," Jamie said. "I know you need some solitude. But I happen to think that you need more than a few hours a day during the AIDS Ride."

"Go on," Ryan said. "I know there's more."

"I think that you should take a week—by yourself—to meditate, and pray and reflect. I think you need it now more than you ever have, sweetheart. You could schedule it during the same time as the AIDS Ride, and spend some of your time praying for the people on the ride—I know that would mean a lot to them, and to you."

"Where would I do this?"

"Anywhere you wanted to, honey. There are a lot of retreat centers within an hour or two of us, or you could be wild and go to Sienna, or Assisi, or to any of the places that have spiritual meaning for you."

"Damn," Ryan said, her eyes glazing over. "It's…too much to consider how much money we have. Let's stay local so I can keep the top of my head on."

"Okay. I'm sure my grandfather has a list of retreat centers, and Father Pender could hook you up, too. Actually, Poppa went to one a couple of years ago that I've wanted to go to. It was a silent retreat, and it was for Christians—but it was conducted on an Eastern model—with guided meditation led by a Buddhist monk."

"Wow, I'd love that," Ryan said softly. "Damn, I haven't been on a retreat since I was in high school—and we just goofed off at that one."

"Will you consider it? I'll be happy to get all of the information for you."

Ryan was quiet for a minute, then nodded her head. "Yeah. I'll definitely consider it. Uhm…could we still give a contribution to the ride?"

"Of course, honey. We can give as much as you want. You know," she said thoughtfully, "there's a retreat center in Santa Barbara. You could go over to UCSB on Saturday and have lunch with some of your buddies—maybe feel connected to them that way."

"That'd be nice," Ryan said, nuzzling her head against Jamie's chest. "So, you wouldn't want to go with me?"

"Mmm…no. I could never keep my mouth shut for a week if you were nearby. I think this is something you need to do alone. Maybe I'll go to a spa with my mom. I'd like to spend some time alone with her this year."

"Wow, we're not even together a year, and we're planning separate vacations," Ryan said, smiling sadly at her lover.

"It's been a unique year," Jamie said, smiling back and adding a gentle kiss. "But next year, you and I are going to be on our bikes—just like normal."

"That'll be nice," Ryan sighed. "I wanna be normal again."

"Me too, sweetie, me too."

"Want me to go pick up the sushi?" Ryan asked, late on Saturday afternoon.

"Sure. That'll give me time to finish a few last-minute details," Jamie said.

"You know," Ryan said, twirling her keys on her finger, "you aren't putting much of your energies into this party. It's not like you to only order a couple of sushi platters when you're entertaining. What's up with that?"

"Well, I don't know most of the girls very well, so I don't know if any of them are vegetarians. I figured there'd be something for everyone with a big assortment of sushi, since I made sure that at least a quarter of the things are veggie."

"Okay." Ryan picked up her wallet. "Whatever."

She started to walk out, but Jamie dashed across the room and grabbed her by her waistband. "Truth?"

"Yeah, that'd be nice—for a change," Ryan said, smiling warmly.

"I think the party's gonna be a big bust, and I don't wanna spend too much time working on it. I'm making an effort to try to draw these girls out a little bit—but I'll admit that I'm not making too much of an effort."

"That's cool," Ryan said, bending to kiss her. "I'm not complaining. I merely wanted to see what was going on in that decidedly pretty head."

"Just being practical. And thanks for helping me out. I'm counting on you charming the pants off a few of these shy little introverts."

"Well, that should make the party interesting," Ryan said. "I didn't know that was allowed under the rules of monogamy—but I'm up for it." She gave Jamie a lecherous grin and palmed her ass, adding a firm squeeze.

"You'd scare these girls half to death if you looked at them that way," Jamie said, chuckling. "That sexy grin had better only come out if you're looking at me."

The sexy grin appeared on cue. "That's the only time it wants to come out. Only you inspire me."

The party had been in full-drone for almost an hour when Mia came downstairs, fresh from a long talk with her beloved. She was feeling quite anti-social, evading everyone in the living and dining rooms to sneak into the kitchen—hoping that Jamie had stowed the excess food in there.

She nearly ran into Juliet, or at least a woman who looked like Juliet—without a tee stuck between her teeth, or a visor covering her face. "Hey," Mia said. "Juliet, right?"

"Uh…yeah," she said, giving Mia a blank look.

"I'm Mia, Jamie's roommate. We played golf together on Tuesday."

"Oh, right. Hi."

Damn, maybe she isn't a lesbian. I didn't even get into her short-term memory. "Were you looking for something? I live here, so I know my way around."

"Uhm…no, not really," she said, her nervousness showing. "I'm not much for parties, to tell the truth. I try to find the quietest place and just hang out."

Sensing an opportunity to probe Juliet's defenses, Mia pulled out a chair and said, "Have a seat. You can sit and chat with me for a while. I don't like crowds, either."

Looking grateful, the golfer sat down, then gazed at Mia, waiting to be led.

"Would you like a drink? Jamie didn't want to put alcohol out, since so many of the girls are underage—but you're a senior, aren't you?"

"Uh-huh." She looked a little uncomfortable, and said, "I don't drink much, though. I never got used to the taste."

"Let's have some fun then. Let's make Jell-O shots."

"I've never had those."

"Well, you will soon. I'll get the Jell-O and the vodka, you put a little water in the tea kettle—and we're on our way."

Ryan caught Jamie when she saw her near the library. Pulling her into the quiet space, she whispered, "I'm about to take poison! Isn't there anything we can do to spice this party up?"

Jamie shrugged her shoulders. "Naked Twister? Body shots? Russian Roulette? I'll try anything. Actually, why don't we take off? Let 'em sit here until they bore each other to death, and then sweep up the bodies."

"Damn, if staying at this party isn't a sign of my undying love, nothing is," Ryan said, her grumbling obviously good-natured.

"I can't believe that no one brought a date. Guys would have at least added a little volume. I've been to livelier wakes."

"Well, let's try to get 'em playing a game or something. Anything to make people start talking about something other than golf."

They started to leave the room, but Ryan pulled her aside to whisper, "Oh, and your friend, Juliet? Big dyke. We've gotta sit over at Sproul Plaza one day so I can teach you how to pick 'em out, baby. If you weren't sure about

Juliet, you clearly don't know what to look for."

While Mia and Juliet waited for the Jell-O to set, Mia decided to probe a little to see if she could get the monosyllabic woman to open up. "So, I've never seen you around campus. What's your major?"

"American Studies."

"Really? That's mine, too. Weird...I would have thought we'd have been in the same classes."

"I always try to get all of my classes in on Tuesday through Thursday. That way I'm free for tournaments and things. I've been forced to take some of the worst classes in the major, just because of when the class meets."

"What else do you do for fun? I know golf takes up a lot of your time, but where do you hang out?"

"Mmm...nowhere, really. I have a room in a private home not far from here. I eat my meals with the family I live with, so I don't go out very much. The couple has two young kids, and I watch them in the evenings when the parents go out. I tend to hang around the house a lot."

"Wow...that must inhibit your...love life. I mean...can you have dates stay overnight?"

"Oh, no, Matt and Patricia have asked me not to do that. It sets a bad example for the kids." She shrugged and said, "It's not a problem, though. I don't date."

"You don't?" Mia asked. "At all?"

"No, not really. Not since I've been at Berkeley."

"You're a senior! You're wasting your prime dating years!"

The young woman laughed softly and said, "I've had other priorities. My goal is to make the LPGA tour. After that I can start to concentrate on my social life."

"Damn," Mia said, shaking her head. "Did you date in high school?"

"Yeah." Juliet got up and pulled open the refrigerator. "Think these are ready yet?"

Mia walked over to her and peered over her shoulder. "Yeah, I think they're close. Let's have one and then put them back in to firm up a little." She cut two generous squares and handed one to Juliet, while letting her own slide down her throat. "Smooth, huh?" she asked when Juliet swallowed.

"Yeah," she said, smiling. "Really smooth. It didn't taste like alcohol at all."

"That's the beauty of the Jell-O shot." Mia sat back down and asked, "Would you be interested in going out on a date or two? I'm sure I could fix you up—if I knew your type."

"Ah...no, really, I'm not in the market. What about you? Are you dating anyone?"

"I'm not dating. I'm in love—big time." She gave Juliet a very warm smile and asked, "Wanna see a pic?"

"Sure." She shrugged, looking less than fascinated, but when Mia went to the refrigerator and removed an action picture from a volleyball game—showing Jordan and Ryan rising in tandem to block a shot, Juliet's eyes nearly popped from her head.

"This…this is your…?"

"Lover," Mia said helpfully. "That's Jordan Ericsson. You might have seen her play volleyball, but if you missed her there's still time to catch her in action. She's on the U.S. Olympic team," she said with a great deal of pride in her voice.

"Wow! She must be great."

"Oh, she is. In many, many ways. Only problem is that she's in Colorado Springs at the Olympic training facility. We can't be together until school's out."

Staring at the picture, Juliet said softly, "It's horrible to be separated from someone you love, isn't it?"

"Yeah, it really is." Mia walked back to the refrigerator and took out the Jell-O. "Care for another?"

"Sure. I didn't even notice that first one."

"They tend to catch up with you," Mia said, offering fair warning. "There's over a cup of vodka in here."

"Is that a lot?"

"It depends on what your goal is," Mia said, wrinkling her nose in a grin. "It's just about right if you wanna get wasted."

"Wasted, huh?" Juliet asked. "I've never been wasted—maybe it's time."

"Stick with me," Mia said, chuckling. "I'll make sure your first trip to Wastedville is a pleasant one."

At ten thirty, Jamie stood in the doorway, waving to the last of her teammates. As she closed the door, Ryan grabbed her from behind, then turned her and pinned her into the corner where she pounced upon her lips. Raining a torrent of kisses upon her sweet mouth, Ryan growled as she pressed her hips against Jamie's, murmuring, "Finally, a way to get my blood moving again."

Jamie slapped her hard on the butt, unable to stop giggling. "You're such a bad girl, Ryan O'Flaherty. I looooove bad girls." She gave her a rough squeeze and said, "Help me clean up a little and I'll let you do as many bad things to me as you want."

"Mmm…motivation," Ryan said, releasing her captive. They started to pick up a wealth of paper cups, plates and napkins, and when Ryan's hands were full she popped the kitchen door open with her hip. She let out a gasp when she spotted Mia and Juliet, sitting—or, rather slumping at the kitchen table. "What in the hell is going on in here?"

Jamie came scampering over, peering around Ryan's shoulder to get a good look. The two drunken women looked up at them, two pairs of unfocused eyes trying to think of an appropriate response. "We're doing Jell-O shots," Mia said, her words slightly slurred. "Want one?" She looked down at the empty glass baking dish and scratched her head. "We made two batches. Where'd they all go?"

"Right to your heads," Ryan said, walking into the room and depositing the trash she carried onto the counter. Turning to Jamie, she said, "Help me load Juliet into the car. I'll take her home." Twitching her head towards Mia, she added, "You can get Sir Drinks A Lot into bed."

"No, no, I'll take Juliet," Jamie said. "I know where she lives."

"All right. Let's get Mia into bed, and we can take off."

"You don't need to go with me. I'd rather you stayed and kept an eye on Mia."

"Are you sure?"

"Yeah, I'm positive. Put the rest of the things in a trash bag, carry Mia to bed, and by the time you're in bed I'll be back."

"I'm not undressing her," Ryan said firmly. "She's so damned ticklish, it's like wrestling a puma."

"I don't need undressing," Mia said, her dignity still intact. "Only Jordy undresses me." As she said those words, she started to cry. "I miss my Jordy." She laid her head on the table and sobbed, with Juliet trying to find her back to pat it.

Ryan met Jamie's eyes and said, "No more parties. Clean-up is a bitch."

❧

With Ryan's help, they poured Juliet into the BMW, then Jamie dashed around to the driver's side. "I'm gonna have to help her get into bed, so it might take me a few minutes. She lives with a family—and I'm sure they wouldn't like to have the kids find her passed out in the hallway."

"Don't be long," Ryan said. "Do you have your cell phone?"

"Of course. I'll be back as soon as I can. Be nice to Mia, okay? She's awfully sad."

"I will," Ryan said, smiling. "I'll nicely dump her butt into bed."

❧

When Jamie pulled into the driveway of the home where Juliet lived, she was pleased to see the lights out. *At least I don't have to attempt this maneuver in front of an audience.* "Okay, Juliet, I'd appreciate some help here." She went over to her friend's side of the car, and found that Juliet was a bit more cooperative than she'd been a few minutes earlier. "The fresh air must have revived you a little."

Working together, they got up to the house, and Jamie got the key into the door—hoping fervently that there was no alarm. When nothing chimed, beeped or buzzed, she smiled to herself and helped Juliet up the stairs. Luckily, she was sober enough to find her own room, and after stumbling and crashing into the wall once or twice, they reached the door. Jamie got it open, then helped Juliet in, looking around quickly to make sure they were in the right place. When all she saw were textbooks on a desk, and an LPGA calendar on the bare walls, she knew they'd hit pay dirt.

"Okay," Jamie said as she got her to the bed. "I'll get your shoes off, then I'll help you with your jeans. After that—you're on your own."

"'Kay," the taller woman said, struggling to get that much out.

When Jamie had her as undressed as she was willing to go, she pulled down the covers and helped her into a horizontal position. Sitting down on the edge of the bed, she asked, "Are you going to be all right? I worry that you won't be able to get to the bathroom without hurting yourself."

"Fine," she said, pointing in the direction of the bath. Jamie got up and made sure the path was unobstructed, then turned the light on, pulling the door halfway closed so Juliet could find it during the night.

Returning to the bed, Jamie said, "I'm gonna go now. I left your keys on your desk there. I assume the front door will lock behind me," she said, trying to think of what she'd do if that weren't the case. Shrugging, she said, "I hope you feel okay, tomorrow, even though I'm sure you won't."

"I have to pee," Juliet said, looking longingly at the bathroom.

Taking pity on her, Jamie helped her up, then waited outside the door, hoping that Juliet didn't lose any of her Jell-O shots. She heard her noisily brush her teeth, which seemed like a good sign, then Juliet emerged, looking a little more put-together.

Jamie got her back to the bed, but Juliet just sat on the edge, rather than lying down. "Thanks for the help," she said, her voice still slurred, but understandable.

"Hey, no problem. I've been in worse shape." Jamie reached over and ruffled Juliet's hair.

Jamie was surprised when Juliet grasped her hand and held it to her cheek, nuzzling her face against the palm. "You're such a nice woman," she said, sighing.

"No problem," Jamie said. "We're teammates. You'd do the same for me."

"No one else would," she said, a few tears sliding down her cheeks. "No one else cares enough."

"Hey, don't say that," Jamie said, her maternal instincts coming out in full force. "You're a very nice person. You don't let people get to know you."

"I…I can't," she said, sounding defeated. "I just can't."

Jamie stroked her back with her free hand, feeling sorry for Juliet—who obviously had some serious problems with intimacy. "Sure you can. You have to be more open with people, and let them get to know the real you. But you can do it."

"No, no, I can't," she said again, crying harder. "I'm so damned lonely."

"Hey," Jamie said softly, stroking her hair, "you don't have to be lonely. You're a nice woman, you're very attractive, and you're gonna be a big success in your field. I think you're quite a catch."

Suddenly, the larger woman's arms were around Jamie's waist, and Juliet was holding on tight, crying her eyes out. Jamie didn't know what to do, so she continued to stroke her hair and her shoulders, murmuring soothing words. "Come on, now, lie down," Jamie said.

Juliet did as she was told, but she failed to remove her arms from Jamie's waist first. The pair tumbled to the bed, legs entwined. For a second, Jamie was too surprised to move, but when Juliet started kissing her chest, making her way towards her mouth, the shock turned to outrage. "Hey!" Jamie got her hands between them and pushed Juliet roughly, then disentangled her legs and stood up. "Don't you ever try anything like that again!" she said, her face flushed with anger. "Only Ryan touches me that way!" She straightened her shirt, then ran her hands through her hair, trying to control her temper.

By this time Juliet was crying helplessly, and Jamie's conscience reminded her that scolding her at this point was a complete waste of time. "Juliet," she said, putting her hand on her leg, "get some rest and try to sleep it off. I know that being drunk can make you do things you wouldn't ordinarily do."

"I'm sorry," she got out, sobbing roughly.

"It's all right. Just go to sleep. We'll talk about this later."

"Do you hate me?" she asked timidly.

"Of course not. Not at all. Now, just relax, will you? I'll see you on Monday morning."

"I'm sorry, Jamie," she said once again. "I'm so sorry. I couldn't help it…"

"We'll talk later. Now, get some sleep, and try to feel better, okay?"

"All right."

A few tears were still sliding down her cheeks, and Jamie gave her a compassion-filled look and said, "It's all right. Please don't worry about it."

"I'm sorry," she murmured, lying down with a heavy thump.

"Goodnight," Jamie said, quickly backing out of the room before she had to hear another apology. As soon as she was on the street, she called the house, and Ryan answered on the first ring. "Hi, speedy. I just left the house, so I'll be home in a few. I didn't want you to worry."

"Oh, good. I wanted to get into bed, but I wasn't gonna take my clothes off until you were home. I wanted to be able to come get you if you ran into any trouble."

"I'm fine. Get in bed on my side and warm it up for me, will you?"

"Will do. Hurry home, baby-doll."

"Baby-doll?"

Ryan shrugged, even though Jamie couldn't see her. "They just pop out. Lord knows why."

"I'll be right there," Jamie said, smiling at the image of her partner, knowing that she had likely shrugged her broad shoulders when she was explaining herself.

🐴

When Jamie got home a few minutes later, her side of the bed was toasty warm—at least it looked warm underneath Ryan's soundly sleeping body. *Well, I guess we're switching sides,* Jamie decided, getting in on the other side. Ryan immediately cuddled up to her, her warm, sleep-heavy body feeling like a familiar, warm blanket. *Damn, Juliet,* Jamie sighed, *I can't believe you had the nerve to make a move on me after you saw your competition. Do you have a death wish?*

🐴

After sleeping in, and taking a few minutes to check on Mia, Jamie and Ryan went to Noe Valley to spend the day with the family. Martin and Maeve and Caitlin had saved them seats at Mass, and the five-some spent the service passing Caitlin from one person to the other—playing the usual game of "who can entertain a sixteen month-old for more than ten minutes."

Ryan had possession of the toddler when it was time to file out of the pew for communion, and as usual, she and Jamie stood side-by-side in the line. It wasn't a common thing at their parish, but a few couples stood next to one another while receiving the Eucharist, and Ryan liked the idea, so she and Jamie had adopted the practice not long after they'd started attending St. Phil's. When they got near the front of the line, the usher directed them to a Eucharistic Minister who stood to the right of Father Pender. Jamie started to go where she was directed, but Ryan tugged on her, staying right where she was. Jamie looked up at her quizzically, then shot a glance at the man from whom they were supposed to receive the sacrament. He gave her a very perturbed look, but she merely shrugged slightly, waiting for Father Pender as Ryan was intent on doing.

After Mass, they went out to the patio to purchase some coffee and donuts from the parish Girl Scout troop. While they waited in line, Jamie asked, "Hey, why were you so intent on receiving communion from Father

Pender?"

"Oh, I wasn't," Ryan said. "I didn't like the alternative."

"Well, that guy was pissed off. He gave me a look like he wanted to throttle me."

"No, honey, he was giving us that look before we were directed to go to him. That's why I refused to do it. That kindly soul is Robert Andrews, Sara's dad."

"Oh! So, I wasn't imagining the look."

"Nope. As soon as he saw us, he started to put a puss on. No way I'm having him try to choke me with a communion wafer."

While they were chatting, Father Pender came up to say hello. Martin and Maeve were sitting at a table with Caitlin, everyone knowing that having the child near the donut table was a recipe for disaster. "Siobhán, Jamie, how are you both?"

"We're good," Ryan said. "Buy you a cup of coffee, Father?"

"That'd be lovely," he said, smiling.

"Could you steer me to a list of good retreat houses," Ryan asked. "I'm thinking about going away for a week this summer, and I'd like to find a good place."

"Oh, certainly. What type are you looking for?"

"Well, I'm not sure how many options there are."

"There are more styles of retreat than snakes in Ireland before St. Patrick," he said, his eyes crinkling up. "Stop by the rectory before you leave. My secretary has a list of all of the places in the Archdiocese."

"Thanks, Father. I will."

Looking at her for a moment, he asked quietly, "How are things going with you personally, Siobhán? Feeling better?"

"Yeah, I'm feeling less guilty about shooting that guy, but my temper's still pretty explosive. I'm about out of cheeks to turn."

"You'll get there," he said, gripping her shoulder. "You're a very forgiving girl."

"Up until now I have been," she said, "but I've never really been tested before."

Jamie gave her a look that questioned her sanity, and Ryan chuckled softly, "Okay, I guess I have been pretty even-tempered before now. My reserves are dangerously low."

"Time and prayer will help you store up all the reserves you need," the priest assured her.

"I hope the reserves are back up before I need them," Ryan said. "I don't want to find out what I'm capable of."

Martin and Maeve stayed behind to socialize, since Caitlin had found a boyfriend and was playing happily with the little fellow. On the walk home, Jamie held Ryan's hand, "How are you feeling?"

"Uhm…good?" Ryan replied.

"Nice and peaceful? Full of good will towards your fellow person?"

"Who am I going to want to kill, and why?" Ryan asked, giving Jamie's hand a squeeze.

"Mmm…maybe Juliet."

Stopping dead in her tracks, the blue eyes narrowed and Ryan turned slowly, gazing at Jamie for several seconds before she asked, "What did she do?"

"Uhm…you know how drunk she was last night…"

Giving her a look that could peel paint, Ryan repeated herself, slowly this time. "What…did…she…do?"

Knowing that she was unable to make it sound better than it was, Jamie told the tale. "I got her into bed and she started crying, saying that no one liked her and things like that. I patted her back and smoothed her hair a little bit—just being nice," she said. "She either got the wrong impression from that, or she just lost it, because she put her arms around me and we fell onto the bed together. She uhm…kissed my chest, and my neck, and was on her way to moving up when I pushed her away and got up. I told her off, Ryan, and warned her to never do anything like that again."

Jamie looked up at her partner, practically able to see steam coming out of her ears. Without a word, Ryan turned and started to walk home, her grip on Jamie's hand just short of painful. Knowing that her partner needed a few minutes to calm down, Jamie didn't say a word. But when they got to the house, Ryan strode up to the BMW and beeped the doors open. As she started to get in, Jamie asked, "Where are you going?"

"We're going to Berkeley," she said, her voice flat, but bursting with menace.

"Oh, no, we're not. No, way, Ryan!"

"There is no way in hell that I'm gonna let her get away with that. You are not some piece of meat that she can paw."

"I'm also not an airhead who can't protect herself," Jamie said, her voice starting to rise.

"Get in the car!"

"I will not!"

"Get in!"

"NO!"

Jamie started for the stairs, not slowing down when she heard the car door slam loudly.

Conor and Kevin were in the kitchen when Jamie entered, and they called out a greeting. Before Jamie could reply, Ryan strode into the house, saying only one word—in a very loud voice. "Downstairs!"

Rolling her eyes at the boys, who each gave her a wide-eyed look, Jamie shook her head and followed her furious partner down to their room. Closing the door, Jamie gently pushed her partner down onto the loveseat and straddled her. "Listen to me," she said, her cheeks pink with anger, "you have every right to be upset by someone trying to touch me against my will, but it was me who was touched. I'm the one who should be indignant—not you. I'm not your property, and I don't like being treated as such. Now, calm down and chill." She got up and went to the built-in drawers, pulling out a sweater and a pair of jeans. While Jamie changed, Ryan didn't say a word, she just sat on the loveseat, looking like she was about to explode.

When Jamie was finished, Ryan rose, changed into sweats and laced up a pair of running shoes. "I'm going out for a run," she said, not waiting for a response.

Jamie shook her head and went upstairs to chat with the boys, trying to think of an excuse for her partner's bad manners that wouldn't reveal anything too personal.

Ryan was gone for a long time—a very long time. Jamie had called her father, her mother, her grandfather, and had made a good dent in her accounting homework by the time the sweat-drenched body returned home.

Jamie looked up from her book, trying to meet Ryan's eyes to see if the dark mood had brightened. From her initial glance, it seemed unlikely, and she mentally rolled her eyes—hoping that their entire day wasn't going to be ruined. But Ryan surprised her; sitting down on her desk chair and gazing at Jamie with a contrite look. "I'm sorry for how I behaved. I don't have a lot of control. My mouth gets away from me."

Jamie reached out and stroked Ryan's wet arm. "I know things are hard for you, honey. Having something like this happen doesn't help the situation in the least."

"No, it doesn't," Ryan said, nodding. "But I'm in bad shape when I can't shrug off some woman making a fairly harmless pass at you. I'm not normally jealous of things like that."

"I know you're not. Don't worry, this will pass."

Ryan sighed, stretching in her chair. "I went over to the church and talked with Da and Maeve for a while," she said. "Then Father Villareal came over, and I asked him for some advice. But even after having three people, whose opinions I trust tell me the same thing—I was still steamed. So, I ran until I could finally feel my anger start to dissipate." She chuckled softly, and said,

"It's a good thing I don't know where Juliet lives, 'cause I could have easily made it to Berkeley—on foot."

"I can handle her. I'm gonna tell her in no uncertain terms that she is never allowed to touch me again. I won't stand for that kind of crap—from anyone. I feel sorry for her because she seems so lost and alone—but I don't feel sorry enough to let her touch me."

"I know you can handle yourself. I have to make the irrational part of my brain listen to the rational side a little more."

"Hey," Jamie said, giving Ryan a sultry smile, "remember when we were on our honeymoon and you told me that your father said you should always get naked to have an argument?"

"Yeah," Ryan said, nodding. "Are we still arguing?"

"Noooo...but it might be a nice way to make up. Let's hop in the shower and see if we can wash away some of the remnants of our little spat."

"But you're not dirty," Ryan said, giving Jamie a sexy grin.

Standing, Jamie extended her hand and pulled her partner to her feet. "I can be as dirty as the next girl—given the right motivation. Come motivate me, hot stuff."

After their make-up shower and a nice nap, the girls went upstairs to socialize a bit. Martin and Maeve had come over to start Sunday dinner, and Brendan, Maggie, Conor, Rory and Kevin were all jammed into Conor's room, watching a basketball game. Since there wasn't room for them in the bedroom, Jamie and Ryan went into the kitchen to chat with Martin and Maeve. Ryan sat on a stool and pulled her partner to her, nuzzling her neck and hugging her constantly. "Looks like someone's feeling a little better," Martin said, giving his daughter a wry look.

"Nah, this is how we fight," Ryan said, kissing a path across the back of Jamie's neck, while Jamie giggled and wriggled on her lap.

"Why don't we fight like that, Marty?" Maeve asked, giving her husband a bump with her hip. "The girls have the best ideas."

"It's never too late to learn a few new tricks," he said. "Maybe we should fight right now." He wrapped his arms around his bride and started to kiss her neck with as much gusto as his daughter had just demonstrated.

"My eyes! My eyes!" Ryan cried, dramatically cupping her hands over the bright blue orbs.

Jamie laughed at her partner's antics, while encouraging the older couple. "Go for it, Martin!"

"I've had to get used to seeing the two of you rubbing against each other like a pair of cats in a sack. It's high time you had a dose of your own medicine," he said, laughing evilly while he continued to kiss the giggling Maeve.

Ryan pushed her partner from her lap and ran from the room. "I'm gonna go watch the game—if my retinas haven't been burned out!"

The only spot available to Ryan was on the floor, next to her cousin. "I haven't had much time to talk to you lately, buddy. How's it going living with us and the boys?"

"Good," Kevin said, smiling brightly. "Better than I thought, really. It's like when Tommy and Michael were still at home. You know, I think I'd rather stay here than move back to my ma's place."

"Have you told your mom that? You know, the whole reason they're gonna move to Niall's is to give you the house."

"I've kinda hinted at it," he said, "but we haven't had a serious discussion. I guess we should, though. I like being around the guys, and it's nice to share the responsibilities, not to mention the expenses. Now that we've gotten rid of that 'no overnight guests' thing, it's perfect living here."

"Do my father and your mother know you've abolished the rule?" Ryan asked with an impish grin.

"What they don't know won't hurt them. Or us."

Tommy, Annie and Caitlin joined the already full house, and while they were eating, Ryan brought the subject up again. "When is Niall's place supposed to be ready?"

"It's going well," Martin said. "I think a few weeks, at the maximum."

"Well, Ryan and I were talking about it, and I don't think I want to move back to the house, Ma," Kevin said. "I like living with the guys."

"Really?" Maeve asked. "Well, goodness, Kevin, if you don't want the house, it doesn't make any sense for us to move."

Ryan had a hard time keeping the obvious signs of relief from her face. A persistent thread of worry had been niggling at her over the thought of her father and aunt moving several miles away, and the possibility that they would stay right where they were was overwhelmingly heartening.

Martin sensed her relief and said, "If we don't have to go, we'll stay right where we are. I need to stay close to keep my eye on you children." He spoke to all, but his eyes were firmly planted on his smiling daughter. "I've been worried about prowlers," he said, scowling a bit. "I saw a young woman walking down the stairs just after dawn the other morning. I think she may have been casing the joint."

Conor, Rory, and Kevin all put on their most innocent faces, no one willing to confess to that particular encounter.

Partially to deflect the focus from his brother and cousins, Tommy piped up and said, "If you don't take Niall's, I think Annie and I might. Our place is too small to change our minds in, and we just found out we're getting another rent increase. We've got to do something."

"Well, that would work, Tom," Martin said. "Although we'd hate to have you so far away."

"Oh, my yes," Maeve said. "Sunset is far too distant to walk to."

"It can't be that far. You were going to live there, Mom," Tommy said. "It's too good of an opportunity for all of us to pass up. The rent is less than we currently pay, and the place is twice as big."

"I realize that," she said. "I just wish there were a better way."

"Well, it's not decided," he said. "Let's see how things go."

"All right," Maeve said, but it was obvious she was very unhappy at the thought of Caitlin being so far away.

Chapter Four

Monday morning, Jamie was hard at work on her golf game, having noticed that Juliet hadn't arrived at her usual, early time. Jamie worked until nine, and when she looked up, she saw Juliet sneaking away, beating a hasty retreat down the path to the parking lot.

Deciding that she was not going to let the incident pass without comment, and wanting to get it over with, Jamie left her clubs lying right where they were and took off after her. She caught up just as Juliet was hurling her clubs into her car. "Hey, wait up," Jamie called out.

"I've got a test this morning. I don't have a minute to spare."

"Fine," Jamie said, "but you and I are going to talk about what happened on Saturday night. When is your last class over?"

"This isn't a good time for me, Jamie."

"I don't care. You can spend a half hour at some point in the day. Now, when will it be?"

"I'm finished by four," she said weakly, staring at the ground.

"Good. Do you know where the softball stadium is?"

"Yeah, I think so."

"Meet me there. I'll be there by four, and I'll stay until six—that will give you plenty of time—even if you get lost."

"Fine," she agreed, nodding.

Out of the corner of her eye, Jamie saw a glimpse of a woman, huffing up the hill on her bicycle. "Uhm…you might want to get going."

"Huh?"

As she said this, Ryan rode up to them, grabbed onto her brakes and skidding a few feet—sending up a flourish of gravel and dust. "Nice morning for a ride," Ryan said to Juliet, grinning like a tiger seconds before it pounces upon a wounded animal. "You guys about done? I thought we could have breakfast, maybe—chat—a little." Her eyes were flashing with unspoken malice, and even though a part of Jamie was irritated, there was something tremendously sexy about the menace that Ryan projected.

Moving to her side, Jamie snaked her arm around Ryan's waist, hugging her firmly. She put her other hand behind Ryan's black-helmeted head and pulled her down, kissing her cheek while she muttered, "Show off."

"I've got to go," Juliet said, looking like she was about to wet her pants. "Big test. Big, big test." She was in her car, pulling out before either woman could speak.

Ryan shook her head, giving Jamie a puzzled look as she asked, "Does she always drive with her spikes on?"

"You are such a brat!" Jamie gave the Lycra-encased butt a firm swat, shaking her head when Ryan looked like she'd enjoyed it. "What am I gonna do with you, you possessive little thing?"

"You can't blame me. You're so beautiful, so desirable, so bright, so clever, so kind, so…"

"Can it, tough girl. I told you I could take care of myself, and I can." She stood on her tiptoes and kissed Ryan on the lips, lingering longer than was prudent, given the venue. "I shouldn't encourage you, but there's something kinda sexy about having my big, tough girlfriend protecting me—even though I don't need it."

"I know you don't need it," Ryan said, staring into her eyes. "But right now—for some reason, I need to do it." She wrapped her arms around her partner and said, "I don't want to make you feel like I think you're a frail, little flower, but I need to bare my teeth once in a while."

Jamie returned the hug, making it nice and hard like Ryan liked it. "You can bare your teeth—once in a while, Buffy. But just for show. I don't want you biting anyone."

"Only love bites," Ryan said, smiling toothily. "Guess what I'm going to do when I get home?"

"No idea."

"I'm going to take off my bike clothes, throw them in the wash, and when they're clean, I'm going to put them away until summer—at the earliest."

Jamie gave her a smile that brightened every inch of her face, then wrapped her arms around Ryan's waist and gazed up at her. "I don't think I could love you any more than I do at this moment."

Bending to kiss her, Ryan murmured, "Your expectations are far too meager. We're gonna love each other much, much more. I'm sure of it."

❧

Ryan had just spent three hours with her math professor, Robin Berkowitz, and Vijay, her graduate student advisor, going over her independent project with such attention to detail that she felt absolutely drained. Spying a rest room, she practically sprinted for it—having been so engrossed in the discussion that she'd paid no attention to her personal needs.

Ryan emerged from the rest room stall and balanced her books on the adjoining sink. Then she bent over and splashed cold water on her face, and patted her strained eyes with a damp paper towel.

As she gazed at herself in the mirror, another stall door opened, and the last person she ever wanted to see emerged. Cassie Martin stood stock-still for a moment, a tiny flicker of fear showing in her eyes, then let her usual nasty personality emerge as she strode across the floor to the sink. "I can't believe you have the guts to show your face around this campus," she said, not even looking at Ryan.

Ryan thought back to her promises—the ones she'd made to Jamie, and Amanda and Father Pender. She'd promised each of them that she was going to do her very best to take the high road in this little soap opera, and not stoop to Cassie's level. So she ignored her completely, acting like she hadn't heard anyone speak—even though her guts were roiling.

"Huh," Cassie grunted, "I guess your 'no comment' thing holds for every area of your life. Buuuuut…that only makes sense when the details of your existence are so sordid."

With shaking hands, Ryan picked up her books and started for the door, wishing the damned bathroom wasn't so long.

"You know, you've even more of a whore than I thought you were. It's bad enough what you did to Jamie, but the things I read about you and that little girl. Tsk, tsk, tsk. Isn't fourteen a little young—even for you?"

Ryan felt her hands whiten on her books, but she continued to walk, not saying a word.

"Or did you have to bring her into the mix for Jamie?" Cassie asked, her voice dripping with venom. "The kid's probably more to her liking anyway—they're about the same age—sexually, at least." She found her comment quite funny, and she was laughing softly when Ryan dropped her books with a thud and quickly reached up to lock the door to the facility.

The laugh was cut off so quickly that it sounded as though her throat had been slit, but Ryan hadn't touched her—yet. In a heartbeat, Ryan was right on top of Cassie, pinning her to the sink with her substantially greater bulk. "You can say whatever you want to say about me, but don't you ever…ever mention Jamie's name again. A slime-dweller like you isn't worthy of licking the soles of her shoes."

Cassie's eyes were wide, and Ryan could see her pulse throbbing on the side of her throat. "D…don't be so touchy."

Leaning in a little harder, Ryan could feel the smaller woman's flesh compress as she pressed against her. She knew the sink was digging into the backs of Cassie's thighs, so she leaned in just a bit more. "Jamie and I've already talked about this," Ryan said, menace oozing from her, "and she doesn't mind if we have to pay a substantial sum of damages to you. She wants me to feel better." Pushing forward until she could hear Cassie gasp in pain, she said, "I've tried to control myself, but it's a losing battle. I think I'll feel better if I hurt you—badly."

Cassie spoke so quickly that her words tumbled from her lips. "You'll go to jail! You can't just beat people up. You'll be in prison—then where will Jamie be?"

Ryan leaned over her, bending Cassie into an inverted "C". "I told you to never speak her name again. I...meant...that."

"Okay! Okay! But you *will* go to jail if you hit me!"

"You don't know much about the justice system. Not many people do time for hitting someone." Ryan leaned even harder against her, smiling when Cassie gasped in pain. "But, given your connections, I guess you could make things tough for me." She appeared to be thinking through the ramifications of her plan. "If there's a chance of going to the slammer I'd better make sure I get my money's worth."

"No! You'll be thrown out of school! Think of yourself!"

Ryan seemed to do just that. "I guess I'll have to make sure no one can prove it was me. It'll be your word against mine, and of the two of us, I have a much better record for telling the truth. The only evidence they'd have is if I scraped my knuckles on your ugly face, or got your blood on me." She looked around the room and her eyes landed on a plunger. "I could beat the crap out of you with that stick..." she said thoughtfully. "Fill your mouth full of wet paper towels so no one could hear you scream...take off my shirt so the blood doesn't splatter onto it..." Her brow furrowed as she said, "Of course, I could drown you in the toilet. That would be all too fitting, wouldn't it?"

"Why are you doing this?" Cassie whimpered, her voice shaking. "What do you want?"

"Want? I don't want anything, other than to cause you pain." She leaned forward with her torso, forcing Cassie's head against the mirror. Ryan was so close she could have bitten her, and Cassie stared at her with round eyes. "You know, I've always wondered which it was. No rational person would care that Jamie and I were together—unless that person was insanely jealous." Pushing forward again, Ryan purred, "Which of us is it? Jamie or me?"

Cassie had to put her hands behind herself to stop the faucets from gouging into her kidneys. Her flailing hands accidentally hit the cold water tap—and the ice cold spray started to pour into the waistband of her khaki's. "Ahhhh!" she screamed, writhing against Ryan, their breasts compressing.

"Oh...it's me, huh? That was always my guess, since you were nice to

Jamie until I came along." Ryan's body ate up the last inch of space, and she murmured, "You've dreamed about being this close to me, haven't you."

"No! No! I'm not like that!"

"Well, we'll never find out, because you make both of us sick." Ryan started to stand up, but she put a restraining hand on Cassie's shoulder, holding her in place. "You know, as much as I want to hurt you physically, and believe me, I do, I think I'd get more satisfaction out of hurting your reputation—sleazy though it is. I'm not sure how I'll do it, but you've woken me from slumber, sweetie-pie, and vengeance will be mine." She leaned over until their noses touched. "Dream of me," she whispered, then swiped her tongue in a long, wet trail all the way up Cassie's flushed cheek. Striding away from the shaking woman, Ryan bent to pick her books up with a remarkable degree of grace. Flicking the door lock open with her hand, she glided from the room—feeling better than she had in weeks.

Jamie was sitting in the stands at the softball stadium that afternoon, giving half of her attention to practice, and half to her real estate text. It was so overcast and cloudy, that they'd turned the lights on—but there was still plenty of light to read by. Ashley and Jennie were sitting about twenty feet away, with Ashley drilling the younger girl for a test. Juliet showed up at four thirty, obviously hoping that Jamie wouldn't have time to talk. When Jamie saw her reluctantly approach, she twitched her head and led her to the grassy area by the ticket window on the outside of the complex. "We can talk here without having anyone hear us."

"Uhm...what do you want to talk about?" Juliet asked, trying to look innocent.

"You know darned well what I want to talk about. Now, let's get this out of the way so we can move on, okay?"

"O...okay."

"What's the deal?" Jamie asked, sitting down on the grass to get comfortable. "You didn't honestly think I was going to let you kiss me, did you?"

"Jamie, I swear I didn't know what I was doing. I've never been drunk before—I lost my mind."

Giving her a long look, Jamie said, "I have some experience in this area, and let me assure you—being drunk doesn't cause you to do things that aren't in your nature. Alcohol lets you do things that you want to do—but don't have the nerve or the sense to do while you're sober."

Juliet looked at the ground, not saying a word.

"Saturday night wasn't the first time I felt that you were attracted to me," Jamie said quietly. "I got strange vibes from you that time you showed me how to hit your seven-wood, too. Is this something that's going to come between us for the rest of the year?"

"No, no, it's not, definitely not," Juliet said decisively. "I was out of line on Saturday, and I promise I'll never let myself get drunk again. I obviously can't handle it."

"What about the other time? You weren't drunk then."

"I...I don't remember that day the way you do. I...uhm...maybe you're ultra-sensitive to things like that."

Jamie smiled and shook her head. "No, I'm really not, but if you don't want to talk about this with me, I can't make you."

"There's nothing to talk about," Juliet said, getting up from the ground. "I got drunk and acted like an idiot. I promise I'll never touch you again. Ever."

"I know you won't," Jamie said, giving her a wry smile. "Your career means too much to you to have my partner lose control and break your hands." She looked at her for a moment and said, "I wish I were kidding, but she's been under a lot of stress. She honestly might hurt you."

Juliet's expression was doggedly earnest, "I promise I'll never be inappropriate with you again. It will not happen!"

"Okay. That's all that I can ask. See you tomorrow."

Jamie started to walk back towards the stadium when Juliet asked, "Why are you hanging out here?"

"Oh, Ryan's on the softball team. Wanna stick around and say hi?"

"No...no..." she said, backing away quickly. "Gotta run." And run she did, jogging at a quicker clip than Jamie had ever seen her move.

As soon as Jamie took her seat, she started to study again, barely noticing what was going on. Heather and Ryan both bounded into the stands at six o'clock, thoroughly startling their fans. "Yikes!" Jamie cried, looking up into Ryan's sweaty face. "Is it six already?"

"Sure is. Hang on and I'll be back in a few. I want to put on some dry clothes."

Jamie patted her butt and sent her on her way, then went over to chat with Ashley and Jennie for a moment. As expected, the jocks were back in a flash, but Ryan had on a clean T-Shirt and her warm-ups, so Jamie wasn't going to press her luck by chiding her for not showering. "Ready to go, slugger?" Jamie asked.

Ryan shrugged, looking a bit uncomfortable. "Wanna see if the other girls want to join us for some dinner on Telegraph?"

"Sure. That'd be fine."

Ryan looked over and said, "Hey, we're gonna get some dinner. You guys up for it?"

"I can't," Jennie said, shaking her head. "I've gotta study every minute for this history test."

"We thought we'd drag Jen back to the dorm with us and drill her over dinner," Ashley said, making Jennie's eyes light up.

"Really? I'll have to call home and ask if I can, but I'm sure Sandy won't mind."

Jamie handed over her cell phone, and Jennie dialed while Ryan smiled at her friends. "You two have really come through with Jen," she said. "We can't tell you how much we appreciate it."

"It's fun," Ashley said. "I want to be a teacher when I graduate, and working with Jennie makes me see that it can be fun to help someone who wants to learn."

Jennie handed the phone back, grinning from ear to ear. "I can go!"

"Let's get moving," Heather said. "We've got over a hundred years to cover."

"See you," Ryan called out, and Jamie waved at the departing trio.

Ryan sat next to her partner, cuddling up to her as the overhead lights switched off. "Let's stay here and neck."

"It's freezing, you goof! You've got to get home and jump in the shower."

"Do you have your car?"

"No, I walked. Why?"

"Let's stop and get some coffee. I can warm up and then we can have dinner."

"Don't you have to study tonight?"

"Uhm…yeah, I could do a little work. We could go to the library after dinner."

"Honey," Jamie said, always attuned to the unspoken messages her partner sent out. "Is there some reason you don't want to go home?"

"Mmm…I'm a teeny tiny bit worried that the police might be at the house," she said, wrinkling her nose.

"The police, huh? Any particular reason they might be paying us a visit?"

"Well, I kinda ran into someone today, and she might have filed a police report against me."

"Did you run into this woman while you were on your motorcycle?" Jamie asked, thoroughly confused.

"No, I was on foot. She might have thought I was threatening her with bodily harm…Well, I was threatening her with bodily harm, but she might not have known it was just a threat. Well…I guess it wasn't just a threat…I was hoping she'd hit me, so I could crack her skull open like a coconut."

Jamie grabbed the closest ear she could find and gave it a yank. "What in the hell are you talking about?"

"I ran into your ex-roommate in the bathroom today," Ryan said, waiting for the words to sink in.

"Oh, God," Jamie said, dropping her head to her knees. "What'd you do to her?"

"Nothing…well…almost nothing. I pressed her up against the sink and leaned on her a little bit. I doubt that she even has bruises."

"Ryan! Why did you do that? You said you were going to control yourself."

"No…I said I was going to try to control myself. I did try, I tried very hard. She pushed me, baby; and if she'd said the same thing to you, you'd have punched her lights out. She did her best to provoke me, and she succeeded."

She said this with such a carefree tone, that Jamie was frankly puzzled. "Why aren't you upset? I thought it would make you crazy to let her get to you."

"Nope. I feel great, actually. She's a big, fucking bully, and sometimes it feels nice to make a bully quake with fear. She was about to wet her pants," Ryan said, chuckling softly. "Well, she did wet her pants, but that was from me jamming her against the faucet. Today was a bad day to wear khakis," she said, shaking her head with false regret.

"You're really okay?" Jamie asked, searching Ryan's eyes.

"Yep. She can't prove I did anything to her, and the police won't arrest me for some idle threat about beating her senseless with a plunger…"

A hand rose, stopping her in mid-sentence. "I don't want to know the details. I'm very glad that you got it out of your system. As long as you don't have to go to jail, I'm happy."

"Uhm…one more little, tiny thing," Ryan said, shrugging her shoulders sheepishly. "If they believe her, they might test me for rabies."

"*What?* Did you bite her?"

"Noooo," Ryan said. "But I…uhm…I…kinda…licked her."

"You…licked…her." Jamie said each word very slowly, her eyes narrowing with each syllable. "You licked Cassie Martin." Her head cocked, and Jamie fixed Ryan with a pensive gaze. "I can't wait to hear this one."

Looking perplexed, Ryan once again shrugged her shoulders. "I honestly can't explain it. There was a moment there when I knew that she was truly terrified. I had to mark her."

"You had to…mark…her."

"Honey, it was either that or lift my leg and pee on her. I felt like a dog, claiming my territory. It was so primal, so instinctive." She shivered roughly. "I can't describe it to you. If you've never felt that way, you don't have the proper frame of reference."

Jamie dropped her face into her hands once again, then sat up and shook her head. "I think we have to put this behind us. I don't think I want to know the part of you that made you do that."

"Just as well. There's a part of me that I don't understand, so I can hardly expect you to decipher it."

Jamie gazed at her partner for a moment, finally lifting her hand to slide her fingers through her bangs. "Are you sure you won't have to go to jail for this?"

"Yep. She can't make this one stick," Ryan said, full of confidence. "And next time, she might have the sense to keep her ugly trap shut."

"Is there going to be a next time?"

Ryan's dark head nodded. "There might well be. I'm still hungry for revenge."

Sighing deeply, Jamie took a minute to organize her thoughts. "Don't tell me about it, okay? You know I usually like to be informed about everything you do—but I don't want to know if you think of some way to get back at her." She stroked Ryan's face and said, "You do what you need to do—but I can't afford to worry about you. We'll deal with the consequences when the time comes—but please do me a favor and make it a civil suit, rather than criminal, okay? I can't bear the thought of having to visit you in prison."

"It's a deal. If I get my revenge, we'll be able to buy our way out of it—and at this point it's worth an awful lot of money to me."

🐴

"Jamie?" Jim Evans' voice boomed through her cell phone, bright and early on Tuesday morning.

"Hi, Daddy. What's up?"

"Well, since I'm coming down for the weekend, I've decided to come a few days early and conduct some business. I thought, if you were free, that we could have dinner together…say, tomorrow?"

"Uhm…sure, I know that I can. Is…do you want Ryan to join us?"

"Oh! I assumed…of course," he said, rather enthusiastically. "I meant both of you."

"Thanks, Dad. You're really making an effort here, and I appreciate it so much."

"I'm trying," he said quietly. He cleared his throat and added, "I have another agenda for the evening, and I hope you can be understanding about it."

"What's that?"

"I've decided to start seeing Kayla again."

She was quiet for a moment, fighting the urge to express her true feelings. "I hope that works out for you."

"That's it?" he asked carefully. "You're not disappointed in me?"

"Dad, Mom's filed for divorce. As long as you're with someone past the age of consent, it's none of my business."

"She's young, but she's not that young," he said with a hint of a tease in his voice.

"How old is she?"

"She's uhm…she's twenty-six."

"Mmm…two years older than Ryan. Well, age is just a number. What matters is that you enjoy being with her, and she with you."

"I don't know if this will last," he said. "But I'm going to try to make a go of it. I'd like to introduce you to her."

She sucked in a breath at that, but did her best to sound calm. "If you can get over your initial feelings about Ryan, I guess I can get over my initial feelings about Kayla. I'm willing to give it a try."

On Tuesday afternoon Ryan walked into her advisor's office and knocked on his cubicle wall. "Hey, Vijay. Got a minute?"

He gave her his usual, warm smile and nodded. "Always, for you," he said, in his clipped, Bombay-accented speech pattern. "What is it?"

"Well, I know you have more work than you can handle, but I was wondering if you could give me a hand with some programming. You're the best programmer I know."

He gave her a curious look and said, "What part of your project needs a program written? Have I missed something?"

"No, no, this is a special project I'm working on. It's a personal kinda thing. I shouldn't need too much of your time, actually. I only need you to help me chart it out and steer me in the right direction."

"Okay. I can spare some time. But you owe me dinner."

"Easy trade. It's a deal."

When Ryan walked into the house on Wednesday night, she went upstairs to get ready for their dinner engagement with Jim. After some negotiation, they agreed to have dinner at Chez Panisse, the site of Jamie's last birthday dinner. This time they had reservations in the more expensive upstairs dining room, and she knew she would have to dress up. Calling out a greeting to her partner, Ryan headed into the bath for a quick shower, then put on her suit, or as she now called it, her uniform. She went with the femmier look, wearing the sterling silver satin tank top and her dressy black flats, and she was just fastening her platinum necklace when Jamie came into her room.

"Zip me up?" Jamie asked.

"Okay," Ryan said, "but you know I far prefer the flip side of the job."

"I wish it were time for the flip side of the job. I *so* don't want to do this."

"Honey, we had trouble accepting Aunt Maeve, and we loved her like a mother. This will take some getting used to."

"My dad and his girlfriend," she said with distaste. "That's so trite."

"Well, it's certainly common. But the only couple we have any control over is us. I'm bound and determined that our kids will always know only Mom and Mama."

Slipping her arms around Ryan's waist, Jamie looked up at her and said, "You've got this all figured out, don't you?"

"What's that?"

"Our names. You've already decided on what our kids will call us."

"Well, no, I haven't," Ryan demurred. "I know they'll call me Mama, but I'm guessing you'll choose Mommy, which will turn into Mom when they're old enough to be embarrassed sounding like little kids."

"Like I said," Jamie insisted, "you've got this all figured out."

They arrived at the restaurant right on time, and as Ryan waited for the receipt from the valet, Jim and Kayla pulled up in a taxi.

"Good timing," Jamie said, giving her father a warm hug.

"Yes, it was," he said, looking very nervous. "Jamie, this is Kayla Horwitz. Kayla, my daughter, Jamie."

They shook hands, and Jamie was pleased to see that Kayla's hand was slightly wetter than her own. Ryan came over and kissed Jim on the cheek, patiently waiting for her introduction. "This is Ryan O'Flaherty," Jim said, omitting her title. "Ryan, Kayla Horwitz."

"Good to meet you," they both said, nearly simultaneously.

They were shown to their table almost immediately, and Jim ordered a bottle of white wine for the table. Jamie knew they could all use a little loosening up, but she'd already decided that she was going to stay completely sober—not liking where her mouth sometimes led her when she was tipsy.

Conversation was at a premium at the table, each person trying to get something going, but each failing miserably. The effort was giving Jamie a headache, and she excused herself to go to the rest room to get a moment alone. To her surprise, Kayla was practically on her heels, and when they reached the confines of the small room she said, "I know this is awkward. If I were in your shoes, and my dad was dating someone almost my age, I would hate it. I know you and I probably won't get to be best buddies, but it's important to your dad that we can reach some kind of accommodation."

Jamie smiled gently and nodded. "I'd like to normalize this as soon as possible. You're not the bad guy here. It wasn't you that caused my parents to split up." *Even though you didn't help matters*, she conceded to herself.

Extending her hand, they shook once again. "I'll do my best."

"Me, too," the redhead said, following Jamie to return to the table.

When Jamie took her seat, things were already going along better, with Ryan having set her mind on getting the conversation moving. She had brought up Jennie, and Jim immediately started to ask a plethora of questions. Kayla had volunteered at a legal clinic that dealt with a lot of child custody and other juvenile law issues, so she was interested, too, asking her own share of questions.

Once they had thoroughly covered Jennie and her progress, they were all more comfortable with each other, and the conversation started to flow. Jim was working on some interesting things, and he and Kayla complemented each other nicely as they jointly talked about their work.

Kayla was Jim's junior legislative aide, but it was pretty clear that she was serving in a greater capacity. Jamie privately wondered what the senior legislative aide thought of the relationship, but decided that really wasn't her concern.

By the time dinner was over, they were all fairly comfortable with each other, and Jim seemed positively buoyant. Jamie and Ryan saw them off in a cab and stood by the valet stand. waiting for the Boxster to be delivered. "Thanks for putting the car in valet. I appreciate not having to walk blocks and blocks in heels."

"Well, I don't like to, but since you insist on going with me to fetch the car, you've tied my hands."

"Mmm…don't give me any ideas," Jamie murmured softly into Ryan's ear.

The blue eyes widened perceptibly as she blinked slowly at her partner. "Do I make you horny, baby?" she said in an imitation of Austin Powers that she used exclusively to annoy Jamie.

"If you repeat one more line from that movie, I'm going to tie your hands and gag you."

"Ooo…big talk. Let's see you back it up with some action."

Jamie shook her head quickly and said, "I was about to make a comment about my father and Kayla, and all of a sudden we're talking like we're in a porn movie!"

"You haven't seen many porn movies, if that's how you think people talk. Actually, you haven't seen many porn movies if you think people talk at all."

"Well, actually, I haven't seen any, but that's beside the point. What did you think of Kayla?"

"I liked her well enough," Ryan said. "She seemed to click with your dad, and after we got over our initial nervousness I thought things went well.

Now about those movies…"

"Focus, tiger," Jamie chided. "I feel pretty good about the evening, too. If she sticks around for a while, I think I can tolerate it."

"I don't see them together long term." Ryan tipped the valet and got into the Boxster.

"How come?"

"I guess it's possible to bridge the age difference, but she's a very young woman. I can't imagine that she won't want kids at some point, and I can't see that your dad will want to have them when he's fifty. I could be wrong, but I think a twenty-year age gap—at this point in their lives—is too hard."

"I don't see it lasting, either," Jamie said, "but for another reason. I can't imagine that she'll keep him interested. He's not very mature, as you may have noticed, and I think the lure of the unknown will always tempt him."

"Time will tell," Ryan said, looking thoughtful for a moment. "Now about those movies…"

Ryan's motor was running by the time they returned home, and when Jamie went into the bath to get ready for bed, she heard her partner banging around in the bedroom. "What are you doing out there?" Jamie called out.

"Getting ready," Ryan cryptically replied.

When Jamie emerged, the grinning brunette was finishing hooking up and plugging in the DVD player. "Have you ever used this thing?"

"Not often. I used to have it in the library, but I rarely watched it down there. I thought I might use it more up here, but I obviously haven't. Advertisers are going broke with us, and we're the prime demographic."

"Mia always has the TV on in her room. She can represent the whole house. Now, we have two choices," she said, eyes flashing with excitement.

"Are we really going to watch a porn movie?" Jamie giggled, looking mildly embarrassed.

"Well, yeah. Don't you wanna?"

"I don't know." She looked down at the ground and said, "It feels kinda weird."

"Because?"

"I don't know. I've never watched one before."

"It's not a difficult thing to master," Ryan teased. "You watch for a while, you get hot, you have sex. It's a snap."

Her chin tilted, and Jamie looked at her partner curiously. "You get hot watching them?"

"Yeah. Definitely. That's the point. They're some of the worst examples of movie making in the universe. If they didn't get you hot, they'd have no value whatsoever."

"I don't know," Jamie said for the third time. "I'm not sure if I'll think it's erotic. I'm not all that fond of penises, and watching straight girls have sex to turn guys on won't do a thing for me."

Ryan gave her a completely puzzled look and asked, "Have you confused me with another? There aren't any men in the movies I own. Geez! Give the girl a break."

"Oh!" Jamie started to giggle. "I thought there would be guys, and girls with big hair and high heels and lacy undies. That's what you always see in the X-rated section at the video store."

"You, my friend, have been going to the wrong video store. Now, I don't want to pressure you in the least. If you want to watch this, fine—if you don't, that's fine too. But, just so you know, it's made by lesbians for lesbians. There isn't a penis in the neighborhood."

"Bring it on," Jamie declared with a big smile.

Ryan stuck the disk in and hit play. Then she climbed onto the bed, and snuggled up next to her partner. They were both wearing T-shirts, but not another stitch, and before the credits rolled, Jamie had to get under the covers. "It's cold in here," she complained. Ryan complied with her wishes, and soon thereafter the screen was filled with the image of a woman, standing out on a redwood deck—a beautiful tree-lined vista filling the sky behind her.

The doorbell of her home rang, and she walked inside to answer. "Here comes the biggest patch of dialogue," Ryan advised.

The woman opened the door to find a friend she had obviously been waiting for. After about fifteen seconds of small talk, they started to kiss. "Oh, they kiss nice," Jamie mused. "I've never watched women kiss before."

"What? Mia and Jordan are attached to each other like they've been super-glued at the lips."

"Yeah, but I don't watch them. I see that they're kissing, and I avert my eyes."

"Heh." Ryan tried to look innocent, but as usual her act backfired.

"You look, don't you!"

"Of course. I mean, I don't stare or anything, but I like to check out a good kiss when I see one. Mia has a style that is…decidedly enthusiastic," she said with a wicked smile.

Jamie slapped at her thigh and said, "You're the last one who needs lessons in enthusiasm."

"Shh! The clothes are gonna start dropping."

"How many times have you seen this?"

"Couple dozen," she guessed.

"A few *dozen* times?"

"Yeah. I bought this when I was seventeen. I had some real dry spells back then. Watching this made me feel like I wasn't the only lesbian in town."

"And it got you off," Jamie added with a smirk.

"Like a charm."

"Hey, where did you watch these movies? Did you have a player in your room?"

"Heck, no," Ryan said, shaking her head as she laughed softly. "I had to wait until Da and the boys were at work or at school. I think that's why I can get turned on so quickly. I had to make the most of my opportunities."

Jamie blinked at her, raising her eyebrows in a look that was partially disbelieving and partially repulsed. "You'd lie on your father's bed and…"

"No!" Ryan cried, slapping her partner's thigh. "That's gross!" She sniffed and tossed her hair over her shoulder. "I sat on the floor." Giving Jamie a randy wink, she added, "Brought me closer to the screen, too."

"Lord, Ryan, with one TV in the house, one of the four of you was probably trying to get a half hour alone to watch porn constantly."

Ryan chuckled, her eyes crinkling up as she nodded. "Mmm…not Conor, but Rory and I were always finagling to get to be the only one left at home."

"Maybe that was your father's plan to keep you all from constant self-abuse."

"You're starting to sound like my granny," Ryan warned, "and she's the last person I want to have in my head when I'm watching porn."

"I'm surprised to hear that Conor wasn't interested in dirty movies. Of course, he was probably too busy actually having sex to bother with it."

Ryan chuckled and said, "No, he wasn't. He just liked getting paid for his pleasure. When he hadn't had a date in a while, he'd go donate sperm. It used to piss me off that he could get fifty dollars to watch porn, and I had to do it for free."

Blinking slowly, Jamie said, "He really did that?"

"Yeah. All the time. He only stopped when Da caught him boasting about it. Conor tried to convince him that he was doing a humanitarian deed, but when Da found out he got paid for pullin' his wire, he put a stop to it immediately."

"Pulling his wire, huh? That's new one." Jamie giggled softly, but then her brow furrowed. "God, I wonder how many little Conors are running around San Francisco."

"Given how often he went, I'd say there could be hundreds. But a donor can only father so many children. I'm not sure how many you can have, but it's not a lot." Cocking her head, Ryan said, "How did we get on the topic of Conor's pleasure? Let's concentrate on our own, okay?"

Jamie turned her head to the screen, and was immediately rewarded by a very appealing sight. "Oh, my," she murmured. "Now that is a nice pair of breasts."

"What makes them nice?" Ryan asked. "Since you're such a breast-o-phile, I'm sure you have criteria."

"Of course I do. Those are nice because they have a nice heft to them. Not too big, but they definitely move. They're fairly symmetrical; they both point the same way, and have nice skin tone. Nice nipples, too. Not as nice as yours, I might add, but nice."

"Why, thank you," Ryan said, grinning.

"Nice. She knows how to play with them too. Oh, I love it when you do that to me."

Ryan shifted around and slid in behind her partner, pulling her against her chest. While the woman on screen played with her co-star's breasts, Ryan mimicked her, tickling and teasing Jamie through her T-shirt. "I'd go to the movies every night if we could do this," Jamie murmured.

"Eleven bucks would seem like a bargain price, too. Pay attention now. The other woman's shirt's coming off."

"Not bad," Jamie said. "A little meager for my tastes, but they'd do in a pinch."

"Speaking of pinching…" Ryan predicted.

"Ouch! That looked like it hurt."

"The pinchee doesn't seem to mind. There go the jeans."

Jamie was completely silent for a few minutes, watching the women strip completely. Once they were nude, they went out onto the deck, tossed some pillows onto the floor, and lay next to one another. Their hands were everywhere, stroking, sliding over each other, playing gently with each other's breasts, and squeezing firm ass cheeks. Ryan noticed her partner shifting around a bit, and she guessed that the movie was having its intended effect. "Damn, it's beautiful to watch two women make love," Jamie sighed. "A woman's body is such a work of art."

"All of those nice curves," Ryan said, drawing her hand over all of Jamie's that she could reach.

"The nice, smooth muscles. Everything's nice and round and soft and squishy."

"Squishy?"

"Yeah, like when my breasts squish against yours."

"Squishy's nice," Ryan murmured.

"Wanna squish together now?" Jamie asked softly.

"Perfect timing." Ryan switched off the player and started to tug her partner's T-shirt off.

"What else do the women in the movie do?"

"They go down on each other in the next scene. Other than that, I have no idea. I've never gotten farther than that."

"In dozens of viewings?"

"Hey, I'm easy. If I can get off in ten minutes, why waste time?" Her eyes grew wide, and she hastened to add, "That only applies to getting myself off. I like you to take all the time in the world."

"Your wish is my command," Jamie said, and proceeded to love her partner nice and slow and unhurriedly.

Chapter Five

On Thursday night, Jamie lay nestled in Ryan's arms, listening to the steady, slow beat of her heart. "I love listening to you breathe," she sighed, making Ryan chuckle.

"I'm kinda fond of it myself. I'd miss it if I stopped."

Reaching up a few inches, Jamie managed to get her fingers up under Ryan's last rib, a sure-fire tickle spot. Amid the startled laughter, she said, "I'm so excited about seeing your first game tomorrow. I charged the battery in my camera, just for the occasion."

"Is this gonna be like the 'first day of school' pictures that Da always made us pose for?"

"Yep. I'm gonna take dozens of shots. I think I'll have you in those action poses like they do on the real baseball cards."

"Well, that will assure that I win the biggest dork competition on the team. But it'll nice to be the best at something."

Jamie hugged her tighter. "You know I'd never embarrass you in front of your teammates. I'll make sure I have you pose in private."

"It's a deal. I won't complain about the pictures, if you don't make me look like a nut in front of my teammates."

"There's only so much control I have over that, but I'll do my best," Jamie said, dissolving into laughter when Ryan returned the favor and tickled her mercilessly.

🐺

On Friday morning, the junior Senator from the state of California met his old golfing buddies near the driving range of the Olympic Club. The first to arrive was Adam Christopher, Mia's father, and one of Jim's oldest friends.

Even though they were close, they rarely spoke for more than thirty seconds on the phone—and it was rare to even do that; they usually had their secretaries make arrangements for them to play golf or go sailing. The status quo didn't change once Jim left for Washington, and as his friend rolled up in a cart, he considered that he hadn't spoken to Adam since he'd left. Thus, they had not discussed the tumult of the carjacking, nor had they broached the subject of Jim's divorce.

As Adam walked towards him, Jim mused that he and Mia didn't have one physical trait in common. He was broad shouldered and lanky, with blue eyes and a shock of fine, straight, blonde hair that constantly tried to fall into his eyes. Having recently spent a little time in Mia's company, Jim decided that even though the pair looked nothing alike, Mia had inherited a good portion of her father's laid-back attitude.

Adam was the prototypical California beach bum when Jim met him during their freshman year at Stanford. Very easy-going, with a razor-sharp mind, the young man had impressed Jim immediately with his ability to glide through Stanford without obvious effort. Always up for a party or a road trip, Adam had been the one to introduce Jim to both marijuana and a long line of beautiful women.

Women found Adam completely irresistible—possibly because he acted like he was fully able to resist every one of them. He was always fun-loving and attentive when he was in a woman's company, but he never sought them out—preferring to make a woman chase him—which many did. Jim learned a lot from watching his worldlier friend, and by the time they were ready to graduate, they had cut a wide swath through the field of eligible women in Palo Alto.

Things didn't change much when they entered law school together. Their brothers of Sigma Chi were not at all surprised when hard-working Jim Evans was accepted to the law school, but many jaws dropped when Adam Christopher was admitted as well. Most of their frat brothers assumed Adam would ride a surfboard for most of his life, with a healthy supply of women to tend to his needs; but that wasn't Adam's plan.

Beneath the carefree exterior was a very competitive, ambitious young man, and when he entered law school that side of his personality started to emerge. He focused his talents for the first time in his life, and was soon near the top of his class…usually a spot or two above his frustrated friend Jim.

Near the end of their first year of law school, Adam met the woman he would marry. A more diametrically opposite pair it was hard to imagine; but for the first time, Adam did the chasing. Anna Lisa Poncirolli was a full-time employee working in the law library, and from the first time he saw her, Adam set his sights on wooing and winning the attractive young woman's heart.

Anna Lisa was a lovely young woman with dark, curly hair, her eyes so dark as to appear black in low light. Her olive-toned skin and petite frame contrasted starkly with the tall, fair, blonde man, and their physical differences were not the only ones that revealed themselves.

Anna Lisa was not a Stanford student—her immigrant parents could never have dreamed of being able to afford the tuition, but that didn't stop her. She had talked her way into a job at Stanford when she was fresh out of high school, and had been spending the last four years taking evening classes through Stanford Extension. It wasn't the same as earning a degree, but she was learning a great deal and improving her mind, which was her main goal. There were many ways she could have obtained a degree, including the affordable city college route, but she saw the respect that Stanford graduates were afforded, and she cast her lot with the school, even though she had neither the grades nor the money to be admitted into a degree program.

At first, Adam's friends assumed that he was stooping below his social class with his determined pursuit of the young, working-class woman. But as more of them got to know her, their opinions quickly changed as they saw what a perfect, albeit mismatched, pair they made.

After a whirlwind courtship, Adam had his prize; and he and Jim subsequently exchanged best-man duties at each other's weddings. Adam and Anna Lisa were married in August of that year, and ten months later, their son Peter was born. Mia came along ten months after Jamie, and to Jim's knowledge, the pair had been happily married throughout.

Adam approached and gave his old friend a hearty handshake. "You look great!" he exclaimed, slapping Jim on the back. "I always knew that senators led a charmed life. You're the living proof of that. Jesus, you look ten years younger."

"I wouldn't let this get around, but it's the truth. I haven't had a schedule this relaxed since we were in law school."

"Really? I was joking about leading a charmed life. But you do look relaxed."

"I have most of my evenings filled with receptions and speeches, but it's not the grinding pressure of practicing law. I don't know how I'll ever go back," he said, shaking his head.

"Well, you can cross that bridge when you come to it. I'm sure there will be plenty of opportunities that come from this. Besides, you could always retire and spend the rest of your life sailing if you wanted to."

Jim decided to get the topic out of the way, so he said, "I could have a year ago, pal, but I don't have Catherine's money to prop me up any longer. The divorce will be final in five months."

"Tough break," Adam said, giving his friend another pat on the back. "How'd it go for you?"

"It went fine. Well, as fine as a divorce can be, I suppose. It was the most amicable divorce in California history near as I can tell. I defaulted."

"You *what?*"

"Hey, people are trying to play golf; lower your voice. You obviously heard me. Catherine filed for divorce...I made a proposal for the settlement... she incorporated my proposal into her petition, and I defaulted. The judge granted her petition, and in a few months it's final."

"Jesus," Adam gaped, "Catherine is obviously the person to divorce if you've gotta divorce someone. What did her attorneys say?"

"She has the most disappointed attorney in the entire bar. She paid the guy for about two hours of work, as a matter of fact. All he had to do was review the document I sent to her and file it."

"Wait a minute. Are you sure that's a good idea? I mean, it's great that you got a good deal, but what if it gets out that a senator screwed his wife over in a divorce? I mean, look what the press did to Newt Gingrich when they found out about him filing when his wife was in the hospital."

"Catherine did not, in any way, get screwed over in this divorce. I asked for my cars and the gifts she's given me. That's it."

"Are you *insane?*"

"No, I'm not. I make a very good living...or at least I did when I was with the firm. If I can't figure out how to live on a million bucks a year, I ought to be ashamed of myself."

"But you're used to so much more!"

"True, but I've had a great ride for twenty-two years. She doesn't owe me more than that, but she very generously transferred title to my apartment in the city, so at least I'll have a place to hang my hat."

"Unbelievable," Adam muttered. "That's going to be some adjustment. Not to say it's not a nice apartment, but..."

"Let's face facts. She's been much more patient than I deserve. Believe me, she's put up with more shit than most women would tolerate. She should have kicked me out on my ass fifteen years ago." He was shaking his head at himself, his remorse visible.

"This has really shaken you up, hasn't it?" Adam asked with sympathy.

"Yeah, it has. It's been a hell of a year."

"All the mess with Jamie sure must have made it worse," Adam said, acknowledging he was aware of the incident.

"Yeah...that was a brutal wake-up call. You don't step back and think how lucky you are until you almost lose a child. I've had more nightmares than I can count."

"Mia says she's doing well now."

"She's great. I'm actually in town mainly because we're having a birthday party for her this Saturday." He looked at his friend and said, "Six months ago I was fixated on her telling me that she was in love with another woman. After everything that's happened, I kick myself when I think about how stupid I was. She's a wonderful young woman, no matter who she loves, and I'm damned lucky to have her."

"I'm glad to hear that," he said, with a smile curling up the corner of his mouth. "I'll try to remember that when Mia pushes me to the edge of my sanity."

The softball tournament was in San Jose, and since Jamie didn't have any classes scheduled, she waited until traffic was bearable, then went down to Hillsborough to pick up her mother.

Catherine was waiting for her—dressed and ready to go when she opened the front door. "Shall we?" she asked, picking up her purse.

"We're not in that big a rush, Mom. Let me go say hello to Marta."

Smiling at her own eagerness, Catherine stepped aside and consigned herself to waiting until her daughter had greeted the cook. *I couldn't be more excited if Ryan were my own child.*

They arrived in plenty of time, and caught up with the team right before they went to an empty field to begin to limber up. "Have you grown since this morning?" Jamie murmured into Ryan's ear when she sidled up behind her.

"Nooooo," she said, turning to give her partner a dazzling grin. "Why, do I look taller?"

Jamie gave her an appraising look, starting at her head, caressing her body with her eyes until she reached her black cleats. "You look like you've got six feet of legs alone," she insisted, dropping her gaze to give the long limbs another look.

"It's the pinstripes," Ryan said, giving Catherine a smile as she arrived. "Good morning, Catherine. Have you ever seen so many softball teams in one space in your life?"

"How many are here?"

"Sixteen. A lot if them are very good, too—Florida State, Nebraska, Iowa State, Ohio State. It should be a good tournament."

"Do you have time for some pictures?" Jamie asked. "I'd like to get you before you're dirty."

Ryan shot a glance at Marge Hellencamp, one of the assistant coaches, and mouthed, "When do we take the field?"

"Fifteen minutes," she replied, then added a wink when she saw Jamie and Catherine.

"I'll be back," Ryan grabbed a bat with one hand and grasped Jamie with the other to lead her back behind where the team buses were parked.

"Is this the best we can do?" Jamie asked, as Catherine chuckled.

"This will be fine. You can shoot towards the berm over there. It'll be a nice, green backdrop."

"All right, hold that bat like you know what to do with it, and strike a pose."

"Such an attitude," Ryan said. "Was she always so domineering?"

"I'm afraid so," Catherine said. "She's always been a natural leader."

"Nice spin on it, Mom," Jamie said sweetly as she framed Ryan in the viewfinder. "Most people would say I'm bossy." As she concentrated on her task, Jamie mused, "You're so darned cute in that outfit. It was made for you."

Catherine cast a long glance at her daughter-in-law, noting the traditional baseball-style white uniform with the crisp blue pinstripes. The pants were very snug, not a wrinkle showing down the long, lean legs. Dark blue stirrups covered plain white socks, with low-rise, black cleats on her feet. A neat, dark blue mock-turtleneck was covered by the sleeveless jersey. Ryan had rakishly left the top two jersey buttons unfastened, letting even more of the dark sweater peek out.

A large, dark blue "9" backed with gold covered Ryan's broad back, and a similarly colored "Cal" was emblazoned in script across her chest. As she loosened up by swinging the bat, the Cal grew distorted, then snapped back into place, with each completed motion.

"Okay, I think I'm ready," Ryan announced. "Is my hat straight, Catherine?"

Moving forward to twitch the bright gold cap a half an inch to the left, Catherine said, "That's a cute hat. I like the tiny blue bear paw on the back."

"I like it, too," Ryan said. "I'm the only one who wears it, though. Everyone else wears visors."

She said the last word with distaste, causing Jamie's head to cock in question. "Uhm…how does that make it a uniform? Isn't uniformity a critical element?"

"No. We have our choice of cap or visor. I guess I should wear the visor, so I look like everyone else, but the bill on the cap is longer. Keeps the sun out of my eyes better."

"Well, I'm always in favor of protecting those baby blues, so I vote for the cap."

"My sentiments exactly," Ryan said, tossing her long braid over her shoulder.

Working quickly, Jamie managed to take a dozen frames, getting her to pose with both bat and glove. As Ryan ran to take the field with her team, Jamie looked at her mother and said, "Well, my work here is done. Think she'd notice if we took off?"

Catherine knew that it would take an act of God to get her daughter to leave before watching Ryan play, so she merely smiled at her and nodded her head in the direction of a game in progress. "Let's go watch that one while Cal warms up."

They found spots in the stands and watched for a few minutes. Catherine's eyes grew wide as she watched the pitcher for Kent State face a short, slim player from Santa Clara. "How on earth does she make her arm contort in that fashion? That's not human!"

"I don't understand it myself. It looks like your arm would pop out of the socket every time."

Since Santa Clara was a local team, the stands were filled with parents and local fans. The atmosphere was fairly casual, people standing around chatting with each other and catching up with old acquaintances. Catherine observed two sets of parents decked out in Santa Clara gear sitting on folding chairs next to the stands. The fathers were studies in anxiety, looking like they were playing the game—even though they were sitting down. They twitched and grimaced when a particular play didn't go their way—and neither had any problem with yelling loudly when disappointed.

The mothers sat between the men, chatting with each other, with hardly one eye on the game. Catherine noticed that each woman paid rapt attention when one of their daughters was at the plate—calling out words of encouragement to the girls—but other than that, they could have been having lunch at an outdoor café.

"Come on, Kelly! Get your head in the game! You know better than to swing at a ball in the dirt!"

Catherine gaped at the man closest to her who had hollered out. She didn't think the girl in question was his child, and she was astounded that he had the temerity to chide her. Leaning over to speak to Jamie, Catherine said, "The atmosphere is quite odd, don't you think?"

"Pardon?"

"I mean, it looks like these people are all members of some big club, even though they're fans of different schools. Why would that be?"

"Ryan says that by the time you reach college most people have been focused on their sport for ten years—kinda like Jordan," she added. "Most of them have very supportive families who get involved; chauffeuring the kid around, raising money for their team. They all belong to a club team, or an AAU team, and are either playing their sport, or preparing themselves to play. It's very focused for most of them."

"But it wasn't like that for Ryan, was it?"

"Mmm…in a way it was—for soccer; but even with that, she didn't do all of the clinics and club teams that most people do. Remember, she went to Ireland for most of the summer, so she wasn't available to do most of that. Plus, playing three other sports didn't give her much time."

"I can't see Martin getting involved like these parents seem to. They look like the outcome of the game is important to them—rather than being happy that their daughters are enjoying themselves."

"Ryan says she's seen parents try to hit an umpire who makes a bad call. For some reason, softball seems to be the sport that parents get most involved in—and get the angriest over. Maybe because they sit so close to the field."

Just then, one of the fathers jumped up from his seat and signaled to the young woman named Kelly, motioning her to the end of the dugout. He appeared to be lecturing her, and Catherine shook her head in amazement. "Some of these people need to find their own hobbies."

"I agree," Jamie said. "Martin and the boys attend the games, as you know, and they care about them, but not like this. Ryan never feels pressure from her family—and I think that's why she still loves sport so much. It's just pleasure for her."

"That's how she plays, too," Catherine said.

Regrettably, Ryan didn't get to experience pleasure, even though they played two games. The day got cooler as the late afternoon game began, and the equipment manager brought out stadium coats for the players to wear when they were on the bench. "There's a couple of extras lying there," Jamie joked as her teeth chattered. "Think they'd notice if I went down and grabbed them?"

"Let's go inside and have some coffee," Catherine suggested, pointing to the two-story snack bar, located right in the center of the complex. "I think we might be able to see the field from there."

"I'm gone," Jamie said, scampering down the bleachers, seeking warmth.

When they settled at one of the Formica-topped tables, Jamie said, "It must be cold, when Ryan puts on a coat. Doesn't she look cute?"

Catherine gazed at the lanky young woman, who now appeared to be at least seven feet tall. The navy blue coat covered her body all the way down to her calves, enhancing the illusion of her endless length. She smiled as the back-up infielder stood next to Ryan at the end of the dugout. Lupe Moreno stood 4 foot 10, and weighed about ninety pounds—with her uniform and coat on. The discrepancy between Ryan's substantial height and bulk and the diminutive woman was comical, but she'd never admit that to Ryan.

"Jamie, look! Ryan's taking off her coat. I think she might be going into the game."

It was the bottom of the seventh, and the score was tied. Cal had a player on second base, and one of their best hitters was up. Ryan strode to the on-deck circle and began to stretch. Jamie was almost disappointed when Julie, the catcher, hit a home run on the next pitch, winning the game for the jubilant Cal players, but prohibiting Ryan from taking a turn at bat.

"I guess I shouldn't be so selfish—but I want to see my sweetie play!"

"With as many games as they have scheduled, I think you'll get your desire soon enough. Now, let's go congratulate the victors."

After the game, the girls dropped Catherine off in Hillsborough and headed on to Noe, managing to make it in time for dinner with the extended family. They ate at Martin and Maeve's, and for a change, both Tommy and Annie were off work, and were able to join them. Over dinner, Annie spoke of the near-constant decision making process that she and Tommy were going through about whether to move to Niall's. "Here's the worst part," Annie said. "Niall can only guarantee that we can stay there for a year. He's not planning on charging nearly as much as the mortgage and interest are, since the place isn't finished. But once it's done, he wants to either move in, or charge market rates. He wants to keep working on it during the entire time, too," she said, her displeasure with that arrangement evident.

"That doesn't sound like much of a deal," Jamie said.

"No, but it's so much nicer than what we have," Annie said. "Getting a big place like that for less than we pay now might be worth the trouble."

Martin narrowed his gaze and looked at Conor and Kevin. "Has Niall had tests to see if any of the paint in the house is lead-based?"

Annie and Tommy exchanged looks, and before anyone else spoke Tommy was already shaking his head in dismay, anticipating the answer. "No, he hasn't," Conor said. "He doesn't think there's lead, but he's afraid of getting bad news, which he'd have to disclose."

Martin turned back to Annie, raised one eyebrow, and gave Caitlin a pointed look.

Annie shrugged and looked at Tommy as she said, "Well, I guess that makes up our mind for us."

"Don't let it worry you," Martin insisted. "We'll find a solution if we all put our heads together."

"I don't know, Martin," Annie said. "The money boom has hit Noe with a vengeance. I can't imagine anyone but high-tech millionaires in the neighborhood eventually."

"Please!" Martin said, lifting his hand. "We're eating here, love. Wait until my dinner settles before you speak of that blight."

🐎

At the conclusion of the tournament in San Jose on Saturday, the girls decided to stop at Catherine's for dinner. They left early, and when they got back home, Niall and Conor were watching the Warriors on TV. Jamie and Ryan kept the lads company for a while, and as usual, the men needed a snack by the time the first half was over. Jamie offered to go make popcorn, and a minute after she entered the kitchen, Niall came in to join her. "Hey, Niall," she said. "What's going on at the house this weekend?"

"Ehh, not much. Now that Tom and Annie aren't going to take the place, I feel like I ought to stop working on it."

"You know, I don't think you need to do half of the stuff you're doing. Why don't you stop?"

He cocked his head and asked, "Truth?"

"Please."

"I can't see myself living there. I mean, if I had a girlfriend who I was serious about…"

"You're a long way from that."

"Yeah," he said, looking sheepish. "I won't get married for years, and I don't wanna live over there by myself. I've got my ma to cook for me, she does my laundry, and I've got my brothers to entertain me when I'm bored. I don't know what got into me in the first place." He shook his head glumly and added, "Don't tell anyone, okay?"

"Our secret," she said solemnly, not bothering to mention that everyone had already guessed why Niall was delaying his move. "But my question remains. Why keep working on the place if it's not what you want?"

"I don't know. I guess I keep thinking that I might change my mind again. Besides," he said with a grin, "it's fun doing the work with everyone. It doesn't seem like work when we all do it together."

"You have a point. Nonetheless, if you don't want to live there, doesn't it make sense to sell the place now—before you put any more money into it? I mean, what you've done so far is great, but you're not going to get your money back from doing much more."

"I guess you're right," he said. "The mortgage for this place is hurting me bad."

Ryan came into the kitchen, asking, "What's hurting you?"

"The mortgage," he said. "Jamie and I were talking, and I think maybe I should sell the place."

"Really? Why now?"

"Well, Jamie has a good point. I've done everything that needs to be done, and from now on I'm not going to do anything more than break even. If I'm gonna sell, I might as well sell now."

Ryan shrugged and said, "Conor knows some good real estate agents. Ask him for a referral."

"Okay," Niall said. "I might do that."

"I think you might be surprised at how much the place is worth," Ryan said. "Very pleasantly surprised."

Later that evening, Ryan sat up in bed, her laptop on her raised knees. "Hey, Jamers?"

"Yeah?" Jamie was sitting on the loveseat, reading a very dry article on the money supply, and was grateful for every interruption.

"How would you like to take a long walk?"

"Okay," she said, checking her watch. "It's a little late, but I'll do it if you need to."

"No, no, not now," Ryan said. "I was thinking of July."

Getting up to sit by her partner, Jamie said, "You're asking me in January if I want to take a walk in July? What's up, babe?"

"I was wondering if you'd be willing to do the Avon Breast Cancer walk with me in July. I thought this could be a nice substitute for the AIDS Ride. I'm sure we're both in good enough shape to be able to do it without too much training—and I'd really like to show my support for the fight against breast cancer."

"That's San Jose to San Francisco, right?"

"Yeah. There's one in LA in October, and that would be the one I'd prefer, but I don't know what we'll be doing in October. I'm pretty sure we'll be in town in July."

"You're on, baby," Jamie said. "Sign me up."

Ryan beamed a grin at her and hit "send". "All done. I had a feeling you'd agree."

"You know me well—and that's just how I like it." She got up and walked over to the bed, sitting on the edge and stroking Ryan's cheek for a moment. "I'm proud of you," she said, gazing into her eyes. "I know what a sacrifice it is for you to give up the ride, and I'm so pleased that you're thinking of your health and your enjoyment, rather than only your commitment. I know how hard this is for you. Thank you."

Ryan smiled sadly, putting her arms around her partner and pulling her close. "I can't only think of myself any longer. We're partners, and the decisions I make affect you, too. It's been hard for me to start thinking that way, but I'm gonna try my best to do so from now on. I know how important it is."

"You're the best partner in the world," Jamie whispered, nuzzling her face against Ryan's neck. "I'm a lucky, lucky woman."

"I think we're both pretty lucky, and participating in the Breast Cancer Walk is one way of showing support for women who aren't as lucky as we are."

Chapter Six

On Sunday morning, Ryan snuck out of bed, sparing a light kiss to her partner's sleeping head. "Happy Birthday Party Day," she whispered before finding some sweats and a T-shirt.

Martin and Maeve were in the kitchen, preparing a small meal before Mass. Giving her father and aunt a kiss, Ryan sat down on a kitchen stool and watched the pair cook, smiling at how well they had managed to accommodate each other in the smallish space. She hadn't apprised him of her demanding schedule yet, so she made it a point to mention, "This is the last weekend we'll be home for over a month, Da."

"Pardon?" Martin asked, his eyes wide. "Why is that?"

"I've got five road trips in a row. Softball's all about tournaments until we get to PAC-10 play. The only way to play good teams is to travel to the various tournaments, and we go to them all."

He crossed his arms over his chest and shook his head as he stared at her. "Is this wise, Siobhán? You admit that you're still not yourself. Why take on yet another activity like this?"

She nodded, agreeing that this probably wasn't the wisest choice. "I know I'm pushing myself, but I think I'm going to like this. You know I like softball, and the other women on the team are nice, and a lot of fun. The coach is my kinda guy, and I fit in well. I think it'll be fine."

"I hope you know what you're getting into, Siobhán. Neither you nor Jamie could take another debacle like you had with that basketball team."

"What can't Jamie take?" the woman in question asked as she entered the kitchen. She was very disheveled, her hair sticking up at odd angles, one of Ryan's volleyball T-shirts and a roomy pair of blue and yellow plaid boxer shorts her only clothing. Ryan looked at her and her mouth curled up in a grin as she privately thought that few things were more attractive than a disheveled Jamie wearing her oversized clothes.

"Da's worried about me biting off more than I can chew with the softball team." Jamie walked over to Maeve and gave her a kiss, then placed one on Martin's cheek. Coming back around to her partner, she sat on Ryan's knee and picked up her coffee mug to take a sip. The mug was so large that she had to hold it with both hands, and Martin stifled a grin as he considered that she resembled a small child sitting on her parent's knee, drinking her morning cocoa.

"I was worried too, Martin, but my sweetie assures me that she'll focus on herself a little more this time."

Martin and Maeve shared a pointed look, with both of them rolling their eyes a bit.

"I know you've heard it before," Jamie said, "but I think she learned a valuable lesson from the basketball team. We're going to have frequent discussions to make sure she's enjoying herself, and not getting too run down." She reached around to pat her partner on the side. "Have you noticed that she's finally putting some weight back on?"

"Yes, her cheeks are filling out a little, now that you mention it," he said. "How have you managed?"

"Hey, they're my cheeks," Ryan huffed. "I have something to do with filling them out."

"Tell us, dear," Maeve said. "What's your secret?"

"I'm not running much, I'm back in the weight room, and I've been getting a lot of sleep. Jamie's been making small meals for me, too, so I can eat more often. I have a nice snack right before practice every day, and that gives me a good boost."

"Ahh, so it is Jamie's doing, just as I thought," Martin said. "Speaking of eating, what would you like, Jamie? You can have whatever you want today, you know, in honor of your birthday."

"Anything?" she asked, green eyes dancing.

"Anything."

"Well, in that case, I'd like pancakes," she said, pursing her lips in thought. "But I only want one, since we'll be eating brunch. Oh, and I want to eat it in bed," she added with a big grin.

"Well, there's a woman who knows her own mind," Martin said. "Go back to bed, girls, your breakfast will be delivered presently."

"I'll wait for it, Da, while Jamie jumps in the shower."

Martin started to comment that it seemed odd to shower before going back to bed, but he caught himself short, his recent experiences with his new wife alerting him to the fact that the girls were probably not going to sleep after their meal. Jamie got up and made for the stairs, encountering Conor on her way. He gave her a birthday kiss and commented, "Don't you look cute this morning."

Patting him on the arm, she shook her head and said, "Yeah, right, Conor. Just because it's my birthday doesn't mean you have to stretch the truth quite that far."

He watched her cross the room and then descend the stairs, his eyes lingering on the slow sway of her hips as she did so. He was gazing so intently that Ryan almost threw her heavy coffee mug at him, but when he sat down, he looked more puzzled than lustful.

Looking at his sister with a bemused expression, he said, "Women don't get how cute they look with that 'just got out of bed' thing going on do they?"

"Jamie sure doesn't," Ryan said, scratching her head as she tried to understand how her partner could fail to acknowledge her obvious morning beauty.

Ryan came out of the shower as her partner was taking a big bite of her pancake. "Save some for me," she said, eying the plate.

"I'm not hungry." She picked up the bottle of Canadian maple syrup and added, "I only wanted an excuse to bring this downstairs."

Ryan jumped the few remaining feet, making the bed groan so loudly that both women were sure it would break. Eyes wide, Ryan said, "It didn't used to do that."

"It didn't used to be thirty years old, and you didn't used to weigh so much," Jamie teased.

"I thought you wanted me to gain weight."

"I do, but the bed frame isn't quite as enthusiastic about it as I am."

"Well, to be honest, it's about time to retire both the frame and the mattress."

Jamie privately thought that event should have occurred twenty years earlier, but she never would have admitted that to Ryan. "I think it's just fine for occasional use, but it won't hold up to the kind of workout you give it."

"Well, I didn't buy you a birthday present—as instructed. Would you like a new bed?"

"Do you know what I'd really like?"

"Nope. But if it's in my power—it's yours."

"Oh, it's in your power. But, you might not think it is."

"Forty questions time, huh?"

"No, not really. I don't think you'll want to do this, so I've been putting off asking you."

"You seem like you're up for it today, so give it a go, babe."

"Okay." Jamie put a bite of pancake in her mouth, then placed another in Ryan's. Chewing thoughtfully, she finally nodded, and said, "I'd like a house."

Ryan nearly spat the bite across the room. "A what!"

"That's the reaction I was expecting," Jamie said, giving her partner a smile. "You never fail to disappoint."

"Jamie! We've got a wonderful house in Berkeley, and there's not a thing wrong with this house, either."

"I agree that there isn't a thing wrong with either place. But neither of them suits us at this point in our lives. Why live in Berkeley if we're not in school there?"

"Well, we might be in school there," Ryan reminded her. "We just won't know that for another year."

"Do you want to live there after we graduate? Or would you rather live here in Noe?"

"If I had my choice, we'd live here. But doesn't it make sense to hold onto the Berkeley house until we decide what our grad school plans are?"

Jamie shrugged her shoulders and said, "Sure, we could do that. But the real estate market is so outrageously high right now, it seems like a good time to sell. If one of us went to school in Berkeley, we could rent a nice apartment, rather than having the upkeep of the big house."

"I guess that's true," Ryan said, nodding thoughtfully. "Okay, let's say that we do sell. Are you saying that you're not happy living here?"

Knowing that she had to tread very, very carefully, Jamie said, "I love living here. And while we're in school, this is a perfect living arrangement. But when we graduate I think we need to have our own space."

"Why?" Ryan asked, her dark head cocking, a completely perplexed expression on her face.

"Baby, it's a lot of fun to live with the boys, but it's more like a dorm than a home. There's someone coming or going at all hours of the day and night—and even though it's nice to have your parents make breakfast for us on the weekends, *I* want to cook for us. I want to have my routine, and I can't do that with a house full of people."

Looking hurt, Ryan shifted her eyes downward. "I thought you liked it here."

Taking her by the chin, Jamie turned her head, staring directly into those big, baby blues. "I do. I've enjoyed it very much. But I don't want to live with Mia, or Jordan, or Conor, or Rory or Kevin for the rest of my life. I want to live with you—only you. I want to cook for you, and eat when we want. I want to sit at the kitchen table and listen to the radio and read my newspapers in the morning. I love your family, honey, but I need my own routine."

Ryan nodded, looking unconvinced, yet resigned. "Okay. Where do you want to live?"

"Noe Valley, of course. I'd like to live on this street if we could find a place."

"Really?"

"Honey, I don't want to move away, but I do want our own place. I won't even lock the door until we go to bed at night—people can drop in whenever they want. I just want to be able to have privacy when we need it."

"All right." Ryan still looked wounded, and Jamie tried another tactic.

"Do you know why I want privacy?"

"Huh-uh."

"'Cause I want to be able to come home and find you in the kitchen, and start undressing you without worrying that someone will come home and find us. I want to be able to make love on the kitchen counters and the sofa in the living room. I want to have a TV in our bedroom, so we can watch all of your dirty little movies—without having Conor lying between us."

Ryan had to laugh at that one. "He would, too."

"I know it! I'm not kidding about that."

"Are you sure you haven't been unhappy here?"

"I'm completely sure," Jamie said. "It's been a lot of fun for college students. But for adults—we need space—and a lock."

Eyes darkening with desire, Ryan asked, "Why don't you show me what you need space—and a lock—for?"

"Well," Jamie said, eying her lover's pert nipples. "I'd like to get the syrup out and make you my big, sexy pancake." She lifted the bottle, then made two golden circles around Ryan's puckering nipples. "I'd like to be able to do this right at the kitchen table, for a nice little after breakfast treat." She leaned forwards and sucked each nipple into her mouth, lovingly whisking away the sticky syrup. Looking up at Ryan's half-closed eyes, she asked, "Wouldn't you like that, too?"

"I don't remember the question, but the answer is yes."

⚜

After another shower, the girls headed off to Mass. When they returned, many of the relatives had arrived, Catherine included. She was in the living room, holding Caitlin, as usual, when Jamie and Ryan went to greet her. Conor came bounding down the stairs and he detoured towards the blondes, making over each of them in turn. Holding Caitlin in his arms, he gave Catherine an admiring glance, saying, "I have never seen you look anything less than marvelous, but today you're reaching new heights."

She smiled at him and gave him a quick head-shake, her embarrassment evident. "You're as generous as your sister is with compliments. Not that I don't appreciate them, of course."

"Ryan, wouldn't you say that Catherine looks as good as you've ever seen her?"

Ryan scratched her head, seemingly giving the matter her utmost consideration. Catherine was wearing a butter-yellow leather jacket—collarless and without buttons—the jacket tickling the waistband of the matching slim-cut pants. A black ribbed turtleneck peeked out from beneath it, the very snug silk knit hugging her body. The pants flared a bit at the hems, and shiny black boots peeked out, the heel low enough to allow for long periods of standing and playing with Caitlin. "I don't know, Con, that's a tough one. Catherine always looks wonderful, so it's hard to decide. I do agree that she looks particularly wonderful today, though. The only thing that's hard to believe is that she could be the mother of a twenty-two year old woman."

"I still don't believe it," Conor said, matching his sister's pose and her look of doubt. "I've never seen a picture of Catherine when she was pregnant, you know."

"I have," Ryan said, surprising Catherine a little. "Down in Pebble Beach, Jamie and I spent a very enjoyable morning looking at old family photos. Catherine was definitely pregnant, Con, but I'll admit that she did look like she could have been the spokes-model for some campaign to eradicate teen pregnancy."

"I was still a teenager," she said in recollection. "If you'd followed my path, you'd have a four-year-old today, Ryan."

The blue eyes grew wide as she said, "That's a scary thought! I *am* a four-year-old."

"I disagree," Catherine insisted. "I think you'd be a fine parent right now. One thing is certain, you'd do a much better job than I did."

"You're doing great now. And no matter how much you denigrate your contribution, I still don't believe that you didn't play a vital role in forming Jamie's character."

Everyone stopped and turned his or her attention to the door at the forceful knock that sounded just as Catherine was going to reply. They all recognized it was someone from outside of the family, since every relative knew the door was always unlocked during a party. Jamie ran down the stairs to open the door and let in a tentative looking Jim, accompanied by Kayla, her confident posture a sharp contrast to Jim's wary look. "Daddy!" Jamie said enthusiastically, throwing her arms around his neck. Releasing her father, Jamie stepped back and extended a hand to Kayla. "I'm glad you could come," she said with a warm smile on her face.

"Thank you for having me, Jamie. Happy birthday."

Ryan hustled over to greet the pair, and dutifully took their coats while Jamie led them over to her mother—deciding to immediately cut the tension that had settled in the room. Jim nodded to his former wife and approached her awkwardly, leaning in for a quick, stiff hug. "Hello, Catherine," he said. "I'd like to introduce you to Kayla Horwitz."

No one made mention of the fact that they had spoken and had been in each other's presence before, but that proper introductions had not been possible. Catherine took in the young woman as she politely extended her hand. The confident, relaxed person standing in front of her bore almost no similarity to the startled, frightened girl that had been nestled in Jim's arms that night at his apartment. If not for the distinctive hair coloring, Catherine would have sworn it was someone else, but it was clearly her, and Catherine followed through on the pledge she had made to herself to be not only polite, but welcoming. "I'm glad you were both able to come," she said. "What can I get you to drink?"

"What type of wine do you have?" Kayla asked.

Catherine chuckled mildly to herself and said, "I'm sorry, I shouldn't have framed the question that way. We have regular beer, light beer, Pepsi and sparkling water. Would any of those be acceptable?"

Kayla's forehead twitched into a small frown and she said, "I suppose I'll have a light beer."

"That's good for me too, Catherine," Jim supplied.

Now that the family was certain there would be no bloodshed, everyone made their way over to Jim, small knots of people greeting him cordially and then departing as soon as polite. Conor gave the pair a warmer welcome. "Good to see you, Jim," he said, shaking his hand firmly.

"Conor, this is Kayla Horwitz. Kayla, this is Conor, Ryan's older brother."

"Nice to meet you," he said, his wolfish grin showing even, white teeth.

Jim tried to convince himself that he was imagining it, but swore he saw an ever so slight widening of Kayla's eyes as Conor loomed over her. *Don't even think about it!* he growled internally.

***

Since Mia now considered herself an honorary member of the family, she knew that knocking wasn't required. She and Jennie stepped into the crowded room, and they both spotted Jamie immediately. Threading their way through the bodies, they both managed to give her a hug. "Happy birthday, James!" Mia said, while Jennie waited her turn.

"Thanks, guys," Jamie said. "You're a little late. What's up with that?"

"Mmm, it took me a while to get going."

The look she shared with Jamie was one of deep sadness, and Jamie picked up on it immediately. "Jen, let's go find Ryan. She'll want to know you're here."

As soon as she caught her partner's attention and sent Jennie over to greet her, Jamie led Mia downstairs. Reaching up to touch her cheek, she asked, "You okay? You don't look quite yourself."

Her head tossed, curls bouncing around her head. "I'm fine."

"You can't pull that one on me. You don't have to tell me what's bothering you, but something obviously is."

"I might only have PMS," she groused, "but I'm so damned sad, that I almost didn't come." A few hot tears spilled out of her eyes, and Jamie got up to fetch a box of tissues for her. "If I hadn't agreed to pick Jennie up, I might have stayed in bed."

"Tell me what's going on? Why are you sad?" The empathy and warm concern in Jamie's eyes broke the dam that had been building in Mia for days, and she let some of her feelings out while Jamie held her in a loose embrace, stroking her back soothingly. "It's okay," Jamie said. "Just let it out until you feel like talking."

It took a while, but she was finally able to speak. "I miss Jordan so much," she whispered. "Coming here reminds me of being with her at parties with you guys…"

"That makes perfect sense," Jamie empathized. "That didn't even occur to me, but I really do understand."

"What do I do? I love her too much to be this far away from her. I've got to make a decision about our future, and I've got to make it soon."

"Mia, it's already February. If you can hold out until May, you can go to Colorado for the summer, at the very least. You don't have to decide your whole future right now."

"Yeah," Mia nodded. "Then what? Do I continue with school? Do I get a job? Putting off the decision isn't making things easier. It makes me feel more out of control."

"What does Jordan think?"

Mia shrugged and shook her head glumly. "She doesn't help at all. She wants me to make up my own mind, but it's so hard to do with so little input."

"What do your friends…" Jamie started to ask, but caught herself short.

"Yeah, right. I can't talk to my parents, I can't talk to my brother, I can't talk to any of my other friends. God, this sucks!"

Jamie nodded sympathetically, now having a better idea of why this was so hard for Mia. Even though she complained about them, Mia was very close to her family. Her brother, Peter, in particular, had been a constant source of advice, and had always been a calming influence between their very volatile mother and the sometimes volatile Mia.

"You haven't been seeing your other friends, have you?" Jamie asked gently. Mia had cultivated a widely diverse groups of friends during their time at Cal, but Jamie hadn't seen any of them around the house lately, and Mia was usually at home in the evenings, a rarity before Jordan.

"No." She shook her head roughly and said, "I don't have the strength to put up a front. Jordy's all I think about, and if I can't talk about her, why bother?"

"But your friends have always been important to you. Heck, some of your guy friends are gay. Can't you at least talk to them?"

She pursed her lips, shaking her head sadly. "I don't know who to trust. I'm so damned confused!" Looking completely forlorn, she announced, "I got accepted to Stanford for next year."

"Stanford? Stanford what?"

"Stanford law," Mia related, the look on her face one of supreme regret.

"What? I had no idea that you'd even applied!"

"Yeah." Mia nodded her head slowly, finally admitting, "I didn't want to tell anyone, 'cause I assumed I'd get dinged. Surprised the shit out of me, to tell you the truth."

"Mia, that's fantastic! What a huge accomplishment!"

"Yeah, yeah, I know; but now I feel like I need to accept," she moaned pathetically. "When my dad finds out, he'll kill me if I walk away from this opportunity."

Jamie nodded, understanding that Mia's fear was probably justified. "Do you want to be a lawyer? I had no idea…"

"I don't know, James. I applied mostly on a whim, and because Peter talked me into it. I mean, I killed on the LSATs, so I figured I might as well give it a try. Who knows?" She shrugged her shoulders and added, "I figured if nothing else, it would give me three years to delay having to get a job."

"I guess you have to tell your dad, huh?"

"If I don't, someone else will. He's got lots of contacts at the school. I'm sure that didn't hurt my chances, either."

Jamie sighed and wrapped her friend in a hug. "I think you need to see Jordan face-to-face to help you make a decision. Can you afford to go?"

"Yeah. I have the tickets that Ryan bought for me, but Jordan's traveling this weekend. She's gonna be at a tournament in Boston, and she won't be back until Monday. We might as well wait until we go to Las Vegas."

"Okay," Jamie soothed, "I understand that you don't have the ability to go see Jordan right now, but I hate to see you cutting yourself off from all of your friends, and your family. That's got to make this worse for you."

"It does." With a heavy sigh, she got up and dried her eyes one last time. "I'm sorry I'm such a grump on your birthday."

"It's okay. I'd be more than grumpy if Ryan were that far away. Think about what I said and consider talking about this with some of your other friends. Don't shut yourself off so much."

"I'll try. Peter's going to be home next weekend, and being around him always perks me up."

"Good," Jamie said. "Will you spend the weekend with your parents?"

"Yeah. I'm looking forward to it. Maybe I'll feel better after a little infusion of family."

"It always works for me." She wrapped her arms around her friend, squeezing her tight.

When Jamie came back upstairs, she decided to take Kayla outdoors to meet the O'Flaherty uncles and the cousins who were supervising the barbecue. Jim chose not to accompany her, having had quite enough of the stilted small talk that no one in the family was very good at. He spied Conor at the edge of a small group and went up to him at an angle, cutting him from the herd. "How are things going, Conor? I haven't had a chance to speak with you in a while."

"Not much to report. Now that things have settled down, and the press isn't outside our door all the time, things have gone back to their normal state of boredom. How about you? I'd guess your life has gotten more exciting since you've been in Washington."

"No, not really. It's just more meetings, more cocktail parties, and more formal dinners."

"Don't you normally drink wine?" he asked, glancing at the bottle of beer Jim held.

"Yes, yes I do, but..."

"Let's go for a walk and buy some. There's a nice wine shop not too far down on twenty-fourth street."

"You don't need to do that."

"You and Kayla are guests. I know you're not a beer drinker, and Kayla doesn't look like one, either."

Jim nodded and clapped the younger man on the back. "I'll take you up on your offer, but I'll buy the wine."

"Deal," he said, smiling. As they walked along on the late winter afternoon, Conor looked at his friend and asked, "How are things really going? I know this is a tough time for both you and Catherine."

"It's been hard for me. I honestly don't know how Catherine's doing, but since she's the one who made the decision, I guess it's easier for her." Conor gave him a speculative look which Jim caught. "She didn't tell you that?"

"Nope," the younger man said. "She's never said a word about what happened or why you decided to divorce. She's not the type to do that."

"Well, it certainly wasn't my decision. I'd be back there in a moment if she'd give me another chance."

Looking at his friend with a skeptical glance, Conor said, "I can't see Catherine booting you out on a whim. I'd guess she had her reasons."

Jim nodded reluctantly. "You've probably guessed this, but I wasn't always faithful. I wasn't ready to be tied down as early as I was."

"That's not uncommon. So Catherine found out about your friend Kayla and called it quits?"

"Well, not exactly," he mumbled. "I mean, yes, that was the last straw, but Kayla wasn't the first."

"Catherine knew about this?" Conor asked, his eyes wide.

"Yes, she knew about some of them. I thought we had an understanding. I guess we didn't."

Chuckling wryly, Conor asked, "What was the understanding? 'Let's be married while I sleep around?' If that were possible, I'd be married!"

"In my defense, she didn't seem to care that much after the first one or two."

"Wow." Conor shook his head slowly. "I've never met a woman who would put up with that. Especially not when she's the one with the money." Jim gave him a sharp look, but Conor explained, "If you were the one with the big bucks, I could see her giving up love to keep the dough. I can't see why she'd share the dough after you cheated on her. That doesn't sound like the Catherine I know."

"She's changed," Jim said. "A year ago, none of this would have bothered her."

"I don't know," the younger man said. "I can't imagine where you've been fishing that you'd throw a woman like Catherine back into the sea. The women you've been seeing must be all-world."

"Some were," he said. "Some were opportunists who wanted me for what I could do for them."

"Which one is Kayla?"

Jim gave him a wry smile and admitted, "She's both."

They walked along twenty-fourth street in silence, finally coming to the wine shop. Conor let Jim go in, since he had nothing to offer concerning the selection. As they walked back to the house, Conor commented, "You said something earlier that's been bugging me."

"What's that?"

"You said that you'd go back to Catherine if she'd take you."

"I would. I swear I would."

"You've probably had more experience with women than I have, but I know one thing—just because a woman tells you that it's over, doesn't mean it is. Sometimes she wants you to prove that you're sincere. That you really will give up everyone else for her." He chuckled mildly and added, "She wants you to show you're suffering."

"What's your point?" the senator asked.

"Well, you claim that you want to get back with her. Yet, not a month after this went down, you're at a family party with the woman she caught you with. If you were serious about getting back with her, if you were broken up about this, why would you do that?"

"I uhm, guess it doesn't look like I'm broken up about this, does it?"

Conor's dark head shook.

"But I am, I really am. I'm not the kind of guy who can go without companionship for months at a time. I believed Catherine when she said she wouldn't give me another chance. I did. And if she was never going to take me back, why should I wait around?"

The younger man patted his friend on the back and said, "That's a good point." As they walked along, he thought to himself, *If you really loved her, you wouldn't even be able to get it up, doofus! Your heart would be so broken that being with another woman would be the last thing on your mind. Catherine's in a lot more pain than you are, buddy, but you'll never hear that from me.*

Ryan was standing near the front door holding Caitlin when she heard a light knock and then felt a rush of cool air as the door opened. She turned, saw Sara and Ally, and waved them in. "Hi, guys, how's it going?"

"Good," Sara replied, leaning in for a slightly tentative, one-armed hug. Ally smiled and did the same, but her hug was generous and warm, and she kissed Ryan with her usual ease. Caitlin leaned towards Sara, and Sara gladly accepted her, smiling broadly as the child vocalized loudly.

"She's got a lot to say, doesn't she?"

"Yeah. She's got mama and dada and goggie down pat." Ryan smiled as she reached over and wiped a string of drool from the baby's chin with her fingertips. "I don't know what it says about us that she mastered 'dog' before any of our names, but she'll get there eventually."

"Hey, she's almost got my name mastered," Jamie said as she came up from behind and caught the end of the conversation. "Hi, Sara, Ally," she said as she gave them each a hug.

"Let's hear you say Jamie," Sara urged, bringing the baby up in her arms until they were nose to nose. "Say Jamie."

"May me," Caitlin dutifully mimicked, her face scrunched up in concentration as she stared at Sara's lips.

"Very good! Now say Ryan," Sara instructed, giving her old friend a wink.

"May me," Caitlin offered, looking a little tentative, but nonetheless pleased with her efforts.

"Oh, close," Sara said. "Very, very close, Caitlin."

Chuckling at the pair, Jamie asked, "Can I get you something to drink?"

"No, I'll go," Ally said. She placed her large hand on the small of Sara's back and asked, "What would you like?"

"A soda or water," Sara replied, smiling warmly. "Thanks."

Ryan fought down the tendril of jealousy that was winding its way around her gut, and tried to make small talk. "So, how's everything going?"

"Good," Sara said. "Really good," she added, wiggling her eyebrows a little. "It's funny going out with someone who doesn't drink and is mostly vegetarian. I've never gone out with someone who encouraged me to have better habits." She looked at her friends and said, "I've already got friends at work who have to have a couple of drinks to be able to relax enough to get to sleep at night. Almost every night, a group of people stops off at a bar before they head home. Being with Ally is really good for me at this point in my life. I don't need to drink to relax when I'm with her, no matter how hard I've worked that day."

No, I bet you don't, Ryan scoffed internally. *Ally has a sure-fire remedy for stress.*

"That's great to hear," Jamie enthused, when it became clear that Ryan wasn't going to say a word. "So, things are going well between you?"

"Yeah," Sara said, sneaking a glance at Ryan to gauge her reaction. "Things are going very well. I mean, it's hard, since this is something neither of us has done before, but we're working through things as they come up."

Deciding to summon her adult self, Ryan leaned over and placed a light kiss on her friend's cheek. "I'm glad you're giving this a chance. I think you can be great for each other."

"Thanks, Ryan," she said, smiling up at her. Her attention was diverted as Ally broke through the crowd; and Ryan couldn't help but notice that Sara's smile grew wider and more intense when she caught sight of her.

Seeing that Caitlin was commandeering both of her friend's arms, Ally held the bottle of water up to Sara's lips and asked, "Sip?"

"You're a doll," Sara said, and took a quick drink. Ally's arm slid around her, and Caitlin cuddled up between them and began to play with the buttons on Ally's shirt.

Feeling like she'd had quite enough evidence of their growing bond, Ryan said, "I need to go check on the barbecue. Be back soon."

"Waitin' for that fence to fall?" Jamie asked, finding her partner standing alone, staring blankly at the fence in the backyard.

Ryan whirled around, startled that Jamie had approached without her noticing. "Oh!" She colored a bit. "I'm giving myself a pep talk."

Jamie patted her side and said, "It hasn't gotten easier for you to see Sara and Ally together, had it?"

Her head shook slowly, a pensive look on her face. "I don't know why it's still an issue. I think that bothers me as much as they bother me. Know what I mean?"

"Mmm, I guess I do. Do you mean that you're mostly troubled by your inability to get over it?"

"Yeah. I know why it bothers me…I know why I'm a little jealous…I know that it will get better over time…but it hasn't gotten much better. That's what concerns me. I'm worried that I won't be able to be friends with them—and that sucks."

"Honey, this is the first time we've seen them since they started dating. That's not giving it nearly enough time. Now, come on, don't be such a pessimist. That's not like you."

Ryan smiled a little, "No, it's not, is it?" She took a deep breath and nodded slowly. "Okay, I'll try to relax and see how things go. I mean, it makes sense it'll take a while. It's not only having to see one ex-lover move on. This is a double whammy."

"Very true," Jamie acknowledged. "I know you'll be fine with this eventually, it'll just take a while." She moved to face her partner, then locked her arms around her neck. "You can talk to me when it bothers you, you know. I'm a very good listener."

"You're the best," Ryan said, bending to kiss her. They kept their embrace chaste, but they were still the recipients of a few catcalls from the assorted cousins gathered in the yard. From behind her back, Ryan shot the men a playful, but rude gesture she pulled away from Jamie's soft lips. "Heathens," she grumbled, her eyes dancing merrily.

"You love every one of them," Jamie said as she gave her a pat on the belly.

When they went back inside, the pair sought Catherine out. "Hey, Mom, could we talk to you for a few minutes?"

"Of course." Shifting her eyes from one to the other, Catherine asked, "Is everything all right?"

"Oh, sure. We wanted to ask you for a favor. Let's go downstairs so we can talk in private."

Catherine took the loveseat, while Ryan lay down across the bed with Jamie propped up against her legs. "We think we might be ready to start looking for a house here in San Francisco. Would you be willing to help us look?"

"Like you could stop me?" Catherine asked with her brown eyes comically wide. "Tell me what you're thinking of."

"Well, we definitely want to live between Noe and Castro."

"All right," Catherine nodded. "I don't know the boundaries of those neighborhoods, but I assume they're close by."

"Yes," Ryan said. "They're within walking distance. That's the bottom line. I don't want our kids to have to get into a car to see their grandparents." Catherine blinked slowly and Ryan hastened to add, "I'd prefer that was true for both sets of grandparents, by the way."

She smiled gently, and reached over to pat Ryan's hand. "I appreciate the thought, but I'm very fond of my yard and my garden. I don't see myself giving them up any time soon."

"The kids will think they're going to Disneyland when they come to your house," Ryan said. "That pool, the great garden. I'd hate for you to give that up."

"I think Ryan likes the house more than our kids ever would," Jamie teased gently. "She loves that pool."

"I freely admit to that. And since we won't be able to have much land, it'll be nice to be able to come down to Hillsborough and run around and feel the grass under our feet."

"I love that you enjoy coming to my home. Now let's talk about yours. In a perfect world, what kind of home would you like?"

"Well, to be honest, we could use a home like yours," she said with a laugh. "We obviously don't need that much space, but we need some place to gather as a family. The problem, as you've seen, is that homes in Noe Valley are all narrow and tall. I don't know how to provide for enough space for us and a couple of kids, and have room for family parties."

"I don't know how that's possible," Catherine said thoughtfully. "When your cousins start having children, you'll need a house bigger than mine. Much bigger."

"This is true," Ryan said, "but we'd like to have as much space as possible. I know it's a tall order, but if you could help us, we'd appreciate it."

"I'm up to the task, girls," she said confidently. "If such a home can be found—I'll find it."

"Before you set off, we should give you a thorough tour of our geographic boundaries," Ryan suggested. "Maybe we can talk Conor into taking us on a tour of the house he's working on. It's an apartment building now, but it was a big Victorian before it was chopped up."

"Sounds great," Catherine said. "I saw him leave with Jim, but as soon as they come back, we'll snare him."

Without too much prodding, Conor agreed to take them to the renovation, but he refused to allow Ryan to bring the baby. "Too many things she could get hurt by," he decreed. The four of them set off in Conor's big truck, with the siblings giving Catherine a tour of Noe Valley on the way to Castro. "The hilly area where we live is called Upper Noe," Conor said. "The flatter areas down by twenty-fourth street where Tommy and Annie live have smaller, newer homes and that area costs a lot less. That's relatively speaking, of course. All of our uncles and aunts live in Upper Noe, by us, but it's going to be very tough for our generation to stay in our neighborhood."

"Has the neighborhood changed, or have prices gone up dramatically?" Catherine asked.

"Both. When our families moved to the valley in the sixties, it was filled with middle income, blue-collar Irish and Germans. None of my aunts ever had to work outside the home to make ends meet. But now, most of the families moving in are two income professionals, like doctors and lawyers, and the tech millionaires. You need a two hundred thousand dollar income to afford a home here now, and none of the O'Flaherty cousins will ever make that kind of money."

"Everyone is in a construction trade, aren't they, Conor?"

"Yes. Everyone except Brendan, Rory and Tommy and Annie." He turned to his sister and said, "I guess we've got another couple of holdouts in the back seat."

"I'd last about a week," Jamie said.

"Ryan could be a good carpenter," Conor mused, "but I think she's gonna make a living with her head, rather than her hands."

"You never know, Conor," Jamie said. "I think she'd like to be a part-time carpenter/part-time mathematician."

"Ooh, that would be ideal," Ryan said wistfully. "But that's a hard gig to find."

They arrived at the building a few minutes later. It was a terrific mess from the outside, and there was construction debris piled up on the tiny front lawn; but even with that, one could tell that this place had potential. "You say this area is Castro?" Catherine asked.

"Yeah. This neighborhood was very similar to ours forty years ago. Very middle class, lots of Irish. But it became the gay Mecca in the sixties, and prices shot up dramatically. A lot of the middle class moved out because of the poor quality of the schools, so as they left, more and more gay people moved in. It's even more expensive than our neighborhood now, and it's a lot more congested, too."

They climbed up the stone stairs to the ornately carved wooden doors. Conor had the key, and he let them in with the admonition, "Watch your step carefully. I try to clean up at night, but there could be nails on the floor."

After a thorough inspection of the first floor, Conor let them take a peek at the second and third floors, which were basically untouched, giving them a flavor for how bad the place had been before work had begun.

"How long has the place been an apartment building, Conor?" Catherine asked, as she found the third kitchen in the building.

"Probably thirty-five or forty years. I'd say the building is a little over ninety years old, and as the neighborhood changed from single family to apartment buildings, they converted tons of these Victorians into three-flats, or even smaller units. We're going to knock out both of the upstairs kitchens and make a huge one on the first floor."

When they went back downstairs, Conor spread out the blueprints for the place. He was very impressed with how quickly Catherine oriented herself, and with her perceptive understanding of the issues involved in making a single home out of three apartments. "I'm very taken with these drawings," she said. "I'd love to speak with this fellow. Can you give me his number?"

"Sure. I think I have some of his business cards at home. I'll get one for you."

As they drove back, Catherine was deep in thought. She asked, "What was the total square footage before renovation?"

"Around thirty-five hundred square feet. But, because of all the hallways, and choppy little rooms the actual living space was pretty meager."

"What will the actual living space of the new layout be?"

"It should be close to four thousand square feet. The rooms will be much bigger, with very few hallways. The first floor will be a kitchen and a formal dining room and parlor. The second floor will hold a library/media room, an office and a guest suite, and the third floor will have two master bedrooms and two huge baths with dressing rooms."

Catherine nodded and resumed her pensive musings all the way home. When they arrived, Jamie slid an arm around her waist and said, "You look like something's perking in your head. Wanna share?"

"No, not yet. I've got the germ of an idea, but I don't want to reveal it if it's not possible. I can assure you two of one thing, though. One way or another, you'll get the house you need, and I'll have a fabulous time helping you get it."

As soon as they returned to the party, Caitlin toddled up to Ryan and asked to be picked up. When Ryan lifted her, she made a face and asked,

"When's the last time you had your nappy changed, sweet pea?"

"Gosh, does she need changing?" Annie asked, handing Ryan the diaper bag while trying to suppress a smile. "I didn't notice."

Blinking her eyes, Ryan reached up and held her nose with her free hand. "The wallpaper's gonna peel off the walls, Annie. If you didn't smell her, you should see an ear, nose and throat doctor at the hospital."

"Oh! I thought the neighbors were tarring their roof," Annie said, the picture of innocence.

"Your momma's full of the same stuff that's in your nappy, Caitie," Ryan said, chuckling as she took the baby downstairs.

When Ryan and Caitlin returned, she saw Jamie standing in front of her mother and Maeve. Both of them looked a little stunned, and Ryan looked to Jamie. "What did you do to those two?"

"I just made a proposal," Jamie said. "They're both a little surprised, but they agreed to it."

"What's the proposal?" Ryan asked.

"Meet your fellow walkers for the Avon Three-Day Walk," Jamie proudly proclaimed.

Ryan nearly fell into a providentially placed chair. "Are you serious?"

"I don't know how she does it," Maeve said dully. "She seems like she's just chatting, and all of a sudden I find myself agreeing to walk sixty miles in three days." She turned to Ryan and said, "How did that happen?"

"As soon as I learn how to say no to her, I'll let you know, Aunt Maeve. But as of now, I don't have a clue."

Jamie was in the living room chatting with Mia, Sara and Ally. Jim walked up, gave Mia a hug, and said hello to the other two women, cocking his head slightly as he looked at Sara.

"I work for Morris and Foster," she said, seeing the vague recognition in his eyes.

"Oh, right," he nodded. "You're in the Litigation Department, aren't you?"

"Yes," she said, brightening slightly. "I am."

"Well, I hope you're keeping an eye on things for me. I'll be back by the end of the year."

"I'll make a point of it," Sara said. "More water, Ally?" she asked, turning her attention to her friend.

"Love one."

As the pair walked away Jim asked his daughter, "Have you seen Kayla?"

"Not for a while. She might still be outside."

"I'll check, but she gets cold easily." Setting off to search for the young woman, Jim stopped abruptly when he reached the landing outside of the kitchen. Kayla was indeed in the yard, sitting at a picnic table, surrounded by an entire flock of eligible O'Flaherty men. Every seat at the table was taken, and several more of the testosterone-laden titans stood around those seated, all of them seemingly intent on catching every word that came out of the beautiful young woman's mouth.

Kayla was wearing a barn jacket, obviously belonging to one of the men, since the sleeves were rolled up so much that the bright red plaid flannel lining showed.

As Jim looked at the tableaux, he wondered to himself, *Where are all of the women? Jamie should have some of her straight friends here—if she has any! Why aren't Mia and…Sara out here? The big woman was obviously a lesbian, but I know Mia isn't, and Sara sure doesn't look like one. Hell, why can't these behemoths get girls on their own? God knows they're good looking enough.*

Ryan wandered outside and caught sight of the look Jim was giving her cousins and Kayla. "Hi," she said quietly, flinching a little when he shot her a fiery glance.

"Oh, hello, Ryan, I didn't hear you open the door."

"We didn't know where you had gone off to. I asked a couple of my cousins to entertain Kayla while you were gone."

"Ahh, I see. Well, that was thoughtful of you. I uhm, was wondering why don't your cousins or your brothers bring women to these events?"

"Oh, they do," she said, "but only if they're seriously dating someone. Only Brendan is hooked up right now."

"Why on earth is that?"

"Once they bring a woman over, everyone assumes it's a big deal, and all of my aunts start bugging them about whether they're going to get engaged and all that stuff. They've all learned their lessons the hard way."

"So not one of those young men is seeing anyone seriously?"

"Nope. Just Brendan, and he's inside with his girlfriend."

"Thanks," he said scampering down the stairs to retrieve his lover before one of the O'Flaherty men changed her allegiances.

"Bad news," Ryan whispered to her partner when she came back inside. "Kayla was outside with the cousins and your dad saw them flirting with her. He looked like he was going to roll up his sleeves and take 'em all on."

"He'd last about three seconds against them," Jamie said. "But, when you date a callipygous girl, you gotta expect to have to fight for her."

Ryan looked at her for a few moments, then gave her a half-smile and nodded. "Can't argue with you there. I'm gonna go get ready, okay?"

"Sure. See you in a few."

Jamie went downstairs a moment later and found her partner nose-deep in her dictionary, idly flipping through pages. Ryan shot a glance at her and colored slightly when Jamie said, "c-a-l-l-i-p-y-g-o-u-s."

Grumbling softly to herself, Ryan found the word and spent a moment committing it to memory. "How do you always know?" she asked plaintively as she sharply snapped the cover closed.

Coming up to wrap an arm around her, Jamie said, "You always wait a beat—like you think I'm going to explain the word that I just used."

"Well, if you know I don't know it, why not tell me what it means?"

"That would be rude. I figure that if you want me to explain something, you'll ask me. Besides, that was the one inflexible rule in my house. If someone used a word I didn't know, I had to go look it up. Both of my parents made it a point to never hand it to me."

"I think that's a pretty good rule. We didn't do that, but I'd be willing to institute it for our brood."

Her one-armed hug turned into a deuce as Jamie looked up into clear blue eyes and asked, "Now we're having a brood? What happened to one or two?"

Ryan sighed and gave her partner her most lovesick look. "I look at you and can't help but wish for a whole house full of cute little Jamie-copies. None of them could ever approach your perfection, of course, but it's sure going to be fun to see how close they get."

"Oh, so now I'm having them all, too, huh?" Her green eyes were glittering with amusement, and Ryan spent a moment regretting that they had a house full of people, and that she had to leave for her game soon.

"You're gonna be so cute and sexy and luscious looking when you're pregnant," she insisted, patting Jamie's perfectly flat belly. "I don't know if I'll be able to resist the urge to pop a little bun in your oven all the time."

Jamie laced her hands around Ryan's neck and stood on her tiptoes for a kiss. "I'm so totally grateful that you don't have a penis," she sighed. "You'd be sneaking up on me constantly, trying to get into my oven."

"Oh, I love your oven." Ryan leered as her hand slipped down between their bodies and found a warm place that she wished she had time to explore. "I just can't help make the buns."

"Thank God for small favors," Jamie giggled as Ryan's fingers hit a very sensitive spot. "At least I've got a fighting chance if I see you sneaking up on me with a turkey-baster."

Ryan came up the stairs from her bedroom at one thirty, dressed in her warm-ups, with a pair of shower sandals on her feet. "You look a little casual to play softball," Catherine teased when she caught sight of her.

"Yeah, I do, don't I? I like to wear these so I have less to carry. I don't know why, but I can't stand to have regular shoes on after I play softball. My toesies have to breathe." Ryan smiled at her approaching partner, and said, "I've got to run, or I'll be late. Will I see you both later?"

"Of course," Catherine said. "I'll stay here a while longer, but I'll be at the game as soon as I can."

"I would tell you that you don't need to come, since it's just the alumni game and it doesn't count, but I already know your answer, so I'll save us both the trouble."

"That's the spirit, Ryan. Now, go play well."

"I'll be there for the end of the game," Jamie said. "I don't want to leave until the party winds down a little. I'll probably come over with Mom, and we'll bring Jennie, since she wants to go."

Jennie heard her name mentioned and popped her smiling face into the crowd. "Could I go with you, Ryan? I love to watch you guys warm up."

"Now that's a fan," Ryan said. "Sure. Come on, sport." She reached into her gym bag and pulled out a T-shirt identical to the one she wore. Handing it to her young friend, she advised, "Since you've become our biggest fan, I thought you should have your own shirt."

"Cool! This is great, Ryan! Thanks!" Her face was beaming with pleasure, reminding Ryan once again how the smallest things had such an impact.

Chapter Seven

Jamie and Catherine were the only family members to make it to the game—the rest of the crowd promising to keep Jamie in their thoughts as they continued the celebration. They arrived as the teams were changing sides at the top of the fifth inning, and immediately spotted Jennie, speaking non-stop to a sweetly indulgent Ashley. "Hi!" she called out loudly when she spotted the latecomers. "We saved you seats."

Jamie and Catherine both smiled at the enthusiasm Jennie conveyed for the smallest of acts, and gingerly climbed the stairs. Jamie had changed into jeans and a sweater, but Catherine had not and was now the clear winner in the best-dressed attendee of a softball game in the history of the sport. Mother and daughter split up, with Jamie taking the seat on Ashley's left, Catherine settling down on Jennie's right.

The youngster had been in school for about a month, and Catherine was anxious to hear a full report on her progress. "So, Jennie," she began, "tell me how things are going at Sacred Heart?"

"Good, Mrs. Evans. Very good."

Catherine patted her knee and asked, "Tell me all about it. Have you made any friends?"

"Yeah," she said thoughtfully. "I have two friends so far—and a bunch of girls I talk to."

"Tell me about your friends."

Her face grew more animated as she expounded. "Dani lives in an apartment pretty close to school. She's originally from France, though. She's been here since she was five, I think, so she hardly has any accent, or anything. Her dad works for some French company here. And Latisha is a scholarship student, who lives near Union Square. We all get along really well—which is kinda funny, 'cause we're all so different." Her high-wattage grin was beaming up at Catherine, and the older woman couldn't help but return a smile with the same intensity.

"Have you considered taking on any extra-curricular sports or clubs yet?"

"No." She furrowed her brow as she revealed, "It's hard for me to keep up. I have to get home as soon as possible to get to my tutoring sessions."

"How is the tutoring going? I see that you and Ashley have bonded nicely."

"Yeah," she said, raising her eyebrows unevenly, in a gesture that was a poor, but adorable attempt at imitating Ryan. "Ashley and Heather are the best. They took me out for pizza last night, and we didn't even talk about school."

"That's wonderful," Catherine enthused, sparing a look at Ashley, who was chatting companionably with Jamie. "Ashley is a lovely young woman."

"Hey!" Jennie jumped to her feet, turning from the field to her companions repeatedly. "Heather's gonna pitch!"

All eyes turned to the dugout, watching the tall brunette leave the warm-up area and head out to the mound. As she crossed in front of the dugout, every player slapped some part of her anatomy for good luck, with Ryan getting in a good swat to her seat with her enormous first-baseman's mitt. "This is her first time in a game!" Jennie cried, her enthusiasm attracting the attention of the other spectators near them.

Heather looked rather fierce as she took her warm-up pitches. Everyone on the bench was calling out supportive messages, and Jennie was soon joining in with them. *"Come on, Heather! You can do it!"*

Catherine tried to ignore the ringing in her ear as the determined-looking freshman stood on the mound, a look of complete concentration on her face. She went into her wind-up and fired the first pitch in for a called-strike, which Jennie celebrated with a scream.

Being a quick study, Catherine stood, reasoning that her hearing would survive better if her ear was slightly higher than Jennie's mouth. The batter popped the ball up high above Heather's head, and the tall woman grasped it firmly in her glove for the first out. The yelling continued unabated, and to Catherine's gratitude, the next two players grounded out after only two pitches each, bringing a blessed moment of peace.

Jennie reached across Jamie to slap at Ashley's thigh. "Wasn't she great?"

"Awesome, Jennie. She was awesome—just like we told her she'd be."

Jennie quieted down a bit after the first rush of enthusiasm. Heather continued her mastery of the plate, mowing down all three batters in the sixth and seventh innings as well. The game was still tied at one to one, but since it was only an exhibition, it would end after the bottom of the seventh, no matter the score.

"Look!" Jennie cried once again. All three women, turned in the direction

she was pointing to watch Ryan snug on a pair of batting gloves. "Ryan's gonna get to bat!"

The foursome watched the her grab an aluminum bat and perform an intricate series of stretches to warm up her muscles, which were probably cold after seven innings on the bench. She looked calm, focused and confident as she squatted a few times, trying to stretch her legs out. As she bent over, her hands splayed along either end of the bat, and Jamie watched with interest as she let her torso hang, again just trying to limber up. *Good thing she wears her underwear with that uniform,* Jamie chuckled to herself. *You can see right through those pants when she does that.*

"Who the hell is that?" an older man behind Jennie asked. "She's playing the wrong sport! How's the weather up there, stretch? Haas Pavilion is behind you."

Jennie whirled and froze him with a glower from her intense blue eyes. "That's my friend, Ryan O'Flaherty. just 'cause she's tall doesn't mean she can't play softball, too."

Not looking embarrassed in the least, the man said, "I didn't mean anything by that, kid. I just think she ought to be playing basketball." His expression grew puzzled, and he asked, "Did you say Ryan O'Flaherty?"

"Yeah," she growled.

"Hey! Did hanging off that car make you that tall?"

"Jerk," Jennie mumbled under her breath.

"It's okay, Jen," Jamie soothed. "Ryan's had a lifetime of tall jokes. It doesn't bother her a bit."

"Bothers me," she grumbled, as she once again focused on the game. Ryan stepped to the plate, calmly knocking the dirt from her cleats with the end of the bat. She stood at the plate, one foot out of the batter's box, while she spent a moment adjusting her gloves, then her helmet, then once again tapping her shoes with the bat. Now ready, she took her stance, and watched patiently as the first ball zinged right by her for a called-strike.

The man called out once more, "C'mon, Kareem! Take the bat off your shoulder!"

Jamie was sure that Jennie didn't know that the loudmouth was referring to a well-known basketball player who stood about seven foot four, but she was also sure that she was going to snap off another retort to him. Trying to forestall her, Jamie tapped her on the leg and said, "Ryan likes to concentrate on a pitch or two to get a good feel for the pitcher."

Jennie nodded. Turning her face only halfway towards the man, she said loudly, "Some people think before they act."

Catherine and Jamie rolled their eyes at each other as Ryan got settled for the next pitch. This one was high, and Jamie shook her shoulders out, feeling the tension knotting there. *It's an exhibition game*, she reminded herself. *Chill!*

Another pitch—another ball, and still the bat had not left Ryan's shoulder. Jamie knew this was exactly the way her partner would be—patient and analytical at the plate—trying to learn as much as she possibly could from the signals that the pitcher was giving her. The next pitch was a little low, and a few inches inside, but Ryan swung at it, sending the ball skittering foul.

Letting out a breath, Jamie gave Ashley a sheepish grin and removed her hand from her leg. "Sorry about that. Hope you don't bruise."

Ashley patted her back and said, "No problem. It's so much harder to watch than it is to play. I'm never tense when I play, but my stomach's in knots watching these guys."

The next ball was right where Ryan wanted it, but the pitcher had disguised her motion to make it look like her usual fastball. In actuality, it wasn't a fastball at all, as she cut the ball just a hair by holding it with her fingers across the seams. Ryan swung, but didn't get all of it. The ball dribbled through the infield, right past the pitcher. The shortstop grabbed it and flung it, but Ryan's surprising speed allowed her to beat the throw by a complete stride of her long legs. As she motored past the bag, the man behind Jennie laughed and said, "She shouldn't be on the basketball team, she should be on the track team."

With a scowl on her face Jennie turned and said, "She could be if she wanted to be!" then folded her arms across her chest as she turned back to the action.

Jamie leaned her head close to Ashley and said, "I think we'd better sit in the car and listen to the games on the radio from now on. Jennie's gonna get punched if she keeps this up."

Ryan reached second on a fielder's choice, and with one out, she stood on the base, looking down at the very short second baseman. The next batter worked the count to two and two, and blistered a low line-drive into right field. The fielder didn't hesitate, firing the ball in with such force that her feet left the ground. Ryan was sprinting around the bases, catching the inner corner of the base as she rounded third, heading for home. She arrived at nearly the same time that the ball did, resulting in a fierce and noisy collision of six foot three inches of lean muscle barreling into a short, squat, muscular catcher. The crowd held its breath as the dust settled, with the umpire decisively calling, "*SAFE!*"

The team streamed out of the dugout, with Heather and Jackie spending a long moment untangling the catcher from Ryan's long limbs. The various members of the winning squad clapped their hands onto Ryan's back and head, congratulating her to the point of abuse, while Jamie, Ashley, Jennie, and a more subdued Catherine cheered in the stands. Jennie, of course, had to turn to the man behind her and gloat. "Told you she could play!"

🐎

By the time the players had exited the locker room, it was five thirty, and the Alumni/Team dinner was due to start in an hour. "I'm barely going to have time to go home, shower and dress," Ryan worried, looking at her watch.

Catherine volunteered, "Let me take Jennie home. Actually, I think this is a perfect night for the two of us to have dinner together. What do you say, Jen?"

"I'd love to, but I have to call Sandy first. She likes to know where I am."

"Use my phone," Jamie said, handing her the little device.

Jennie looked at Catherine as she dialed and said, "I have to be home by nine. That's my curfew."

Catherine smiled at her earnest face and said, "I think three and a half hours is plenty of time to have a nice dinner. How do you feel about French food, Jennie?"

"Umm…" she hesitated, clearly trying to get the answer right. "I like french fries," she offered tentatively.

"I know just the place," Catherine said as she draped an arm around her shoulders and gave her a gentle squeeze.

🐎

Late that night, walking home from the team dinner, Jamie tucked her hand into Ryan's, enjoying the crisp, cool, evening. "I can see why you like your new teammates. They seem like a lot of fun."

"Yeah, they are. It…uhm…wasn't too boring for you, was it?"

"No, not at all, honey. Everyone was really friendly. Admittedly, the whole purpose of the dinner was to talk softball, and I don't know a heck of a lot about it, but it was fun to watch you charm everyone."

Giving her partner an adorably embarrassed grin, Ryan said, "I tend to talk a lot when I'm with people I don't know. It makes me feel more comfortable."

"Face it, honey, you're a charmer. You can't help it."

"As long as I charm you, I'm a happy girl."

When they reached the house, they were both pleased to find a note from Mia that said she had gone out with friends for the evening. "That's a relief," Jamie sighed. "She's abandoned her entire support system. I gave her a pep talk today, encouraging her to reach out to her friends."

"She has seemed down lately. This is the dark side of a new relationship."

"It can be dark," Jamie nodded. "She was in a very bad place this afternoon."

She considered the note, saying, "I hope she's out with her friend Aaron. He's always been good for her."

"I don't think I've met him."

"He's been a good buddy of hers since we were freshmen. He's a little wild, but he's a very sweet guy."

Ryan's eyes bugged out. "He's wilder than Mia?"

Laughing gently, Jamie said, "No, I'd say they're about equals in the wild department. He's a lot like she is, really. Very open, always willing to try something new, but also a good friend. You'd like him."

"Well, maybe I'll get to meet him if she abandons her self-imposed isolation."

"I sure hope she does. Mia is a very social creature. She doesn't do well when she's alone too much."

When Jamie came downstairs the next morning, Ryan was standing at the kitchen sink, her attention sharply focused on something in the back yard. "What's up?" Jamie asked, startling her partner.

"Oh," Ryan said, her attention still riveted, "I was just wondering if I'd be into penises if I were straight."

"Huh? Why are you wondering that?"

"'Cause there's a pair of guys playing with each other in the back yard. I was wondering if I could get into it." Before her last sentence was out of her mouth, Jamie was pushing her aside to get a look.

"Jesus!" the smaller woman cried. "I've never...Jesus!"

"They do look like they're having fun," Ryan said. "But they're investigating each other like they're in slow motion. Kinda weird."

She was obviously trying to understand the dynamic, but Jamie was a bit more focused on figuring out why there were two men in their backyard in the first place, regardless of their state of undress. "You don't happen to know those guys, do you?" Jamie asked.

"Of course not!" Ryan gaped at her. "You mean, you don't?"

"No! Jesus! Maybe they're strangers who wandered into the yard!"

"Oh, great. Now what do we do? I mean, should we let them finish?" She took a long look and said, "The darker skinned guy doesn't look like he could walk with that chubby."

Jamie took a glance and agreed. "It is odd, the way they're caressing each other. One of them looks like a pro, but the other doesn't appear to have ever done this before. He looks very amateurish." She started to turn away, but whirled back to the window and ordered, "Don't you two drip anything on my lawn furniture!"

Ryan chuckled at her outrage, but stayed right where she was, watching the men intently.

"Ryan! You can't stand there and watch."

"Why not? They're in my yard. I've always wondered what it looks like when a guy gets wood, and this is probably my only chance to find out." After a few seconds a grin creased her face as she said, "It's kinda hot. That one guy looks like he's having a fabulous time."

"Come on, you little voyeur. If you're not going to roust them, let them have their fun."

"Oh, I'll roust them, all right," Ryan said. "But first I'm going to go figure out if they're invited guests. I think our roommate holds the key to that puzzle."

Striding up the stairs, Ryan reached Mia's room and cracked open the door. Jamie was right behind her, and she nearly stumbled when Ryan backed away, paling noticeably. "What's wrong?" Jamie whispered.

Eyes wide, Ryan jerked her head in the direction of their bedroom. Jamie led the way and resumed her questioning. "Honey, you look like you've seen a ghost. What's wrong?" she repeated insistently.

"Mia's in bed…with a guy." She looked like she was torn between punching something and crying, and Jamie grasped at her arm, holding on tight.

"In bed with a guy? Are you sure?"

Shooting her a perturbed look, Ryan nodded quickly. "I might not sleep with them, but I recognize them. There was a nice looking, sweet-faced guy in her bed. She was cuddled up behind him, with her arm draped over his hip." Sitting down heavily on the bed she muttered, "I thought she was serious about Jordan. Jesus! She's gonna be devastated."

Jamie's concerned look lightened a bit as she asked, "Did he have curly hair?"

"Yeah. Curly, blonde hair, pink cheeks. He coulda passed for sixteen."

"That's Aaron!" Jamie cried, now looking massively relieved. "He and Mia don't have sex. He's as gay as you are."

Ryan blinked at her for a moment as she absorbed what Jamie had said, then asked, "I thought you were gay too?"

"I am," Jamie said, placing a kiss on her cheek. "I'm just not as gay as you are."

Shaking her head, Ryan mumbled, "Whatever. All I know is that I wouldn't be happy about you being sprawled all over a guy, no matter how gay either of you were."

"I'll go talk to her and ask if the guys in the yard are her friends. Be right back."

As she walked away, Ryan mused, *I think poor Jordan might have been right to worry about Mia's ability to remain monogamous. No matter what Jamie says, that scene didn't look right. And as Jennie learned the hard way, you can get into plenty of trouble playing around—no matter what your sexual orientation is.*

🐎

Jamie slipped into the dim bedroom and stood quietly for a minute, letting her eyes adjust as she decided how to awaken her friend. She was relieved to see the tiny strap that drooped low on Mia's shoulder, indicating that she was wearing some form of clothing.

Approaching her friend from behind, Jamie placed her hand on Mia's shoulder and gave it a squeeze. That attempt received no response, so she increased the pressure and gave her a shake. Again—nothing. She finally had to resort to tapping her cheek with her open hand—continuing the annoying contact until Mia finally lifted her hand from Aaron's hip and weakly swiped at her. Knowing that she almost had her, Jamie leaned over until her lips were near Mia's ear. "Come on, wake up. I need to talk to you."

A low, tortured groan was the only reply, but Jamie kept it up—entreating her again and again until Mia stopped fighting and allowed herself to wake. "What?" she husked out when she realized Jamie was leaning over her.

"Are the two guys out in the backyard your friends?"

"Oh, fuck!" With an unhappy growl, Mia tossed the covers from herself and got to her feet. "Just what I fucking need. Try to do somebody a favor…" Grumbling under her breath, she paced in front of Jamie, heading for the stairs.

Jamie gently grasped the waistband of her thin cotton pajama bottoms, urging, "Hold on a sec. What's going on?"

She accepted the detour that Jamie was indicating, and shuffled into the bedroom to flop down next to Ryan. Running her hands through her hair, she muttered, "Maybe I'm better off not seeing my friends, huh?"

Mia's brow was furrowed, and her eyes had yet to fully open. From her posture and grumpy mood, Ryan deduced that she was either hung over or currently drunk. Gently, Ryan urged her over onto her stomach and started to massage her neck and shoulders.

"Thank you, thank you, thank you," Mia murmured, letting out several deep groans as Ryan loosened her up.

"I assume you know the boys in the yard," Ryan said.

"Not really," Mia replied, her speech a little thick and distorted. "But Aaron does. He used to date Bobby. The other guy is Mike, or Mark, or something with an 'M.'" She groaned loudly and rolled away from Ryan's soothing hands. "I'm very sorry they're in the yard, but they were too fucked up to let them loose on the streets."

"Where were you?" Jamie asked. "At a party?"

"Yeah. A rave."

Suddenly, Jamie's expression sharpened. "Mia," she said in a low, threatening tone, "you didn't…"

Giving her a scowl, she said, "Of course not. I made a promise. My parents would never forgive me if they knew I was into that again."

"But the guys in the yard…?"

"Oh yeah. They both took another hit right before the party broke up. I don't know what happened to the woman Mike or Mark, or whatever his name is, was with. We lost her at some point."

"Are you implying that he's straight?" Ryan asked dubiously.

"Oh, yeah. He was trying to hit on me all night. I was about to deck him." She shook her head and said, "Maybe that's why his girlfriend disappeared. I woulda ditched him, too."

"If he's straight, he's obviously a member of the Open-minded-Straight-Guys'-Society," Ryan said, getting to her feet and going to the window. "Take a peek." Mia got up with some difficulty and walked over to stand next to Ryan, peering down into the yard.

"Oh! That is open-minded, isn't it? Jeez, Bobby could give lessons on how to give a hummer. Great technique." She turned to Ryan, wrinkling up her nose as she asked, "Do I really have to stop 'em now?"

"No, don't bother," Ryan said. "But don't leave them there all day. Even though it's February, they could still get sunburned if they're outside too long. That's some virgin skin there."

"Shit, I hope Mike or Mark doesn't freak out about getting blown when he comes down. That could get ugly."

"What are they on?" Ryan asked, turning to observe the men again. "Acid?"

"Mmm…I'm not sure. They took 'E' when Aaron did, but that was hours and hours ago. Either they took more, or they scored some acid. There was a lot of it floating around last night. It was quite a scene. We were out all night—just got to bed at five thirty. What time is it, anyway?"

"Six fifteen," Jamie said, casting a glance at her watch. "Ryan, for the last time, get away from the window!"

"No wonder I'm tired," Mia complained. She started to head back to bed, but Ryan put a hand on her shoulder.

"How would you feel if Jordan slept with a guy—even if he were gay?"

She thought about that for a second, then rolled her eyes and climbed into their bed, pulling the covers up under her chin. "Don't tell her, okay?" she asked tentatively.

"Of course I won't," Ryan said, scowling a bit. "But you should."

"What was that about?" Ryan asked when they returned to the kitchen.

"You looked like you were ready to jump down Mia's throat."

Jamie rolled her eyes and said, "She promised her parents that she'd never do Ecstasy again. I was worried that being depressed and going to a rave would be a combination of circumstances where it would be too tempting for her to resist."

"What's with the promise? Did she have a drug problem?"

Jamie sipped at the juice that Ryan had poured for her. "Yeah, well, I'm not sure it was a problem, but she made it into a problem."

"Explain, please."

Jamie nodded, took another sip of juice, and said, "When we were sophomores, she did Ecstasy every weekend for months. It didn't bother her at first, but she started having these hangover kinda things. Then she started taking Xanax along with the Ecstasy. I think she called that parachuting, or something like that. She said it made the Ecstasy last longer, and made the hangover less severe. She got caught trying to fill a fake prescription for Xanax." Jamie rolled her eyes and said, "The goofball created prescription forms on her computer, and used her real doctor's name on it. There was some problem with the form, probably because she wrote the prescription directions in English, rather than that weird Latin they use. So, the pharmacy called the doctor and he said he'd never prescribed Xanax for her. When she went to the pharmacy to pick it up, the Hillsborough police were waiting for her. I don't know how she thought she wasn't gonna get caught—but you know Mia. Thankfully, her dad talked the police out of charging her. Good thing he has connections."

"That must have been fun," Ryan said. "Given what you've said about her mom, I'm surprised she didn't kill her."

"It was close," Jamie admitted. "But Mia made a solemn promise that she'd never do Ecstasy again—and when Mia makes a promise, she keeps it."

"Maybe we shouldn't have kids," Ryan sighed, letting out a deep breath. "I'll be worried sick about all of the trouble they can get into."

Jamie smiled over at her and reminded her, "At least we have enough money to have them followed around the clock."

Ryan nodded, sparing a smile for her partner as she thought, *Yeah, and your dad has just the guy.*

🐎

The comment Jamie had made about their ability to have their children followed stuck with Ryan as she got ready for her day. Idly mulling over the implication, she made a phone call during her lunch break that surprised her, even as she dialed the phone. "Hi, Jim, it's Ryan," she said when she reached her father-in-law on his cell phone.

"Hi, Ryan. Is everything all right?"

"Oh, sure. I wanted to ask your opinion on something. Is now a good time?"

"Sure. What is it?"

"Well, I feel a little odd even asking the question, but what I'd like is some advice on how to exact revenge against someone."

There was a significant silence, then he said quietly, "I suppose I can understand why you'd think I'd be an expert on the issue, but it still smarts to have you think that."

"I'm sorry if that hurt your feelings, really I am. But, I know that you've worked with a private investigator before, and I thought you might be able to tell me if hiring one would be a waste of my money."

"My feelings are a little hurt, but I made that particular bed, so I can't be upset with your assuming I lie in it. Now, who would you like to have investigated, and what do you want to find out?"

"Cassie Martin is the person, and I want anything I can use to wipe the nasty, smug smile off her face."

"Right. Jamie's told me that you're having a tough time getting over your anger at that creature. I'm so angry with her myself that I'd be willing to pay for the investigation. What she did was unconscionable."

"I agree, and I'll admit that most of my anger is because of what she said about Jamie. I can't stand to see someone I love hurt."

"What's your plan? What do you think you might be able to use?"

"I'm not sure. I'm working on something to embarrass her, but even while I'm doing it, I know that it's incredibly immature. I feel like a nine-year-old, but I can't stop myself. I get a great deal of satisfaction from working on this little project—dreaming about the look on her face when she sees it."

"Tell me about your project. Maybe there's something we can come up with to make it work for us."

She shrugged her shoulders and confided everything to Jim, and at the end of the discussion he said, "I think your focus is misdirected. If I were you, I'd make this a two-pronged approach. I'd not only want to humiliate her, I'd want to take a pound of flesh."

"Hmm. That sounds pretty harsh." She paused for a moment, and let the evil smile that was begging to get out settle upon her face. "I'm in."

Jordan sat in her room, trying to keep her eyes open long enough to call Mia. They tried to keep their nightly calls brief, and they'd taken to making them right before bed, but that time was getting earlier and earlier. Finally deciding she couldn't wait any longer, Jordan dialed Mia's number and waited for her always-perky voice to answer. To her surprise, the always-perky voice was a little subdued, and she quizzed, "Hi. Did I catch you at a bad time?"

"Oh, no," Mia said unconvincingly. "I'm just a little tired tonight."

"Did you go out last night?"

"Yeah. We had Jamie's party yesterday, remember?"

"Uh-huh. I remember. But I also remember that it was over in the early afternoon. You didn't call me last night, and it was your turn. I called you right before I went to bed, but you didn't answer." Even though she had only a slight feeling that Mia was dissembling, her stomach was in her throat and her heart beat heavily in her chest. There was a short pause, then Jordan asked, "Is something going on?"

The fifteen seconds that it took for Mia to compose her answer felt like an eternity. Jordan knew that something was amiss, and as she often did, she catastrophized the possibilities; running through a list that covered everything from fatal illnesses to outright betrayal.

"Uhm…I did something last night that, in retrospect, I shouldn't have done," Mia began. As she spoke, Jordan had to lie down, the blood rushing to her extremities so quickly that she felt faint. "It's no big deal, but Ryan pointed out that you might not like it."

"For God's sake, Mia, what is it?"

"Honey, honey, calm down," she soothed. "It's nothing horrible."

"Then tell me," Jordan got out through gritted teeth.

"Okay. You've met my friend Aaron, remember?"

"Yes," she said tightly. "I met him on campus one day."

"Right. Well, he and I went out last night, to a rave," she added tentatively.

"Mia, you didn't…" Jordan began, but Mia stopped her immediately.

"No, I didn't do anything crazy, Jordy. I got drunk, and so did Aaron. He had a couple of friends there, and they'd done a lot of E, so we all came back to my house."

"What happened?" Jordan snapped, her patience ebbing.

"Uhm…Aaron and I slept in the same bed." Mia said this very quietly, stunned by how bad it sounded, compared to how innocent it had been.

Jordan swallowed, then a full minute ticked by before she could find her voice to ask, "Why?"

Mia's words came out in a rush. "We always have. It didn't even cross my mind. We were both drunk, and we stumbled into bed like we always do. Aaron's like a brother to me, Jordy, and he's the gayest man alive. Neither of us has ever touched each other sexually, and neither of us would ever want to. I swear!" she finished plaintively.

A tired-sounding sigh left Jordan's lips and she said, "I believe you, but it still hurts my feelings."

"But why?"

Jordan wasn't sure what hurt worse. The fact that Mia had slept with Aaron, or that she didn't understand why it bothered her. "That's an intimacy that we should keep for each other," she finally said, her voice very thin. "Did you touch him or cuddle up to him?"

"Yes," she said. "It's very, very fraternal, Jordy, but we did cuddle a little."

"Would you mind if I did that with one of my straight roommates?"

"I get your point," Mia sighed. "I'm sorry."

She sounded very contrite, but Jordan cursed their distance once again. Not being able to see Mia's face made this so hard, and she knew they'd get past this quickly if they could hold each other again. "I know," she said. "I know you didn't mean to hurt me."

"That's the furthest thing from my mind, Jordy. You're my girl."

"I am," she whispered, and Mia could hear the tears in her voice. "I'm gonna go now. Sleep well. I love you."

"I love you too, Jordan. I'm so sorry that I hurt you—I'll never do something like that again."

"I know you won't," she said, relieved that she was confident Mia would honor her promise. "G'night."

"Night." As she placed the phone back in the cradle, Mia flopped to the bed and stared up at the ceiling in frustration. *Nice job*, she chided herself. *You hurt Jordan's feelings and made Ryan think you're an asshole. Not bad for a day's work.*

When Jamie got into bed that night, Ryan was lying prone, her hands laced behind her head. Her eyes were fixed on the ceiling, and she gave a start when her partner crawled in with her. "What's going on behind those baby blues?"

"Oh." Ryan rolled onto her side and braced her head on her hand, "I was thinking about double standards."

"Is that a math thingy?"

Ryan chuckled and shook her head. "Huh-uh. I was thinking about how you must have felt when I told you that Jordan and I slept together on road trips."

Jamie lay down on her back and snaked an arm around her partner, pulling her onto her chest. When Ryan's head was comfortably pillowed on her breast, she began to stroke her hair. "It wasn't my favorite thing, but I was so new at being a lesbian that I thought it might be a common occurrence with your kind." She chuckled mildly to show that she didn't harbor any ill feelings about the incident. "I knew you weren't doing anything that I should be suspicious of—so I forced myself to swallow my unease."

"I'm sorry for that," Ryan murmured.

"It's okay, babe. I slept with Mia when you and Jordan were on that one road trip. Did that bother you?"

"No," Ryan said thoughtfully. "I know you've never been attracted to each other, and you've been friends for so long that you seem very much like sisters. Jordan and I didn't have that kind of history, though, and I think it was quite obvious that she was pretty flirty when we first met."

"All an act," Jamie said, having seen through Jordan's facade.

"Yeah, but it still doesn't feel the same to me. Even if you didn't mind, I should have at least asked you first."

"Do you want me to ask you first if I ever sleep with Mia again? I might want to sometime when you're on a road trip."

"No, it doesn't bother me at all. If you're feeling lonely, I want you to get comfort." She looked thoughtful again and said, "I don't have anyone in my life that seems like a sister, and it doesn't seem right to me to share my bed with another woman." Nodding to herself, she looked at her partner and said, "It's taken me a while to begin to understand what it means to be monogamous. I'll never do that again."

"It's okay," Jamie said. "If you ever did, I know it would be because the person really needed some comforting. It's your nature to soothe someone who's hurting. I don't want you to stop being who you are."

"I think it's best to limit it to warming someone who has hypothermia. Knowing me, that's not outside the realm of possibilities."

"It's a deal. Next time you're climbing Everest, you have my permission to share a sleeping bag."

"If I ever climb Everest, I want you right by my side."

"Then that's one place to knock off your list of possibilities," Jamie said. "You're the tallest mountain I want to climb."

Chapter Eight

Senator James Sloan Evans stood in front of the microphone, gazing out at the sea of semi-interested faces as he addressed the students at Cal State University-Los Angeles. His scheduled remarks had just concluded, and he braced himself for the questions from reporters that were sure to follow.

His advance staff had tried to keep the members of the press to a minimum, since the senator was still trying to get comfortable with the pugnacious style that most reporters displayed. He was used to a very civil style of discourse, both at the firm, and in his daily life, and he was having a little trouble adjusting. On more than one occasion, a staff member had to catch his eye and make a discreet "kill" sign to urge him to stop talking about an issue that they were not ready to have made public, and he was slowly learning to dance around every question, revealing little, if anything.

After the expected questions about the economy, his support for Vice President Gore in the November election, and his insistence that he would not be running for re-election, a young man, probably a student, finally was allowed to step to the microphone. "Senator Evans," he began, his voice shaking from nervousness, "could you describe your stance on the proposition to ban gay marriage?"

Jim hid a smile, pleased that he was up to date on the party line, and comfortable with the position the administration had decided upon. "My stance on this proposition has been consistent. I am unequivocally opposed to it. Even though this is a state, not a federal matter, I think it's a wrongheaded ploy by a small group of right wing zealots to push their agenda forward—at the expense of gay men and lesbians. This proposition is totally unnecessary, and will lead to nothing less than an increase in divisive rhetoric. I think we have quite enough of that in the country at the moment," he concluded firmly.

The young man nodded and went back to his seat, his place taken by a newspaperman from the Los Angeles Times. "Could you explain how the proposition would divide the state, Senator? The wording couldn't be simpler," he explained. "It merely states that in the state of California, marriage is defined as a union between a man and a woman. That doesn't seem so divisive to me."

"If the backers of the proposition were merely trying to clear up a point of confusion, I would have no argument," Jim said. "But case law and judicial opinions have consistently held that marriage in this state is only valid between men and women. The backers don't want to clarify the law—they want to make this a referendum on behavior that they don't approve of. I guarantee that they will tout a winning vote as evidence that the people of the state are opposed to gay rights—even though gay rights are not addressed in this proposition. I assure you that the backers of the plan are using this to advance their own goals. Why else would the advertisements imply that this proposition is the only thing stopping people of the same sex from marrying? That's not so—and that's why I think the measure is mean-spirited and divisive."

Several other reporters now started shouting questions at him, but Jim's handlers decided that he'd said enough for one afternoon. The last question was loud enough to be heard even over the din. "Does the fact that your daughter is a lesbian influence your vote, Senator?" The small band began to play, and soon the noise overwhelmed the shouted questions, and the senator was able to leave the stage after waving to the moderately enthusiastic crowd.

"Wow," Jason Farlington sighed as he settled into the roomy leather seat of the limo that would take Jim and Kayla back to the airport. "My life flashed before my eyes. Anyone else?"

Jim gave his chief aide a sharp look and asked, "What do you mean by that?"

The younger man sat up straighter and cleared his throat nervously. "Oh! just that uhm…well, that we're vulnerable on the proposition. We've got to avoid it, Senator, at all costs."

"Vulnerable?" the low, slow voice asked. "Vulnerable how, Jason?"

"Everyone knows that your daughter is gay, sir. It's a live grenade. Every time this issue has come up, we've managed to dodge it, but that can't last forever. I'm hoping we don't get dragged into a big thing before the primary. The Veep doesn't need this shit."

Jim's eyes narrowed, and his nostrils flared as he spat, "Al Gore can kiss my ass! My daughter's private life is her business. Not yours—not anyone's."

"Of course, of course," Jason backpedaled. "No one with any brains cares about her sexual preference, Senator. But it's still a weak spot, and I'd like to continue to run every time it comes up." He cleared his throat and seemed to hesitate for a moment. "You said something that's not on message, sir, and I…"

"Now what?" he growled, sick to death of being dictated to by underlings.

"You said two words that can't ever be used to your advantage, especially given your daughter's uhm…"

Eyes narrowing to slits, Jim cocked his head, waiting for the younger man to finish his thought.

"You said 'gay rights', sir," he swallowed. "It's bad enough to say 'gay', but it's a time bomb to ever merge the word 'gay' with 'rights'. The other side will find some way to take your statement out of context and…"

Jim held up a hand, as Kayla shifted uncomfortably in the seat next to him. "Enough. I get the message. You won't have to tell me again." Closing his eyes, he allowed his head to drop back onto the seat, as Kayla and Jason shared an anxious look over his head. His quiet voice startled both of them. "This god damned proposition means nothing, and how my daughter spends her time means nothing to the people of this state."

"That would be nice," Jason said, his voice as soothing as he could make it. "But, it's not reality, sir."

Now that Ryan was feeling so much better, she and Amanda had tapered off to speaking three times a week on the phone. Much to her surprise, Ryan struggled a little with the diminution of their contact, but she knew she had to get used to dealing with her feelings on her own, so she did her best to express how she felt about the reduced sessions, rather than give in to the temptation to increase them again.

They had consciously tried to limit their discussions to focusing on the carjacking, and all of the fallout from the event. Now, nearly eight weeks since the trauma, there was only one thing that Ryan had on her agenda. Placing her Wednesday morning call to Amanda, Ryan decided to broach the topic. "I've decided on my plan for revenge," she said quietly.

Amanda didn't rise to the bait, merely saying, "Yes?"

"Uh-huh. I know we've talking about this several times, but I don't think I can let go of my anger without some satisfaction."

There was a long silence, then Amanda said, "I understand your impulse, but as I've said before, it's awfully difficult to exact revenge. I only want you to be certain you've thought this through."

"I have. And, strangely enough, Jamie's father has helped me focus my feelings. He's helped me to see that it's not merely revenge that I'm seeking. At this point, I also need restitution."

"Jamie's father, huh? That seems like a curious alliance."

"Yeah, I guess it is. But he was quite helpful. He has a certain uhm… expertise in this area."

"Do you want people to say the same thing about you? Would you like it if your family or friends thought you were the person to see to get advice on how to pay someone back for doing them harm?"

Ryan thought about the question for a moment, finally saying, "You know, a few months ago I would have said no. But now, I think I'd be fine with people acknowledging that I won't lie down and let someone screw me over."

"I'm not making any judgment about your seeking revenge. I'm only trying to make sure that you can deal with the feelings you'll have. You have an awfully gentle soul, Ryan, and I don't want this experience to scar you."

"Thanks. I do have a pretty gentle soul, but I have a tendency to be too forgiving sometimes. In this case, I think it would be good for me to get a little retribution, as well as a little revenge. I think it's my due."

"I can't argue with you, and it appears you've give quite a bit of thought to this. I hope you get some satisfaction."

"I do, too. But even if I don't get any satisfaction from the revenge, the restitution angle will make me feel better. Of that, I'm certain."

"Okay," Amanda agreed. "Other than that, how are you feeling?"

"Mmm…pretty good, I guess. I still struggle with my guilt feelings, but I've resigned myself to having to live with them."

"Do you honestly believe that?"

"Yeah, I do. I'm profoundly disappointed in myself, and I don't think I'll ever think of myself as a brave woman again. I'm going to have to live with that."

"We've talked about this before, but at this point I'm going to push you a little. I think you need to get into a small group setting and talk with other people who have been through traumatic situations."

"No, I really don't wanna do that," Ryan said immediately. "Besides, it's hard enough to find the time to talk to you. I can't spend any more time on therapy."

"Then we can reduce our sessions to give you more time. I don't normally try to coerce you into doing things, but at this point I have to concede that we're not making progress on this point. I truly believe that you'll be better served by talking to other people who've been through what you have. I feel strongly about this."

There was dead silence on Ryan's end for a full minute. "I don't want to."

"I know that," Amanda acknowledged. "But you also don't want to spend the rest of your life feeling guilty, do you? You owe it to yourself to get past this, and I believe this is the way to go."

"Fine," the younger woman said with no enthusiasm. "How do I find a group?"

"I have some contacts. Let me make a few calls and see if I can find a group for you. Would you prefer for it to be in Berkeley?"

"Yeah, I guess so. But, I don't have much free time. Actually, the only time I have available is before eight a.m."

The doctor laughed softly. "Don't think that will put me off. I'm as determined as you are."

"I feel sorry for your loved ones," Ryan said, finally giving in and laughing as well.

On Wednesday evening, Ryan ate hurriedly, since her advisor, Vijay, was coming over.

"What are you two little math nerds working on tonight?" Jamie asked.

"Actually, it's not math tonight. He's helping me with a program I'm writing."

"A program? A computer program?"

"Yep," Ryan confirmed, as she stood to collect the dishes from the table.

"Is it for your independent study?"

"Nope. It's…extracurricular," Ryan said, finding the word particularly apt. She walked into the kitchen and started to do the dishes, turning to meet Jamie's eyes when she walked in behind her. "You can hang out if you want. It's no big secret. It's something I'd like to learn, and Vijay is a programming genius."

"Maybe I will. I'd like to see how you two work together."

Jamie had a load of her own studies to concentrate on, but she had a niggling desire to observe her partner working with another person. She had the faint hope that listening to Ryan have to put words to her thoughts might help her to understand the way her mind worked.

Vijay and Ryan had been upstairs for about an hour when Jamie went up with a plate of cookies and a glass of milk for Ryan, and a Coke for Vijay. "Keep working," she said when she entered the room to two pair of eyes meeting hers. "I thought you'd like a snack."

They nodded almost identically, and Jamie had to hide a smile. *Math nod*, she thought to herself. They had a long stream of flow-chart paper laid out on the floor, and the pair started speaking to each other in a language that had some familiar elements, but certainly did not sound like English. *I'm sure she doesn't speak Urdu or Hindi,* Jamie mused, resisting the urge to scratch her head in puzzlement. After a few minutes, she stepped out of the room, unnoticed by either of the programmers. Passing Mia in the hall she said, "Wanna get a brain cramp? Stick your head in there and listen to those two. They are otherworldly."

Jamie had been studying in the library and, finding herself in dire need of some form of caffeine, she made for the kitchen, coming in the seldom-used side door of the room.

She thought she heard some quiet sounds emanating from the room, and her suspicions were confirmed when she spied her lover standing at the sink. About to speak, she instead concentrated on the show her quirky partner was putting on.

Ryan was focusing fiercely, her concentration complete, as she attempted to peel a large navel orange—all in one, long piece. That part wasn't so odd, and Jamie had grown used to her partner's need to devise games and tests of various arcane skills. Jamie pondered that the dance Ryan was performing may have been part of her need to challenge herself, but the longer she watched, the more she was sure that her partner only needed to go to the bathroom.

Ryan was hopping from foot to foot, her butt twitching as she shifted her weight back and forth repeatedly. Her tongue was sticking out about a half of an inch, and a low hum came from her partially open mouth.

"Ryan." A startled gasp came from the oblivious woman, and Jamie had to laugh at her expression.

"Don't disturb me! I'm almost done."

Jamie strode over to her, and extended both hands. "Give it to me right now and get into the bathroom. I swear, you're worse than Caitlin."

Thoroughly chagrined, Ryan handed it over like a guilty schoolgirl, dipping her chin as she peered at Jamie through her long bangs. "Don't ruin it," she ordered, then promptly ran for the blessedly convenient bathroom. She emerged minutes later, a look of sublime pleasure on her face. "Does anything feel better than that?" she moaned.

"I can think of several things," Jamie contradicted. "And if you didn't ignore your body's signals so frequently, you'd give that experience the scant regard it deserves."

"You don't know how to have fun," Ryan insisted, sniffing pointedly as she held out her hands for her prize. With another few seconds of concentrated effort, the orange was perfectly peeled, and she regarded it with satisfaction. "I'm an artist," she declared, holding the end of the peel with her other hand, letting it dangle.

"You're a lunatic," Jamie insisted with a wide smile. "Did Vijay leave?"

"Uh-huh. He's gonna come back next week and check on my progress."

Jamie walked to the refrigerator and took out a Diet Coke. "Hey, did you remember that next week is Valentine's Day?" She was trying hard to sound casual, realizing that it was a challenge to put anything over on her hyper-alert lover.

"Nah. Can't be. It's in two weeks," Ryan insisted, stopping to look at her watch. She made a face, then looked up at Jamie. "Guess you're right. Do you want to do something?"

"You don't?" Jamie asked, more than a little shocked and slightly perturbed.

'Well, we'll just be getting back from Florida late the night before." She shrugged, looking slightly bored. "Anyway, does it matter now that we're together? I thought Valentine's Day was for people who were dating."

Jamie set her bottle down on the counter and crossed her arms, glaring at Ryan with fierce green eyes. "Hell, yes, it matters! What's wrong with you, anyway? I thought that being with a woman would relieve some of the 'I'm just a guy and I don't know how to be romantic' shit that I've had to put up with my whole life."

"Okay, okay!" Ryan soothed, holding up her hands in supplication. "I didn't know the rules, but I can learn. Don't take my head off."

She sighed and shook her head slowly. "I'm sorry. It's our first Valentine's Day together," she said, deeply wounded, "and I've never had a nice one. I thought you'd…" She trailed off, staring at the floor, thoroughly dejected.

"Hey," Ryan murmured, crossing the room quickly to slip her arms around her partner. "I'm just messing with your mind. I've already got something planned." *Thank you Catherine and Mia*, she said in silent offering.

"You do?" she asked suspiciously, looking up into Ryan's eyes to gauge her sincerity.

"Yep. I really do. We don't have practice that night, since we're just back from a three-day tournament, so I arranged for us to do something a little different that afternoon."

"Okay," Jamie said slowly. "I was going to take you out to dinner. Can we do that, too?"

"Sure. This thing is over by five or so. Dinner would be great."

"Should I make reservations for someplace local?"

"I'd rather go someplace in the city, if it's all the same to you," Ryan said. "My thing's in the city, and I don't want to have to drive back over here during rush hour."

"I'll think of someplace nice and romantic," Jamie promised. She snuggled up close to Ryan and murmured, "Sorry I was being such a baby. I was so stunned that you didn't think it was important."

"I do think it's important," Ryan whispered as she held her close. "Any chance I get to tell you how much I love you is very, very important."

🐎

Ryan knew it was wrong, but she snuck into Mia's room later that night and closed the door behind her. "Do you have any idea where Jamie's taking me to dinner for Valentine's Day?"

The curly-haired brunette looked up from her book with exaggerated indifference. "I might. What's it worth to you?"

"Mmm, it's worth Jamie having a memorable night, and since you're her best friend, that should be reason enough for you."

"Keep going," Mia said. "You're not there yet."

Ryan reached into her wallet and extracted a calling card that she kept for road trips. "This one has about twenty dollars left on it. That would let you spend the evening talking to your sweetheart on Valentine's Day."

"Sold," Mia declared. "You're going to Farallon. Nice place from what I've heard."

"Thanks," Ryan said, heading for the door. "I won't tell Jamie that you sold her out for only twenty."

"She's known me for almost eight years now. She'll be surprised I held out for that much!"

🐎

"Farallon. How may I help you?" the cultured voice answered, when Ryan called later that night.

"Uhm, hi," Ryan said. "My partner and I are having dinner at your restaurant on Valentine's Day. I'd like to do something special for her that night, and I was wondering if you have any suggestions for how to surprise her with a ring. I'm sure you've seen every trick in the book."

"Ah, yes, Valentine's Day. Yes, I would say that, over the years, I have seen that day commemorated in every possible way. Did you have anything particular in mind?"

"Is there any way to surprise her with a ring during the meal?"

"I could go on," he sniffed dryly, "but the easiest way is to hand it to her. Much less fuss."

"Is that the best you've got?"

"I have many, many suggestions, I assure you. But handing it to her is the only way that I can guarantee your success." He paused dramatically and added, "If she accepts your proposal of course. I can't help you at all in that area."

"What could go wrong?" Ryan wondered.

"Again, I could go on. There are problems too numerous to mention."

"Uhm…I know you're the expert, but I'd like to surprise her in a non-traditional way."

He sighed, then said, "Well, we have a very nice heart-shaped flourless chocolate cake that we make that night. We could bake it into that."

"Bake it? Wouldn't that hurt it?"

"Is the ring plastic?" he asked archly.

"No, it's a very nice stone. In a gold band."

"Then it won't be harmed by a little heat. If you like the idea, you can drop the ring off early in the day, or you can excuse yourself and come into the kitchen to drop it off before you order dessert."

"I think I'll come into the kitchen," she said, not liking the idea of leaving the ring unsupervised for any length of time.

"You can join the crowd," he said. "It's a complete madhouse in that kitchen, with nervous men watching to make sure their ring gets into the correct dessert."

"No women?" Ryan asked, chuckling.

"I think you'll be the first," he admitted. "But we at Farallon thrive on variety."

Before bed, Ryan went into the kitchen to make some cocoa, and before she was half done, both Jamie and Mia were sitting at the kitchen table, waiting for their portions. "You two sure do have keen senses of smell. You're like bloodhounds."

"You make the best cocoa in the world," Mia said, licking her lips.

"My mom taught me to make it," Ryan said, a thoughtful look on her face. "It was the first thing I ever learned to cook."

Jamie got up and slipped her arm around her partner, holding her close while Ryan stirred the rich mixture. Mugs in hand, they were halfway up the stairs when the phone rang, and Mia dashed to answer, thinking it might be Jordan. "Oh, hi, Conor," she said, her normal enthusiasm tamped down. "Yeah, she's here. Hold on."

Ryan grasped the offered phone and said, "Hey, Con."

"Did you hear what that sneaky cousin of ours did?"

"Nope. I've heard nothing. What's up?"

"Niall sold his house! He got an all-cash offer with a thirty day close. The agent I referred him to really came through for him."

"That's great," Ryan said. "Why are you pissed?"

"After…I repeat…after…broker's fees he's gonna make two hundred thousand dollars! Two fucking hundred thousand!"

"Jeez, that's a boatload of dough. What's he gonna do with it?"

"Who cares? That's not his money!"

"Whose is it?"

"It belongs to all of us! Maybe not you and Jamie, and some of the boys didn't do all that much. But Frank, Donal, Padraig and I have put in hundreds of hours working on that dump! I didn't mind doing it when I thought it was gonna be his home, but to line his pockets? No way!"

Ryan sighed, having a feeling that the other cousins probably felt as put-upon as Conor did. "I assume you've expressed your displeasure to Niall?"

"Of course I did. If you think I'm mad, you should hear Frank! I was afraid he was going to knock him senseless."

"What does Niall have to say?"

"Oh, he gave us some load of crap about how he was going to live there, but it didn't work out. I don't think he was ever serious about it, and now he's got a nest egg that none of the rest of us will ever be able to match. It sucks!"

Ryan rolled her eyes at her partner, who had come to sit next to her on the stairs. "Conor, you know as well as I do that Niall isn't a long-range plan kinda guy. He bought the house before he thought it through, he fixed it up more than he ever should have, and as soon as someone suggested it—he sold it. He didn't put ten minutes of thought into any element of the entire thing! Now, come on, I understand that you're pissed to have put that kinda time in, but you'll be paid back someday. If you ever want to have your own place, I'm sure all of the cousins will help you as much as they helped Niall. Think of your time investment as money in the bank. When you want to make a withdrawal, the family will be there to repay you."

"Yeah, you're right on that point, but Niall can withdraw something a little more tangible than I can. I swear, if he buys a hot car and starts flaunting it…"

"Niall is the most frugal of all of us. He's not going to do that. Now, chill, will you? You can't turn back time, and other than giving you a share of the money, there isn't much Niall can do to make it up to you. If he offered you money, would you take it?"

There was a short silence as Conor had to admit, "No, I wouldn't. But he didn't even offer."

"I understand that, and I'm sorry you're so bummed. I just don't think Niall thought this through."

"Nah, he didn't. It clearly wasn't his idea to sell." There was a short silence and then he chuckled and said, "Don't think I don't remember who put the idea into his head, either. Tell Jamie I've got a bone to pick with her."

"She was only trying to help," Ryan said, snaking an arm around her partner and giving her a squeeze. "She didn't know that Niall was so malleable."

"Oh, he's malleable, all right. And he'd better have his malleable little ass right in the front of the line if I ever need his help."

On Thursday afternoon, Jamie struggled through the small aisle of a 737, trying to keep up with her partner. For once, Ryan had much more luggage than she did, so they had checked their bags. But she had a thing about keeping her gloves in sight, and somehow Jamie wound up carrying the gym bag, rather than her own carryon. The bag wasn't particularly heavy, but it was ungainly—since the gloves were bulky and irregularly shaped. Ryan's computer and a number of her books were also in the bag, so Jamie had to be careful with it as she walked.

They reached their seats, and found that a civilian was sitting in the window seat. Jamie thought about trying to switch, but she decided to play nice and go along with the flow on this trip.

The last few stragglers made it onto the jet and Coach Roberts strolled up the aisle, counting heads. Satisfied that all were in place, he took his seat at the rear of the section and wasn't heard from again.

"I don't know why, but I had an image of this being a charter flight, with only you guys on it," Jamie said.

"No such luck. We don't have enough players to need our own plane. We would if we shared with Stanford and St. Mary's or San Jose State, but we tend to go to tournaments that they aren't in."

"Are you looking forward to the tournament?"

"Yeah. It's a lot of softball crammed into a weekend, but with five games in three days I might get to play. How about you? Sure you don't mind having your birthday away from home?"

Jamie squeezed her hand and said, "You're my home. As long as we're together, I'm happy."

The flight was uneventful, and things were well organized when they landed. After waiting for their luggage, the motley-looking crew made their way to a chartered bus that was waiting outside the terminal. When they were all settled in their seats, Coach Roberts stood at the front of the bus and said a few words.

"Okay, we've got five games over the next three days, so we've got to focus. We're playing some powerhouses, so I hope you all get some rest tonight. We'll have a light dinner at the hotel, and breakfast starts at nine. Neither meal is mandatory, but I want you all to eat healthy meals while we're here. If you can't manage to get yourself fed properly, then you'd damned well better be eating with us. If I catch any of you eating a bag of chips and a Coke for breakfast, the meal is gonna be mandatory, and that's a promise.

"The bus leaves for the complex at ten a.m. sharp. If you're not ready, we leave you behind. Oh, and curfew is midnight for everyone. I'm not going to do bed checks, but if I hear that someone stayed out much later than twelve, you'll be sitting in your room instead of playing."

"One last thing." He scanned the players' faces, making sure that everyone was paying attention—which they all were. "O'Flaherty has her girlfriend here with her."

Jamie could feel her cheeks coloring and she mentally rolled her eyes, wondering where this train was headed.

"I know most of you aren't petty little whiners, but just in case, I want you to know that O'Flaherty isn't getting any special treatment here. As you all know, the NCAA expressly prohibits any player from receiving benefits that a regular student wouldn't receive, and I take the NCAA rules very, very seriously. Blondie paid for her own plane ticket and she's paying for their room and her own meals. It doesn't cost an extra dime to let her ride on the bus, and I'd gladly give a lift to any Cal student who wanted to hop on, so I'm not gonna charge her anything for that. Now, if any of you want to bring a boyfriend or a girlfriend or a family member, you have the same opportunity." He looked at every face once again, sparing a slight wink for Jamie, then nodded and sat down.

"Well, he's certainly to the point," Jamie said. "Any chance of getting him to remember my name?"

"Only if you can play softball."

Their arrival at the hotel was a study in organized chaos. There was a tremendous amount of luggage stored under the bus, and it took quite a few minutes to get everything sorted out. Ryan grabbed her suitcase and crawled over a dozen bags to fetch Jamie's, then started for the main entrance. "Honey," Jamie said, "you had two bags. You had a huge duffel bag, too."

"Oh. Yeah. Jackie's gonna take that one for me. I've got some of her stuff in it."

"Huh?"

"It's cool. Everything's under control."

Jamie took another glance at the milling players still trying to locate their bags, and doubted Ryan's words, but it was her bag so she shrugged her shoulders and followed her into the motel.

The student manager had gone inside as soon as the bus pulled up, and now she stood in the lobby handing out room keys. "You've got your own reservations, right, O'Flaherty?"

"Yep. We're good." Ryan strode up to the front desk and got squared away, and a few minutes later they arrived at their room. To Jamie's surprise it was a very spacious layout, with a nice sitting room and a separate bedroom.

"Did you do this on purpose?"

"Yeah. I know you're not used to hanging with the poor folks, so I thought I'd at least get you a big room. I thought it might ease your transition into the lower class."

Jamie gave her a hug and said, "I appreciate your efforts to cushion my culture shock, but you don't have to do this in the future. I think you'll get along better with your teammates if it doesn't look like we're livin' large. I mean, Coach Roberts must be a little concerned since he made a point of saying something on the bus."

"Nah. I don't think that'll be a problem with this group. He's only being proactive. But I won't splurge on rooms anymore. This is a special occasion."

"Oh, right." Jamie giggled, popping her open hand over her mouth. "I forgot it was my birthday tomorrow."

"I didn't. I know it's not the same as being at home, but I want you to have a fun day."

"All I have to do is be with you, and fun is sure to follow."

They were about halfway through putting their things away when Ryan went to answer a knock at the door. "Hi. Put it right on the table," Jamie heard her say. She popped her head out of the bedroom to see a man placing the largest gift basket she had ever seen onto the small dining table. The basket was obviously very heavy, because even his impressive musculature couldn't quite handle the lift, and Ryan had to help him.

"What's this?" Jamie asked, a delighted grin on her face.

"Oh, they do this for everyone," Ryan teased.

The server wiped his brow and said, "If we did this for everyone, I'd find a new job."

Ryan tipped him and sent him on his way, and by the time she saw him to the door, Jamie was already deep into her exploration. "Wow! Look at all of the cool things in here."

"Catherine comes through again," Ryan said, peering at the delights over Jamie's shoulder.

"Did you know she was going to do this?"

Ryan gave her an enigmatic smile and said, "We've had a few discussions about your birthday, and how to make it special for you. We share a common goal, you know."

"What's that?" Jamie linked her hands behind Ryan's neck and leaned back to be able to observe her face.

"To make sure you're as happy as possible every minute of the day."

With a few gentle kisses and a firm hug, Jamie said, "You're both doing very, very well."

They were sharing lazy kisses when another knock startled them. "Now what?"

Yet another man entered the room, this time carrying a large square box. "Put it right there," Ryan instructed, while reaching into her pocket for another tip.

"Ryan!" Jamie said after the man had gone. "It's a cake big enough to feed the whole motel."

Ryan checked her watch and proclaimed, "Then I guess it's time we invited the whole motel in for a party." She opened the door and the entire team started streaming in, each woman bearing a neatly wrapped present and offering a hug for the birthday girl.

Jamie was too stunned to move, and every time she cast a glance at her partner, Ryan was smiling like the cat that ate the canary. When the last of the guests had entered, Ryan called them to order. "We've got enough food for a small army here, and I want every crumb gone by midnight. The kitchen is sending up drinks, but if there's anything you want that we don't have, just let me know. Enjoy!"

Jamie had sidled up next to her while she spoke, and Ryan reflexively draped an arm around her shoulders. "Surprised?"

"Yeah. I'd say that surprise covers it. You are too much sometimes."

"You know what I always say," Ryan said. "Too much of a good thing is juuuuuust right."

The party was in full swing and Ryan was the perfect hostess, making sure that everyone had food and drink at all times. She had to climb over bodies to tend to everyone's needs, but she was graceful enough that she was able to manage it.

Jamie caught her during a quiet moment and said, "That's a pretty impressive mound of presents there, sport."

"Yeah," Ryan said. "You've obviously made an impression on them all."

"Oh, I'm sure that's so. I've even inspired them to use matching paper, and wrap the presents in an identical manner. Remarkable."

"Yep," Ryan said, going along with the joke. "You've inspired them to uniformity. Wanna open them yet?"

"Nah. Let's wait until most of the food is gone. It will be easier to move around when people aren't balancing plates on their knees."

"Having fun?" Ryan asked, bending to kiss the top of Jamie's head.

"Absolutely. I think we should do this for every road trip."

Ryan gulped, her eyes wide. "I'd better get busy then, 'cause this took me weeks to plan."

They combined the gift opening with a test of Jamie's memory. The memory test was, of course, Ryan's idea, and Jamie shot her a few lethal looks, but played along.

Ryan handed her the first gift and pronounced, "This one is from Stephanie."

Jamie accepted it, and scanned the crowded room. She pointed at a very slim, dark-haired woman and said, "Stephanie Simon. Pitcher. Senior. From…somewhere in Southern California." Smiling she cocked her head and asked, "How'd I do?"

"Excellent," Stephanie said. "I'm from San Diego, by the way, but I won't deduct anything from your score."

Jamie rolled her eyes and said, "Softball players. Always keeping score."

She got through the pile of gifts with very few errors, although she had a pretty tough time with hometowns. Ryan had obviously bought and wrapped each of the gifts; and while each was only a small thing, Jamie was deeply touched by the effort and thought her partner had put into the endeavor.

Heather approached as the guests started to leave and pressed a small gift into her hands. "I wanted to get you a little something on my own, Jamie," she said nervously. "I uhm…hope you like it." She gave her a hesitant hug and took off before Jamie could get a word out.

Ryan saw the interchange and approached her partner, whispering, "Glad to see that she's got that shyness thing licked."

"She's so cute," Jamie said. She tore the wrapping off the gift to expose a CD. "Ooo, the new Katy Perry. Cool!"

I owe you one, Heather, Ryan growled internally. *I hope Jamie plays that when I'm out of the house.*

The next morning, they were almost ready to head downstairs to wait for the bus when the phone rang. "I'll get it," Jamie called. "Hello?"

Martin's voice greeted her. "Happy birthday to you, Jamie."

"Oh, thanks for calling Martin. It's been a great birthday so far, thanks to your daughter. She had a huge party for me last night, with the whole team. It was great."

"You bring out the best in her, and for that I'm forever grateful to you."

"She does the same for me. That's the only way it works."

"Wise thoughts for one so young," he teased. "Of course, that extra year you put on today might have done the trick."

"Most likely."

"Maeve wants to say hello, too," Martin said. "Here she is."

"Happy birthday, Jamie dear. How was the party?"

"Ahh, you knew about it, huh?"

"Not in detail. But we knew that Ryan had arranged for something with the team. Was it fun?"

"It was a blast. It was a nice way to get to know everyone, too. As usual, Ryan had several agendas she was serving."

"That's our girl," Maeve said. "We'll let you go now, dear. I'm sure you have a million things to do."

"Yes, the bus is leaving soon, so I'd better run. Thanks again for calling. I appreciate it."

"Think nothing of it," Maeve insisted. "Have a lovely day, Jamie."

"I haven't had many bad ones with Ryan by my side. She's my perpetual birthday gift."

When she hung up a pair of warm hands settled on her bare waist. "Perpetual birthday gift, huh? I like it."

"I like it too, but if I don't get dressed I'll miss the bus. Something tells me that Coach Roberts would ditch me, even on my birthday."

When they arrived at the softball complex Jamie found a quiet picnic table and started to study. She quickly got lost in thought and barely noticed when Ryan sat down next to her. "Hi," she said, all decked out in her softball gear. "Do you want to study today, or would you like a more interactive experience?"

"I could be convinced. What do you have in mind?"

"Wanna be our bat girl?"

"Are you serious?"

"Yep. Coach says it's okay if you want to. You could even wear a uniform."

"Can I sit on the bench with you?"

"Yep. Right next to me."

"I think I'll pass on the uniform," Jamie said, "but I'm all about sitting in the dugout with you."

They found a navy blue Cal Softball polo shirt that fit well, and the khaki shorts she had chosen nearly matched the ones the coaching staff wore. So Jamie looked very much like the supporting members of the team. Her duties were few—run out to the plate and retrieve the bat when a player hit the ball. She took her cues from Ryan, who watched the game so intently Jamie wondered what could possibly be going on in her head since there was so little action.

She got a clue into her partner's mental processes when Jackie sat down next to her. Jackie Maloney was probably Ryan's best friend on the team so far. She was from Salinas, California, and Jamie was sure she'd never seen anyone look less like an athlete—at first glance, that is.

Jackie was a farm girl, who had spent her early years helping out around her family's large spread. She had to weigh at least two hundred and twenty-five pounds, and she was only about Jamie's height. Her long, wavy, medium brown hair was usually worn in a heavy braid that trailed down her back, but having all of the hair pulled off her face so severely made her look even more imposing. When she wore her uniform, the vertical stripes looked more like a series of parentheses, but upon closer inspection Jamie had quickly decided that she wasn't truly fat. She was simply a very large girl with a substantial bone structure and heavy, thick muscles.

As Ryan had said, it was a shame that Jackie was straight, since many lesbians were partial to large, powerful women, while most young men didn't find the look attractive. But Jackie was clearly straight, albeit frustrated by her inability to find a man who could appreciate her.

Jackie had struck out in spectacular fashion in the first inning, nearly managing to fall onto her butt when she flailed at a pitch in the dirt. Upon her return to the bench she sat next to Ryan and the pair stared at the opposing pitcher for a few minutes, not a word spoken. Finally, Jackie said, "I can't read her. You got anything?"

"Yeah," Ryan nodded, "I got a little. She's got an 'oh, shit' sinker that you bit on your first time up."

"No kidding?" Jackie said, giving Ryan an elbow in the ribs. "I felt like a pretzel."

"Yeah, she messed you up bad on that one. But I've been watching her carefully, and she has a little bit of a tell when she throws it. You've gotta watch carefully, but it's her favorite pitch and she gets a little excited when she's gonna throw it. Right before she goes into her windup, she loosens up her shoulders, like she doesn't want anything to interfere with the delivery. Watch her," Ryan instructed. They sat quietly for a few minutes, and sure enough, the next time the pitcher threw the sinker she nudged each shoulder a little, trying to settle her shirt. "Here goes," Ryan predicted. Lupe flailed at the ball, and Jackie gave Ryan a warm grin.

"Good work, Rof," she said as she slapped her hard on the back.

"Rof?" Jamie asked when Jackie went to grab a bat.

"Yeah. I told you they were calling me the Notorious R.O.F. before I even joined the team. Well, that got shortened to Rof."

"You jocks are all about nicknames, aren't you?"

"Hey, you're a jock, too. Don't you have nicknames for your golf teammates?"

"None I've ever heard. Maybe I'll start a trend."

"Yeah, tell 'em your nickname is Cinna Bunz. That oughta make you popular."

"If that gets out, you're toast," Jamie threatened, her green eyes flashing.

"Don't worry, you've got more on me than I have on you."

When Jackie took her next turn at bat, she managed to hold off on every sinker thrown her way. The pitcher was getting frustrated, and after Jackie had worked the count to three balls and two strikes, the hurler made a mistake and sent up a fat fastball—right over the heart of the plate. The pitch was so juicy that Jackie almost swung too soon, but she held back a heartbeat and crushed it. The ball left the stadium so quickly that the left fielder didn't even move. She merely let her eyes rotate to watch the missile zoom over her head.

The whole team rose to greet her, and Jackie reserved a special thump on the back for Ryan. "You rock, Rof. Thanks!"

"I only gave you a tip. You're the one who ripped the cover off that poor ball. I think it's still rolling around out there in a field somewhere."

Jackie went to get a drink and Jamie looked over at her partner, who was sitting calmly, a broad smile covering her face. Patting her on the thigh, she said, "You really don't mind not playing, do you?"

Ryan shrugged and said, "I'd rather play than not, but I'm cool with it. Jackie's a better hitter than I am, and she's a good fielder, despite her size. She's been with the team for four years, and works her butt off to perfect her hitting. I don't have a word of complaint."

"You're a good teammate."

"Hey, I've pushed a lot of good players to the bench in my day. I don't mind seeing what it's like to be on the other side. Besides," she said, "I get to sit with my best girl when I don't play. That's a deal I'd make any day."

Chapter Nine

Mia sat in the vaguely comfortable seat in the United terminal, and craned her neck towards the doors where she expected passengers to arrive to pick up their luggage. Although she was eagerly anticipating this visit, she still felt a little ill-at-ease, an emotion that she couldn't ever remember experiencing around her older brother.

She was lost in thought for quite a while, shaking her head in amazement when Peter tapped her on the shoulder, grinning widely. "Bored?" he asked.

"Peter!" She leapt to her feet and rose to her toes, stretching to reach his face. With generous kisses to both of his cheeks, she released him for a moment before she leaned back in for a hug. His carryon was draped over his shoulder, restricting his movement, but when he saw how desperate his sister's embrace was, he dropped the bag with a thud, and wrapped his arms around her.

"Hey, are you all right?" he asked when she nuzzled her face against his jacket.

"I've missed you," she mumbled. "This is the longest we've ever been apart."

"You're the one who didn't want to go to Europe over Christmas," he reminded her gently.

"I know. I'm not blaming you. But I've really missed you."

He stooped to pick up his bag, then slung an arm around her shoulders. "Please don't think I doubt your sincerity, Mop Top," he teased, reverting to a once-hated childhood nickname. "But when you miss your big brother, it's usually because you're in some kind of trouble that you don't know how to get out of. What is it this time?" His blue eyes were gentle and filled with equal parts affection and resignation.

"Nothing!" she said sharply, her eyes sparking with indignation. "Can't I simply be happy to see you?"

Pulling her to a quiet corner of the waiting area, he placed a hand on each of her shoulders and said, "Of course you can, and I'm happy to see you, too. But you haven't been calling, you haven't been writing, and you haven't been going home. It doesn't take too much extrapolation to leap to the conclusion that something's going on with you. It might be good, or it might be bad, but it's something. Do you want to tell me now, so I can help deflect the Grand Inquisitor?" he joked, referring to their mother. "Or do you want to wing it?"

She sighed heavily and took her cell phone from her bag. Speed dialing a number, she rolled her eyes at him and said, "Hi, Mom, it's me. Peter's flight's delayed, so don't expect us home soon. No, it's no problem. I'll wait in the bar." With another sigh she met her brother's amused smile and added, "I'm legal now, Mom. You won't have to bail me out, it's not against the law to have a drink in an airport." She couldn't help but chuckle as she said, "Yes, you're right. It's not a single drink that lands me into trouble. I'll behave." She took Peter's arm and led him to the first bar they encountered. "Okay. I'll call when we're leaving. I love you too, Mom."

She snapped the cover closed and sighed, "Don't you dare laugh! She doesn't watch you like a hawk."

"She doesn't need to," he said, leading her to a corner table and signaling the waitress.

They chatted companionably while they waited for their drinks, with Mia occasionally reaching over to give his hand a squeeze. Peter wasn't nearly as openly demonstrative as his sister, but he gracefully accepted her loving touches, and occasionally gave her a gentle pat as well. Their drinks were nearly ready for a refill when he asked, "Ready to spill the beans?"

She shrugged her shoulders, not feeling ready, but knowing that it didn't help to delay. "I've fallen in love."

As his head cocked, his eyebrow lifted. "So far, so good. I assume there's more?"

"Yeah. There's a little more. Uhm, it's someone from school. One of the nicest people you'll ever meet. Bright, sensitive, funny, and very gifted athletically."

"You with an athlete? That's a shock. You've always hated jocks."

"*Very* gifted. A member of the Olympic volleyball team," she added, completely avoiding the use of pronouns.

Recognition dawning in his gentle blue eyes, he reached across the table and grasped her hand. "I assume Mom and Dad don't know?"

"Don't know what?"

"That you've jumped the fence." His lips twitched into a small smile. "You were so certain that you were only interested in experimenting with women. What pushed you over?"

"Jordan," she sighed dreamily. "Jordan Ericsson, the most beautiful, loving woman on the planet."

His smile grew as he watched his sister's face. Her gentle, warm, peaceful expression reflected a calm he had rarely observed. "This is the real thing, huh?"

"Oh, yeah. There's not a doubt in my mind about her. I'm just worried about—everything else," she grimaced, the restless, slightly agitated look back in force.

"Don't go off the deep end. If you're sure about this, it can work out. Tell me about her."

The warm sparkle came back into her eyes as she wrinkled up her nose and asked, "Wanna see her picture?"

"Sure. I'd love to." He didn't know what to expect, having seen his sister run through the gamut of 'types' when it came to men. His forehead twitched into a frown as he observed her take the latest issue of Martha Stewart Living out of her bag.

She thumbed through it until she got to an ad for "Polo" by Ralph Lauren, then pointed to the tall, lean woman in a strapless, black velvet evening gown, straddling an equally gorgeous wavy haired young man dressed in a tuxedo, sitting on an old wooden swing hanging from a huge tree branch. The man was grinning at her like he was barely able to stop himself from ravishing her, and her head was thrown back, allowing her long, golden hair to drape down her bare back. Peter's eyes popped out as he considered that he would have gladly traded places with the man in the picture, or with his sister, for that matter. "*This* is your girlfriend?"

"No, that's the perfume she wears," she scoffed, slapping his shoulder. "Actually, they gave her enough of the stuff to fill a bathtub. Or a trash can."

"Your girlfriend is a model, *and* an Olympic athlete?" he mumbled, unable to take his eyes off the lovely woman in the picture. Jordan's hands were grasping the sturdy rope that held the swing up, and her well-defined biceps curved a bit to very good effect. The bustline of the dress swept across the tops of her full breasts, creating a delicious-looking expanse of cleavage. Full lips beckoned the man in the picture, and Peter imagined having those lips…He was ripped from his musings by being hit sharply with the rolled up magazine.

"She's mine, you know!"

Rubbing his hand over his face, he fought down the flush that he knew was rising on his cheeks. "Shit. I'm sorry, Mia, but when you show me a picture like that you can't expect me not to react. Dad will do the same."

"Great. Just what I need. The three of us can sit around and drool over her while Mom loads the gun."

He chuckled, shaking his head. "We don't have a gun. You know Mom's more the butcher knife type, anyway."

Even through her anxiety, she couldn't help but laugh at that. "I guess you're right. I don't have to be able to outrun a bullet. I only have to be able to outrun you and Dad."

"Are you gonna tell them?"

"Not yet. I'm not ready yet. I mean, I'm not unsure about Jordan, but I don't have answers to the questions that I know they'll ask. I feel like I need an iron-clad case before I bring it up."

"They love you, Mia; you don't have to defend yourself to them. I know it'll be hard at first, but they'll get over it."

"Maybe, but I've seen what happened to Jamie this year, and I worry that it'll be the same for me."

"How's she doing? I wrote her a note after the car-jacking. She sent me a nice one back."

"Yeah, she told me." She gave his knee a squeeze. "That was nice of you. She's doing better now. Ryan's still having a tough time, though. She doesn't say anything, but she's a lot jumpier since it happened. Not that I blame her," she said, shivering at the memory.

"Is Jamie happy? Is this all working out for her?"

Her lips curled into a wide grin as she said, "I've never seen her happier. She finally seems to know who she is, and she's growing and changing in ways that truly amaze me. It's been great to watch and be a part of."

"The same might happen to you. I mean, yeah, it'll be hard for Mom and Dad to accept, but if this is who you are, they need to know it."

Her chin tilted up as her brow furrowed. "Who I am?"

"Yeah. They need to know that you're a lesbian."

"I'm not, Peter," she said quietly. "That's part of the problem."

"But I thought that…"

"Look," she said, folding her hands on the table and rubbing her thumbs together as she organized her thoughts. "I'm in love with Jordan. I would happily remain in a monogamous lesbian relationship for as long as we can make this work. But I'm not a lesbian. I love men, and I always will. I just don't want to love them while I'm with Jordan."

"I see," he said, scratching the back of his head in an indication that he actually did not.

"That's my problem. If I were a lesbian, I wouldn't have a problem with telling Mom and Dad. They'd flip out, but they'd get over it. It's much, much harder to explain to someone that you're in a lesbian relationship—that you love a woman—but aren't gay. I don't think they'll get it."

He nodded slowly, and Mia saw that he was finally understanding her point. "I think I see one potential argument they'll have."

"What's that?"

"It's one thing if you're only attracted to women. But if you can love men, why choose to love a woman? You're voluntarily putting yourself into a group that society in general doesn't approve of."

"Exactly! That's exactly what Mom will say. I can hear her now."

"Is your girlfriend a lesbian? She sure doesn't look like one."

The scowl on her face made him wish he could suck his last statement back in, but it was out now and he tried to explain, "I didn't mean that like it sounded. That was, well, that was a stupid thing to say."

She patted his hand and said, "Don't feel bad. Everybody does it. I've done it myself." She reached into her wallet and found the schedule for the volleyball team that showed a fierce looking Jordan elevating to go for a kill. Gazing at it fondly for a moment, she handed it over, saying, "This is how she looks when she's not in makeup and a gown. I'm the first woman she's been with, but I'm pretty sure this is a life-long commitment for her."

He looked at the photo for a long while, finally saying, "I can't imagine what that would be like. I mean, I knew I liked girls when I was in pre-school. I can't imagine how weird it would feel to one day wake up and find out that I was into guys, but hadn't known it."

She chuckled and said, "I think it's a little more involved than that. She's had lesbian leanings for a long while. She's just now ready to commit to it."

"How does she feel about the fact that you don't feel like a lesbian?"

"Mmm, she says she's fine with it, but I think it bothers her more than she lets on. I think there's a part of her that worries I'll find some guy that I like better, and dump her."

"That's not how you are. You hang in there and try to make things work."

Mia beamed a smile at her brother and nodded. "Yeah. I know I do, but she's never known me when I'm in a relationship. This is all new for both of us."

He reached across the table and grasped her hand, giving it a squeeze. "I think you should wait to tell Mom and Dad. I think you need to see how this goes and make sure you're in it for the long haul before you freak them out."

She nodded briskly, her curls tossing about her head. "I think I'd already decided that. Now I have to figure out how to plan for next year without them finding out."

"Next year?"

She checked her watch and said, "I'll tell you in the car. I know Mom will freak about Jordan, but Dad will freak about the other little matter that's come up."

"Little matter?" he asked as he got to his feet and grabbed his bag.

"Not so little, actually," she said, knowing that deciding to attend Stanford Law would ameliorate any wrongs she committed, at least in her father's eyes.

A gentle hand stroked languidly through her curls, causing Mia to sigh heavily and curl her body around the warmth that she unconsciously sought. "Mmm, nice," she murmured, as she tightened her embrace while arching her back in a long stretch. Her head shook to clear the cobwebs, then she rolled onto her back and looked up into Jordan's clear blue... "Mom!"

Anna Lisa Christopher gazed fondly into her daughter's dark eyes and moved her hand from her hair to her cheek. Brushing the backs of her fingers along the smooth surface she said, "God willing, some day you'll have a daughter, and you'll know the feeling I get in my heart when I watch you sleep."

A slow, drowsy smile settled onto Mia's face and she nuzzled against her mother's hip. Her relaxed, unguarded posture left her totally unprepared for the sharp sting when her cheek was grabbed and pinched firmly. "Pray that your daughter doesn't keep secrets from you like you do from me!"

"Ow! Ow! Ow!" she cried trying to follow her mother's hand to relieve the pressure on her face. "Lemme go!"

Releasing her, Anna Lisa leaned forward until their nearly identical brown eyes were inches from each other. "Who are you sleeping with so often that your body thinks he's beside you in bed? Is this why you don't come to visit anymore?"

"No!" she scowled, rubbing her cheek. "I don't come home because I don't like to be assaulted!" Throwing off the covers, she exited the bed from the other side, trying to stay as far away from her mother's strong grip as possible.

The two fiery women stood at opposite sides of the bed, regarding each other warily. "Mia," Anna Lisa warned, "you know we have a deal. It's obvious you haven't kept up your end of the bargain. Now who is he?"

Mia rolled her eyes, mentally kicking herself for promising that she would always keep her mother informed when she got serious about anyone. In exchange for her promise, Anna Lisa had agreed to never question Mia about her sex life. It had seemed like a good idea when she had struck the deal in high school, and hadn't had the money to purchase birth control on her own. But now she deeply regretted both having made, and then having reneged on, the agreement. Considering how to extricate herself from this dilemma, while her mother's dark eyes bore into her, she decided to adopt one of Ryan's tactics.

"Okay," she sighed. "You're right, Mom. There is someone, and we are serious about each other."

Anna Lisa's hands went to her hips and she glared at her child with a triumphant expression. "I knew it!"

"I'm sorry," she added, her genuine sincerity boosted to the highest level she could summon. "I haven't told you, and that was wrong."

The rigid stance shifted, then softened, then Anna Lisa opened her arms and beckoned her daughter to come to her. Mia did so, letting her mother envelop her in a warm hug. "Why didn't you tell me? It hurts me to have you keep your life so secret."

"I'm sorry, I really am. I…well, I have some things that I have to work out before I'm going to be ready to talk about this." She pulled away and gazed directly into her mother's eyes and promised, "That doesn't mean that I don't love you, or trust you. It only means that I'm confused about this, and talking about it now won't help."

"Since when can't I help you get through something? We've been through so much together. I've worked so hard to listen to you, and try not to judge you."

"I know," she soothed, leaning in for another hug. "I swear that this isn't about you." Releasing her mother with a gentle pat, she straightened up and said, "There are just some things that I have to work out on my own. This is one of them."

"All right. I won't ask again."

"Really?"

"Yes. Really. You're old enough to know what you need at this point in your life. I'm here for you, and I know that you know that. I must know one thing, though," she said, an unyielding expression in her eyes.

"What's that?"

"You're not in any trouble, are you? You're not pregnant or using drugs again, or…"

"Mom," she said firmly, holding up a hand. "Stop. Nothing is wrong, I swear. I'm very happily in love with a wonderful person, who I know you and Dad will love. It's other…circumstances that are the problem, and as soon as I figure out all of the details, I'll tell you everything. I promise," she vowed. "I'm very happy, Mom." The smile she beamed at her mother was a clear indication of her veracity, and the older woman reached for her once again.

Stiffening, Anna Lisa grabbed her shoulders and held her at arm's length. "He isn't married, is he?"

"No. Definitely not. This is an issue between the two of us. No angry lovers, no spiteful ex's. I swear. I'm very happy, and I'm sure we can work things out."

"If you're happy, I'm happy. That's all I want for you."

They stood quietly, holding each other for a long while, until Anna Lisa released her, but not before slapping her gently on her butt. "You're too skinny. Come down for breakfast right now, and eat something substantial for a change."

Anna Lisa stood in the bedroom she shared with her husband of twenty-five years and said, "I think she's all right. She admitted that she's fallen in love, but she won't talk about him."

"She won't?" he asked slowly, knowing that his wife could make a rock talk if she set her mind to it.

Sighing deeply, an expression of resignation on her face, she said, "It's time I stepped back and let her make her own way. She'll tell us when she's ready."

With a broad smile, Adam wrapped his wife in a warm embrace, then tilted her head up to kiss her. "That must be hard for you, but I think it's the right thing to do. If she doesn't feel like she's going to be questioned so intently, she might be willing to come home more often."

Returning the soft kiss, Anna Lisa shook her head, while giving her husband a smile. "No, that's not it. She doesn't come home because she wants this man in her bed. She's not ready to tell us, so she can't bring him home with her. As soon as she figures out whatever it is that she has to figure out, I think we can convince her to visit more often and bring him with her."

Adam smiled at his wife, frankly amazed at the change in her attitude. "You'd let her sleep with her boyfriend in the house?"

Shrugging her shoulders, she admitted defeat. "I want my daughter to come home more often. I'd rather have her here with a man, than there with the same man. We can't stop her from having sex," she said. "Although Lord knows we've tried."

"So what will it be?" Adam asked as his entire family sat in the kitchen, digesting their breakfast.

"What are our choices?" Peter asked.

"We can play golf…"

"No golf!" Anna Lisa declared. "I want all of us to be together."

"Okay," Adam said. "I've got the keys to Jim Evans' boat. How about a day on the bay?"

"That's my vote," Peter said immediately.

"I'm game," Mia said.

"Let me pack a lunch and we can be off," Anna Lisa said, hopping to her feet to get started.

Following the script that she had worked out with Peter on the ride home the previous evening, Mia waited until they were on the water to make her announcement. "Mom, Dad, I've got good news," she said brightly.

"What's that?" Adam asked.

"Either Stanford has dropped a few hundred notches academically, or there was a terrible screw-up in the Admissions Office, but, either way, I was accepted into the law school." She waited expectantly for the words to register with her father, grinning widely when his face practically exploded with glee.

"Oh, my God! I didn't even know you'd taken the LSATs! I'm astounded! Overjoyed, but astounded," he repeated.

"That's wonderful, baby," Anna Lisa echoed. "We're both very proud of you."

"That's the good news," she hedged. "Now the news you might not like so much is that I'm not sure I'm going to accept."

Adam looked like he was ready to jump overboard, and he said, "You can't turn down an opportunity like this! You can't!"

"Why would you turn it down?" Anna Lisa asked. "You wouldn't have applied if you didn't want to go. This has something to do with this boyfriend, doesn't it?"

"No!" Mia shouted to be heard above the snapping sails. "Well, maybe a little," she said. "We're having a tough time figuring out where we'll both be next year."

"He won't be in San Quentin, will he?" Anna Lisa asked suspiciously.

"Mom, I said nothing was wrong. That includes dating a felon."

"Mom, Dad," Peter said, "give her a chance here. Committing to three more years of school right away is a tough thing. Wouldn't you rather she make the decision before she goes, or do you want to waste a year's worth of tuition if she drops out?"

"Yeah," Mia piped up. "I'm trying to think things through for a change, but I need a little time."

Adam nodded. "All right. You let us know if you need any help in making the decision. Obviously, I'd love for you to go and be successful at Stanford, but I only want it if it's right for you."

"That's very generous of you, Dad," she said, wrapping him in a hug. "I know it would mean a lot to you if I went there."

"It would, but no matter what you do I'm very proud of you for even being admitted."

"Thanks, Dad," she said, smiling broadly, wondering why on earth she hadn't come home weeks earlier.

"I've got it!"

Ryan turned her head slowly and gazed at the near-joyous look of satisfaction on her partner's face. They had been in the air for over an hour, and Ryan had been nearly asleep for most of that time. Jamie, however, had been busily making notes in her journal, the soft, consistent scratch of her fountain pen lulling Ryan to sleep.

"Care to share?" Ryan said, knowing that it would be impossible to stop her.

"I know how to get Niall out of the doghouse!"

"I know you're good, but I don't see how even you can accomplish that. I've spoken with at least six of the lads, and they're well and truly steamed. I think this is going to have to wear off gradually."

"That's where you're wrong. When they hear the plan, they'll think he's a hero."

"Give," Ryan demanded, sitting up a little straighter in her seat.

"Okay." The dark blonde eyebrows twitched vertically a few times, then she turned a few pages in her journal and began. "The main issue is that he made two hundred thousand and they all made squat, right?"

"Right."

"But being hard-headed O'Flahertys, they wouldn't consider accepting any of the money, even if Niall offered, right?"

"Well, I don't necessarily agree with the descriptor, but the facts are correct," Ryan said. "And at this point, even if they wanted the money, they wouldn't take it as a matter of pride."

"So how about this," Jamie said, the excitement flowing from her in waves. "Niall takes the entire chuck of money, and uses it to make a down payment on another fixer-upper, either in Noe or the Mission. We form a collective, and we all contribute to the mortgage and expenses of the new place. All of us work on the house, and when it's done, we sell it. Niall would get his investment back, and the rest of us would split the excess."

Her wide eyes and happy, expectant grin would have made Ryan say it was a marvelous idea, even if it wasn't, but as luck would have it, she thought it was just short of brilliant. "How long has this been rolling around in your mind?"

"Ever since Conor called to say they were all mad at Niall. I can't stand to have the boys angry with one another." Her expression was so sincere, so guileless, that Ryan couldn't help but lean over and give her a gentle kiss.

Jamie returned it, the soft, moist meeting of their lips creating barely enough noise for Jackie to hear and immediately lean over the seat back to give Ryan a rap on the head.

"No funny stuff on public conveyances, O'Flaherty!"

"Everybody's a critic," Ryan called back over her shoulder.

Touching her nose with a fingertip, Jamie said, "We should behave. I don't want to make the other women uncomfortable."

"I'm the one who's uncomfortable," Ryan said, rubbing her head.

"So, given the kiss, I take it that you approve of my idea?"

"I think it's absolutely brilliant. And I think the boyos will go for it. Conor told me the other day that he missed working with the fellas on the weekend."

"Now I haven't worked out the details, but I think we should propose the rough framework to Niall to see if he's willing. I'll call him as soon as we get home."

Ryan leaned in again, but then remembered where they were. "I owe you one," she promised, blowing a kiss instead of delivering one.

🐎

"Niall is in!" Jamie crowed the second she hung up.

Ryan found it completely adorable that Jamie was the one to take the lead and call Niall, and she thanked the heavens once again that her partner was so very comfortable with her extended family. "What now?"

"I think I'll call Brendan next, and see if he has any ideas for how to structure it. Are you up for having him and Maggie over for dinner to discuss it?"

"Always," Ryan said. "Other than practice, I'm free through Thursday."

🐎

Mia came home not long after that. "Hey, you two!" She offered hugs to both women, then went to the table in the entryway and picked up a key. "Something's waiting for you in the garage," she said. "It's blue...and hot... and it's from Germany..."

"My X5!" Ryan snatched the key that Mia teasingly dangled, and in the blink of an eye, the door flew open and she was running down the front stairs, heading for the garage.

"I think she's excited," Mia said dryly as she and Jamie set off at a more moderate pace.

"Get in," Ryan ordered when they approached. Chuckling softly, both women did so, "Who delivered it?" Ryan asked when she met Mia's eyes in the rear-view mirror.

"It was cool. They brought it in on a flatbed truck and pushed it into the garage. It was mighty tempting, but I resisted the urge to take it for a spin."

"Good thought," Ryan said, not even able to think of a punishment severe enough to fit that crime. "There's only 1.7 miles on it."

"It's really nice," Jamie said. "Can I play with the buttons?"

"Can I stop you?" Ryan asked.

Jamie stuck her tongue out and started to play, opening and closing the sunroof a few times and discovering the CD player hidden in the glove box.

"I've never had a new vehicle," Ryan marveled, her hands running all over the matte black, leather-covered dash. "It's so sweet."

"Don't you want to drive it?" Jamie asked.

"Of course. But first, I want to make sure I know where everything is. I don't want to wreck it my first day out." She proceeded to figure out how to position the mirrors and her seat, while Jamie and Mia both punched every button they could get their fingers on.

Ryan was finally confident, and turned the key. "Ooo, nice purr, huh?"

"Sounds a little like you when I rub your belly," Jamie joked.

They went on a short spin around the neighborhood, and to Mia's amazement, Ryan let both her and Jamie do a lap around the block. "Great ride," Mia enthused when they returned. "It could be a real neck-snapper if you gunned it."

"Thanks." Ryan was distracted, but she managed to send a smile Mia's way. "It's got a good-sized V-8 in it. That gives it some pep."

"Ready for bed?" Jamie asked.

"Heck no. I've got to play."

"Have at it, but I'm going to bed. Kiss me when you get there."

"Uh-huh," Ryan said in her 'I'm not listening to you so you'd better not be telling me anything important' tone.

Jamie draped her arm around Mia's shoulders and said, "I wonder how long it will take her to notice we're gone?"

"Given the size of the owner's manual, I'd say about three a.m."

"You may be right," Jamie said. "I'll give you a report tomorrow."

🐎

When Jamie saw her roommate the next day she said, "You weren't off by much last night. Ryan woke me up at two with this totally puzzled expression on her face. I honestly don't think she had any idea she'd been alone out there for three hours."

"She's no slouch in the concentration department. Did she have a good time?"

"You know, I think she enjoyed getting to know her car as much as she enjoyed driving it. She seemed quite blissful today. Tired, but blissful."

🐎

On Valentine's Day afternoon, Ryan stood in her room at her family's home. "Ready to head out?" she asked brightly. Jamie finished hanging up the dress she planned on wearing that night, and gave her partner a broad grin.

"The event you planned takes place outside?"

"Yep. Make sure you dress warmly. We'll be out until it's dark."

"Okay," she said, making sure that her warm gloves were in her pockets. "Should I take my little camera?"

"Yeah. I'm pretty sure there'll be some photo opportunities."

Finally resigned that her cajoling had been to no effect, and that Ryan would not reveal their destination prematurely, Jamie took her partner's hand as they set off for points unknown.

Ryan was not yet ready to take her new car on its maiden voyage across the Bay Bridge, so they'd come in Jim's loaner. Since parking was so scarce, they parked in Niall's driveway at his house in Sunset. Taking off on foot, they passed a building that nearly filled a block. "This is the Irish Cultural Center," Ryan indicated. "This is where I took ceili dancing lessons when I was a little ankle biter."

Jamie laughed at her choice of terms and said, "Knowing how tall you were, you were a butt biter by the time you were old enough to take dance lessons."

"Good point. I guess I was about four when I started. That would definitely put me within butt biting range of most people."

"Wow, I can't imagine getting a bunch of four-year-olds to concentrate long enough to teach them how to dance. What did you call it again, kay-lee?" she asked, pronouncing it phonetically.

"Yeah, traditional Irish step-dancing."

"Like Riverdance?"

Ryan sniffed. "Hardly. If ceili dancing is like classical ballet, Riverdance would be like interpretive dance based on a ballet. Riverdance takes the elements of ceili and runs wild with it."

"Your tone implies you don't think much of Riverdance."

"No, it's not that. It is what it is," Ryan said. "I only hope that kids stay interested in the tightly controlled style of the traditional dance. I think they have to know the elements before they can start riffing on them."

"Show me a few steps," Jamie begged. "I've never seen you dance that way."

Ryan patted her and said, "I'll show you at home. I'd look like a nut standing out on the street doing a step dance."

Jamie nodded soberly. "Oh, I understand. You never want to look like a nut." She ran all the way to Sloat Street, barely managing to stay one step ahead of her lover's pinching fingers.

🐉

"Wanna take a picture of the pup?" Ryan asked, a big grin splitting her face.

"If this is where we're having lunch, you're in more trouble than you can imagine," Jamie scolded as they stood outside of the Carousel Diner on Sloat.

"No, we're not going to eat here," Ryan said. "I like the dog. I used to come here for a soda after dance lessons while I waited for the bus."

"When you were four?"

"Nah. Conor took lessons with me until he was in high school, and we went together most of the time. I wasn't allowed to ride the bus alone until I was seven or eight."

Jamie shook her head as she considered letting their children ride alone on a city bus when they were in second grade. Drawing her attention back to the topic at hand, Ryan pointed up. Jamie's eyes drifted up the rusted, paint-peeled steel pole, to gaze at the giant dachshund head that rested at the top. The dog wore a chef's hat, and was clad in a neat bow tie. "It's very nice," she said with a forced smile.

"You have no sense of history," Ryan chided her gently. "This is the last intact Doggie Diner dog head in the world."

"Imagine that," Jamie said. "Are the others in museums? Perhaps the Louvre?" She batted her eyes ingenuously, causing a scowl to form on Ryan's face.

"I really like it," she said, her feelings obviously hurt. "Da brought my Mama here when they were dating." Her mouth was turned down into an adorable pout, and Jamie couldn't help but kiss the frown from her face.

"The O'Flahertys have always known how to treat their women, haven't they, tiger?"

"Hey, he was a young guy. He took her to the zoo, and Golden Gate, and any other place that was free. Heck, she still had the Irish soil on her shoes. I'm sure she thought it was a lovely spot compared with the chipper in Killala." At Jamie's raised eyebrow, Ryan explained, "When she was growing up the only restaurant in Mama's town was a fish and chips takeaway. Now, fifty years later, the only restaurant is a fish and chips takeaway," she added with a grin. "But it's owned by a different guy. That's progress for you."

"I'm sure your mother thought it was the nicest place she'd ever been so long as your father was with her. That's how I feel when I'm with you," she added, sparing a warm kiss for Ryan's chilled lips.

Ryan took her hand to start up again, but Jamie paused to take several pictures, mildly disappointed when she was unable to get Ryan in the shot—since the head was so high above the ground. She grasped Ryan's offered hand and leaned against her shoulder, "I like the doggie, too."

They proceeded up the street, with Jamie still having no idea of where they were headed. "I used to go out with a woman who understood my doggie devotion," Ryan sighed.

"Oh, did you now?"

"Yep. She understood the cult. Heck, she had the dog tattooed on the back of her shoulder."

Jamie turned repeatedly to look at the dog head as it shrank in the distance, then back to her partner, finally asking, "Really?"

"Yeah," Ryan insisted. "The dog's a big deal around these parts, honey."

"Huh." Jamie took her partner's hand as they continued to walk, finally asking, "Why did you and your fellow doggie worshiper stop seeing each other? It sounds like you shared a belief system." She said this with a face full of studied innocence, making Ryan smirk at her.

"Honest?"

"Yeah. Of course."

"Uhm…I uhm…couldn't keep up with her," Ryan said, shrugging her broad shoulders. "She was…wow…she was all that." Her mouth twitching into a wistful smile. "If I hadn't been trying to do well in school as well as work a lot of hours, I would've hung in there. But with my schedule, she almost killed me!"

"Is she still single?" Jamie asked suspiciously.

"Nope. She found a great woman about a year ago. They seem very happy together." Waggling her eyebrows, she added, "Her girlfriend seems very, very satisfied." She waited a beat and added, "Not as satisfied as I am, but that's understandable." Lifting Jamie's hand to her mouth, she kissed it gently and said, "No one's as satisfied as I am."

"Good recovery," Jamie said. "I'll let you buy me lunch."

"We're here," Ryan declared a few minutes later as they stood in front of the entrance to the San Francisco Zoo.

"We're going to the zoo? For Valentine's Day?" Jamie gazed at her partner, waiting for the punch line.

"Don't you like animals?" Ryan asked, cocking her head.

"Well, yeah, but…"

"Come on," she insisted, tugging at her hand. "We're gonna miss the show."

"Show?"

Ryan was moving at such a quick pace that Jamie had a difficult time keeping up with her. They walked past every display and habitat, not slowing until they reached an out-of-the-way spot where a uniformed woman asked for their names. Jamie was too out of breath to even question her partner by this time, and after they were waved into a small grove, Ryan grinned at her and asked, "Isn't this a nice place for lunch?"

Jamie looked around and saw buffet tables laden with all sorts of delectable looking goodies, ice sculptures in the shapes of various zoo residents, and a champagne bar, where several other couples stood, sipping wine.

"Ryan, why are we having lunch in the zoo? Not that I mind, of course," she hastily added. "It looks fabulous."

"It's a tour the zoo puts on every year. We have a nice lunch, then we go on a tour with a guide, who explains the mating rituals of a selection of animals."

"Mating rituals?" Jamie asked with one severely raised eyebrow.

"It's Valentine's Day. Birds do it, bees do it, even educated fleas do it. Or so I've been told. I've never actually seen fleas do it," she added, grinning cheekily.

Jamie led her over to the champagne bar and took a pair of glasses from the tray. Leading Ryan to the nearest space heater, she clinked their glasses together and said, "Happy Valentine's Day, sweetheart." Taking a sip, she added, "I'm very glad that you brought me here. This is so...so you," she said. "A little off-beat, a little wild, very non-traditional. All of the reasons I fell in love with you, all in one package." She smiled up at her and said, "I should have known you'd never forget Valentine's Day."

"I never will," Ryan pledged, bending slightly to offer a soft kiss. "It gives me a marvelous excuse to kiss you in public."

As she pulled away, Jamie looked around at the assembled couples and said, "I think we're the only lesbian representatives here. Two gay couples, but that's it."

"That's nice," Ryan sighed, not having heard a word she said. She was gazing at her lover with a besotted smile, letting the warmth of their bond pervade her body. She had never considered Valentine's Day a memorable one on the calendar—always managing to be blessedly single when the day rolled around. But now, as the lovely blonde gave her a bemused smile, she decided that she quite liked the holiday. Going out of her way to show Jamie how much she loved her was something that she knew she could become very used to.

"What's that cute little grin for?"

"I was wondering if many animals feel love like we do," she commented thoughtfully. "I mean, I know that many species pair-bond, and some mate for life. I'm just wondering if they experience love." She sighed and cocked her head a little, saying, "I hope so. It's a delicious feeling."

A uniformed woman approached and lightly tapped Ryan on the shoulder, interrupting their warm embrace. "The tour's going to start soon. Why don't you two go on over and hop on the tram before everyone else."

"Thanks," Ryan said, taking Jamie's hand to lead her to the front seat. "We might be the only lesbians on the tour, but we're not the only ones in the house. Sister's looking out for us."

Ryan asked so many questions that Jamie was afraid the guide regretted her decision to offer them their choice of seats. Luckily, the patient woman clearly loved her job, and was very well schooled in her subject. The discussion about whether animals felt love lasted for over a quarter of the tour, with no real resolution, but it was fun to watch Ryan and the guide use their logical, scientific minds to try to think the question through.

When they finished, the guide offered to take a couple of photos of them, then Jamie snapped one of Ryan with her new friend. It was almost dark when they left, and the zoo was shutting down for the night. As they walked out, Ryan called out and waved to every creature that she saw, "G'night. Thanks for sharing your home with us."

"You are one of a kind, Ryan O'Flaherty. I'm so glad that you're mine."

Chapter Ten

Daniella Ericsson considered her address book for a moment, then muttered to herself as she searched the living room for her reading glasses. Once she found the half-frames that she hated as much as cellulite, she peered at the book again and dialed the unfamiliar number.

"Jordan? It's Mom, honey. I wanted to discuss this Olympic situation with you."

"This isn't Jordan. If you hold on, I can get her for you, though."

"Oh, well, that's fine. Please do."

She waited for the few minutes it took for the woman to locate Jordan and call her to the phone, finding her temper growing shorter as she waited. "Hello," the slightly more familiar voice said.

"Jordan, I'm calling from Los Angeles. When you know it's me, I'd appreciate it if you'd hurry to the phone."

"I was going to the bathroom, Mom," she sighed, not usually the type to reveal personal matters like this, but already exasperated, even though they had only been speaking for moments. "It's awfully cold here, and it takes me a minute to get bundled up again."

"Right," she said, not hearing the reply. "I'm calling about this ticket offer."

"Ticket offer?"

"Yes," she said, impatiently. "The offer from the Olympic Committee to purchase tickets to the Opening Ceremonies for the parents of all of the athletes."

"Oh." She'd hoped that the Committee would leave it to the athlete to inform her parents of the offer. "Yes, I'm familiar with it."

"Well, what does this include? It only mentions the tickets. Surely they don't expect us to pay for our own plane tickets and hotels."

Jordan cleared her throat, knowing she'd be getting a lecture momentarily.

"That's exactly what they expect. They only offer the tickets to the Opening Ceremonies because they're so hard to get. To do just that is gonna cost them over three million dollars."

"Well, in that case, I don't see how we can come. That would cost an exorbitant amount."

"I realize that," she said, trying to keep at least a note of regret in her voice. "In a way, it's a shame the games are so far away, even though it will be fascinating to see Australia."

"I suppose I'll have to watch it on television," Daniella said. "Gunnar will be so disappointed."

"Well, I'll take plenty of pictures and show him the next time we all get together," Jordan said, rolling her eyes as she played along with the family fable. "It won't be the same without you two there."

"Your father isn't going, is he?"

The question hung out there in space. Jordan knew that the chances were good that her mother would never find out the truth, but she also knew that her life would be hell if she was caught in a lie. "He's still thinking about it." This was a bold-faced lie. Jorgen Ericsson had promised his daughter that he would attend the competition as soon as she told him she had made the team. As a matter of fact, she already had his flight and hotel information. Regrettably, his stunningly young girlfriend Candy was going too, but she would at least keep Jorgen entertained.

"Jordan," her mother said, in a tone that indicated her limited patience was at its terminus. "Is he going, or not?"

"I think so."

Alas, Daniella immediately said, "Well, we might have to investigate this a little more." Jordan felt her heart sink, knowing that no good could come of this development. Her parents had not been in the same room since her high school graduation, and she still had occasional nightmares about that little get-together. "This will break my budget for the whole summer, but I hate to think of you going all that way and not having your family there for you."

Uh-huh. And if you didn't think Dad would be there, it would be fine with you if I were all alone. A small smile crossed her face as she considered one guest whose presence she was most happily looking forward to. *They can do whatever they want. They can fight to the death, for all I care. I'll have Mia with me, and nothing else matters.*

As her mother droned on, Jordan spent a moment letting herself savor the thought of looking up into the stands to see Mia's sweet face. As the reassuring images flitted through her brain, she was struck by the thought of how it would be when her family met her lover. *If she'll agree to meet them as my lover,* she considered. *She might just want to act like she's a friend from school.* A wave of unfathomable sadness washed over her as her mother's words continued on. For some reason it was suddenly desperately vital that Mia not only acknowledge, but be proud of their relationship—if not in all situations, then at least when she met Jordan's family.

"Jordan...Jordan! Have you heard a word I said?"

"Huh? Oh, yeah, sure I did," she said, feeling sick to her stomach.

"Well, will you do it, or not?"

"Sure. I'll do it," she muttered, not caring what she was agreeing to.

"Fine. I'll let you know how much the tickets cost."

"Tickets?" she asked, finally coming to her senses.

"Yes. I'll have Gunnar pay for the hotel, and you can pay for the airfare for the three of us. That seems fair, doesn't it? Now, since we have so far to go, I think we'll need either first-class or business-class, don't you?"

"Yeah. Sure. Whatever," she mumbled, unable to say no at that point.

"You certainly don't sound very happy about this. Is something bothering you?"

"No. Nothing's bothering me. I'm only wondering how I'm going to pay for the tickets since I don't have many opportunities to work here in Colorado."

"I saw that ad for Ralph Lauren," her mother said. "How many days was that shoot?"

"Two."

"And what's your quote now?"

"Two thousand dollars an hour for a national print campaign."

"So, you made at least thirty-two thousand for that one ad alone. I know the business, honey. Don't try to pull one over on me."

"I know how much I've made. But I've got some expenses coming up that are gonna make it tight."

"Oh, Jordan, you've been so sheltered. You don't know what it's like to have to maintain a house this size on the pittance that your father..."

Once again Jordan went into her little private world, letting her mother's voice provide the white noise to her musings.

⚜

Jamie was dressed and ready to go to their second engagement by seven o'clock. Ryan had fallen behind since Jamie hadn't let her into the bathroom for nearly a half hour. When she emerged, Ryan forgave her dawdling, spending several moments gazing at her partner appreciatively. "I was going to compliment you on your dress, but I don't even know what to call that color. It's what...jade?"

"Somewhere around there. Jade, emerald, malachite."

"It makes your eyes look greener than I've ever seen them," Ryan sighed as she took in the twin pools of verdant green that blinked up at her. "Once again, it feels marvelous," she added as her hands roamed all over the slightly slick-feeling silk. "Of course, that sensation might not come from the wrapper so much as the filling."

"I don't think I've ever been called filling. Yet another new one."

"I've got a million of 'em," Ryan said, dashing into the bath so she'd be on time.

Minutes later, Ryan slipped her long legs into the new slacks that Jamie had purchased for her in Pebble Beach, then tried to decide on what blouse to wear. "I know I should wear my suit, but I'll be too hot if I have to keep the jacket on," Ryan said, staring at the closet, waiting for it to divulge its secrets.

Jamie came up behind her and gave her bare waist a hug. "I have a couple of suggestions."

"Suggest away."

Going into her side of the closet, Jamie extracted a pair of blouses; one, white with French cuffs, the other a small blue and white check. "I had a couple of blouses made for you. You can't wear nice slacks with your shirt sleeves rolled up."

Ryan smiled gently at her partner and said, "One little decision leads to many more, eh? First it was the suit, then it was shoes, then another pair of slacks. Now it's blouses. Oh, I forgot—we're getting a new house to keep all of my clothes in."

"Funny," Jamie said, tweaking her nose. "Which blouse do you want for tonight?"

"I think I'll take the white one. Do you have any cufflinks?"

"But of course," Jamie chided her gently. She fastened the links after Ryan had put the blouse on, then stood back and watched her lover contort her body wildly.

"I've never had a blouse I could do this in," she mused as she extended her elbows and lifted her arms high into the air.

"Why have you wanted to?"

"Good point," Ryan conceded. "But if this restaurant needs any wood chopped tonight, I'm their woman." She mimicked the action she would have to make, and nodded, very satisfied that her new blouse allowed her complete freedom of movement.

"I like this collar on you," Jamie said, stepping back to admire the cut. "It's very feminine, but also tailored. Your necklace will look perfect with it." Jamie retrieved her partner's jewelry and fastened the necklace, settling it under the collar. Slipping the diamond earrings into her lobes, she stood quietly, letting her eyes roam up and down her lover's body. "We could always order a pizza."

Ryan smiled at her wanton leer and shook her head. "No way. I'm not going to have our grandchildren hear the story of how Grandmom got stuck with a pizza on Valentine's Day. I know you're the type to regale several generations of O'Flaherty/Evans offspring with that story." Her hands settled onto Jamie's hips and she added, "Besides, you look too wonderful not to share you with the world a little bit. I can't be that selfish."

Jamie smiled up at her and brushed her cheek with her lips, taking care not to leave any trace of her lipstick. "Thank you," she said, smiling demurely. "We're about ready here. One more little touch. Now, don't have a stroke, but I had a winter coat made for you." She gulped visibly and reached into her closet, pulling out a beautifully made, lightweight coat.

Raising an eyebrow, Ryan fingered the charcoal gray fabric, finding it deliciously soft and slightly furry. "A winter coat? I've never had a winter coat that didn't have a big zipper and a lift ticket or two hanging from it."

"A ski jacket doesn't look very good over your nice clothes. As Ryan continued to feel the fabric, Jamie prayed, *Please don't ask what it's made of... please don't ask.*

"Will this never end?" Ryan sighed dramatically.

Jamie turned her around and looked into her eyes, relieved to see nothing but gentle teasing in the cool, blue orbs. "You're not mad, are you?"

Ryan hugged her tight and said, "No. I'm not mad at all. I find that I understand your motivations more now that I'm serving this same function for Jennie. She thought I was crazy when I gave her seventy-five dollars for a pair of shoes, but I knew she'd look like a dork if she had some ten-dollar cardboard-soled shoes on at Sacred Heart. You're doing the same thing; trying to make me look like I fit in with my peers, in this case, you and your mom."

"Baby, you class up any room you enter," Jamie said sincerely. "I just like to dress you up a little bit once in a while."

"I'm pretty happy about the coat. I used to have to run from my car to where I was going during the winter, and that was if I could borrow a car. I've been on more than one date where I had to stow my ski jacket somewhere before I went into a nice restaurant."

"Well, I think you're set now," Jamie said, feeling like she had dodged a bullet. *If she knew that coat was cashmere she'd have a fit!*

As Jamie and Ryan walked down the street to retrieve the car, Martin and Maeve spotted them in the distance. They were on their way to Martin's brother Francis' house for dinner, and were too far away to catch the girls' attention without shouting—definitely not Martin's style. He squeezed his wife's hand and commented, "Have you ever seen a greater transformation in a shorter time period than the one our Siobhán has undergone?"

"Ahh, she hasn't changed so much, Marty. She's the same sweet little sprite she's always been."

"I hardly recognize her, sweetheart. Six months ago she was just another hooligan in the pack. I honestly had to sometimes remind myself that she was a girl. Now…look at her."

Maeve did as he asked, trying to think of how her niece had looked and behaved before she met Jamie. The girl was wearing a beautiful, double-breasted coat that enhanced her already impressive height, and a pair of well-tailored slacks draped gracefully across her shoes when she walked. "Where did she get that beautiful coat?" Maeve asked. "I've never seen her in anything but a ski jacket."

"I don't know where she got it, but it looks like it was made for her. I assume Jamie had something to do with it," he said, chuckling softly.

Even though Ryan's clothing was crisply tailored and bore very simple lines, the style highlighted every facet of her lushly feminine body. "She's simply stunning," she sighed. "She's not a girl any longer, Marty."

"No, she's truly not. Jamie's brought out the woman that's been hiding inside. She's so much more mature now." He smiled warmly, watching the way she held Jamie's hand in her own. "She's more loving, too. It took long enough, but I think she finally understands that it's no accomplishment to merely win a woman's body. Claiming her heart is all that matters."

Maeve nodded, feeling tears sting her eyes. "She's an adult now. Our little Siobhán isn't a child any longer."

Ryan stopped when she reached the passenger door of the stately, black BMW sedan and held the door open for Jamie. Then Ryan closed the door and dashed around to the driver's side. She got in and carefully guided the car up the street, catching sight of her father and aunt. Suddenly, they heard her voice over the external speaker, Irish accent firmly in place. "Off to the rub-a-dub-dub again, are ya? Sláinte!"

The couple looked at each other, both rolling their eyes as the car sped by. "Maybe she's got a bit of childhood left in her after all," Maeve said.

"What in the heck is a rub-a-dub-dub?" Jamie asked, giggling along with Ryan, even though she didn't know why she was laughing.

"Oh, that's one of the many, many terms for going to a pub."

"Rub-a-dub-dub…" Jamie looked at her and asked, "Is that a reference to the nursery rhyme? I don't get it."

"Nope. It's a form of rhyming slang. Dub rhymes with pub." She gave her partner a thoughtful look and said, "I guess we don't do that here, do we?"

"What?"

"Come up with little rhymes to refer to certain words. The Irish do it constantly."

"Uhm…why?" Jamie asked.

"Dunno. It's just a thing. Da doesn't do it much, but my Uncle Patrick does. Haven't you ever heard him?"

"I don't think so. Give me an example."

"Oh…he says 'dog and bone' instead of phone. He sometimes will call one of his kids a 'current bun'…"

Jamie started laughing, and in seconds she was slumped down in her seat, holding onto her stomach. "Oh, my God!" she gasped out. "I've heard him say things like that, but I never knew he was making a rhyme. I thought he was a little goofy!"

Ryan was chuckling along right with her, and she said, "Well, he is a little goofy. But he also rhymes a lot."

"I heard him call one of the boys a current bun and I thought it was a pet name, like my dad calls me cupcake."

"No, no," Ryan said. "Current bun rhymes with son. Like my dad might refer to me as a bottle of water. It rhymes with daughter. Sometimes Uncle Patrick calls me his long term lease, because lease rhymes with niece."

"Odd," Jamie said, shaking her head. "That's just plain odd."

"So you don't want me to refer to you as my struggle and strife?" she asked ingenuously.

"I'm guessing that means wife," Jamie said, her eyes narrowed. "I wouldn't recommend it if you want to get weekly paid."

"Weekly paid…weekly paid…what rhymes with paid…?" Ryan's eyes widened as recognition dawned. "I'm very fond of getting paid, sweetheart. Struggle and strife is hereby stricken from my lexicon."

Chapter Eleven

Ryan rolled her eyes when she handed the keys to the valet parking attendant in front of the restaurant. If she had been alone, or if Jamie had not had on heels, she would have never consented to the twelve-dollar fee, but she was feeling magnanimous, considering it was Valentine's Day.

As soon as they stepped inside the large space, they both unconsciously gasped in delight as they took in the huge chandeliers that ran the length of the main room. The massive lamps looked exactly like jellyfish, trailing long, glowing tentacles over the heads of the diners. Their eyes met in a shared memory as their thoughts returned to their last morning in Eleuthra, when they had been startled to have a sizeable jellyfish pass right before their eyes.

Unable to stop themselves from staring at the dramatic interior, Jamie's eyes took in the huge coral-tinted columns, covered with something that looked like kelp; while Ryan's gaze flitted to the dramatic, lengthy marble bar tucked away on the right side of the room.

When Jamie was able to tear her eyes away from the spectacle, the host, who was well used to diners being unable to focus on him, greeted her. "Good evening," he said. "Have you a reservation?"

"Yes," she said. "Evans for two."

He scanned his list, and she caught the twitch in his brow when he came to her name. "Mrs. Evans?" he asked cordially. "Will Senator Evans be joining you?"

"Actually, Mrs. Evans is my mother," Jamie explained, gracing him with her most confident smile. Gripping Ryan's hand, she added, "She made the reservation for the two of us."

"Marvelous. Come right this way," he said, leading them up a graceful, curved staircase covered with black beads that resembled glistening, fat caviar eggs. Ryan's mouth was nearly hanging open as she took in the strands of coral and barnacles that draped over the wall sconces leading up to the mezzanine.

Once they were situated in the most private corner of the space, he bade them have a pleasant meal and disappeared, leaving a stunned Ryan and an amused Jamie looking over the half-wall to survey the diners below.

"Happy?" Jamie finally asked her partner.

"I feel like I'm in the ocean again," Ryan managed to get out. "Look at the fish scales on the hood over the kitchen!"

"It is spectacular, isn't it? Mom was right, as usual."

Coming back to reality, Ryan cocked her head and asked, "What was that about your mom making the reservation?"

"Oh, I wanted to make sure we got a special table, so I asked her to call. She knows the maitre d'."

Ryan rested her chin on her hand and gazed at her partner for a long minute. "You two are quite the pair. I pity the poor soul who gets in the way when you have a goal."

The waiter appeared as Jamie was going to respond, and they spent a few minutes discussing his recommendations for appetizers. Ryan listened with less than half of her attention, content to stare out over the assembled diners and people watch. No business diners were in attendance, only couples and a few foursomes. She noticed a table or two of gay men, and was watching one pair share an order of oysters when Jamie's voice called her back. "Does anything on the appetizer list appeal to you?"

Ryan grinned at her and said, "Order for me? You do a much better job."

The waiter bit back a smirk and turned his attention back to Jamie, waiting patiently while she rattled off the items she'd like. After settling on two glasses of wine, he was off, and they were once again able to focus on each other.

"Do you like for me to order for you?" Jamie asked.

"I prefer it. You know what I like, and you know what goes well with other dishes. I've never been disappointed with what you've chosen, so why not?"

"Okay," she said. "Just know that I'll gladly step aside if you want to take over."

Ryan gave her a rakish grin and said, "You can be the top when we're out, as long as I take my rightful place when we're making..." The waiter arrived with their wine, and Ryan finished her statement non-verbally, with a slight twitch of her eyebrow and a crooked grin. As he left, she took a sip of her wine, savoring the various notes of the complex bouquet on the back of her tongue. "Oh, this is nice," she purred. "You've started to show me what the big deal about wine is, and I'm very grateful for that."

"It's the least I can do," Jamie said as she clinked her glass against Ryan's and tasted her own selection. "You've awakened my senses to so many pleasures in the past few months that I have to return the favor." She held her glass up to the light and observed the color of the wine, and the way it clung to her glass when she swirled it. "Nice, indeed," she said. "Want to taste mine?"

"We don't have the same thing?"

"No. We're both having Bourgogne blancs, but I thought the one I chose for you would go better with the appetizer you're having."

Ryan cocked her head slightly and sighed, her eyes growing slightly hooded as she reached across the table and grasped Jamie's hand. "Being with you is such a sensual experience. I feel so alive when we're together, like every nerve is singing with pleasure."

Jamie bit her lower lip as her eyes fluttered closed. With a matching sigh, she gazed at her partner and said, "You have the most beautiful way of expressing yourself. And even though you might deny it, you're the most romantic person I've ever met."

Ryan blushed, averting her eyes to once again look out over the restaurant. "The ceiling is simply stunning. How did they ever afford that kind of tile work?"

Glad that Ryan hadn't looked at the menu, Jamie mused, *You haven't seen the prices, honey. They could afford to move the Sistine Chapel over here.* "They didn't have to," she said. "This was the old Elks Club, and that was the mosaic that used to be over the pool. They added a floor, and curved the walls to give the room the cave-like feel that it has. Didn't they do beautiful work?"

"They sure did," she said, unable to take her eyes from the space. "I should bring Conor over here to see the workmanship."

"I like the sea urchin chandeliers," Jamie mused. "And they did such a nice job with those huge windows. They actually look like waves."

"You know, the food could suck, and this place would still be worth a visit."

As she spoke, a plate was placed in front of her, and she decided that even if the food was inedible, it was certainly gorgeous. A sea urchin shell was centered on the frosted glass plate, and Ryan delicately flicked at the ingredients. "What am I eating?" she asked as she picked up her fork and tried to decide how to attack her plate.

"Those are truffled mashed potatoes; with crab and a sprinkling of orange salmon caviar. I don't think you've had truffles before, but I thought they'd be fantastic with crab."

Ryan took a tiny bite, letting the earthy musk of the black truffle settle onto her palate. The sweet, fresh flavor of the crab hit her next, followed by the bright, salty burst of the caviar that practically exploded in her mouth.

The tangy caviar soothed the richness of the other ingredients, leaving a clean, yet complex feeling in her mouth that she decided she could grow very fond of.

While all of this sensory information was flooding her brain, her body was unconsciously performing her usual paroxysms of delight. Jamie fully expected her to moan and slide to the floor, but Ryan managed to remain upright in her chair and attract little attention.

"I haven't even tasted mine, but with that face, I've got to have a bite of yours," Jamie said, reaching across the table to snitch a forkful.

Ryan watched the fork travel back across the table, then saw the precious morsel disappear between her partner's coral-tinted lips. "I think that's the biggest sacrifice I've ever made for you," she sighed as she watched Jamie's face contort into a multi-layered expression of pure pleasure.

"Oh my God," Jamie husked as the flavors burst against her taste buds.

"That's the same look you get on your face when I first touch you with my tongue," Ryan whispered in her sexiest voice.

"Check!" Jamie looked around for their waiter, but Ryan grasped her hand and pulled it to her lips for a kiss.

"Don't rush, baby. Think of this as foreplay."

Jamie twitched in her seat and roughly shook her head, trying to force some blood back into her brain from whence it had settled near the apex of her thighs. "That's a foregone conclusion," she murmured throatily. She sank back against the cut velvet cushions of her chair and tried to concentrate on her own dish.

A shimmering seafood pyramid glistened in the soft light, the quivering mass of seafood aspic holding floating chunks of shrimp, scallops and lobster. It was centered on an oversized plate, surrounded by a bright yellow saffron vinaigrette and a sprinkling of salmon caviar. As she took her first bite, she closed her eyes and nodded slowly, her mouth curling into the half-grin that Ryan so loved. "This is fine. You need a little bite." Loading up her fork with a healthy portion, she reached across the table to offer it to her partner. Ryan scooted her chair closer and accepted the bit from Jamie's fork, pursing her lips as the tines slid from them. Before she could blink, Ryan had shifted her chair even closer, then brought her place setting and wine with her, so that their chairs were touching.

"We need to share," she announced soberly. And so they did, feeding each other, sipping each glass of wine in turn as accompaniment to the dishes. By the time they were finished, they were practically sharing the same chair, but neither moved when the dishes were removed from the table. A few of the diners on the mezzanine shot surreptitious glances at them, but they were hidden from view of the crowd on the first floor, for which Ryan was very grateful.

They were lost in each other's eyes, nearly drowning in the depths that reflected their love, their desire, and their utter happiness at being together, when a sharp flash of light nearly blinded Jamie. She blinked up in surprise, trying to focus through the spots that clouded her vision. In a split second, Ryan was on her feet, stalking the short distance to a table behind them to glare at a woman who was trying to quickly put her disposable camera away.

Folding her arms across her chest, and summoning every shred of intimidation she could muster, Ryan fixed the flustered woman with her laser-like gaze and demanded, "How much do you think you'll get for that little prize?"

"Get?" she asked, looking to her husband for protection.

"Well, taking our picture while we're trying to have a nice, romantic dinner implies that you want to do something with it. I'm asking what your plans are."

Now Jamie was beside her, holding onto her arm in case Ryan tried to deck her. "I...I don't have any plans," she stuttered. "I only wanted to show my friends that I saw you."

"I can't imagine why, but if you're telling the truth, I'd like to offer an alternative." The energy was rolling off of Ryan, and her prey looked more than a little intimidated. When she didn't speak, Ryan offered, "I'll ask someone to take our picture with you. Then you can show your friends that you didn't only spy on us and invade our privacy, you actually spoke with us. Surely, that's worth more than a shot of the back of my head." She looked confused by this offer, and shot a glance at her husband who shrugged his shoulders. "In exchange for that, you give me the camera. I'll have the pictures developed and returned to you. Minus, of course, the shot of us when we didn't know we were being photographed."

The woman was nearly frozen with indecision. She seemed slightly embarrassed, but the prospect of having a posed shot with these two, who had been the topic of conversation around the water cooler at her office in Los Angeles for several weeks, appeared too tempting to pass up. "All...all right," she said, as Ryan signaled for their waiter.

"Will you take a photo of us with these...people?" she asked, handing him the camera.

"Of course."

The other couple stood, and Ryan led Jamie to stand next to the man. She then guided the woman next to Jamie and stood on the other side of her. She nearly spit when the woman slid an arm around both her and her partner, then tilted her head towards Ryan, but she honored her pledge and even managed a thin smile. When the waiter handed the camera back, she held it tightly and asked for an address. Looking longingly at the camera, the fledgling paparazzi had the nerve to say, "Why don't you let me have them developed? I promise I'll throw that other picture away..." Ryan's glare increased dramatically, and she bit off the rest of her statement and began to write her address on a slip of paper.

"Thank you," Ryan said insincerely as she placed her hand on the small of Jamie's back to lead her to their table.

Luckily, the other couple was on the verge of leaving when they took the picture, and they departed moments after Jamie and Ryan sat back down. Ryan gave her partner a look filled with sorrow—so like the haunted, anxious gaze that had settled on her face after the car jacking. She looked like she was on the verge of apologizing, but Jamie lifted a hand and placed two fingers against Ryan's lips to stop her. "You handled that beautifully, and no, it didn't ruin my evening." Ryan tried to contradict her, but she held firm. "It really didn't. Actually, in a weird way, it enhanced my appreciation of you. If that's possible," she added with a playful wink.

"Please, go on," Ryan said, summoning a half-smile.

"Okay," Jamie said, making her voice as bright and cheerful as possible. "I got to see how quick you are to protect me and come to my defense. By the time that flash finished clicking, you were across the room, and I know that was because you thought I'd be upset. Right?"

"Right," Ryan nodded, her smile increasing steadily.

"I got to see how quick-witted you are, too. It was fascinating to see you figure out how to get that camera away from her without force—that was sweet."

"Force was next on my list," Ryan said, with a note of chagrin in her voice. "She wasn't gonna leave here with a picture of us on the night I..." She pulled back from the brink, mentally slapping herself as she realized she had almost blurted out her plans for the evening.

"On the night you what, sweetheart?" Guileless green eyes peered over at her, and Ryan cudgeled her brain to come up with an acceptable answer.

"On the night I got to share Valentine's Day with you for the first time," she said, wincing at the inelegant way that sounded, even thought it was the literal truth.

"But she'll get a picture of us, if you follow through on what you said you'd do."

"True," Ryan said. "But that one was posed. We both knew it was being taken. I just didn't want to have a photo taken when we were so unguarded. It's too personal."

"So, you do think she'll try to sell it," Jamie said, an unhappy frown on her face.

"Yes. She probably will. But she and her husband are in it, and it would be hard to crop them out without making it look like it had been doctored. That's why I had her stand between us," she said, an eyebrow twitching. "Now if she sells it, she'll know what it feels like to have strangers coming up and pointing at her in the grocery store. Justice," she added firmly.

An elegantly dressed man hurried over to the table, apologizing profusely even as he approached. "I am so very sorry, Ms. Evans," he murmured. "I'm Banks Rein, and your mother and I are well acquainted. If you will allow me to, I'd like to offer your meal compliments of the house."

"It's nice to meet you, Monsieur Rein. This is my partner, Ryan O'Flaherty."

He grasped Ryan's extended hand and began to lift it to his lips. A startled look from Ryan, however, caused him to change his plans and shake it lightly. "I'm very pleased to meet you, Ms. O'Flaherty."

"It's not necessary to pay for our dinner," Jamie demurred. "We're used to being harassed by now."

"Frankly, I'm shocked that someone would have the nerve to invade your privacy like that. I'm very, very sorry for the intrusion."

"Don't give it another thought," she said once again. "It's not something that you could have controlled."

"You're equally as gracious and charming as your mother," he said as he took her hand and kissed it gently.

Ryan watched him walk away, giving him a narrow-eyed glance. "Do you like to have your hand kissed?" she asked, still looking in his direction.

"I don't mind a bit. It's pretty common in Europe, so I'm used to it."

"Hey, I'm more European than you are, and he almost got more of my hand in his face than he wanted."

"Ireland's a whole other Europe," Jamie teased, grasping Ryan's hand and kissing the inside of her wrist, making the buss as delicate and sensual as she could manage.

"On second thought…" Ryan murmured with her eyes half closed.

"I knew you were open minded."

The entrees were as spectacular as the appetizers, and the wine that Jamie chose perfectly complemented both of their selections. Ryan was about ready to curl up on the table for a nice long nap now that her stomach was full and the wine had so thoroughly relaxed her. Regrettably, she had to sneak down to the kitchen and arrange to have the ring placed into their dessert. She excused herself to use the facilities, grimacing when Jamie pointed her away from the stairs, and towards the rest rooms on the second floor.

"I want to see what the place looks like from down there," she said, and Jamie nodded, sparing a smile for her inquisitive nature. Before she got to the stairs, she ran into the maitre d' and pulled him aside. "I'm trying to arrange to have a ring baked into my partner's dessert."

"We're making heart-shaped fallen chocolate cakes tonight. They're fantastic. Let me take care of it for you," he offered. "I'll make sure that it's handled properly. It's truly a madhouse in the kitchen tonight."

She extracted the dark blue velvet covered container from her pocket and handed the ring over, smiling when he exclaimed, "Goodness! What a beautiful piece. Ms. Evans will be thrilled."

"I sure hope so."

"She will," he said, grasping her hand and beginning to lift it to his lips. Suddenly, he stopped himself and flipped her hand around and caught it in a handshake, smiling as he scurried away for the kitchen.

"How did you get to the rest rooms without me seeing you?" Jamie asked when Ryan returned.

How much wine did I have? I'm not thinking things through! "Uhm…I decided I didn't have to go. I spent a minute looking around up here a little bit. Did you see those wall light thingies?"

"The sconces?" Jamie asked.

"Okay…if you say so. Whatever you call them, they're awesome."

The waiter approached and asked, "Can I interest you in dessert?"

"Oh, I should say no," Jamie began as Ryan's eyes widened. "But, I could be persuaded."

Whew! This is nerve-wracking!

Jamie surveyed the menu, then turned to the waiter and said, "The chocolate cake for my partner, and the passion fruit cake for me."

"I think you should have the chocolate cake, too," Ryan said, her eyes widening again.

Jamie lowered the menu and stared at her for a moment. "Uhh…why?"

"You love chocolate," she said, even to her own ears the argument sounding lame.

"Yes, yes, I do. But I had golden pike for dinner, and I'd prefer something to cleanse my palate of the oiliness of the pike. You, on the other hand, had the lamb shank, which chocolate would complement quite well. Don't you think so, Robert?" she asked the waiter, who she was now on a first name basis with.

"I would tend to agree."

Okay, now I have to figure out how to get the damned ring onto a spoon and feed it to her. I can do it, I know I can! "All right. Passion fruit it is. I guess that's appropriate for Valentine's Day, too."

"We'd like some champagne, Robert. This is a very special occasion, so we'd like something extraordinary. Do you have any recommendations?"

He pursed his lips for a moment and said, "I can't recommend one bottle that would perfectly suit your dessert choices. The passion fruit and chocolate have very little in common."

He looked so sad at this admission, that Jamie took pity on him. "Ignore our dessert choices then. Bring us the most extraordinary bottle of champagne that you have."

"That I can do," he said, looking positively giddy.

As he dashed away, Ryan rested her chin on her braced hand and said, "Extraordinary, huh?"

"This is a very special occasion, Ryan O'Flaherty," Jamie said. "This is the first of many, many Valentine's Days we'll spend together. I want to start off right."

"No arguments. It is a special night." Her eyes darkened with emotion, and she took Jamie's hand in hers. "I love you so very much," she whispered. "I know our love with continue to grow, but my heart is already filled to bursting. I don't know where more love can fit."

She had such an adorable expression on her face that Jamie couldn't resist the urge. She had to rise a few inches and lean across the table to kiss her lover soundly. She was about to lean in for another when she noticed Robert returning. Sitting up, she gave him a warm smile to show she didn't mind being interrupted. "A Krug brut blanc de blanc," he said with obvious pride. "Clos du Mesnil, 1988. A truly wonderful year."

He opened the wine soundlessly, and poured an ounce or two into Jamie's glass. She let the wine sit on her tongue for a moment, then gently swirled it around. "Oh, Robert," she said in a tone that she usually reserved for Ryan alone. "This is glorious."

Beaming a smile at her, he started to pour, but Jamie stopped him with a hand on his arm. "I'd like to wait until dessert arrives. It will stay cold in the ice."

He looked aghast and said, "Then I'll bring you another bottle. It will be ruined if it sits open for that long."

"No, really, it's fine," she said firmly. He looked like he wanted to argue, but ultimately controlled himself and left the table.

Jamie looked around the restaurant, her eyes narrowing as she twitched her chin towards the staircase and said, "Doesn't that woman remind you of Brendan's girlfriend?"

Ryan's head swiveled around, and as it did so, Jamie plopped Ryan's ring into the open bottle of champagne, hoping that her partner's sensitive hearing hadn't picked up the sound.

"That chubby, middle-aged woman with the mousy brown hair?" A dark eyebrow lifted, as she said, "Yeah. They could be twins." Looking pointedly at the champagne, Ryan added, "You've had enough. Tell your new friend to put the cork back into that baby."

A startled squeal caught their attention, and they both turned to see a young woman throw her arms around a blushing young man and squeal once again. "Yes!" she cried. "Yes, I'll marry you!"

Ryan turned back to her partner with an amused smirk on her face. "Sign of the season," she said. The woman was so exuberant that her voice could be heard all through the mezzanine. "How did you know this was my favorite stone? It's so unique! I love the square cut!" she added. "How on earth did you ever afford this, Sam? Three stones! Three stones!" she exclaimed again.

The young man looked completely stunned, and suddenly it hit Ryan that one good reason to look stunned was if you had not intended to ask someone to marry you at all. She strained her eyes and saw the chocolate cake, and before she knew what she was doing, she was on her feet, crossing the room to stand in front of the couple. "Congratulations!" she said, trying to look calm as they looked up at her. "May I see your ring?" she asked, knowing that she had mere seconds before the couple called for security.

The woman reluctantly extended her left hand, and Ryan nearly kissed it when she saw the ruby surrounded by diamonds. "It's magnificent!" she gushed, "Congratulations!" Then she ran back to her own table, to try to explain to a startled looking Jamie why she had gone berserk. "It's an old Irish custom," she said, trying to think of a reasonable one. "The sooner someone congratulates you after you get engaged, the longer your marriage will last."

"Then they'll see the next millennium in," Jamie dryly observed, thinking that perhaps they had both had enough to drink.

Robert returned with their desserts, and when he barely had the plates down, Ryan was digging in, looking more like an excavator than a diner. Her spoon slid through the still-warm cake until she finally felt it hit something metallic. She secured the ring onto the spoon, smoothing her fingertip across the edge of the utensil to make sure it was hidden, then extended the spoon towards Jamie, while Robert began to pour.

"No! I'll do it!" Jamie said, eyes wide with alarm as she reached for Robert's arm. But he had already filled Ryan's glass, and was starting to pour hers. She looked up at him, then shrugged her shoulders and sighed. "Go ahead. Fill mine, too."

As he did, a heavy ring slipped through the neck of the bottle and landed in Jamie's glass with a splat. Robert's eyebrows lifted dramatically, then he gave Jamie a chagrined look and stood stock-still, waiting to be dismissed.

"Thanks," she said unenthusiastically.

Robert rocked back and forth on his heels for a moment, then left as quickly as he was able.

Ryan took one look at the frustrated expression on her partner's face, then another at the chocolate covered ring on her spoon, then a third at the ring lying in the bottom of Jamie's champagne flute, and she started to laugh. She laughed harder and harder, finally placing the spoon into her own mouth and sucking the chocolate off of it while she giggled. Taking it from her mouth, she dropped it into her own champagne flute, then extended the glass towards her stunned partner. "Wanna trade?"

Ryan was still chuckling softly when the valet handed her keys over. The door closed with a thunk and she fastened her seat belt, then spared another amused glance at her partner. "This must be the first case of someone actually taking a ring back because the presentation was ruined. I didn't even get to look at it!"

"I'm not taking it back," Jamie explained patiently. "That attempt was a complete failure, so we're gonna try again when we get home."

"It wasn't a failure. It was funny."

"I'm not looking for funny, sport. I'm looking for romantic. This didn't cut it, and we're gonna keep trying until we get it right."

Ryan rolled her eyes and gave in; knowing that the determined look on her lover's face was insurmountable.

"Hi," Jordan said, her voice a little quieter and less animated than usual. "Happy Valentine's Day."

"Hi, baby," Mia said as she put her earphone/microphone in and lay down on the loveseat in the living room. "How's the sweetest, cutest Valentine I've ever had?"

"I'm okay," she said, sounding anything but. "It doesn't seem like we're celebrating when we're apart, does it?"

"No, not really. I miss you so much. Las Vegas can't come soon enough for me."

"Me, neither," Jordan said softly, suddenly feeling like she wanted to cry.

"Hey, hey, talk to me," Mia demanded. "What's going on? You sound very upset."

With another long sigh, Jordan said, "No, not very upset. Only a little. I talked to my mother today, and she's decided to come to Sydney, with my brother and grandmother."

"Oh." Mia was quiet for a moment, not quite sure of how to react. She knew that Jordan's relationship with her mother was strained at best, but she still had a vague thought that it might be important to her to have her family with her at the games. "Does that upset you? It sounds like it does."

"Mia," she said, her voice shaking with emotion, "how do you feel about me telling my family about us?"

Once again, Mia was silent for a moment, not being able to get a good read on Jordan. From the tone of her lover's voice, she realized that her answer was important, so she decided to be as honest as possible and hope the answer was correct. "Honey, I haven't given it much thought. I guess I figured you'd decide when and how you wanted to do it." There was stark silence from the other end, so she kept going. "I guess I thought I'd follow your lead. Any way you want to handle it is all right with me."

"Any way?" Jordan asked, her soprano voice even higher than normal.

"Sure. Any way. I want this to go as well as possible for you. Do you want me to be there when you talk to them? I will be, if it will help." She kept her voice low, and soothing, and as if her partner's voice was coated with ice, she heard it begin to melt.

She began with a long exhalation, then asked with a healthy dose of incredulity, "Would you honestly do that for me?"

"Of course! Of course I would, Jordan. I'd do anything for you. I love you, you know."

"I…I don't know why this is so important to me," Jordan's whisper was raspy. "It means so much that you're not ashamed to be my lover. It means so much, Mia."

"Oh, Jordy!" Taking a breath to calm her racing heart, Mia murmured, "How can you even think such a thing? I've already told my brother, and you know how much he means to me."

"I know," she murmured shakily.

"You're the best person to ever come into my life. I'm so proud of you—proud of us, Jordan. Please believe me."

"I'm…I'm feeling bruised and battered today. I don't know why, but I desperately need you tonight. This is so hard."

"I know, sweetheart, I know. It is hard, harder than I ever imagined." She could hear Jordan give a little gasp, and she knew immediately what she was thinking. "But it's worth it. It's worth every lonely night to be your girlfriend. I'm so proud of you."

"Thanks. That means a lot."

"Don't you dare thank me for loving you," Mia soothed gently. "I'm so lucky to have found you. You're the best thing in my life."

"Me, too," Jordan sighed, her voice quavering.

"Honey? You sound like you're freezing. Are you in bed?"

"Yeah. It takes me a while to warm up." She chuckled gently and said, "I'm in my usual sexy attire, long underwear, a turtleneck, and two pairs of socks. God, I didn't realize I was such a delicate little thing until I got to Colorado."

"You're my delicate little thing, and I wish I was snuggled up next to you, warming you up."

"I wish I was next to you so I could sleep naked and feel your skin against mine." Her voice had grown low and soft, giving Mia chills.

"Just a few days, and you'll have your wish. It'll be warm in Las Vegas, and even warmer when we're in bed together." She paused briefly and said, "Would you like to hear what I'd like to be doing if you were in my arms right now?"

"Right now?" Jordan asked, her voice cracking like a twelve-year-old boy's.

"Yeah," Mia purred. "Right now."

"That would be nice." She paused for a second and asked, "Are we gonna have phone sex?"

"No, we're gonna love each other. But this time we have to do it over the phone."

"I like the sound of that," Jordan sighed again. "I love loving you."

"I love loving you, too, baby. And tonight I need you to stand in for me and love yourself."

"I will if you will," Jordan said quietly, and Mia smiled when she heard the excitement in her voice.

"Oh, I will. I hope the girls don't come home early, though, 'cause they'll get a show."

🐴

Mia was still lying on the sofa in the living room when her roommates returned home, having made herself presentable after the more heated parts of her phone call had taken place. She scampered from the couch, grabbing at each woman's left hand. "What?" she demanded when she saw that both were devoid of adornment. "No, Jordy, I can't tell you what the rings look like on them, because they're not wearing them! What in the heck is going on?"

Ryan disconnected the earphone to avoid having Mia interpret and said, "Hi, buddy. No, we didn't turn each other down. We had a little comedy of errors, and decided to take another stab at it once we were home. Piece of advice that I was given but chose not to follow. If you ever want to ask a woman to marry you—hand her the damned ring."

🐴

Ryan called dibs on the bath, and she spent her usual five minutes getting ready for bed. Jamie took a much more leisurely approach, so Ryan tried her best to beat her to the punch most evenings. As usual, Jamie left the door open while she was brushing and flossing her teeth and washing her face, so that she could chatter away. "What are the odds of us having the same idea for the same day without ever having discussed it?" she asked, still amazed that things had worked out as they had.

"Well, the Valentine's Day thing is a pretty big motivator. I mean, if you were planning on getting engaged anytime between January and April you'd probably do it on Valentine's Day. Women really like that."

That caused Jamie's head to pop out of the bathroom, an amused smile on her face. "Oh, is that so? Do you speak from your personal perspective as a woman, Ms. O'Flaherty?"

"Well, no. I kinda don't get it, but Mia assured me that it was a girl thing, and that I should give up and go along with it."

"Mia did this, huh? How did you happen to ask for her advice?"

She went back into the bath as Ryan answered, "I was going to ask you on your birthday, but she said that girls liked Valentine's Day better for things like this."

"Hmm, I hate to bow to stereotypes, but in my case, she's right. I'm glad that you followed her advice."

She closed the door to finish her tasks, and Ryan ran out of the bedroom, went down the hall, and snuck into her own room; rifling through her dresser until she found her prize. A few minutes later, Jamie walked out of the bath, ruffling her hair with her hands as she crossed to her dresser. She was wearing only a pair of lipstick pink bikinis, and Ryan decided that her choice of attire was perfect. "Leave those on," she purred, causing Jamie to snap to attention.

Her eyes went to the dark figure sprawled against the cushions of the loveseat, a vision of long black hair, sparkling blue eyes, bright red and black satin. Ryan was sitting against one arm of the piece, one long leg drawn up under herself. A red satin chemise topped a black satin thong covered with tiny red hearts. A vivid red rose was held lightly between her white, even teeth, and the look in her eyes spoke of love, desire, and passion waiting to explode from her voluptuous body.

Taking the rose from her teeth with an elegant hand, she offered it up to her partner as she said, "Happy Valentine's Day, Jamie."

Jamie closed her eyes and patted the skin over her heart with the flat of her hand. "Looking at you makes my heart skip a beat."

"That's the general intent," Ryan purred, gazing at her with frank, open longing.

"Let me slip something sexy on," Jamie offered as she started once again for her dresser.

"What you have on is the pinnacle of sexiness. You couldn't possibly improve on it." Ryan patted the seat next to her and gave Jamie an encouraging smile.

She stood rather awkwardly, rocking back and forth as she tried to make up her mind. "Uhm…I'd rather…"

"Go on. I don't want you to feel uncomfortable."

Jamie went to her dresser and removed a sheer white camisole, the fabric nearly diaphanous. Slipping it over her head, she twitched her butt tauntingly, knowing that Ryan was staring at her.

"Ooo," the low, honeyed voice purred.

"You are so predictable," Jamie teased, sitting down on the small sofa, imitating Ryan's posture.

"It's not that I'm predictable. It's that you know me so well." She shifted slightly to be able to face Jamie fully. "As well as you know me now, I'm truly looking forward to eventually having you know every single thing about me—every dream, every hope, every wish, every desire." She slid off the sofa and dropped to a knee; taking Jamie's trembling hand in hers, shaking her head as she realized how very nervous she was.

Surprising Ryan completely, Jamie slid off the sofa as well, and once again mimicked Ryan's pose. Each woman on one knee, they faced each other, neither sure of who should begin, their carefully planned speeches evaporating under the pressure. Ryan lifted a hand and began to trace the graceful, smooth planes of Jamie's face, smiling into the touch when her lover's hand returned the caress. They shared whisper-soft touches, generously interspersed with warm, moist, lingering kisses.

Ryan finally lifted her head to speak, but found such complete and utter understanding in the verdant eyes that gazed back at her, that she immediately recognized that words were completely superfluous. She removed the ring that she had tucked inside the strap of her wristwatch, and smiled warmly when Jamie turned her hand to remove hers from the identical spot on her own wrist.

Without a word, each woman extended her left hand, the ring fingers lifting slightly as they each settled a ring into place. As they shared nearly identical smiles, their arms slipped around each other's waists and tightened into a tender embrace. Jamie lifted her head, seeking Ryan's lips, which were gladly delivered. They kissed—gently, softly, but with a depth of emotion that touched each of them to the core.

Jamie finally broke the silence, gazing up into Ryan's bright eyes to whisper, "One lifetime isn't nearly enough."

Ryan beamed a smile back at her, a hint of longing in her dark blue eyes, as she shook her head the tiniest bit. She wanted to speak, to share the joy that filled her heart, but she was completely unable to form her feelings into words. Finally realizing that she was more fluent in her actions than her words, she tightened her embrace and pressed her lips against Jamie's, letting her body convey the feelings that words could never express.

When the lingering kiss ended, they let their heads rest upon each other's shoulder, each woman breathing in the scent of her partner for long moments. Without thought, Jamie's hands began to move, and soon they were gliding across Ryan's body. The dark-haired woman matched her actions, her hands greedily feasting upon the delights of her lover's body. But even though her hands were ravenous for the dips and curves they encountered, Ryan didn't feel the usual thrumming of sexual desire coursing through her body. It wasn't sex that she craved this night—it was love. She desperately wanted to merge with her partner, to somehow slip into her skin and feel her blood pounding through her own veins; to know each nerve, each muscle, each cell that made up the woman who held her spellbound.

Jamie seemed to echo her quest, her hands tracing a whisper-soft path over Ryan's sensitive skin. The green eyes shifted up and locked onto blue and they stared, transfixed, looking into the essence of each other's souls.

Ryan's head slowly dipped, and she tilted her chin to allow her lips to press against her partner's. Slowly, every other sensation faded away. The only thing that existed for Ryan was the pair of soft, sweet lips that she feasted upon. It seemed as though her very survival depended upon remaining fastened to the warm mouth, and her hands went to cradle her partner's head to ensure the connection.

After a very long time had passed, Ryan regretfully pulled away, gazing at her partner for a moment before saying, "Let's go to bed."

Jamie nodded and got to her feet, waiting for Ryan to rise and take her by the hand. When they reached the foot of the bed Ryan ran her hands over Jamie's body and asked, "Can I undress you?"

Jamie head nodded. "Please," she whispered. With tender hands, Ryan slipped the scant covering from her partner's body, smiling gently when her lovely form was fully exposed.

"So very beautiful," she sighed. "You're absolutely magnificent."

Blushing warmly, Jamie let herself be tugged onto the surface of the bed and into Ryan's embrace. She rested her head upon the red silk that covered her partner's breast, and relaxed into the gentle touch that once again began to work up and down her skin. Then Ryan lowered her head and began to kiss her once again, but this time her caresses fell upon skin rather than lips. Starting at the hollow of her collarbones, she worked her way to the tips of her pink toes; again, not trying to enflame Jamie's ardor—seeking only to communicate the deep, abiding love that burned in her soul.

Ryan climbed on top of her lover's body, supporting most of her weight on her forearms. For a long while she gazed at her, her face composed, her look almost curious. Jamie's hand reached up and tenderly brushed a few stray strands of hair from her eyes.

As often as she looked at her lover, Jamie's opportunities to study her were relatively infrequent. As she did so now, she found herself nearly breathless—practically in awe of Ryan's loveliness. But as her eyes searched Ryan's, she was struck, not by their beauty, but by the complete confidence she saw in them. Placing her hand on Ryan's cheek she said, "You're not afraid any more, are you?"

A smile twitched at the corners of her mouth. "No. Not anymore." Admitting to the feelings she'd been trying to hide, Ryan said, "Even though I've been able to be intimate, I've been holding back a little." She lowered her head and kissed the moist, pink lips. "But tonight I finally feel free. I'm all yours, Jamie. Every part of me."

"I can tell. It feels like it used to." She reached for Ryan's lips and kissed her softly. "Maybe even a little better."

"That's my goal," Ryan murmured. "To give myself to you completely every time we make love. It's hard sometimes, but it's so fulfilling when I can do it."

"I know it's been hard for you," Jamie said softly.

Ryan's eyes blinked slowly, and she said, "It has, but I could never let something so wonderful fade away. Being intimate with you is vital to me."

"It is to me, too. That should be our lifelong goal. To always try to be as open and vulnerable with each other as we possibly can."

"I promise to try," Ryan vowed. She smiled gently and dipped her head once more, meeting Jamie's lips tenderly. "Sealed with a kiss."

"I promise, too," Jamie whispered. Wrapping her arms tightly around her partner, she rolled her onto her side and kissed her for a very long time. "I love you so much."

Ryan smiled warmly and said, "And I love you. More and more every day."

"A whole lifetime of loving you a little bit better with every day that passes: that's my idea of heaven."

Holding her tenderly, Ryan nuzzled her face into her partner's neck, composing herself enough to whisper, "I see heaven in your eyes."

Chapter Twelve

As she tried to make her bleary eyes focus, Ryan jogged down the stairs to answer the doorbell. *Who in the heck is at the door at this time of the morning? Oh well, at least it got my lazy butt out of bed. If left to my own devices, I would have been tempted to bag my whole morning schedule.* As she flung the door open, she was surprised to come face to face with a huge bouquet of flowers, her nose twitching as a spider mum poked her cheek.

"Delivery for Evans-O'Flaherty," the invisible deliveryman announced.

"That's me," she replied, and placed her hands around the substantial vase, relieving the now visible man of his burden. She turned and placed the vase on the hall table, then made eye contact with the visitor. "Do I need to sign for it?"

"No need," the attractive, well-dressed man said. "I own the shop."

Ryan shook her head, a smirk covering her face. "Let me guess," she drawled. "Catherine Evans is behind this special delivery."

"She said it was important that they arrive before you left for school. My delivery guys don't start until eight, so I thought I'd drop them off on the way back from my daily visit to the flower mart."

"Catherine has a way of making things happen."

"For what she spends at my shop, I could afford to go to Holland to pick up those tulips," he said, nodding his head toward the arrangement. "Her complete satisfaction is very important to me." Ryan started to grab her wallet from the table, but he saw what she was doing and said, "No, really, there's no need to tip me. But, I would appreciate it if you let Mrs. Evans know that you were happy."

"I'll make sure to give her a good report," Ryan promised. "Thanks for going out of your way." She closed the door and stood back to assess the gift, marveling at the remarkable assortment of flowers the elaborate ceramic vase held. Snatching the large card, she trotted back up the stairs, dropped her sweats and slid into bed.

"Mmm…good morning to the future Mrs. Evans," Jamie purred lazily as she snuggled close.

"Good morning to you, the future Mrs. O'Flaherty," Ryan murmured. "How's my fiancée this morning?"

"She's good," Jamie mumbled through a yawn. "How's mine?"

"She's very good." Ryan wrapped her arms around her still-drowsy partner and cuddled her to her chest. "She's well-loved, well-rested and ready to blind a few of her classmates when the sun hits her hand." Extending her left hand, she admired her ring, amazed that she felt perfectly at ease to have the substantial investment resting on her finger.

"Do you really like it?" Jamie asked, with the faintest note of worry in her soft voice.

Giving her answer thoughtful consideration, Ryan said, "It's certainly not what I would have picked for myself."

Jamie's heart picked up, suddenly chagrined at having asked Ryan such a direct question. She knew her partner was always frank about issues of style; and while she applauded her honesty, for a moment she wished this was one of the times Ryan would humanely lie to spare her feelings.

Ryan continued in her slow, analytical fashion, "I'm sure I would have tried to get away with something much more modest, if I consented to a ring at all." Now the smaller woman's heart began to thud in her chest, beating so loudly that Ryan noticed it. "You okay?"

"Uh-huh," she said tightly. "Go on."

Ryan shrugged and continued. "I'm so glad that you didn't consult with me before you bought it. It would have been a shame to let my frugal nature stop me from wearing something this gorgeous. This is a little much for me right now, but I'm going to wear it for the rest of my life, and I'll slowly grow into it. If you bought me something I was comfortable with now, it would look kinda silly when I was in my forties or fifties."

"So you do like it?"

Lifting her head up so that she could look into Jamie's eyes, Ryan cocked her head and asked, "How could I not like it? It's stupendous! Haven't I made that clear?"

"Well, you seem a little hesitant…"

"Look," Ryan said, lifting Jamie's chin with her fingers. "I'm hesitant to get used to this kind of lifestyle. That's no news flash. But being your spouse puts me into this economic stratum, and I've got to work on getting comfortable with it. It is what it is, and I refuse to have this be a chronic issue between us. I'm gonna try to chill a bit and look at the long view."

It took a little maneuvering, but Jamie managed to get Ryan's hand close to her face. She spent a moment looking at the ring, admiring the way it looked against the long, elegant fingers. "It suits you," she said softly.

Ryan chuckled and nodded her head. "It does, strangely enough. I don't see myself as the kind of woman who's suited to diamonds of this size. I'm gonna have to do some mental adjustments." She gazed at the three oval diamonds, the center stone nearly two and a half carats, with each of the flanking stones over a carat. In color, they perfectly matched her diamond earrings, and the platinum band stylistically tied them to the platinum collars of the earrings as well. "I'm very glad that you bought it for me. And I'm flattered that you see me as an elegant enough woman to be able to pull off wearing it." They kissed gently, their lips barely brushing against each other. "What about yours? Are you happy with it?"

"Of course I am!" Jamie brought her hand up to rest between them, so they could both view the new ring. "I'm glad that we didn't try to make them match. We would have both had to compromise to get something we both liked. I think it's cool that they're so different—they're as different as we are."

"Yeah. A square cut emerald with two square cut diamonds in a yellow gold setting is about as far from mine as you can get. Do you really like the square cut? I was torn between the square and the round."

"I prefer the square," Jamie said, "and I'm very glad you went with the Princess cut. It has so much more fire than the flat emerald cut. I don't know why, but I've always pictured a square cut emerald when I thought about my engagement ring."

Ryan chucked as she said, "I can honestly say that the thought of an engagement ring had never crossed my mind. I don't think that's a common lesbian daydream."

"You're my lesbian daydream," Jamie sighed as she wrapped Ryan in her arms, only to be poked by a sharp object. "Ow!"

"Oops." Ryan giggled as she took the card out from between their bodies. "Forgot about that."

Jamie removed the card from her hand and batted her eyes at her. "Oh… you bought me a card. How sweet."

"Can't cop to that," Ryan said. "It's from your mom. She had a bouquet the size of a truck delivered this morning."

"Really? That's cool," Jamie said, opening the card. She cleared her throat and read, "Congratulations, Jamie and Ryan. I know that your marriage will bring both of you unlimited happiness. I love you both, Catherine."

"She's a peach," Ryan said.

"There's more. We need to get together immediately to start planning your wedding! Dinner at my house tonight?"

Ryan pulled the covers over her head and muttered, "She was the soul of restraint for Da and Maeve, but I know she's gonna take off the gloves now. Heaven help me!"

"Good news, Poppa," Jamie giggled into the phone later that day when she caught her grandfather in. "She said yes!"

"I'm speechless. I thought you'd have to spend weeks convincing her."

"No, she jumped aboard without a complaint. Gullible little thing, isn't she?"

"I happen to think you both have excellent taste. I take it you're both on cloud nine today?"

"Yes, except that mother wants to discuss our wedding plans tonight. I have a feeling that's going to be a bit of a struggle with Miss 'Can't We Order a Pizza And Be Done With It?'"

"At least you don't have to worry that she loves you for your money. Unless she's a fabulous actress."

"No, she's a pretty awful actress, actually. She genuinely doesn't like having this much money. But she was very sweet about the ring I bought her. Nary a complaint."

"That's good to hear. It's not that common for couples to have the issue of fighting over too much money, but it can be as bad as having too little. I'm glad that you're both trying to find a middle ground."

"We are. Still, Mother might try her patience with her plans for the ceremony. Can I convince you to join us for dinner—say, around eight?"

"I'm happy to. We have a few things to discuss, anyway, and we can wrap up my issues at the same time."

"Great. Meet us at Mother's.

"Hi, Mom, it's me," Jamie announced late that afternoon. "Poppa's on board, so we'll be there around eight. Should we coordinate our ideas before we get together?"

"Why would we want to do that? Isn't that the point of the meeting?"

"Not when Ryan's involved," Jamie said with a chuckle. "She thought Martin and Maeve's reception was ostentatious. I think we're gonna have to struggle to get her to agree to anything fancy."

"I don't want to make her uncomfortable. We can keep this very low key."

"But I don't want low key, Mom. I want something memorable. It doesn't have to be opulent or anything, but I've dreamt about my wedding since I was a little girl. It's important to me."

Catherine paused, thinking that perhaps it was unwise to discuss the issue until they had both come to a private agreement about the tone for the ceremony. "I don't want this to cause trouble for you. Maybe we should hold off until you and Ryan agree."

"Don't worry about that," Jamie said. "We don't fight about issues like this. Ryan acts like she's making a huge sacrifice, then I thank her profusely. It all works out."

"If you're sure," Catherine said warily.

"I am. I don't want her to be unhappy. I can tell if she's really uncomfortable, or being dramatic. I have found one trick that works, though. She likes to be able to compromise about issues like this."

"That's good to hear."

"So, what works is to ask for something outrageous," the younger woman revealed. "Then, the compromise is close to what I wanted anyway."

With a tone that was only partially teasing, Catherine said, "That's frighteningly devious, sweetheart. Are you sure that's a good idea?"

"Absolutely. She's still talking about how fabulous Martin and Maeve's wedding was. She loved the fact that it was a special day and that they had a party that was different from all of their other gatherings. She's programmed to say that she doesn't want it. If she could let herself go and say what she truly wants, I bet it's nearly identical to what I want."

"You know her well, but try not to push her too hard. There's nothing more unattractive than a woman who constantly manipulates her spouse."

"I understand that. We do tend to manipulate each other a little bit, but we get over it quickly if we don't get our way. I'll be fine with it if we end up having a barbecue in the back yard. But I'm going to ask for more than I want and see where we end up."

🐎

"Hey," Ryan called as she ran up the stairs after softball practice.

Jamie poked her head out of the kitchen and called up the stairs, "One day of being engaged and I no longer merit a hello kiss? This bodes ill, Ms. O'Flaherty."

"I'll make it up to you later," Ryan hollered as she dashed into the shower.

"You'd better," Jamie chuckled in a normal tone of voice, since Ryan couldn't hear her anyway.

🐎

The first stop was to dash by Martin and Maeve's to make their announcement. On the drive over the traffic-clogged Bay Bridge, Ryan said reflectively, "This is kind of an odd situation to be in, isn't it?"

"What is?"

"To tell people that we're engaged. It's kinda bass-ackwards, isn't it? I mean, we've told people that we're, in essence, married. You already wear a wedding ring. We refer to each other as spouses. Yet, now we're engaged. It's odd."

"I don't think it's much odder than a straight couple who lives together, is it? They probably consider that they're spouses, too."

"I guess," Ryan said. "I do kinda like the formality of being engaged, to tell you the truth. It's cool to think of you as my fiancée. It's like we get to do the whole thing over again. And having our families with us is going to make it special." She shot Jamie a wide grin and said, "I'm really looking forward to this. It's one bit of heterosexual privilege that I want to claim."

Jamie grinned back at her, charmed by how much the ceremony meant to her partner. "You know, I was thinking about it today. I suppose I should take my wedding ring off until we make it official." She caught Ryan's startled look and immediately followed up. "But I can't. I couldn't bear to."

A luminous grin lit up Ryan's entire face. She reached across the car and captured her partner's hand, bringing it close to her lips for a soft kiss. "I'm glad. I don't want you to ever take it off."

"I'll take off the engagement ring when I play golf, but I leave the wedding ring on all the time. I'm developing a nice callus at the base of my finger, as a matter of fact. I like it."

Since the hand in question was still available, Ryan tickled the callus with the tip of her tongue. "I look forward to developing my own. One more small reminder of my love for you."

"Only you could make a callus sound romantic," Jamie sighed as she unbuckled her seat belt and leaned over for a warm kiss. "Might as well give the other drivers something to talk about on their cell phones."

🐉

"Anybody home?" Ryan called out as she popped her head into her aunt's house. As usual, the front door was unlocked, but she didn't want to fully enter without permission; trying to give the newlyweds some level of privacy.

"Siobhán?" Martin's voice carried from the kitchen.

"Yep." She and Jamie entered the house as Martin and Maeve exited the room.

"Did you come for dinner, girls?"

"No. We're headed over to Catherine's place for dinner, but we wanted to stop by and show you something first." She was smiling broadly, and Martin's smile reflexively broadened to match hers.

"What is it?" Maeve asked.

"Last night we proved that we truly belong together. We both had the same thought at exactly the same time."

"Get on with it," Martin ordered.

"We asked each other to marry," she announced proudly, with both her and Jamie extending their hands to Martin and Maeve's astonished eyes.

"Holy mother of God!" Martin reached for both hands simultaneously. "I've been blinded!" he cried dramatically, as the light hit the substantial stones.

"Oh, girls," Maeve gushed, "I've never seen two more beautiful rings." She tore her eyes away from the jewelry to gaze at her niece. "And you didn't talk about this beforehand?"

"No, that's why it's so funny. We knew that we wanted to have a commitment ceremony, but we hadn't discussed it at all."

"Well, this is grand, just grand," Martin enthused, wrapping each woman in a hug, as Maeve did the same. "Congratulations, girls."

"Thanks, Da," Ryan said as she pulled away. "We're running late to get to Catherine's, but we had to stop by to let you know."

"Will you be home this weekend, love?"

"No. Another tournament. We're gonna have to start coming over for dinner during the week so I can see you two."

"We'd be happy to bring Caitlin over to you some evening," Maeve offered. "She misses you fiercely when you don't come home. She associates you both with church now. She was anxious all during Mass on Sunday, and I think she was looking for you."

"I'd love it if you'd bring her over," Ryan said. "But I hate to have you sit through that much traffic."

"We'll come early and watch your softball practice," Martin suggested. "I'm off next Tuesday and Wednesday. Maybe we can do it then."

"Sounds like a plan," Ryan said as she kissed him goodbye. "We've gotta run now."

As they ran back down the stairs, hand in hand, Martin found himself transported to the morning that Ryan had announced that Jamie was the one for her. It was the morning that they'd left for Pebble Beach, and father and daughter had been able to carve out a few private moments in the midst of doing laundry and packing.

"I can't say I'm surprised, but I didn't know you were ready to make a permanent commitment at this point in your life," Martin began.

Ryan's clear blue eyes were slightly wide, and her expression was one of pure determination. "This is it for me, Da. You know I don't enter into relationships easily, but this was the most natural thing in the world. I barely had to think about it."

"That's how it was for me with your mother. Getting married was the furthest thing from my mind, but after a few weeks, it seemed like something I had to do."

"Had to do. That's exactly it," she said reflectively. "This is something I have to do."

"I'm happy for you both," he whispered into her ear as he hugged her close. "I know you'll be happy together."

"I know we will," Ryan said, sniffing. "I had a very good example of a successful marriage."

"I wish you would have had that example for many, many more years, darlin'." *He held her close as the tears started to fall. "Your mother would have been so happy for you. And she would have loved Jamie like her own. I'm sure of that."*

"Thanks, Da," she whispered, her voice too raw with emotion to speak any louder. "If it's okay with you, I want to give Jamie Mama's wedding ring. I want to always have her with us, and having Jamie wear it will always remind me of her."

He didn't answer verbally—too choked up to speak. He just hugged her so tight she was nearly bruised, giving her his enthusiastic permission.

※

"Marty…Marty." Maeve's hand on his arm startled him from his reverie, and he shook his head to clear it.

"Sorry. I was wandering a bit."

"It's hard to see her grow up so soon, isn't it?" she asked softly.

"It is. Luckily, she's chosen well. I have every confidence that they'll love each for their whole lives."

"I do, too," she said, taking his hand. "Jamie's a very lucky young woman. If Ryan's anything like her father, and I know she is, Jamie's going to be very well loved."

Martin gave his blushing bride a very enthusiastic kiss, giving complete credence to her words.

※

After Marta had worked her magic with a perfect paella, the foursome got down to business.

"Why don't you start, Poppa?" Jamie suggested. "I know you have some thoughts about the timing of the ceremony."

"All right. Normally, I have an unwritten rule about marrying people who have only been together a short time. I generally request that a couple be together for two years, and be members of the congregation before I'll agree to join them." Ryan's eyes widened a bit, but he quickly said, "There is a benefit to being my granddaughter, though. I know that neither of you are behaving frivolously here and, given what you've been through in the past few months, I think there's been a very good indication of the stability of your partnership. So I'm willing to waive my two year rule. I would, however, like to wait until you have a full year together. Is that something you can live with?"

"That's fine," Ryan said immediately, and Jamie nodded her consent as well. "We could actually have the ceremony on the anniversary of our..." She searched for words to explain their bonding on that June day in Pebble Beach, finding herself completely tongue-tied.

Jamie came to her rescue, saying, "We pledged our permanent commitment to one another on June the fourteenth. I think it would be a great idea to have our wedding right around then."

Ryan nodded at this suggestion, and Charles agreed. "That's fine, girls. Now the only other thing I need to have you do is participate in our marriage preparation class."

Looking a little ill, Ryan managed to say, "Another class? I don't mean to be difficult, but I've got about all I can handle on my schedule now, Charlie. How big of a time commitment is this?"

"It's two hours a week for eight weeks. We've got a class starting up on the first week of March for all of the couples marrying in June." He gazed at her thoughtfully for a moment, then said, "I don't feel comfortable waiving that requirement, especially since you've been together such a short time. I think it's important, and I think it can help assure the success of your relationship."

"Oh, I'm not trying to get out of it. I'm trying to figure out how on earth I can participate."

"It won't be easy for me either, Poppa," Jamie said. "When is the class?"

"It's on Thursday nights."

"That clinches it," Ryan said, shaking her head. "We either play on Thursday, or are on a plane going to a tournament. I'd have to quit the team to participate."

"No, no, don't be silly," Jamie insisted. "We'll figure this out."

Catherine piped up with a suggestion. "Why rush, girls? Now that you've decided not to go to graduate school yet, why not take it easy and have the ceremony later in the summer? That will give you time to plan and relax a bit after you graduate."

"Well, I like the idea of having it be on our anniversary, but I don't see any way around this," Jamie said. "How about August, Ryan? Does that work for you?"

"August the twenty-sixth is a perfect day," Ryan said, grinning widely. "It's not only a Saturday, it's my parents' anniversary."

Reaching across the table, Jamie grasped Ryan's hand and gave it a squeeze, locking her eyes on her as she said, "That's a wonderful suggestion, sweetheart." Looking at her grandfather, Jamie asked, "Could we do a class that would allow us to use that date?"

"Yes," he said, looking at his schedule. "I can start another near the end of June. That'll be just about right."

Giving her partner a big smile, Jamie said, "Let's do it."

Charlie penciled the date in, as Catherine jotted the day down in her massive Filofax. "I think that's a better time anyway, girls. It gives me six full months to plan." Her eyes were twinkling, and Ryan knew the tag-team harassment was about to begin.

"Can I have a glass of wine before I'm beaten into submission?" she asked with an aggrieved expression on her face.

Charlie rose from his chair and patted her on the back. "Buck up, Ryan. You've marrying into a family of very determined women. You can either submit now, or submit later. Either way, the outcome is predetermined."

❧

After taking a sip of her wine, Ryan said, "We haven't discussed a pretty important element here. Since I'm broke, and Da isn't flush, we either have to have a very modest affair, or the Evans family will wind up paying for the entire thing. How do you two feel about that?"

"I want to pay for it," Catherine insisted. "I want you to have exactly what you want, and I don't want you to give the finances another thought." Looking at her daughter-in-law, she asked, "Can you live with that?"

"Yeah, I think I can. At least, I'll try my best." Looking at her partner, she said, "Having a wedding has never been a dream for me, but it has been for Jamie. I want this to be perfect for her."

"I want it to be perfect for you, too," Jamie said. "Let's get to it, then. I suppose we have to decide on the location. I'd prefer to have the service in Poppa's church, and then move to the reception. What about you, honey?"

"Agreed," said Ryan. "Weddings in an informal setting don't seem real to me."

"Excellent," Jamie said, giving her partner a wink. "See how easy this is?"

Charles made a note in his calendar and nodded for Jamie to continue.

"Next is the venue for the reception. We could do it in Hillsborough, but I was thinking that it might be nice to have it at a hotel, or a club. I'd like for Marta to be a guest, and she would never be able to let strangers into her kitchen to cater without closely supervising them." She braced herself for Ryan's rejoinder, expecting her opening volley to be a suggestion that they have the party in the backyard in Noe.

One dark eyebrow rose, then she nodded her head slowly. "How about the Olympic Club? After all, we are members."

Jamie nearly fell to the floor in amazement, but she managed to cover fairly well. "You're okay with having it at Olympic?"

"I suggested it," Ryan said, blinking her big blue eyes ingenuously.

"All right. What do you think, Mom?"

"I think it's a good idea. Olympic has a lot of family memories for us, too, Jamie. It'll be rather homey." Giving Ryan a quick glance, she offered, "My only other suggestion is the Ritz-Carlton. They have a lovely room, and the food is better than it is at Olympic."

Ryan shrugged and said, "Either one's fine with me." Then she relaxed in her chair and took a long sip of wine, smiling serenely at her stunned partner.

Going for an item that she knew would provoke controversy, Jamie said, "I'd like to have a formal reception. What do you think, Ryan?"

"I'm not sure I know what that means."

"Well, everyone in the wedding party would wear formal attire. Tuxes for the men and gowns of some sort for the women."

"What about the guests?" she asked, looking very dubious.

"The men would have the option of wearing a suit or a tux, and the women could choose between a dress and a formal gown."

Her eyebrows remained in their hitched position as she enunciated clearly, "Some women will be wearing slacks, Jamie. One of them is in the wedding party."

"We can work that out," she soothed. "I know you wouldn't feel comfortable in a bridal gown with a big train."

Once again, Ryan stunned the assembled group when she shrugged her broad shoulders and said, "Okay. As long as I can wear slacks, whatever you want to do is okay with me."

"You don't mind that your cousins will have to wear suits? And your brothers will have to wear tuxes?" This was too much agreement for Jamie's brain to process, and she took another swallow of wine to calm herself.

"Nope. Won't kill 'em." Another small, satisfied grin took up residence on her face, and Jamie wondered once again who this impostor was.

"Well, maybe we should discuss how many people we want to invite," Jamie suggested, giving Ryan another quick look. "I was thinking about two hundred and fifty."

Now Ryan's familiar scowl settled on her face, and Jamie was reassured that the tall beauty at her side was really her partner. "I don't know about that. I think we might have to go higher."

"Higher?"

"Well, yeah," Ryan said, ticking the categories off on her fingers. "Family on my side alone will be over fifty. If we invite all of my aunt's people, I could easily get to a hundred. I want to invite my volleyball team and all of the coaches, my softball team; the basketball team can kiss my Irish ass," she added with a grin. "A lot of people from the AIDS Ride, some of the people from my old gym…" Blinking at Jamie, she hesitated and asked, "Is that too many?"

Jamie held up a hand, trying to make the words coming out of Ryan's mouth fit with her usual parsimony. "You don't mind having three or four hundred people at our wedding?"

"Why would I mind?" she asked, cocking her head. "I want to share this with everyone who's important to me. Don't you?"

"Of course I do, but I thought you'd want to keep it simple and quiet."

"Heck no! This is a very big deal to me. I never thought I'd get to have anything like this, and now that I can, I want to blow the lid off! I want this to be a party that people will remember for years." Her face was beaming such a wide grin that Jamie's astonishment faded away, to be replaced with a matching smile.

"I want that, too," she said, leaning over to press her lips against Ryan's. She kissed her cheek several times, adding a firm hug. "I want everyone we care for to be there with us."

Ryan nodded, slipping an arm around her to return the hug. "We've had the private ceremony. This one's a party."

As she sat upright, Jamie spared a glance for her mother and grandfather, who were both doing their best not to laugh. "The only consistent thing about Ryan O'Flaherty is her consistent inconsistency," she announced. "Thank God I love every one of her adorable quirks."

By the time they left, they had decided on either the Olympic Club or the Ritz, depending on availability and capacity; hiring a band so that Rory didn't have to work; a noon church service, with the reception beginning at six o'clock; a full dinner with dancing afterwards; and a honeymoon trip of undetermined length and destination.

They were settled in the Boxster, and Ryan had dropped the top, even though the night was cool. She'd been going non-stop since six a.m., and thought the cool air might help revive her. Since Jamie was tired as well, she didn't complain, even though the weather was quite brisk.

Riding in companionable silence until they reached the bridge, Jamie leaned over as far as she could and tucked her left hand under Ryan's jacket, knowing that her body heat would warm it in seconds. "You pleasantly surprised me tonight, tiger," she said reflectively.

"How so?" Ryan asked over the whipping of the wind as they passed by the massive supports of the bridge.

"I thought you'd have a lot of problems with the ideas I suggested for the reception. I'm still amazed at how agreeable you were."

Sparing a warm smile, Ryan said, "I'll take that as a compliment."

"That's how I meant it."

"I meant what I said earlier. This is the first and last time I'll ever have a huge party like this. We might as well do it up right."

"You're honestly okay with all of the elements we decided on?"

"Well, the formal dress is a little much, but I want you to be happy. If you get pleasure out of that, I figure it's the least I can do. After all," she said, "the bride pays for the wedding. You should have the bigger say."

Giving her a pinch, she demanded, "If I'm the bride, who are you?"

"Mmm...I'm not sure. I only know that I'm not the bride."

"Maybe we'll have the ushers ask the guests whether they want to sit on the bride or the non-bride's side."

"Works for me. I'm neither a bride, nor a groom. Those terms don't fit me."

"The title doesn't matter. All that matters is that you love me and I love you."

"That's a title I can get behind," Ryan said, gracing her partner with a winning smile. "I'm a Jamie-lover."

When Ryan came home from her morning class on Wednesday, the phone rang just as she was wrestling with the key in the lock. Grabbing it, she said, "H'lo?"

"Hi, Ryan, it's Amanda."

"Oh, hi. What's up?"

"I think I've found you a group that will fit your stringent requirements."

"Oh, boy," Ryan said, letting her decided lack of enthusiasm show.

"You don't have to go. I won't think badly of you if you're not able to commit to this. But I believe that at this point, you'll get more from the group than you will from me."

Ryan sighed, and chided herself for giving Amanda a hard time. "Let's hear the details."

"It's in Oakland, which shouldn't be too inconvenient; and the best news is that it meets at seven a.m. on Monday and Thursday. How does that sound?"

Forcing herself to be polite, Ryan said, "It sounds like you went to a lot of trouble to find this for me. I might not sound very enthusiastic, but I appreciate that. I guess the group meets tomorrow?"

"Yes, it does. Bright and early."

"Uhm...Jamie and I are going to Las Vegas tomorrow for a softball tournament...I'm not sure I can..."

"When does your flight leave?"

Blowing out a breath, Ryan admitted, "Late afternoon. I guess you'd better give me the address—since I suppose I'm headed over there in the morning."

⚔

Later that afternoon, Ryan rushed around the house, getting her gear packed for the short bus trip to Moraga for a double-header against St. Mary's. The day was very overcast, and promised a good drenching, so she made sure she took the new rain jacket that Jamie had purchased for her. She was almost out the door when the phone rang; and when she heard her father's voice on the machine, she dashed over and picked up. "Hey, Da, I'm about to head out. What's up?"

"Your aunt and I talked about it today, Siobhán, and we're not willing to wait another week to see you. I arranged to take the afternoon off, so we're going to come see your game."

Smiling brightly at his thoughtfulness, she warned, "I'd love to have you, but it looks like we might get rained out. I hate to see you drive that far for nothing."

"Not to worry. I know it's a risk, but one you're well worth. Tell Jamie we'll see her there."

"Okay. I love you, Da. Thanks for being so supportive of me."

"Always a pleasure, love. Now see what you can do about getting your coach to let you play an inning or two, okay? I want to see you stretch those long legs."

"Will do," she said, knowing that he was kidding.

⚔

On the bus ride to St. Mary's, Ryan sat in the seat behind Jackie, and they played one of their favorite games—"guess who's driving the car." The point of the game was to guess the sex and approximate age of the drivers of the cars they passed, and over the weeks Ryan had gotten quite good at it. But she was still no match for Jackie, who beat her every time out.

Nearing their exit on the freeway they approached a black Nissan mini truck, and Ryan called out, "Two people...no, three. A man, a woman and a baby. Both of the adults are in their late fifties, and the baby is..." she scrunched her nose as she appeared to concentrate, "about a year and a half." Nodding, she added, "The baby's blonde." The bus passed the truck, and Jackie shot a quick look at the occupants, then turned to Ryan with her mouth hanging open. "My parents and my cousin," the taller woman laughed heartily.

"Your parents, huh? Have they been to any of the other games?"

"Nope. They came to almost every volleyball and basketball game I played in, but these games are a little harder for them to get to, since they're usually in the afternoon. Besides, since I generally don't play, I hate to see them waste a trip to see me sit on the bench."

Jackie gave her a concerned look and asked, "Do you ever resent not playing? I mean, it's obvious that you have a ton of talent, Rof."

"No, I really don't. I played my ass off in volleyball and basketball. I'm enjoying being part of the team." She smiled and said, "I think my father would enjoy getting to see me play, but he won't be disappointed if I don't."

"I don't think my parents will get to make it to a game this year. This is calving season, and you don't leave the farm when you've got a bunch of animals giving birth."

"How about later in the year?"

"They promised they'd go to Oklahoma City if we make it to the College World Series. That'd be sweet."

"Well, we're undefeated," Ryan reminded her. "If we keep playing like this, we're a lock."

"Uh-huh," Jackie said, knowing that Ryan was joking. "It's one thing to do well in the early season. It's a whole 'nother thing to kick ass in the PAC-10."

"St. Mary's…Arizona…UCLA…no difference," Ryan said, pumping up the bravado. "Just a bunch of girls who can't touch us!"

Cal was beating St. Mary's 3-0 in the fourth inning when the rain started to fall. It was a light drizzle, not enough to halt play, but it looked like it was the front edge of a much bigger storm. Cal was at bat, and when Jackie went to the on-deck circle to warm up, she took a few tentative swings and signaled the trainer. After a brief consultation, she headed back to the dugout, and Ryan heard Coach Roberts call out, "O'Flaherty! Grab a bat and earn your keep!"

"Yes, sir!" she yelled back, getting to her feet so quickly that she almost tripped over her own bag. Sparing a glance a Jackie, she saw her friend give her the okay sign, relieving her worry about her injury. Ryan dashed to the bat rack and pulled out her favorite, then ran to the on deck circle and started to warm up. She didn't have much time to spare, but she did manage to find her family in the stands and give them a ghost of a wink.

Of course, Martin, Maeve and Jamie all waved excitedly, and Ryan hoped that her teammates didn't notice their exuberance. Softball, above all of her other sports, was about being cool—and having your family hooting and hollering was far from cool. Inwardly, however, Ryan was tremendously pleased that her family was there to see her finally get to play in a real game.

Julie, the catcher, made the second out, and as Ryan narrowed her concentration to approach the plate, it hit her—Jackie was faking her injury.

Her friend had obviously wanted Ryan to get to play in front of her parents—and she had decided to take the matter out of the coach's hands. Ryan shot a quick glance to the bench and saw her friend sitting at the far end, grinning widely. *Damn!* she thought, approaching the plate and knocking the mud from her spikes. *She did that just for me. Well, no matter how it happened, I'm in the game. I might as well take advantage of it.*

Standing at the plate, she focused intently, trying to see only the ball. The pitcher had a rough, irregular motion, and she forced herself to ignore all of the twitches and jerks and concentrate on that yellow orb. Ryan had been studying the pitcher throughout the game, and she smiled inwardly when she threw a fastball off the plate, the same as she had with Jackie at her previous two at bats. Assuming that she'd follow up with the same second pitch slider that she had throw her predecessor, Ryan focused even more intently, and was ready for the ball when it reached her. She swung and made solid contact, knocking the ball over the head of the shortstop, where it fell, untouched. Lupe, who had been on second, ran for all she was worth, and scampered across the plate moments ahead of the desperate throw from the left fielder. Ryan knew they'd throw home, so she headed for second as soon as the ball left the fielder's hand. The catcher fired down to second, and Ryan arrived a split second before the ball, sliding in safely.

She asked for a time out, and then hopped up, trying to brush the dirt from her once-pristine uniform. But the drizzle had turned the dirt to mud, and she could already feel it seeping through her uniform. *That's more like it,* she thought to herself. *Nothing like a filthy uniform to make you feel like you contributed.*

After thumping Jackie on the head with her oversized first baseman's mitt, Ryan ran out to take her position in the field. Sparing a glance into the stands, she made eye contact with Jamie, who blew her a huge kiss, and then tried to get Caitlin to do the same. It was hard to concentrate with the adorable blondes in the stands, but she managed to block out everything except the game, not even noticing when the rain picked up by the end of the inning.

They had a long rain delay, and after having a word with the coaches, she ran over to the fence to speak to her family. "You might as well pack it in. If we can finish this one, we will; but they're pretty sure they'll call the next one."

"You were awesome!" Jamie crowed.

"It was only a single," Ryan demurred, but it was obvious to all that she was pleased with herself.

"You did well," Martin said. "And thank that coach for finally coming to his senses."

"Will do. Love you," she said in parting. As she dashed back to the dugout she mused, *It's Jackie I have to thank. Coach still thinks I'm a bench ornament.*

Departing Moraga, Jamie drove to Berkeley to prepare for the second wave of O'Flahertys visiting the East Bay. With all of their demanding schedules, this was the only night the girls were able to get together with Brendan and Maggie to discuss the real estate plans, so Jamie rushed to the store to buy enough groceries to make a simple dinner for the small group.

By the time the second game was finally called due to darkness and rain, Jamie nearly had dinner ready. Brendan and Maggie arrived well before Ryan returned, and Jamie and Mia entertained the pair with an extended retelling of the engagement ring fiasco. It amused Jamie to no end that the story had already become Mia's to tell, but she didn't mind, since her friend did a marvelous job of recounting the tale. They were still laughing when Ryan finally arrived, hair wet and slicked back off her face, but clothing completely dry—sparing her a swat from her disciplinarian lover.

After dinner, Mia retired to spend her evening on the phone, while the foursome sat around the table, with Jamie furiously scribbling notes.

Maggie had worked on a few real estate investment partner deals, so she had some valuable insight as to how the deal should be structured. Most of her ideas made perfect sense, but both Ryan and Brendan balked at her idea of how to assign partnership interests.

"I know it makes logical sense to have each cousin get a share equal to the hours he puts in, but that's not a good idea with this bunch," Brendan said, with Ryan nodding her agreement. "The boyos do better when it's all for one, one for all."

"If they have to keep track of hours, they'll be squabbling constantly," Ryan said. "I propose that they each get an equal share. They'll police themselves into working harder that way. I'm certain of it."

"Okay," Maggie said, while Jamie continued to write away. "There's no reason that can't work. My family would probably do it the same way."

"So, how should we do this legally?" Jamie asked.

"I think we should form a real estate investment trust," Maggie suggested. "Everyone gets an equal share of the proceeds after expenses. Niall would put up the capital, but he wouldn't get any return on his investment per se—his return would come from his work on the house—the same as the other guys."

"Is that fair to Niall?" Jamie asked. "That's like providing an interest free loan."

"I think it's fair," Brendan said. "The cousins are really angry about what they consider his unfair profit. If he doesn't make any additional money off of his principle I think they'll be much more amenable to the deal."

"Yeah, I guess I see your point," Jamie said. "Hopefully, Niall won't squawk about it."

"Would all of you want to be partners, too?" Maggie asked.

"No, no, not us," Ryan averred. "We're not skilled enough to contribute as much as the boys will, and if we go to grad school in a year we won't want to spend our weekends working that hard. We'll help, but out of solidarity—not obligation."

"I don't want to join either," Brendan said. "I don't need the extra money enough to give up all of my weekends. Rory might want to, but he's gone half the year, so we have to figure out how to work that out."

"He's gone half the year, but he's available nearly full-time when he's home," Ryan reminded him. "I think he should get a full share if he's willing to work during the week when he's home—rather than weekends only."

"Sounds fair to me," Brendan said. "So, now what do we do?"

"I think we have a family meeting—how about next Wednesday?," Ryan suggested. "We can have everyone over for pizza—say seven o'clock?"

"I can make it," Brendan said, and Maggie concurred.

"I'll start dialing for cousins," Ryan said and picked up the phone to commence.

"Wait, honey," Jamie said, walking over to stop her in mid-dial. "I don't think we should do that."

"Huh? But I thought you wanted to…"

"Oh, I do. I just don't think we should be the ones to make the proposal. I mean, the whole point is to have the boys forgive Niall, right? So let's have Niall make the offer, over at his house." She was beaming at Ryan, her green eyes dancing with pride at her brilliant idea.

The grin that met her was nearly identical in its intensity. "That is a fabulous idea." She handed the phone to Jamie and said, "Call the man and make it happen."

Chapter Thirteen

Early the next morning, Jamie reached out and tucked her arm around Ryan's waist. "Are you sneaking out of bed this early?"

"Yeah. I've uhm…got to go to a meeting."

"What?" Jamie sat up and switched on the bedside light, rubbing her eyes as they adjusted to the brightness. "What meeting do you have at this time of the day?"

"Amanda wants me to go to a…group…or something, I guess." Ryan slid out of bed, gazing down at her partner with an unreadable expression on her face.

Seeing the hesitancy and unease on Ryan's face, Jamie gentled her expression and said, "It's okay, honey, you don't have to tell me about it if you'd rather not. I know you like to keep things between you and Amanda."

"No…it's not that…it's…well, I'm nervous about it."

"Do you want me to go with you? Drive you there?"

"That's sweet," Ryan said, her expression softening into a smile. "But, I think I have to do this for myself. I might want to talk about it—but I might not, okay?"

"Okay. You're entitled to your privacy."

"Thank you," Ryan said, sitting down on the bed and stroking Jamie's cheek. "That means a lot to me."

Jamie turned her head to kiss Ryan's palm. "I know." Giving her partner a hug, she asked, "Want me to make you breakfast?"

"Thanks, but I don't think so. My tummy's a little upset, and I don't feel like eating. I'll stop and get a latte on the way."

Jamie put a hand on her lover's bare shoulder and gazed into her eyes for a moment. "Baby, whatever comes up today, I'm sure you can handle it. No matter what life throws at you from now on, you've been through worse."

"You have a good point there, partner. Talking about the carjacking can never be as frightening as that night was." She kissed Jamie soundly, and said, "Thanks for reminding me of that."

"All part of the job description. I'm merely trying to suck up to my supervisor."

At five minutes to seven, Ryan paced up and down the sidewalk in front of a small office building in downtown Oakland. She held a large latte in her hands to warm them, desperately wishing she'd worn gloves. A middle-aged woman approached and asked, "Are you Ryan, by any chance?"

"Yeah, I am." Extending her hand, she said, "Ryan O'Flaherty. Are you Doctor Moss?"

"Yes, but feel free to call me Ellen. Everyone in the group does. Come on in and let me introduce you."

Swallowing nervously, Ryan followed her in, and made eye contact with the four other women she'd seen enter the building while she waited. Ellen opened the door to the office and the group filed in, with the others chatting companionably. Ryan shrugged out of her down vest, then took off her ski cap and muffler. She noted that a few of the other women gave her puzzled looks for wearing shorts on such a cold morning, but Ryan was very glad she had done so when the room started to heat up past her comfort level.

"Okay," Ellen said, "it looks like everyone brought coffee this morning, so I won't make my usual offer. We have a new member of the group that I'd like to introduce. This is Ryan," Ellen said, smiling at the newcomer. "To give you a little time to acclimate, we normally go around the room and introduce ourselves when we have a new member. So, why don't we do that? Helen, would you mind starting? Just say who you are, and what brought you to the group."

A cheerful looking, middle-aged woman smiled at Ryan and said, "I'm Helen, and I've been with the group for almost two years. My husband, God rest his soul, had been embezzling from his company. Things had been going poorly for Stan for a couple of years, and he was sure he was going to be fired. I'll never know what caused him to do what he did, and I'll never know why he didn't trust me enough to tell me how frightened he was." She took a deep breath, and gave Ryan a sad smile. "But, he didn't. When he was found out, he hanged himself in our home. We lost our house and our car; and I had to find a job to care for our teen-aged children." She looked into Ryan's eyes, as though she could see the dark places in her soul, and said, "This group has saved my life."

Ryan nodded, feeling her stomach start to churn from hearing Helen's tale. The woman next to Helen then spoke. "Hi, I'm Pamela. I've been with the group for about six months now. I was…" She looked out the window for a moment, took a deep breath, then looked up and continued. "I was raped and severely beaten by my ex-husband. I'd recently gotten into a relationship with a man I liked, but Jerry couldn't stand to have me move on with my life." Ryan looked at the angry red scar that ran from Pamela's eye to the base of her ear. "I really like the group—but it's…hard…it's hard to come here and talk about it. I know it's something that I need to do, and I know it will help me, but it's still hard to get to sleep on Sunday and Wednesday nights."

Nodding even more dramatically, Ryan tried to unclench her hands from the arms of her chair, feeling her muscles contract painfully.

The next woman said, "I'm Arlene, and I'm about to leave the group. I've been here for a little over a year, and I think I'm ready to graduate." Her comment drew nods and smiles from the others, and she continued, "I was in a very bad auto accident. The driver of the car that hit me was killed, and I was badly injured. But I'm nearly healed physically, and I'm feeling pretty good mentally, too."

"That's good to hear," Ryan said, smiling nervously.

The woman next to Arlene shifted in her seat, looking tense and unsettled. "I'm Barb, and I've been coming here for two months." She looked around the room, her gaze brushing the top of each head, but never meeting anyone's eyes. "I am…or I was…a police officer. I'm on disability, but I don't think I'm going to go back." She shrugged her shoulders and said, "I change my mind about that every other day, so maybe I should keep my opinion to myself." She gave a stilted laugh, then took a breath and studied the carpet for a moment, then said, "I shot…and killed…my partner during a robbery. The review board declared that I wasn't negligent in Phil's death…but, I'm not the review board."

The room was completely quiet, so quiet that Ryan could hear her own heart beating. Her anxiety increasing by the moment, she was about to grab her jacket and run, but Barb's voice pulled her back from the brink. "I hate coming here, but it's helping. It really is." Ryan met her eyes, and could tell that the older woman could see the fear and anxiety that poured from her. "Hang in there, Ryan. We all help each other here."

Biting her lip, Ryan tried to twitch her face into a smile, but it didn't come off very well. "I'll try," she said. Knowing it was her turn, Ryan looked at Ellen, hoping for a reprieve, but the psychologist merely nodded encouragingly, so Ryan took a big breath and told her tale, in a very abbreviated form. "My lover, my niece and I were carjacked. All of us made it out alive, but I made some choices that night that still haunt me. I'd…I'd like to get past my guilt. I've also had a few people betray me—mostly to get money from the tabloids, and I'd like to get a better handle on my anger." She took a nervous breath and said, "I know I should be grateful that we're all alright, but some dark urges keep pulling at me." Unable to think of another thing to say, Ryan looked at Ellen, hoping to be rescued.

Smiling warmly, Ellen said, "We all welcome you, Ryan. Now, this might surprise you after hearing the stories, but everyone in this room has experienced some level of guilt and anger over what happened to them. Every one of us has a different story, but there is some part of your experience that each of us can empathize with. I think you'll find that this is a safe, caring place to talk about what's troubling you. I only ask that everything we say here stay in this room. The only way we can trust each other is if we keep each other's confidences."

"I understand that. I've had a little experience with having my privacy invaded, so I'm hypersensitive to that."

Ellen smiled at her and said, "Well, after that glaring understatement, let's begin. We normally spend about ten minutes each, checking in and talking about anything that's come up in the last few days. Helen? I think it's your turn to check in first."

Ryan hadn't been out of the session for five minutes when her phone rang. "Guess who loves you?"

A big smile covered Ryan's face. "An adorable, sweet, kind woman loves me. I never have to guess."

"Good answer," Jamie said. "How you doin', buddy?"

"I'm all right. A little shaky, but all right. I can't talk about the group, because I promised to keep everything confidential, but I think there's a chance this might help me. Hearing these other women talk about their struggles put some of mine into perspective."

"So, you're okay? Need me to hang around for a few minutes to hug you?"

"Do you have time?"

"I'll make time for you. Are you coming home?"

"For one of your hugs? No question. I'll be home in ten, then we can walk to school together."

"Hurry home, baby. I love you."

"I know that. I know it in my soul, Jamie."

Jamie scampered down the stairs that evening, still shoving things in her open duffel bag. "Are you sure you don't want to come with us tonight, Mia?" she called down to her roommate, who was sitting in the living room.

"Nah. I have to go to class tomorrow. Besides, you two probably want to have an evening alone in Las Vegas. You can use all the togetherness that you can manage."

"We haven't really been apart all that much, since I've been going on road trips with my sweetie. I feel like her groupie."

"Let's go!" Ryan poked her head in the front door, pointedly glaring at her watch.

"Bye, Ryan," Mia said, getting up to offer a kiss and a hug.

"See you tomorrow. I'll try to leave some money in the casinos for you to win."

"My little jackpot is a sure thing," Mia said. "As soon as I pick her up from the airport—I'm gonna get lucky."

Standing with the group of people gathered around the flight gate, Jamie said, "When I see your coach tomorrow, I'm going to thank him again for treating you like an adult."

"It has been nice, hasn't it? It's pretty cool to be able to go a day early and enjoy the sights."

"Are you excited about seeing the Cirque de Soleil show?"

"Yeah," Ryan said, actually more excited about Jamie's excitement than she was about seeing a circus act. "I haven't been to the circus since I was a little kid. Michael took me," she said wistfully. "He, of course, had to constantly critique the clowns' makeup, but we still had a ball."

Jamie squeezed her arm and said, "I've told you, sweetie, that this isn't your typical circus."

Ryan shrugged amiably. "Whatever. If you're excited about it, it must be good."

She wasn't paying rapt attention, and after a moment, Jamie started to look around, trying to determine what Ryan was looking at. Backhanding her in the stomach, she hissed, "Will you quit staring at the women!"

"Oh!" Ryan turned back to her and said, "I wasn't staring at them for the usual reason. I'm trying to figure out why they're here. Is there a convention or something in Las Vegas this weekend?"

"Hundreds of them." But as she took yet another look, she had to admit that she couldn't guess what kind of convention the women would be attending. Young, thin, well built...very well built, actually, uniformly blonde, and dressed in a manner that could only be called...revealing; the collection of women stood around looking very bored. There were about ten of them, and they seemed to know each other, but they didn't, for the most part, seem like friends. When Jamie turned back to say something to her partner, Ryan was gone. It took Jamie a moment to locate the tall brunette up at the check-in counter, and a few minutes later she was back.

"The attendant says we're on the 'call girl express'," Ryan said.

"What?"

"Every Thursday night, sex workers from here and L.A. apparently fly to Vegas for the weekend. They're commuters, after a fashion. Wanna strike up a conversation...get some tips?"

Raising an eyebrow, Jamie regarded her partner for a moment. "Are you inferring that I need tips?"

"Makeup tips," Ryan said slowly, clearly trying to be quick on her feet. "I thought they could give you some tips on how to get those long fake eyelashes to stay on."

"Pitiful save. Truly pitiful."

They boarded a few minutes later, and managed to take off nearly on time. Ryan had to stop herself from laughing at the parade of men who happened to stop by some of the working girls' seats on their way up and down the aisle to nowhere at all. When she tired of the show, she popped the last of her peanuts in her mouth and eyed Jamie's unopened package. One twitching eyebrow convinced the smaller woman to hand them over. "How have you avoided coming to Las Vegas?" Ryan asked.

"Mmm...I didn't have any desire to come until I could gamble. I'm not even sure my mother has been here, as a matter of fact. She's not much for gambling. We were in Monaco a couple of years ago, and she sat in the bar while Daddy and I blew our bankroll."

Grinning playfully Ryan mused, "Some heavy hitters in Monaco, right?"

At Jamie's cautious nod, Ryan commented, "Must be weird, not being the richest people in the room, huh?"

"Yes, it was very traumatic," Jamie said, rolling her eyes. "Now I understand how people in developing countries feel." She slapped her partner hard on the thigh, whispering, "Brat."

They landed at McCarran Field, and after a short cab ride, were delivered to their hotel. In return for agreeing to stay with the team on Friday and Saturday, Ryan allowed Jamie to book them into any hotel she chose for Thursday. She wasn't terribly surprised when the cab dropped them off at The Bellagio, an elegant, massive hotel, situated on a calm, seven acre lake. Having guessed that they would be staying somewhere nice, Ryan had dressed up, wearing her neatly pressed chinos, a crisp blue and white checked blouse and her marine blue crew neck sweater, one of Jamie's favorites.

The lobby was massive, and filled with people lined up in neat queues to check in. The lighting was provided by a spectacular canopy of blown glass flowers—of every type and color. As they stood under the warm lights, Jamie found herself lost in her partner's bright blue eyes, made even bluer by the sweater. "These lights are beautiful, but they pale in comparison to you."

"Excuse me," the clerk said when the previous customer departed. "Ma'am. Ma'am!"

"Oh! Sorry," she said, blushing madly while Ryan chuckled. "I wasn't paying attention. We're checking in for tonight, and friends of ours will join us tomorrow. It should all be noted in your system."

"You were paying attention," Ryan whispered into her ear after Jamie had handed the clerk her credit card and he stepped away. "You were paying attention to me—and that's exactly how I like it."

Pressing her finger against the shirt button that peeked out of Ryan's sweater, Jamie let it slip into the placket and reach in to tickle the soft skin. "Ahem. Ma'am?" the clerk asked as the flush grew once again.

"Yes?"

"I can upgrade you to a suite with a spa tub for a fifty dollar additional charge. Would you be interested in the upgrade?"

"Uhh, sure," she said, still looking at the magnificent color of Ryan's eyes.

The clerk scampered away again, and Ryan whispered, "You can't catch a break. He's gonna think you're one sexually frustrated woman."

"I am," Jamie said, grinning wickedly. "I'm intensely sexually frustrated. Don't you think it's time to satisfy me?" As if on cue, the clerk returned, and his expression made it clear that he'd heard every word.

She looked at him, shrugged her shoulders and twitched her head in Ryan's direction. "Do you blame me?"

"Not in the least, Ma'am," he said, smiling primly. "I hope that all of your needs are completely satisfied this weekend."

"Well, that was the first time in my life that a check-in clerk said he hoped I got lucky during my stay," Jamie said, rolling her eyes at Ryan on the way up in the elevator.

"It's happened to me a time or two, but never in a place that didn't charge by the hour."

"Such a life you've led," Jamie said, grinning at her randy partner.

Ryan's ego had been thoroughly stroked by the interactions with the desk clerk, and she was ready to spend the better part of the evening fulfilling Jamie's stated wish. Her hands were already probing some sensitive spots as the otherwise empty elevator whisked them to their floor, but Jamie had other plans. "You'd better calm down, hot stuff. The show's at eight, and we've got to get going if we're going to have time for dinner."

Glancing at her watch, Ryan said, "It's only six. Can't we go to one of those four dollar and ninety-nine cent buffets I keep seeing signs for? That shouldn't take long."

"I assume you're kidding. Tossing her head she said, "It doesn't matter if you are or not—because we are never—I repeat—never—going to have dinner at a four ninety-nine buffet."

"You're no fun."

Jamie stood on her tiptoes and kissed her extended lower lip. "I'm plenty of fun, and you know it. When we get back to the room I'll remind you of exactly how much fun I can be."

The bellman with their luggage was waiting for them when they exited the elevator, and Ryan gave him a puzzled look. "We have a separate set of elevators for luggage," he explained. "Let me show you to your room."

The room was absolutely gorgeous. Sumptuous, yet understated by Las Vegas standards, it reminded Jamie of a four-star hotel in Rome or Milan, with twenty-first century amenities. They passed through the marble foyer into a large sitting room, with a small dining area off to the side. "Let me show you some of the room's features," the bellman said. His short tour took only a few minutes, and Jamie left Ryan to push all of the buttons and investigate the room while she called the concierge desk to arrange for dinner. After a short discussion, she called out, "Honey? Can I have some input here?"

"Yep." Ryan dashed out of the bath and leapt onto the sofa, causing Jamie to juggle the phone to keep it from falling to the floor.

"Brat!" she whispered. "We have a few choices for dinner. We can go French, Italian, Chinese, Japanese, or American."

"Doesn't matter to me. Your choice."

Picking up the phone again, Jamie said, "I think we'd like to dine at Le Cirque. I assume it wouldn't be difficult to be seated now, would it?" She nodded her head and said, "Yes, we're ready. That's great. Thanks a lot."

Hanging up, Jamie stood and extended her hand. "We're on. Let's chow down."

"Can I go like this?" Ryan asked.

"Well, I wouldn't think of going to Le Cirque in New York dressed this casually, but this is Las Vegas. I think we'll be fine."

"You look great," Ryan said, eyeing her partner. "But, then, you always do." She put her hand on the shoulder of the simple but elegant-looking vivid blue, linen shift that Jamie was wearing, smiling gently at her partner. "You look fantastic, honey. Are you sure I'm okay?"

"You look adorable. Really." Standing on her toes, Jamie gave her partner a few, quick kisses. "You look so comfortable in your skin that I don't think people notice what you have on. You command attention, no matter what you're wearing."

"It's because I'm so tall. When you're taller than ninety-nine percent of all women, people always look at you."

"Yeah, that's probably it," Jamie agreed, not believing it for a minute.

As Jamie had expected, the restaurant was nearly empty at the early hour, having opened only a half hour before. The maitre d'hôtel was very accommodating, seating them at a table right next to the window, where they could overlook the lake. The restaurant was decorated in a whimsical fashion, with a multicolored re-creation of a circus big top dominating the entire ceiling of the smallish room. "This place is beautiful," Ryan said, craning her neck to see everything. "I'm guessing that Le Cirque means the circus?"

"Good girl," Jamie said, nodding. "That semester of French is paying off."

Chuckling, Ryan said, "I've barely figured out what 'Le' means. Good thing I'm not fixated on grades, 'cause I might get my first *C* this term."

"Wow. Your first *C* in college."

Ryan's dark head shook, and she took a drink of water, continuing to look around the room.

"High school?"

Another shake of the head.

"Oh, please! You've never had a *C*?"

"Nope. It won't kill me if I get one, though. I'm not going to let little things like that bother me any more."

"I thought your grades went down when you were a senior in high school. Are you not counting that?"

"No, I'm counting that. I got two *B*s and two incompletes my first semester. Those were my first *B*s," she said, shrugging sheepishly.

"I hope to God our kids get your brains."

"Well, the ones that I have might, but you're rolling the dice if you use my brothers or my cousins as sperm donors. Donal and Declan barely got through high school, and Padraig is dyslexic. He had a hell of a time in school. Conor's bright, but he was no scholar. Come to think of it, Brendan's the only one who had any desire to go to college. The boyos were glad to be done with it after high school. I'm an anomaly for the O'Flahertys. The Ryans are the ones with the book-smarts. Maybe we should consider my cousin Cormac."

Jamie's lower lip stuck out. "He doesn't look like you. Remember, my main goal is to have a carbon copy of your sweet little face."

"Then, you'd better stick with Brendan. He at least likes to read. I don't think the lads have opened a book since high school, unless you consider Playboy and Penthouse a book."

"I don't," Jamie said, smiling sweetly. "And you'd better not, either."

"I'm completely unfamiliar with the genre," Ryan said, boldly lying. "I prefer Scientific American."

When their server arrived, Ryan, as usual, left the ordering to Jamie.

Jamie chose a five course tasting menu; accompanied by five wines chosen for their compatibility. The pair was happily consuming a delightful cream of watercress soup when something caught Jamie's eye. Signaling for their server, she asked, "Could you possibly open this door?"

"Of course, Ma'am." The man pushed the drapes aside, letting Ryan see what had captivated her partner. As the door opened, they were delighted to see a massive, synchronized, water show from the normally hidden fountains of the lake. There must have been a thousand huge streams of water; some going so high that Ryan supposed they must be forced from fire hoses. As the streams of water danced against the night sky, powerful speakers broadcast Frank Sinatra singing "Luck Be A Lady, Tonight."

"Not too cool," Ryan said, smiling warmly at her partner. "Of course, my lady always brings me luck."

Reaching across the table, Jamie grasped her lover's hand and gave her a somewhat shy smile. "Are you having fun, sweetheart?"

"I am. And I'm very glad that we didn't go for the four ninety-nine buffet. This meal is fantastic, and I'm happy that you didn't let my cheapness carry the day."

"You're not cheap. You're careful, and that's not a vice. It's just that we don't go out very often, and when we do, I like to make it memorable."

"I'm certain this will be a very memorable weekend. Being with you for four days will guarantee that."

"Such a romantic little Irish heart you have."

"I don't have it any longer," Ryan said, her eyes sparkling in the reflected light of the fountains. "I gave it to you."

Just as Jamie had predicted, Ryan was in thrall during the entire performance of "O." Cirque de Soleil had constructed a theatre at The Bellagio expressly for the elaborate water-themed show, and they had done a masterful job. Every seat had excellent sight-lines, the music was perfectly suited to the theme, and the performances flawless. At the end, Ryan turned to her partner, and said, "There's an eleven o'clock show. Can we go again?"

Jamie would have moved mountains to satisfy the hopeful expression on her lover's face. But she'd already had to move a mountain of greenbacks into a ticket broker's pocket to secure the tickets to this performance, and she knew that Ryan would have a fit if she learned how much that had cost. "They're sold out," she said. "I can try to see if there's a ticket broker…"

"No, no, that's okay," Ryan said, looking like Jamie had suggested armed robbery. "It's better to leave wanting more."

"If you're sure…"

"Positive. Let's hit the blackjack tables and let me win back what this evening cost us."

You'd better be one very, very lucky woman.

Ryan was a very lucky woman, and after playing for two hours, she had recouped over half of what they'd spent so far. Jamie didn't let on, however, praising her abilities lavishly. "Your cousins think you cheat," Jamie teased when they were outside watching yet another performance of the fountains.

"I do not! They think I cheat because I have such a good memory." Her lips curled into a grin, adding, "Those boys are some of the worst card players you'll ever find. I was born into the perfect family. They think they're great, and they can't back down from a challenge, but they suck! Absolutely perfect," she said, humming with satisfaction.

The soft click of the door woke Jamie the next morning, and she pushed her hair from her eyes to witness her grinning partner trying to sneak into the room. "Where have you been?"

Eyes wide with delight, Ryan ran over to the bed and dumped two huge plastic cups filled with quarters onto Jamie's startled body. "I won a jackpot playing video poker. A great, big, fat royal flush. twenty-five hundred quarters!"

"Ryan!" Looking at the clock, she saw that it was six thirty, and was none too happy to have been woken by having a few pounds of dirty metal thrown onto her. "Why do you run out on me like that?" she asked grumpily. "I don't like to wake up and not know where you are."

"I left two notes."

"Can't you stay in bed like normal people? The dawn can come without your help, you know."

"I'm here now." The grin that had won her heart began to form, and Jamie felt her own lips respond in kind. "I'd love to stay in bed and cuddle you until I have to go to the game. Isn't it better to be in this nice, soft bed when we're both awake?"

Jamie's bad mood began to lift. She glanced at her watch and asked, "How long do we have?"

"Four and a half hours. But I should get a bite to eat before I go."

"Oh, I'll give you a bite," Jamie purred, drawing her partner down on top of her coin-covered body. "I'll give you a bite to remember."

The pair enjoyed one of the best mornings that either could recall. A large helping of each other, a long, playful shower in the sumptuous bath, and a delightful dim sum brunch in the hotel's Chinese restaurant.

With great regret, Ryan hopped into a cab to head to the softball complex, with Jamie promising to meet her after she'd checked into the team motel.

Jamie liked to watch the games, but watching warm-ups, batting practice and two seven-inning games while sitting on a backless bleacher was a little much—even for her.

After she got settled into their small, utilitarian room at the team motel, she flipped on the TV to while away an hour. The bed was firm, and the room was overly warm, but neither fact stopped her from falling asleep almost immediately. She woke slowly some time later, her neck stiff from the odd angle she'd been in. Stretching languidly, she looked at her watch and nearly jumped out of bed. "Two o'clock!"

Jumping into her shoes, she grabbed her backpack and ran for the lobby, only to have to wait twenty minutes for a cab. By the time she reached the field, the first game was in the top of the seventh, and she was almost relieved that Ryan was sitting on the bench, still in her warm-up jacket. *At least I didn't miss seeing her play*, she thought in relief. *I never would have heard the end of it.*

The game was over in moments, and she waited patiently by the entrance to the locker rooms. *Ryan might not have even noticed that I didn't come on time. I don't think she can see all of the stands from the dugout.* The players started straggling out of the locker room, all of them giving her a friendly hello and a wave. Heather came out, obviously looking for her. "She's okay, Jamie. It looks worse than it is."

Jamie's eyes grew wide as her lover came limping out of the locker room, one ice bag secured to her knee, another to her elbow. Ryan's face was a stoic mask of nonchalance, but Jamie ran to her, grasping her frantically. "Honey! Are you all right?"

"Hell, no, I'm not all right," she said, wincing in pain. "Would you be all right if that had happened to you?"

"Well…" She started to say that she hadn't seen what had happened, but she didn't have the nerve to admit it at the moment.

"Have you ever seen such a collision? Jesus, it's a wonder that I wasn't carted away in an ambulance." Ryan was shaking her head, grumbling to herself the entire time. "I guess you're going to want me to go to the hospital, huh?"

"Didn't a doctor look at you?"

"Nah. No doctor was available. I'll probably be okay," she said, not looking very convinced. "I'm still a little woozy, but the double vision's about gone."

Just then Coach Roberts came out of the men's locker room, took one look at Ryan and asked, "What the hell's wrong with you?"

"Nothin'," she said. "Only injury I might get is splinters from sitting on the bench."

"I'll give you a splinter," he grumbled, cuffing her affectionately. "I thought maybe you'd sprained your arm playing the slots last night."

"Nah, I'm all about poker and blackjack."

"Doesn't surprise me a bit, O'Flaherty. Go get those ice bags off and warm up. You might get off your butt for a change in the second game."

"Cool!" she cried, turning to share a smile with Jamie. She winced noticeably when she saw the cold fury in the jade green eyes. "I was playing a practical joke on you. Funny, wasn't it?"

Jamie didn't say a word, but she took off after her, chasing her lover all around the field; nearly catching her several times since the ice bag on her knee slowed her down. "You're gonna need those ice bags when I'm done with you!"

"Can't you take a joke?" Ryan gasped, leaping over a low bench.

"Yeah, I can take a joke," she panted. "Now we're gonna see how well you can take one."

"What are you gonna do?"

"Be ready, O'Flaherty. That's all I'm gonna say. Be ready."

Ryan did indeed get the nod to start the second game, taking over for Jackie, who needed a rest after the heat of the Las Vegas sun proved to be too much for her. Ryan looked so darned cute with her cap pulled low over her eyes that Jamie couldn't bear to be angry with her, even though she would have been well justified. Right before the game started, she called her over to the fence and handed her the present she had been carrying ever since the start of the season. "I've been saving this for the first game you started," she said, pushing the package of 'Big League Chew' through a link of the fence.

Ryan smiled broadly and opened the foil packet. She took out a huge wad of the shredded bubble gum and stuck it in her mouth, chewing noisily until she got it down to a manageable size. "Thanks," she said, her expression bordering on a leer. "Hey, you busy after the game? I've got a single room." Merrily dancing eyebrows indicated that she didn't expect to be alone in the room for long, and Jamie played along.

"It depends on how you play. I'm a Cal groupie, you know. I'm going home with the star of the game. If that's you—fine. If not—that's fine, too." With that, she tossed her head and went to her seat, turning before she sat down to confirm that Ryan was, as usual, staring at her ass. Giving it a twitch, she sat and waved her off. "Play well," she drawled.

To prove her star status, Ryan ran out to first base full-tilt, performing a flawless flip right before she reached the bag. Jamie heard Coach Roberts yell, "For Christ's sake, O'Flaherty!" and she knew he too had seen the extemporaneous performance.

Luckily for Ryan, she was the star of the game, thanks to a single in the sixth inning, which knocked in the winning run. She was filthy, as expected, having slid into second base, and Jamie was surprised to see yet another ice bag when Ryan emerged from the locker room, Heather in tow. Jamie grabbed the younger woman by the arm and pulled her close. "An accessory after the fact still goes to jail, kiddo." Heather looked at her with wide eyes, but Jamie slapped her on the seat and said, "I know, she's impossible to say no to."

"She really is, Jamie," Heather insisted. "I don't know how you ever do it."

"I don't very often. She has an odd, but effective, charm."

"Hey!" Ryan scowled. "Who you calling odd?"

"Shoe fits—wear it," Jamie tossed back. "Now what's with the ice?" Ryan's makeshift ice bag was a zip-lock plastic bag, taped to her knee with a strip of what looked like clear plastic wrap.

"No biggie. When I slid into second, I banged it a little. It's not even swollen, but the trainer loooooooves to make us look goofy."

"Not a long trip when you're involved. Bus or cab?"

"Bus. The way I look, I don't think I could get a cab to stop."

Jamie took a long look at the sweaty, bedraggled woman and shook her head. "You've got a point there, sport. Thankfully, Heather is still fresh as a daisy. I think I'll sit with her." She grabbed the young woman's arm and led her to the bus, sparing a teasing wink at her smirking partner.

🐎

As soon as Ryan was clean, she lay down on the bed and stretched out. "Time for a nap?"

"Yeah, I think so. Jordan's flight comes in at seven, and Mia's is due right around then, too. I told them we'd be in the casino at Mandalay Bay, since it's close to the airport—and that you'd probably be playing poker."

"No probably about it. You gonna nap with me?"

"I had a pretty good one earlier in the day," she reminded her. "I fell asleep sitting up watching TV."

"Come snuggle for a minute, then," Ryan said, giving a hopeful look. "You can watch TV or read once I'm out."

"Love to." Taking one of her textbooks, she lay down on the bed next to her always-cuddly partner and smiled when Ryan soon had her pinned firmly to the mattress. Ryan was asleep in seconds, and Jamie knew that her study plans would go unrealized. *She could run a sleep clinic for insomniacs,* she mused before she nodded off. *Ten minutes of cuddling with her could knock anyone out.*

🐎

They were waiting for a cab in front of their motel when Jamie asked, "Isn't it kinda funny how much freedom Coach Roberts gives you guys? Not many coaches would let you all run wild in Las Vegas. You don't even have a curfew."

"It's a little odd, but it's how I'd run the team if I were in charge. Seniors don't have a curfew, but the rest of the team does. He likes to give each class a little more freedom so he can keep an eye on them until he's sure they can handle it. The juniors have to be in by two, the sophs by one, and the freshmen by midnight."

"Huh. But, doesn't that preclude the freshmen going out with any of the upperclassmen?"

"Yep. That's part of his plan," Ryan said. "He wants us to play as a team, but he doesn't think it's mandatory that we all hang out together. He realizes that since the seniors have the ability to go to casinos and have a drink, they'll be resentful if they have to stay home because the younger players can't come with us. Plus, if he keeps the freshmen on a short leash, they're less likely to get into trouble by tagging along with the older women. His style is unconventional, but it's worked for him."

"Coach Hayes should work for him for a few years after her lame ass is fired."

Ryan laughed, "He wouldn't put up with her for five minutes. I've never met two coaches with such different styles. You'd think she'd take a look at his consistently successful record and take a clue, but that's not gonna happen."

"Her loss," Jamie shrugged.

"Literally."

Jamie was playing the slots when Mia and Jordan arrived. "Hey, girlfriend!" Jamie smiled at Mia's bubbly voice, gathered up her cup full of quarters, and went to greet her friends.

"Wow! You look fabulous, Jordan," Jamie said, staring openly at the lanky blonde.

"Free product," she said, giving Jamie a quick pirouette to show off her new clothes. "I got a suitcase full of things after that Polo ad that I did, so I brought everything with me. This is the first chance I've had in weeks to be out of sweats or warm-ups."

"I think I've only seen you dressed up at Martin and Maeve's wedding," Jamie said, eyeing her critically. "You should get out of sweats more often."

"Can you see why Ralph Lauren wanted her?" Mia asked, letting her eyes wander up and down the long body. "The clothes were made for her."

Jamie had to admit that the items fit Jordan perfectly. She wore a beautiful cashmere crew-neck sweater and a pair of pleated wool slacks, both in a warm, winter white. A well-cut, navy blue blazer with the large RL crest on the pocket was draped over her shoulders, making her look more like her model-self than her athlete-self. "You're sure not going to get carded tonight. You could pass for thirty."

"What about me?" Mia asked rather petulantly.

Jamie gave her a fond glance and said, "You and I could both pass for twenty. Regrettably, we're twenty-one and twenty-two. You do look way nice, though. That suit is great on you. You should buy one like it." Mia was wearing one of Jamie's favorite outfits, since it was, in fact, Jamie's. The dark emerald pants suit made of very fine velour was marvelous on Mia, very sophisticated; but she still looked a good ten years younger than Jordan.

"I didn't have anything that Jordy hasn't seen before," Mia said. "You don't mind, do you?"

"You know I don't. Besides, it looks great with your eyes. Gives them some green highlights."

"It does," Jordan sighed. "I've been staring at her ever since we met in the airport, and it just dawned on me that it's because her eyes look so complex tonight."

Mia squeezed her hand and said, "You can admire them all night, honey— 'cause we're staying up 'til dawn."

It took a while, but they finally found the poker tables. The Mandalay Bay followed the custom of most of the Vegas casinos, and had created a separate room for the game. Blackjack, pai gow poker, Caribbean stud, three-card poker and Texas hold 'em could be played at any one of a number of tables dispersed around the gaming floor. But, regular poker was still king, and it was treated as such by the casinos. The poker room was raised up a few steps from the casino floor, and surrounded by a half wall. They found Ryan at a table near the back of the room, seated with six men and one young woman, deeply engrossed in her game. "Odd crowd," Jamie said, looking around at the players.

Mia nodded, a look of faint distaste on her face. "They look like a bunch of guys who should be pluckin' chickens."

Jamie took another critical look and had to agree with her friend. The room contained about twenty tables, and the vast majority of them had a game going on. The average age of the players was around sixty-five, and very few of the men had bothered to shave—that week. The players contrasted so dramatically with the younger, wealthier looking crowd that populated the rest of the casino, that she was unable to reconcile the variation.

Something about the way the room was set up made Jamie reluctant to go in and tell her partner they were there. The place was very, very quiet—also strange for a casino. Oddly, there was a no smoking sign prominently displayed; the only place Jamie had seen such a restriction. Gazing at her partner again, Jamie said, "She looks hot, doesn't she?"

Due to the angle of the table, they had a side view of her, and both women agreed with Jamie's assessment. Ryan was wearing a cream-colored, heavyweight silk blouse and her leather pants, which gleamed in the muted light of the room. Her hair was loose and draped around her shoulders, the highlights almost blue where one of the pin-spots hit her. She had a long, thin cigar in her mouth, but Jamie noticed it wasn't lit—due to the prohibition. Rather than smoking it, she seemed to be using it as a prop of some sort. But whatever her motivation, it made her look sexy and confident—two of Jamie's favorite attributes.

The hand was over quickly, and Ryan stood and started to put her chips in a plastic carrier. Another man stood and approached her, motioning with his head towards a small room labeled "High Stakes." Ryan's brow furrowed and she shook her head, but the man didn't want to take no for an answer. He gestured towards the room again, but Ryan held her ground, sticking her chin out the way she did when her mind was firmly made up. Disgusted, he stalked away, passing by the three spectators as he did so. "Fuckin' bitch," he grumbled to himself.

Ryan looked up as she walked away from the table, and gave her friends a beaming smile. "Wow, three of the best looking women in Las Vegas—all in one spot." With warm hugs and kisses for Mia and Jordan, she draped her arm around Jamie and said, "Let me take you all to dinner. The sky's the limit." She pointedly eyed her chips, giving Jamie a wink.

"Who was the guy talking to you?" Jordan asked. "He was cussing you out when he left."

"Sore loser. I cleaned him out, and he wanted to play for a hundred dollars a hand in the high stakes room. I never bet that much," she said, shaking her head. "You can lose your shirt in ten minutes. Besides, if my luck held, he'd probably be betting the mortgage on his house. I hate to play with compulsive gamblers, and he had all the signs."

"How much did you win?" Jamie gaped, seeing chips of many different colors in the tray.

"Enough." Her self-satisfied smile was all Jamie was going to get out of her, and she let Ryan cash out in private—since she obviously didn't want to share the extent of her success.

They decided on drinks at The Red Square, an opulent vodka bar and Russian restaurant at the hotel. The chic, trendy bar was filled with the beautiful people of Las Vegas, and to Ryan's surprise, her foursome fit right in. Her burgeoning wealth and social status didn't hit her very often, but in a setting like this, she was unable to exert her powers of denial. *Face it, O'Flaherty, Jamie's always going to be one of the beautiful people, and since you're her spouse, you're at least mildly attractive.* She laughed softly, and Jamie caught her eye, giving her a raised eyebrow.

Leaning over, Ryan said, "I was having one of my 'I can't believe this is my life' moments. It'll pass."

Jamie leaned right back into her, saying, "I can't believe that you're my lover, and I hope that's a feeling that never passes."

"Let's skip dinner, and go make out," Ryan whispered.

"Oh, no! You're gonna need all of your stamina tonight. I need you well fed."

"Then let's get some food, 'cause I'm all about goin' home early."

Jamie had been busy during Ryan's poker game, making reservations at a lovely restaurant in the hotel. Aureole was known for both fantastic food and a very unique wine cellar. The cellar was actually a four story glass tower, located right in the middle of the room, and Ryan was spellbound by the display. "If I had to move to Las Vegas, that's the job I'd have," she said, her voice filled with longing.

Jordan was imitating her stare, and she nodded her complete agreement. "Without a doubt."

Jamie and Mia exchanged aggrieved looks, each of them rolling her eyes. "Jocks," Mia said.

"Well, it is kinda cool," Jamie had to admit, "but I think I'd get tired of it."

The foursome stared for a few more minutes, watching a lithe, graceful woman glide up and down the tower via a system of pulleys; her athletic body secured by a nearly invisible harness. The lovely sylph wore a headset, and was obviously being given instructions by the sommelier. Up and down the tower she went, barely pausing long enough to slip a bottle from its cache and return to the ground. "I could do that for twenty-four hours straight," Ryan said, transfixed.

"Easy," Jordan agreed. "I'd do it for free."

"Let's go, you two," Jamie said, tugging on her partner's hand. "You're goofy enough to try to wrestle the poor woman out of that harness."

That comment got Ryan's attention, and she leaned over and whispered, "You have no idea how many times I've wrestled a woman out of a harness."

Jamie swatted her on the seat, no longer caring if people saw her. "Big talker," she whispered back. "I think you've made up half of your supposed debauchery."

Not rising to the bait, Ryan waggled her eyebrows, "Wanna bet?"

"No thanks. I don't want to lose my shirt like that poor old chicken farmer did."

"Chicken farmer?" Ryan asked, scratching her head as Jamie tugged her over to their table.

🐎

Leaving the restaurant, Ryan clutched the complimentary box of handmade chocolates to her breast, leaving no doubt that they were hers alone. Deciding to walk their dinner off, they began the long stroll back to The Bellagio.

On the walk along the crowded Strip, they passed a near-constant stream of young Latin men, handing out full-color ads for prostitutes. The men were respectful, doing their best not to give the ads to children or women. But there wasn't one who didn't try to thrust one into Ryan's hands. After the twentieth such encounter, her friends were laughing helplessly; and the look on Ryan's face was as funny as the situation. "Do I look like a guy? Or can everyone tell I'm a big dyke looking for a woman?"

"Neither honey," Jamie assured her. "It's your height. They don't look at your face; they see that you're a foot taller than they are, and shove a flyer at you."

Ryan stopped in the middle of the sidewalk, giving Jamie a scowl. "Jordan's a half inch taller than me, and she hasn't gotten one."

"Hmm…I guess you look like a big dyke then," Jamie said, giggling, 'cause you sure don't look like any man I've ever seen."

"Thanks, I think," Ryan said, and shrugged her shoulders, only to have another young man put a particularly lewd picture in her hand. "I don't have to pay for it!" she shouted, waving the picture at him.

"I'd pay you. Any price, any time."

"That's more like it," Ryan sniffed, her dignity somewhat restored.

🐎

When they reached The Bellagio, they walked past the throngs of people waiting to enter the theatre to see "O." Ryan walked over to the ticket window while Jamie paused to regale their friends with how much they had enjoyed the performance, and moments later she was back, beaming a grin. She extended a pair of tickets to Jordan and said, "Eleven o'clock tonight. Be there."

Jordan gaped at her. "Jamie said they were sold out. How did you…?"

"They had some cancellations," she said. "Never hurts to ask."

"Ryan, you didn't have to do this!" Mia said.

"I enjoyed the show so much that I want you to see it, too." Her face grew serious and she said, "I love winning money—but it's like a gift—it doesn't feel like mine. It gives me a a lot of pleasure to share it with my friends."

Mia wrapped her in a hug and grasped her hand as they walked towards the elevators, the pair a few steps in front of Jordan and Jamie. "You know," she said thoughtfully, "I used to worry about Jamie. I honestly never thought she could find anyone as generous and loving as she is—and I thought she might not be able to share that part of herself with her husband. It's so nice to see her with someone who's as kind as she is. You two deserve each other."

Ryan leaned over and placed a kiss on the crown of Mia's curly head. "Thanks. I appreciate that. Being compared to Jamie is the nicest compliment you could give me."

⚞

After Jordan and Mia dropped off their bags in the room Jamie and Ryan had vacated, they prevailed upon their friends to do a little gambling before returning to the team hotel. The found a bank of slot machines in a quiet corner of the casino, so they could talk while they gambled. Ryan and Jordan were sitting on the cushioned, brocade chairs, while their girlfriends each perched upon one of their athlete's legs. "We're starting to make plans for Sydney this week," Ryan said. "I'm so damned excited about coming to watch you. I don't think I'd be any more excited if I were going to compete."

Jordan gave her one of her most luminous grins. "It's gonna be so great to have you all there."

"Are your parents' coming?" Ryan asked.

"Yeah. And my brother and my grandmother."

Mia rolled her eyes, and Jamie could tell something was up, but she didn't want to pry. Switching to what she assumed would be a safer topic, she asked, "What does your brother do, Jordan? I don't think I've heard you talk about him much."

Jordan pursed her lips, her brow knit into a frown. "He's kind of an actor."

"Kind of?"

Jordan turned to Jamie and shrugged her shoulders. "There's a breed of people in LA who manage to live with no visible means of support. He claims that he's an actor, but I've never heard of him appearing in anything. I think he's still in Actor's Equity, but last I heard he was in danger of losing his card since he hadn't worked."

"And he doesn't do anything else?"

"Not that I know of. He has an apartment in Brentwood, and he always has a nice car, but I don't have a clue how he pays for it."

"Maybe your father...?"

That got a laugh from Jordan. "Not hardly. I don't think they speak."

"Oh." Jamie knew this conversation had run its course, but she didn't want it to end on such a down note. "Maybe he takes jobs here and there that you don't know about."

"I'm sure that's true," Jordan said, smiling enigmatically, and letting the issue drop.

🐴

"This game is too dull," Ryan declared. "Let's play blackjack together."

"I don't know a thing about it," Mia insisted. "I'll go broke in two minutes."

"No, no, no, it's fun. Let's find some good blackjack slot machines, and I'll explain it to you. You've gotta play a few hands of a real game on your first trip to Las Vegas. Come on."

She confidently led the way, and her friends dutifully joined her when she'd located the right type of machine. A cocktail waitress came by, and Ryan gave her a charming grin and said, "If you'd bring us a bottle of water every time you come by, we'd sure appreciate it." She slipped the waitress a five dollar bill, and received a warm, friendly smile in return.

"I'll be back in a minute," she said, and Jamie could see a brief flash of connection between the women.

Leaning in, Jamie asked, "You could get her if you wanted her, couldn't you?"

"Mmm, I'm not sure," Ryan said thoughtfully. "You can never tell with women who work for tips. Most of them have a very well developed sense of people. If they pick up that you're gay, a lot of them will play with you, to make you think you can get them."

Jamie gave her a curious look, and asked, "Do you ever want to try to pick a woman up to see if you still have the magic?"

Ryan smirked at her, shaking her head. "Nope. No interest." At Jamie's pleased smile, she added, "I know I've still got it."

🐴

Ryan launched into a rather detailed explanation of her usual strategy, but quickly realized that she had lost both Mia and Jamie. Jordan was paying rapt attention, however, so she kept going, figuring that she'd think of another way to keep the stragglers involved.

Mia had disconnected so thoroughly, that she didn't notice when all eyes turned to her.

"Mia, why are you staring at that couple?" Jordan asked when she caught her attention.

"Oh!" Mia actually blushed—not an easy thing to make her do. "Uhm...I was...thinking."

"About what, baby?" Jordan asked. "You look like something's bothering you."

"No, I'm okay." She looked uncomfortable, but all three women were looking at her, and she swallowed and said, "I was thinking about attraction and...stuff."

"Huh?" Jordan cast another glance at the extremely attractive couple playing the nearby slot machines. The dark haired man looked Italian or Spanish, and his fair-haired companion appeared to be a typical California actress/model. They were beautifully dressed and both oozed sex appeal. The man was playing the machine, with the woman leaning on a column, watching him intently. She gave off a vibe that said she was waiting for him to finish so that she could take him to their room and have her way with him.

"I was thinking about sex appeal and sexual orientation and things like that," Mia explained vaguely.

Jordan's look was still blank, and Jamie and Ryan's exhibited similar confusion.

"Okay," she explained, knowing she'd painted herself into a corner. "When you look at a couple like that, who do you notice first?"

Jordan scratched her head and said, "I don't look at other people very often. If I don't know them, I hardly notice that someone's there."

Mia knew this was true, even though she didn't understand it. She loved to look at people, and she noticed nearly everyone she encountered on a given day. Jordan, on the other hand, seemed to glide through her own little world, concentrating on something or other that only she was aware of.

"What about you?" Jordan asked Mia. "Who do you notice?"

"Mmm..." she said, wishing she hadn't gone down this path. "It depends."

Jordan grasped her hand and gave it a squeeze. "It's okay. Who do you notice? It won't hurt my feelings. I'm interested."

She nodded and told the truth. "I see the guy. I always see the guy. If the woman's extraordinary I notice her, too, but it's the guy who catches my eye." She shrugged her shoulders, looking slightly bothered by this fact.

Trying to take the spotlight off Mia, Jamie piped up. "I see them both. It's like my mind looks at them as a couple, like I'm trying to assess their chemistry—then I check out the woman...thoroughly. What about you, Ryan?"

Ryan took in the scene, letting her mind assess it as she normally would. The man was giving off a powerful vibe, his attention fixed on the spinning reels, his fit, muscular body beautifully displayed in a tight black T-shirt and black slacks. His companion was very much in the background, most of her energy fixed upon him. He pulled on the handle with gusto, thrusting his hips with each forceful yank. Ryan noted that he was playing three coins in a ten-dollar machine, tossing away thirty bucks with each unsuccessful spin. Satisfied with the information that her brain had registered, she shrugged and said, "I see a really hot woman leaning against a pillar." That drew a hearty laugh from her friends, but Ryan wasn't trying to be funny. She didn't notice men most of the time—unless there weren't any women around to capture her attention. "I'm being serious, guys. It's how we're programmed and how we've trained ourselves."

Still looking concerned, Mia turned to Jamie. "After you came out, did the way you look at people change?"

"No to be really, really honest," Jamie said, drawing out her answer, "No. It didn't. I've always noticed women. I used to try to convince myself that I was checking out their clothes, or their style, but in reality I was looking at their asses," she said, giggling. "I'm more honest about it now, but nothing has changed."

Ryan loved to hear her partner talk about her still-developing sexual personae, so she encouraged her to continue. "What do you look at when you see a nice-looking woman?"

"Hmm…" Jamie turned her attention to a lovely brunette standing at a slot machine. She cocked her head and let herself look at her like she normally did, then relayed the process. "I start at the top and think, 'Ryan's hair is much nicer.'" She shot a grin at her partner, and continued, "Then I think, 'Ryan's face is so much prettier.' I go down her body, comparing her bit by bit. And let me tell ya, not many parts ever beat yours out."

"That is absolutely adorable," Ryan said, leaning it for a kiss. "I had no idea that you did that."

"Do you do that, too?" she asked, a hopeful look on her face.

Oh boy! "Well, I uhm…I guess that I kinda…"

"Never mind," Jamie said, shaking her head in disappointment.

"Hey, there's a very good reason that I don't compare you to other women," Ryan said, trying to rescue herself. "First off—it's not a fair comparison. I love the whole you—not only your beautiful face or fabulous body. I don't know the women I see on a daily basis, so it's like comparing apples and oranges. They'd lose before the comparison could even begin."

"Should I accept that answer?" Jamie asked her friends.

"Yeah, give the poor thing a break," Mia urged. "She's been very nice to us tonight."

"Okay," Jamie said, sparing a glance at the puppy-dog look on Ryan's face. "I accept your rationale."

"I'm being serious. The women I look at are merely bodies and faces. They don't touch me or move me. They're only assemblages of protoplasm."

"Wow!"Jamie gasped as a woman with a massive assemblage of protoplasm arranged on her chest walked by. "Were those real?"

"If you mean real versus illusory, then yes, they were," Ryan teased. "But if you mean real versus manufactured—no, they weren't."

"How can you be so sure? Maybe she got in the breast line twice when God was handing them out."

"Nope. You can tell. Look at the movement. Breasts that large have to move when you walk, and hers don't. They're far too firm and rigid to be real."

"Have you ever…sampled a surgically enhanced pair?"

Ryan shrugged and said, "Only partially."

"Explain."

"Well…at my old gym, one of my clients had hers done. She told me I could feel them—so I did."

"A client let you feel her tits?" Jamie gasped in surprise.

"Well…I think she suspected that I was an aficionado. She'd recently had them done, and she asked if I'd like to give her some feedback. So, we went into the locker room when we were done with our session, and I felt them."

"Amazing," Jamie said, shaking her head.

"They were kinda weird. Not bad weird—different weird. They had a very, very different feel—much more resilient than natural breasts. I'd have to get used to them before I could enjoy them."

"Not to worry," Jamie said. "I won't be having mine done in the near future, and we've agreed that you don't get to sample anyone else's."

"Not true. We've agreed that I don't want to sample anyone else's. Small, but vital difference. You don't force me to want only you. It's the simple truth."

They walked over to the blackjack tables together, with Jamie asking Ryan a few detailed questions about enhanced breasts. She knew she'd never experience any, but she was a more avid aficionado than Ryan, so she felt it mandatory to live vicariously through her partner.

Finding an empty table, the foursome took their places, Mia and Jamie agreeing that Ryan would signal them when she wanted them to hit. They played for quite a while, and managed to lose only about a hundred dollars among the three of them. Jordan, however, was on a roll—even though she'd never played before. She didn't ask for Ryan's help, and proved that she didn't need it—getting up to five hundred dollars before she cashed out. "What a rush," she moaned to Ryan when they stood in the cashier line. "That was hot!"

"It does feel good, doesn't it? I think gambling is one vice I could easily become addicted to. Thank God I'm too cheap to be able to tolerate losing money."

Jordan peeled off two hundred and extended it towards Ryan. "Let me pay you back for the tickets to 'O.'"

Ryan firmly pushed the money back at her. "Nope. Use it to buy a plane ticket to come home. Mia misses you something fierce."

"I know. It's hard to tell which of us is more miserable."

"I think it's a tie," Ryan said. "We're gonna head home now. You two have a great time tonight, okay?"

"We will. We'll try to get to your game tomorrow…" she began, but Ryan hushed her.

"Please don't come. I'd like it if you stayed up late and made love until dawn. You need to spend your time together."

Jordan nodded and gave Ryan a kiss. "I would have had a best friend years ago if I could have had one like you."

"You've got one now," Ryan promised, wrapping her in a hug.

🐴

After they left, Mia and Jordan went to another quiet bar to have a drink before the show began. Mia sipped her Cosmopolitan, deep in thought.

"What's going on behind those pretty eyes?"

"I didn't hurt your feelings when I said I noticed men first, did I?"

Reaching across the table, Jordan took her hand and gave it a tug. Mia smiled and moved her chair closer until they were shoulder to shoulder. "Do you have any desire to break up with me to be with one of the guys you notice?"

"No! Of course not!" She leaned her head against the soft wool of Jordan's jacket. "I apologize for bringing the topic up. It was tacky. I feel like I'm fixated on sexual desire and orientation these days."

Stroking her thigh, Jordan leaned in close and asked, "Why, babe?"

"I've been thinking, and sometimes I wish I were gay. It would make things easier."

Laughing gently, Jordan said, "That's a new development. You know things have changed when being gay is easier than being straight."

"Not for everything. But it'd be easier for things like telling my parents about us. I think they'd understand if I told them I was a lesbian. It's this damned mixed-up orientation that I have that's hard to explain."

"Baby, you're not mixed up. You're perfectly, logically, you. You are what you are."

"I know. But I think it's gonna be hard to make them understand my Mia-ness."

"Are you thinking about telling them? I uhm…thought that you were certain that you didn't want them to know."

"Things are different now, Jordan," she said, reaching down to grasp her hand. "We're not just dating now. I've never kept anything important from them—and you're very, very important."

"Thanks," she whispered. They sat in silence for a few minutes while each tried to think of a solution. "Maybe you could wait until the summer's over. That'll give you six months to prepare—maybe drop a few subtle hints."

"That won't work. I have to tell them before that because I have to make a decision about grad school."

"What do you mean?"

Mia shifted in her chair, as though she were sitting on a string of barbed wire. "I'm not sure I'm going to go."

"Pardon me?" Jordan gasped. "You've got to go!"

"But school starts at the end of August. I'd have to take over a week off to go to the Olympics, and believe me, I'm going to the Olympics." A smile broke through when she added, "I don't think law school is going to be like college. Missing a week might actually matter at Stanford."

Jordan let out a sigh and forced a smile onto her face. "We'll figure it out. I'm not sure how we'll do it, but we'll figure it out."

Chapter Fourteen

The Saturday softball games went as well as the Friday ones had. Once again, Jackie was toast after the first match, and Ryan ably took her place. They beat the University of Virginia handily, 6-1, with Ryan getting her first home run of the year, a solo shot in the first inning.

As usual, Jamie was waiting outside the locker room when Ryan emerged; grimy, sweaty and smiling. Jamie tossed a ball at her, which Ryan caught defensively. "What's this?"

"Your home run ball. You don't think I'm going to let them throw it back in with the rest of the balls, do you?"

Ryan blinked at her, surprised and puzzled. "But how...?"

"I saw a kid who works at the facility run out there to retrieve it. I caught him before he entered the clubhouse and gave him twenty bucks for it." She waggled her eyebrows Ryan-style, breaking her partner up, as usual.

"You're the best," she said, giving her a sweaty squeeze.

"I'm inspired to greatness."

After a quick clean-up, the pair headed to The Mirage to meet up with Jordan and Mia. "Have a nice day?" Ryan whispered into Mia's ear when they found them playing quarter slots.

"Yipes!" She turned and gave her a light slap in the gut. "You scared me!"

"Well, did you?" Ryan asked, unrepentant.

"Yes, we did, as a matter of fact. We've been vertical for nearly an hour now." She had a very pleased smile on her face, and Ryan nodded her approval.

"Good job. Now I won't feel bad demanding that you come to the game tomorrow. We swept today, so we're in the championship game tomorrow. It's not until two, so you can get your beauty rest."

"In my case, the correct term is resting with my beauty, but I get your point. We'll be there. Did you play?"

"Yep. Started the second game. Hit my first home run."

"Way to go, Boomer!" Jordan said. "You rule!"

"Thanks. We've been playing great. Haven't lost one yet."

"We'll definitely be there to root you on. I can't wait to see Heather, too. How's she doing?"

"Good. I wish we could have brought her tonight, but she skipped a grade and hasn't even turned eighteen yet—much less twenty-one. By the way, she and Ashley are tutoring Jennie, just like they said they would. She's a great kid."

"Does she get to play much?"

"Nope. She hasn't played in a real game yet, but she doesn't seem to mind. Coach likes to go with a hot hand—and Stephanie and Courtney are mowing people down. She'll play plenty if she sticks with it next year, though. I think she'll be good once she matures into her body a little bit. She pitched in the alumni game and did very well."

"So, what do you guys want to do tonight?" Jamie asked.

"I wanna go see 'O' again," Jordan said. "That show was so totally fine. We can't thank you guys enough."

"It was great, wasn't it?" Jamie asked. "Once Ryan got over her disappointment at not having lions and tigers and bears, she was goofy for it."

"Let's see if we can get tickets to see that freaky magician guy," Mia said. Jordan rolled her eyes and Ryan's mirrored her. "No interest," Jordan said.

Jamie sided with Mia's desire. "Come on, you two. It'll be fun."

"Doesn't sound like fun to me," Ryan said. "I don't like those big, staged shows."

"You enjoyed 'O' more than I've ever seen you enjoy anything."

"It was awesome," Ryan said, "but watching magic isn't in the same category. I wanna play poker, blackjack, or maybe craps."

"Me, too," Jordan said. Turning to Ryan, she asked, "What's craps?"

"Fine. We'll see if we can snare a couple of tickets," Jamie said. "And we won't tell you any of the cool things that happen."

Ryan had a perfect mental image of Jamie as a six-year-old, snubbing her little friends for refusing to go along with one of her ideas. Unable to resist her allure, she bent her head and kissed her soundly, pressing their bodies tightly together until Jamie relaxed against her. "I would have loved to have known you when you were a little girl."

Struggling to get her bearings, Jamie responded, "I didn't do things like that with my little girl friends. Elizabeth would not have approved."

"I'm glad she went back to England," Ryan said. "She doesn't sound like any fun at all."

Giving Ryan a squeeze, Jamie sent the jocks on their way. "You two have fun. The show's over at ten, so we'll come find you at either the poker or the blackjack tables."

"Okay," Ryan said. "Miss you already."

"Uh-huh. That's why you don't want to come with me."

"How can I miss you if you won't go away?" Ryan teased over her shoulder, drawing a fierce scowl that quickly turned into a smile and a blown kiss from her partner.

Ryan's luck was holding, and she amassed quite a nest egg from her two hours at the poker table. Jordan stuck with blackjack, making the hundred dollar bankroll she'd started with triple over the course of the evening. It was not yet ten o'clock, but because her concentration was beginning to wander, Ryan decided to cash out. She and Jordan went to the slot machines that bordered the blackjack area, thinking that Jamie and Mia would try that area first.

Jordan went to fetch some mineral water for them, since the free drinks were slow to come. Ryan wasn't paying much attention, slowly putting one quarter at a time into the machine. She felt a warm hand on her shoulder and turned, expecting to find Jamie. To her surprise, the woman now touching her back was part of the reason her concentration had flagged at the poker table, and she swallowed hard when she found herself face to face with the object of her distraction.

She looked like a model or an actress, and Ryan had a very vague sense of having seen her somewhere. She racked her brain, trying to remember any recent movies she'd seen, but came up blank. "You play well," the stranger said in a very friendly voice. Ryan swallowed, trying not to stare at the long, lean legs, shapely body, and generous breasts; or the long, light brown hair held back in a simple braid, showing off the well-defined planes of her face. Her eyes were hazel, and they were gazing avidly at Ryan.

Ryan shrugged, trying to avoid looking into the woman's beckoning eyes. "Anybody can pull a handle. The skill is in designing the computer program that sets the random payout for the machine."

The hand returned to her shoulder and squeezed a bit, sending a shiver down Ryan's spine. "I meant that you play poker well. I think you saw me watching you…didn't you."

A faint flush climbed Ryan's cheeks and she nodded. "Yeah. I thought maybe you were looking at someone else."

"No. Only you. You held my attention."

Ryan made a show of holding up her left hand, flexing her ring finger— hoping to blind this interloper with her diamonds. "Thanks. Uhm…but my attention is taken. I'm permanently partnered."

A tiny frown crossed her face and she said, "You've been by yourself all night…I assumed…"

"That makes perfect sense." She rose from her stool and started to move away, wanting to remove herself from this discussion as soon as possible.

The woman moved right with her, however, and put a hand on her arm, stopping her. "Are you forbidden to talk to people?"

"No, no, of course not," Ryan said, slightly flustered. She honestly didn't know what to do in this situation. She didn't want to be rude. Something inside told her that Jamie wouldn't be very happy to find her spending time with a beautiful stranger, no matter how innocent the situation. "I can talk to whomever I want, but you're wasting your time talking to me."

"You're pretty fond of yourself, aren't you?" she asked, tilting her head.

"No, I'm not," Ryan insisted, backing away. "But I have a lover, I don't live around here, and we'll never see each other again; so why not find someone who can show you a better time than I can?"

The woman tried unsuccessfully to hold back a smirk. "I don't think I've ever met anyone more henpecked than you are. Does she beat you for having fun?"

Ryan's eyes darkened, and she gave her a withering look. "That's not even remotely funny. I'm in love with my partner, and I've never met a woman who I'd prefer to spend my time with. Including tonight." She brushed past the woman, who followed right along beside her, trying to get in one last dig. But when they got to a small seating area, the stranger tripped on something, banging into Ryan, who fell onto the cushion of an overstuffed chair, the other woman falling right into her lap. Those dangerously long legs were now exposed up to mid thigh, and Ryan struggled to catch her breath.

"Did I hurt you?" she asked, feeling gently around Ryan's body to check for damage.

Trying to remove her wandering hands, Ryan sputtered, "No! Now, please get off my lap."

"I fell. I'm not trying to assault you! You're a good-looking woman, but I've had better. Get over yourself!"

Ceasing her attempts to extricate herself from the chair, Ryan gave her a chagrined look and said, "I'm sorry if it sounded like that. Really. I'm sorry."

"That's okay. You just shot me down awfully quickly. I'm…not used to that." She was sitting across Ryan's lap, with one arm draped around her shoulders. "Damn, my watch snagged on your sweater. I think I've almost got it…okay. I'm free."

As her admirer started to get up, Ryan heard Jamie's outraged voice. "Ryan! How could you!"

Grasping the woman by the waist, Ryan pushed her to her feet, calling out after her lover's departing form, "Jamie! It's not what it looks like! She fell onto my lap."

"Is that the best you could come up with?" Mia growled, giving Ryan a menacing look before she ran after her friend.

Ryan quickly made sure the woman had regained her balance, and ran as fast as she could, barely able to see Jamie's blonde head in the distance. Her heart was pounding so hard that she felt faint, but she kept going until she lost her partner near the progressive slots. Not having a clue of where to look, she started back for where she'd left Jordan. She got no more than ten feet when a pair of hands pushed her into a quiet corner. Now, a very familiar pair of lips met hers, and she immediately relaxed into the kiss. "You got me back, didn't you," she mumbled as her knees began to weaken.

"Yep." Jamie kissed her again, ratcheting up the passion. "You've been had."

"You can have me any time you want me," Ryan said, smiling down at her. "And, for the record, I'll never play another practical joke on you. You're fucking vicious!"

"Sure am. I've got to pull out all the stops when I'm dealing with the likes of you."

Both laughing, they walked back to find their friends, Ryan pausing to ask, "How did you find someone to play that joke on me?"

"I recognized her from the Bimbo Express," Jamie said. "Cost me a hundred dollars." She cocked her head at Ryan and said, "See how serious I am about getting revenge? I could have had sex with her for twenty minutes for that price, but I spent my whole allotment getting back at you."

"Thanks, I think."

"She assured me that she was the best in the business, but she's a rank amateur compared to you. I know you're the tops."

"Even though your opinion is based on pure speculation, I'm very glad to hear it," Ryan said, giving her lover a blissful smile.

After they saw Jamie and Ryan off for the evening, Mia asked, "Where to now?"

Jordan shrugged. "I don't want to gamble any more. I'm up five hundred and I'm using it for a plane ticket." At Mia's raised eyebrow, Jordan tapped Mia's nose with her finger, then placed a tiny kiss there. "A plane ticket to come see you. I can't bear to be away from you for longer than a month."

"Let's not talk about being apart right now, okay?" Mia asked gently, her face reflecting her sadness over their impending separation. "Let's try to stay upbeat. I hate to waste any minute that we have together."

"You're right. Let's go back to our room. There's nothing that appeals to me more than being alone with you."

When they reached the room, Mia said, "Let's fire up that spa tub. Jamie said they didn't have time to use it, and I hate to see it go to waste."

"Good deal. I'll go get us some ice while you fill it. I brought a bottle of white wine."

Several minutes later, the pair was comfortably ensconced in the deep, whirling waters of the tub, sipping at the wine Jordan had brought. "I've been thinking about what you said last night," Jordan said. "I hope you know that I'll do anything I can to help you if you decide to tell your parents."

"I do," she said quietly, "but I don't know how to do it. I need to think about it for a while."

"What about Peter? Could he tell them first?"

"I've considered that, but I think it would hurt them to think I was afraid of telling them. I'm sure he'd do it, though. He's always willing to go to bat for me."

"I can't wait to meet him," Jordan said. "He sounds like a great brother."

"He is. You know, I think you'll like my parents, too. They're nice people, Jordy, and once they get over their shock, I'm sure they'll be fine." She gave her a squeeze and said, "Someday we'll be sitting around the dinner table at their house, laughing about how afraid we were to tell them about our relationship."

Jordan had been cupping her hand and pouring water over Mia's shoulders, but she stopped abruptly. "Do you honestly see that happening?"

"Uhm...yeah. What's wrong? Don't you want to have a relationship with them?"

Letting out a long sigh, Jordan closed her eyes and shook her head. "Of course, I do. I just didn't know that you wanted to have a...normal relationship. You know, like Ryan has with her family, and like Jamie has with her mom."

"Normal?"

"I don't even know what I'm talking about," Jordan said quickly, her head shaking roughly. "Forget it."

Grasping her arm, Mia held her still and said, "No, I don't want to forget it. What did you mean?"

"I guess I'm still fixated on what you told me when we were in L.A. with Ryan and Jamie. You were so clear that you didn't want anyone to know about us, and it throws me when you talk about things like we're a regular couple."

"We are a regular couple, sweetheart." She looked into Jordan's eyes. "When I said those things in L.A. I was in a very different place. I thought we were only playing, and I didn't want things to get complicated between us. It seemed to me that if no one knew, it wouldn't be a big deal if it didn't work out. Do you know what I mean?"

Nodding briefly, Jordan waited for her to continue.

"We're not playing any more," Mia whispered, snuggling closer as she tilted her head upwards. Her breath was warm and sweet, and Jordan was drawn towards her, their noses nearly touching. "I'm deeply in love with you, and you can take everything I said in L.A. and trash it. I want to tell my parents about us. I want to tell my friends about us. I want everyone I know to know how special you are, and how much you mean to me." A few hot tears slid down Jordan's face and Mia kissed them away as they fell. "I love you," she whispered between kisses. "I want to share my life, and all of the people in my life, with you."

"How much of your life?" Jordan's faint voice asked.

"All of it," Mia promised. "I want to share everything with you."

"For how long?" The look on her face was one of pure terror, and Mia couldn't answer fast enough.

"Forever," she whispered. "I want to love you forever."

The sun peeked over the mountains, spreading a warm orange glow over the room. The heat radiated through the large window, painting the glistening bodies with a vivid, golden light. "Is this what being in love feels like for everyone?" Jordan's lazy, soft voice asked.

"Don't know." Mia was lying on her belly, too enervated to even think of moving. Not that she could move much even if she'd wanted to, since Jordan was sprawled on top of her, her head pillowed between Mia's shoulder blades. When she spoke, the vibrations hummed against Jordan's cheek, making her smile serenely. "It's never been like this for me."

"Am I crushing you? Not that I could move if I were."

"Uh-huh." Mia's voice was a little wispy from her inability to take a deep breath, but as Jordan tried to roll off, she placed a restraining hand on her hip. "I like it."

"You like to be crushed?"

"No, but I want to share your skin. This is the closest I think I can get."

"Let's try it the other way." Summoning a burst of energy, Jordan rolled off and lay on her back, then pulled Mia on top of her. "How's this?"

Nuzzling her head against the softest breast imaginable, Mia sighed deeply. "Preferable. My ribs thank you."

"Tell me how it's been for you before."

She tried to recall the way she'd felt in the past, finding those thoughts elusive. It felt like it had been years and years since she'd been in love. "I've thought I was in love before, Jordy. But, now I'm not so sure. It never, ever felt like this."

Jordan reached up and started to run her fingers through Mia's curls. Immediately, Mia moved to optimally position herself so Jordan would be encouraged to continue.

"Give me more," Jordan said. "How's it different?"

"Mmm…lots of ways. But it's hardly fair to make the comparison, because I know that I wasn't really in love before."

"But you thought you were."

"Yeah, yeah, I did. I was just wrong. I think it's easy to confuse desire with love—especially when you're young."

"Did you think you were in love with your high school boyfriend?"

"Who, Mark?"

"Maybe. Was he the guy you were with during your senior year?"

"Yeah, that was Mark. It's hard to believe that was only four years ago. Looking back, I was only a girl then. I'm starting to have more empathy for my parents." She started to laugh, making Jordan's body jiggle as well. "They knew I was just a kid, but I was sure I was an adult, and should be able to make all of my own decisions."

"Tell me about Mark," Jordan said. "You've never spoken about him much."

"That's because there isn't a lot to tell. He was a good catch: tall, good-looking, popular, a good athlete—and a total goof-off in school. My ideal man," she added, giggling. "I liked him, we got along pretty well in bed, and he was a lot of fun when we went out."

"When did you realize that you didn't love him?"

Mia thought for a minute, trying to recall the chain of events. "I guess I was certain that I didn't love him when I started wishing he and Trey would leave so I could be alone with Melissa. I don't think that's the normal reaction of a woman in love." She gave Jordan a sad, wistful smile, and Jordan squeezed her a little tighter.

"Does it make you sad to talk about this?"

"Mmm…a little I guess. I…I wish I'd had the guts to let myself face my feelings for Melissa. I think I could have loved her."

"Do you really? I got the impression she was only a sex partner."

"Well, that's the impression I wanted *her* to have. And that's what I tried to make myself believe. But I had feelings for her, Jordy. I felt so much when she held me—so much more than I did when I was with Mark." She shook her head, her ringlets trailing across Jordan's chest. "I wish I'd let myself explore being vulnerable with her. I'm not sure it would have worked out, but of the people I've slept with, I felt more for her than for anyone else, until you, of course."

"It's okay if you loved her, Mia, you can be honest with me."

Lifting her head so she could stare into Jordan's eyes, Mia said, "If I'd loved her like I do you, I wouldn't have been able to be in the kind of denial I was in. I'd risk anything for you, Jordy. I wouldn't even give Melissa a hint that I had feelings for her. That's not love."

"I guess you're right. You have to be able to risk to love someone."

"You do. You also have to be kinda selfless. That's another big difference for me. I think of you first. That's never happened to me before. Like with Jason," she said. "I spent a lot of time trying to make sure he wasn't getting the better end of the deal. I used to try to protect myself in case he hurt me, too. But I don't do that with you. I'm as open with you as I am with my family, and that's very different for me." Seeing the cautious look in the blue eyes gazing at her, she added, "It's good different."

"I think of you first, too. I get up and turn on my computer every morning, and I have the weather for San Francisco on my start page. I think about you waking up, and I actually say, 'It's gonna be chilly today, Mia. Make sure you wear a jacket to school.'" She laughed softly and said, "I don't normally notice if the people around me are even clothed. But I'm fixated on your comfort and your safety and your happiness. I've never ever felt this close to anyone." Her eyes showed pure terror. "It scares me to death."

"I know," Mia whispered. She tucked her hands under Jordan's body and rocked her gently. "I know it's hard for you to trust me not to hurt you."

"I feel so exposed. I've never let anyone in like I have you. I'm not used to being so vulnerable."

"We're both vulnerable, baby," Mia said. "We have to treat each other's heart like it's the most fragile thing on earth. I promise to do everything I can to make it safe for you."

"I do, too," Jordan whispered. They sealed their promises with a tender kiss, then Mia began to relax, and in a few minutes she was sound asleep, her body limp and heavy. Jordan wrapped her arms around her and forced herself to remain awake, savoring the weight and feel of Mia's body, the scent and texture of her skin, the pattern of her breathing. As the sensations flooded her brain, she sighed and allowed herself to experience the depths of emotion she felt for her lover. A small grin split her face, and she gratefully acknowledged, *This is what it feels like to love and be loved.*

They were nowhere near on time, but Jordan and Mia finally arrived at the stadium as the third inning began. "Did we miss anything good?" Mia asked Jamie as she squinted into the amazingly bright sun.

"Nope. No hits, no runs. Ryan and Heather are both on the bench."

"Sorry we're late," Jordan said. "We had a hard time getting organized."

Jamie grinned back at her. "It's happened to me a time or two. Sometimes Ryan organizes me so thoroughly that I'm nearly paralyzed."

Jordan blushed fiercely, but she didn't dispute Jamie's tease. "Softball's kinda slow moving, huh?" she said, to take the focus off herself.

Jamie showed the textbook on her lap. "It can be like watching paint dry. I'm only interested if Ryan's playing."

"You're a good partner," Jordan said, patting her thigh. "I'm sure Ryan appreciates that you come to her games."

"Oh, she'll have her fill of watching me play golf. That's not her favorite thing in the world, either. The only difference is that I actually get to play."

"Doesn't it bother her to sit on the bench? It would drive me crazy!"

"It honestly doesn't seem to," Jamie said. "It surprised me, too, but she seems perfectly fine with it. I think she enjoys the team experience as much as the playing experience, and she likes her teammates a lot."

"I like my teammates as long as I'm on the court," Jordan said. "If I were on the bench for long, I'd be plotting a debilitating accident for one of them."

As usual, Mia needed something to munch on, and she went in search of junk food. Jamie looked at Jordan and noticed a peacefulness to her expression that was quite rare. She patted her leg and commented simply, "You look happy."

A wide smile telegraphed her reply. "Mia makes me happy."

"I think it goes both ways. She talks about you with a depth of emotion that I've never heard from her. You're good for each other."

Jordan cocked her head a bit, and looked at Jamie speculatively. "I assume you know about her getting into Stanford?"

"Yeah. Pretty awesome, huh?"

"It didn't surprise me. I know she's capable of anything that interests her. She's a very bright woman."

"She is. She doesn't always want people to know it—but she is."

"Do you think she wants to be a lawyer?" Jordan's face reflected her doubt, and Jamie wasn't able to reassure her.

"I've known her for almost eight years, and when she told me she was admitted, that was the first time she's ever mentioned the idea. If it's been a burning desire, she's kept it well hidden."

"That's what I'm afraid of," she mused. "I don't know what's behind her desire to go—maybe it's only to please her father."

"Maybe. She's very fond of him, and I know he's thrilled." She shrugged her shoulders and said, "I think it might be a way to stay in school for a while. She's not crazy about school, but I know she's not terribly interested in any particular line of work. Maybe a few more years of school will help her make up her mind about what she wants to do." Jordan nodded, but didn't look convinced. Jamie patted her leg and asked, "What about you? What do you want to do when your time with the team is over?"

"Oh. I'm going to be an architect." There wasn't a glimmer of doubt in her statement.

"I've never heard you mention that. Is that a new goal?"

"Oh, no. I made up my mind when I was in grade school." She gave Jamie her usual enigmatic smile, and Jamie mused that she didn't know one thing about Jordan that she hadn't learned as a result of a direct question. Jordan would reveal her secrets—but you had to know exactly what questions to ask.

"You'll be quite the power couple. An architect and an attorney."

"The power part means nothing to me, but the couple part means everything." She turned her attention back to the game, and Jamie gave her another puzzled glance. *There's a lot going on behind those blue eyes, and Mia's just the one to pull it out of her.*

Ryan didn't get the call until the top of the seventh, when Coach Roberts sent her in to pinch-run for Jackie. All three of her fans focused their attention on her, with Jordan commenting, "God, she looks like she's seven feet tall."

Jamie giggled at her comment, but she had to admit that it was accurate. "I think it's because so many of the women are particularly short. This obviously isn't a tall woman's game."

"It's kinda cute," Mia said. "She's so comfortable with her height that it looks very natural."

"She is. I'm not sure how Martin did it, but he helped her have confidence in her body." Turning to Jordan, she commented, "You seem very much at ease with your height, too."

"Yeah, I am. Probably because I got so much acclaim from my sport. It's a good thing to be a tall volleyball player, and I got praise heaped on me when I grew an inch. Plus, my mother's tall, and she thought it was a good thing if I wanted to model."

"She encouraged you to do that, honey?" Mia asked. "You never told me that."

"Yeah," she said absently, her attention focused on Ryan. "She was a pretty well-known model when she was young. She thinks it's a great way to make a living."

"Your mom was a model?" Mia had never heard a whisper about this fact.

"Yep. Cover girl. Most of the important ones are framed and hanging in a very well-lit wall in her house. She quit when she had Gunnar." She turned to Mia, and added, "My dad says that she was planning on going back, but she got pregnant with me—unexpectedly. Apparently, she wasn't aware that she was pregnant; she was so thin that she often missed a period. She didn't know she was pregnant until she was four months along—too late to have an abortion." She shrugged and gave Mia a half smile. "Good thing she didn't gain much weight, huh?"

"Oh, Jordy, why would anyone tell you that?" Mia reached out and grasped her lover's hand, giving it a squeeze while looking at her with tears in her eyes.

"I don't know," Jordan said quietly. "But I remember her telling me dozens of times that she would have been one of the top models of her era—if it hadn't been for me. She had to make sure I knew I'd screwed up her plans."

Mia stared straight ahead, her eyes focused on Ryan, who was moving around on her base, but her mind filled with thoughts of a young Jordan. "I'd sacrifice anything to have a daughter as wonderful as you are," she sighed. "I wish she appreciated what she has."

"Not gonna happen," Jordan said briskly. "No sense wishing for what will never be." She said this so matter-of-factly that only Mia noticed the flash of pain and longing that briefly flitted across her features.

Ryan was dancing around first base, trying to distract the pitcher, but her tactics were ineffective. The next two batters struck out—leaving her stranded. Jamie sighed and shrugged. "Oh well, at least she didn't get hurt."

"That's not a small accomplishment for her," Jordan said. "Coach Placer used to get so pissed off at her. She'd go running up into the stands to return a ball—nearly breaking her neck to get to it—and this was during warm ups. She gets so focused that it doesn't matter to her that the play is meaningless."

"She's like that about everything," Jamie said, sparing a fond glance at her partner, who was throwing the ball around the infield to warm up. "If Ryan does something, she does it with every bit of effort and concentration that she has." She thought about her statement for a moment and added, "It's her best and her most frustrating trait."

Mia giggled and tucked an arm around Jordan, giving her a squeeze. "My Jordy's no slacker in the effort and concentration department, either. I'd have to say it's all good in her case."

Jordan looked down and acted like she hadn't heard the compliment. Jamie added, "I admit it's a wonderful thing most of the time—but I'd like to see you try to pull her away from her computer when she's working on a math problem. She doesn't know I'm talking to her—she doesn't see me if I stand right next to her—and if I touch her, she nearly jumps out of her seat. I swear I'm going to give the poor thing a heart attack."

"You've gotta take the bitter with the sweet," Mia said. "Having the full concentration of these big girls is worth whatever little problems we have to put up with."

"Can't argue with you," Jamie said, delighted to wring yet another blush from the usually unflappable Jordan.

The bottom-half of the seventh inning passed without incident, securing Cal's victory. Ryan was upbeat and relaxed when she emerged from the locker room, Heather in tow. The three former teammates started chattering about volleyball, the Olympic team, and some of their former pals. Jamie and Mia finally sat down on the bleachers and watched the threesome for a few minutes. "Heather sure comes out of her shell when the topic turns to volleyball, doesn't she?" Jamie asked.

"I've never heard two words from the girl," Mia observed. "She's pretty bubbly when you get her going."

"We'd better break up the party soon. We're gonna have to rush to make the plane."

Mia shook her head, staring at Jordan as she said, "I'm on the verge of dropping out of school to go to Colorado with her. It's tearing me apart to let her leave."

"I know, but I'm sure she doesn't want you to do that. You've only got three months left. Can't you tough it out?"

"I'm gonna try, but I can't guarantee anything. I feel so good when I'm with her, Jamie. She…makes me see the world in a whole new way. Everything is brighter when we're together."

"I know exactly what you mean. There's nothing better than being loved."

"And there's nothing worse than being away from the one you love." With a dejected slump to her shoulders, Mia went to fetch her partner so they could get to the airport in time for yet another parting.

Mia was able to secure a seat on the plane taking the team back, and after a few ticket swaps the threesome was able to sit together. Jamie preferred the window, and Ryan was partial to the aisle, so Mia sat between them. She was uncharacteristically glum and non-communicative; and once the plane was in the air, Ryan took one look at her face and tucked an arm around her shoulders. "Come here," she urged, drawing Mia close. The smaller woman raised the armrest and cuddled up to her body, resting her head on Ryan's shoulder. Jamie gave her partner an appreciative grin and started patting Mia's leg, to show her support. "It'll be okay," Ryan soothed, her voice soft and gentle. "You'll be together soon. As soon as you graduate, you can go to Colorado and be together."

"This will be the longest three months of my life," Mia sighed, and both Jamie and Ryan knew that statement was the absolute truth.

When they were lying in bed later that night, Jamie cuddled up next to her partner and asked, "How'd you make out this weekend? I saw a lot of greenbacks bulging in your wallet."

"Mmm, I'd say I came out even. I had about a hundred dollars of change that I'd collected before I started, and now I've got a hundred dollar bill and a pocketful of change."

Jamie sat up abruptly, her hand on Ryan's chest for support. "What? I didn't see you lose a lot. Where did it all go?"

Ryan shrugged, and made a non-committal gesture. "Easy come, easy go. I'm happy."

With a quick knock, their door flew open, revealing a sobbing Mia. She was holding some papers in her hand and she shook them in the couple's direction. "Which one of you did this?" she asked, her voice nearly incomprehensible.

"Did what?" Jamie asked.

"No biggie," Ryan said simultaneously.

Mia gave both of them fervid hugs, reserving a bone-crushing one for Ryan. "You are the most thoughtful woman on earth," she murmured, her lips pressed against Ryan's hair.

"I told you before, money I win gambling is like Monopoly money to me. It gives me a lot of pleasure to share it with my friends."

"Anybody want to clue me in?" Jamie asked, still befuddled.

"Your girlfriend bought me a roundtrip ticket to Denver," Mia said. "You are a remarkable woman, Ryan O'Flaherty."

"She has a point, Jamie," Ryan agreed, drawing smiles from her audience.

Chapter Fifteen

Early the next morning, Ryan paced in front of the Oakland office building, waiting for the therapist to open the door. She had staked out a spot as far as possible from the door, giving herself the ability to see when Ellen went inside. From her previous visit, she knew that the lobby was open, but she didn't have any interest in making small talk with the other women, so she paced and drank her coffee, trying not to look as nervous as she was.

She nearly spit a mouthful of latte when a quiet voice right behind her said, "Hi, Ryan."

Whirling, she stared, wide-eyed, at Barb, the police officer who had accidentally shot and killed her partner. "How did you get behind me?" she asked, her heart racing. "I can always hear when someone's near me."

"I'm a cop...or I was a cop," Barb said, looking towards the door of the building. "The lobby's open, you know."

"Yeah, I know."

"Nervous?"

Ryan nodded, saying nothing.

"I was, too. Still am, sometimes. Every Monday and Thursday morning, I have to give myself a pep talk to make myself come here again."

"I only come because I don't want to disappoint my lover. I know she wants me to get over my anger and my guilt, and I want her to know I'm doing all I can to work through this."

"It'll get easier. That's a promise." She took a long look at Ryan and said, "If you're anything like me, having strangers know about your demons is really painful."

Ryan nodded again, her hands shoved into the rear pockets of her jeans. "It sucks."

"The most encouraging thing I can tell you is that over time, these women won't be strangers any more. They'll be your friends."

"I've got all the friends I need," Ryan said, giving Barb a half-smile. "I'm only looking for someone who can help pull me out of this funk."

"It might take a while, but I think we can be more help than you might imagine."

"Ellen's here," Ryan said, twitching her head towards the door. "Let's go spill our guts."

Barb laughed softly, saying, "You remind me more of a cop than a student at Berkeley. Aren't you supposed to be into that touchy-feely stuff?"

"My dad's a firefighter. We don't go in for touchy-feely much."

"No wonder I liked you immediately," Barb said. "My dad was a firefighter, too. What house is your dad with?"

The pair walked towards the building, talking about the fire department, and laughing in surprise at the large number of people they both knew. As they got to the office door, Ryan took a breath, feeling significantly lighter than she had mere minutes earlier.

When Jordan reached Mia that evening she was uncharacteristically lethargic. "Hi."

"What's up, Jordy?" Mia bubbled. "How was practice?"

"It was okay. Hey, I got a call from my agent tonight and she's got another ad for Ralph Lauren lined up for me."

"That's great! Are you gonna take it?"

"Yeah, I guess I have to."

"What's up? You don't sound like yourself."

Jordan yawned loudly, unable to stop herself. "I'm so tired. I had a great time with you this weekend, but I'm paying for it today. I felt like I had lead shoes on at practice." She chuckled softly, but Mia knew her well enough to recognize that Jordan was not a whiner, and would only mention a problem if it was extreme.

"Jordy, if you're complaining about it, it must be bothering you a lot. Now what's going on?"

"I guess it's hard for me to get used to the pace. Even though I've played the sport for years, I've never focused on it to the exclusion of everything else, you know?"

"I'm not sure I do. Tell me what you mean."

Jordan sighed and said, "We practice twice a day, for two hours at a time. There isn't a moment that we're not flying around the gym like lunatics, either. It's very high intensity stuff. Then I have to weight train three times a week, and I work on my jumping twice a week. We also run three days a week; and in this thin air, that's tough to get used to. I need my weekend to veg," she said quietly. "I wish I didn't have to, but I can't keep up if I don't sleep for most of the weekend."

Fighting the hurt that her lover's words caused, Mia said, "I understand. We won't schedule any more weekend trips. I don't want you to wear yourself down."

"No, that's not it. I get such a boost from seeing you that it's worth the fatigue. It's the modeling that's worrying me. This shoot is in LA, and it's three full days. That's good money, but I'll be sitting or standing around most of the time while they adjust lights and fuss with my hair. It's truly mind numbing. God, I wish I didn't have to do this crap."

"Jordan," Mia soothed. "You don't have to do it. It's only money. Don't let that be the only factor you consider."

"It has to be. It's gonna cost a load to buy business class plane tickets for my mother and grandmother and brother…"

"You're paying for all of them?"

"Well, yeah," she said defensively. "Gunnar's gonna pay for their hotel, but I have to pay for the air fare and tickets to the opening ceremonies. Then I'll have to pay for all three of them to go to whatever other events they're interested in. And believe me, if Gunnar doesn't come through, I'll have to pay for the hotel too."

"Jordan, you don't have to do that. If you want to, that's one thing, but you don't have to."

"But, I said I would," she said quietly. "I have to. You don't know…"

Realizing that she was pushing too hard, Mia backed off. "I'm sorry. You're right. I don't know what it's like for you. But that doesn't stop me from worrying about you."

"I'll be okay," she said. "I'm gonna grab a bite and go to bed. I'm thrashed."

Looking at her watch, Mia saw that it was only seven thirty in Colorado Springs. "Please take care of yourself. You can't afford to get sick."

"Don't I know it. I've got to make an impression on the coaches. The last thing I want is to be an alternate on the damned team. I've got to start kicking ass."

Pausing a moment, Mia asked, "When do you have to go to LA?"

"Thursday night," Jordan said through another massive yawn. "I got permission to miss practice on Friday."

"I'm going to drive down to be with you. I want to make sure you're eating right, and that you're in bed early every night."

Jordan paused for a beat, unable to wipe the smile from her face. "I have to go to bed early to sleep. That's not what we're best at. Don't you remember seeing the dawn on Saturday and Sunday?"

"Holding you while you sleep is the second most pleasurable thing we do in bed. I'll take that over sleeping alone any time."

"If you're sure," Jordan said, her voice taking on a hint of her normal sparkle.

"I'm positive. I'm your support team."

The next morning, the ringing phone woke her earlier than she would have liked, but Mia stumbled to her feet and croaked out a hello.

"Oh-oh," her brother's amused voice replied. "Someone was still in bed."

"That's okay," she yawned. "What's up?"

"I had an idea, and I thought you could investigate it a little."

"Shoot," she said, struggling to wake up, since Peter's ideas were usually very sound.

Mia headed down to Palo Alto that afternoon and spent quite a while speaking with a sympathetic woman in the admissions office of Stanford law school. When she was satisfied with her answers, she headed north for Hillsborough.

Anna Lisa seemed shocked, but very pleased, to see her daughter stroll into the kitchen. "Mia! Is everything all right?"

"Yep," she said, snitching a carrot from the salad her mother was making. "It's the four a.m. phone calls from the lock-up that you have to worry about. An in-person appearance is usually good news."

Her mother gave her a playful swat on the seat and said, "So, tell me some good news."

"Is Dad home?"

"Yes, he's upstairs changing."

"Is that Mia's voice?" Adam called out as he descended the stairs.

"Sure is," she replied, going to meet him for a hug and a kiss.

"What a nice surprise! Are you staying for dinner?"

"Of course. I even brought one of my books. I thought I'd hang out with you guys this evening." Adam and Anna Lisa exchanged puzzled glances that Mia caught. "I miss you both. Is that okay?"

"Of course it is, honey, but you haven't been around much lately. Is everything all right?"

"Yes, Dad, everything is fine. As a matter of fact, I'm in the neighborhood because I spoke with the people in the admissions office at the law school, and they've agreed to let me defer my admission for a year."

"What does that mean?" Anna Lisa asked.

"It means that I'll enroll next fall instead of this one. I'll still go—I'm merely going to wait a year."

"Does this decision make your boyfriend happy?" Anna Lisa asked, guessing that the unknown boyfriend was directing Mia's decisions.

She looked at her mother for a few moments, then said, "I haven't discussed this with anyone but you. You know, you might not see it, but I've grown up a lot in the last year. I think I need a year off before I can throw myself into law school. My brain's tired."

"How about coming down to the firm and clerking for a year?" Adam asked hopefully.

Peter had warned her about this potential development, and she had a ready answer. "No, as tempting as that sounds, I'd like to do something different—something that I'll never be able to do once I'm in the working world."

"Like?" Anna Lisa asked suspiciously.

"I'm not sure yet." *Especially since Peter just gave me this delayed admission idea this morning!* "I might do some volunteer work," she suggested, hoping that her father would bite the hook.

"I think that's a fine idea. I'd be more than happy to support you while you did that, Mia."

Yes! "Okay, Dad, I'll check out the opportunities, and see if there's something I can do for a year that'll be rewarding."

He tucked his arm around her and gave her a gentle hug. "You're turning into a fine young woman. We're lucky to have you."

Late the next night, after a long discussion with the cousins, and more beer than she should have drunk, Ryan suppressed a yawn as she followed her partner up to bed, switching off the lights as they moved through the house.

"That went better than I had hoped," Jamie said, falling onto the bed.

"Me, too. It was so nice to see Frank and Niall walk out together with their arms around each other's shoulders. If Frank's excited about the concept, everyone else will be, too."

"I'm glad they decided to think about it over the weekend," Jamie said as she walked into the bathroom to begin brushing her teeth. "I didn't want them to jump into the plan too quickly. Better to make sure they all agree."

"I think it'll work. And I want you to know how grateful I am that you've worked so hard to make this happen. There's no better way to show me that you love both me and my family."

"Right on both counts," Jamie said. "And thanks for letting me drive home. I guess I'd better get used to being the designated driver when we're with the boys, huh?"

"Not a bad thought," Ryan said, smiling slowly. "I don't normally drink this much on a school night. I kept looking at you, and thinking about being away from you for five days. I kept drinking so I didn't start crying."

"I've been trying not to think of it at all. I didn't used to mind your being away for a few days…but now…"

"Yeah, that's it. I feel like my mental health is dependent on having you near. I'm freaked about leaving."

"This should be the last time this happens," Jamie reminded her. "It's bad luck that my first spring tournament starts on Sunday. I would have gone with you—even for a couple of days, but I can't miss class tomorrow."

"That's all right. I need to get some of my confidence back. Being alone and surviving is good practice."

"You'll survive," Jamie whispered, pressing her lips against the edge of Ryan's ear. "You have me in your heart, baby. I'll watch over you every moment."

"Will you hold me tight tonight, Jamers? I need to feel your arms around me."

Quickly, Jamie stood and undressed, then she undressed her partner as well, looking into Ryan's eyes with total understanding. "Come on, love," she urged, pulling back the covers. She scooted up higher than normal, and patted her chest. Ryan gratefully lay alongside her and placed her head just above Jamie's soft breast.

"I don't want to leave you," Ryan murmured, and Jamie felt her partner's warm tears roll down her skin.

"I don't want you to leave. But we'll both be fine. I'm only a phone call away—any time of the day or night. Promise me you'll call if you're feeling scared or lonely."

"I promise," Ryan said, sniffling softly.

"Come on, now and try to relax. You've got to get up early to go to your group."

"Oh, great! I get to sit in a room with a bunch of strangers when I'm feeling this bruised. Now I feel better."

❧

At three a.m., Mia woke to feel a shivering body slide into bed next to her. "Hey, what's wrong?" she mumbled, trying to clear her mind.

"Nightmare," Jamie said, her teeth chattering noisily.

"Why are you so cold? You're shivering."

"Not cold…scared."

"Oh, come here," Mia said, wrapping her arms around her friend. "Cuddle up tight, James, it's gonna be all right."

"I'm worried about her, and about me," Jamie muttered. "We're gonna be apart for five days, and she won't have anyone to watch over her."

"She has friends, James. Isn't Jackie her roommate?"

"Yeah, but she's a jock roommate. I'm sure Ryan would never tell Jackie about her fears. My baby is a long, long way from normal, and I'm worried that being all alone will hurt her progress."

"Can't you go with her for the first couple of days? I know your golf thing is on Sunday…"

"No, I can't. I've got a full day of class tomorrow, and I have a test in the afternoon. The last flight's at five thirty, and I'd never make it." She fell back against the pillow and said, "I thought it would be okay, but Ryan was very fragile tonight. Damn! I should have prepared for this. I could manage to go on Friday morning, and come back on Saturday night. I should get on the computer and make reservations."

"But that would only give you one night together. That's a hell of a trip for one night."

"I know, and that's why I didn't do it. But, isn't one night better than none? I was being selfish," Jamie muttered. "I hate to spend the better part of two days flying to and from New Mexico when I have so much homework to catch up on. The flight takes at least five hours, with a stopover in Phoenix, and I know I wouldn't get any work done on the plane. I was honestly looking forward to having a couple of days alone." She shook her head, wiping at a few tears. "I wasn't thinking of her."

"Hey, hey, you're always thinking of her," Mia insisted. "You need to think of yourself, too, James. It's not a sin to want some time to catch up on things."

"Fuck! What am I gonna do? I'll be worried about her all weekend if I don't go for at least one day."

"Look, let me call Jordan in the morning and tell her I'm going to go to New Mexico, instead of LA. I can stay for the whole weekend. It's what Jordan would want, James. I'm sure of it."

"No, No, I can't let you do that. Jordan needs you right now, and you need to see her."

"Yeah, we do, but neither of us is traumatized like you two are. I'd be happy to do it, James. Ryan means so much to me."

Jamie slipped her arms around her friend and cried softly, while Mia gently ran her fingers through her hair. "I love you. You're the best friend I've ever had."

"I love you, too, and so does Jordan. I'll call her in the morning and tell her about the change of plans."

Jamie sat up and straightened her hair. "No, you don't have to do that. You've given me an idea that I think can work. Thanks so much." She leaned forward and kissed her friend tenderly on the lips. "Thanks for being my friend."

"That's one job that has no down-sides, James. It's always a pleasure."

Thursday evening found Jordan standing in front of a heavy hotel room door, with Mia standing in front of her, mouth agape. The bellman had just departed, and Mia was obviously having trouble adjusting to their accommodations at the luxe Bel-Air Hotel. "Damn, Jordy, this is living large!"

"Yeah," she said, "I actually haven't traveled for many jobs, and I wasn't sure what to expect. This is pretty sweet."

"I'm starved," Mia said, peeking into the mini-bar. "Can I raid the bar?"

"You can, but why don't we go down to the pool and have an early dinner? They serve until five."

"Cool. I wish it were warm enough to swim."

"No such luck. We used to start swimming in April or May, just like the rest of the country. You get an occasional ninety degree day, but it's still usually fifty at night—not warm enough for the pool to retain any heat."

Mia grasped her hand as they exited the room and headed towards the pool. "It's hard for me to picture you growing up down here." Cocking her head slightly, she said, "Maybe it's because you don't talk about it much. It's like your life started when you got to Berkeley."

With a half-smile, Jordan tossed her blonde hair over her shoulder and said, "In a way it did. My bad memories about growing up are as plentiful as the good ones. I guess I try to erase them all."

"Would you show me around a little?" Mia asked tentatively. "I'd like to see the house where you grew up, where you went to school…stuff like that."

"Okay, we can do that. I can have the limo drive us by my mother's home—but I'm not going in." She lapsed into pensive silence while they walked, not speaking again until they were seated at a nice table right on the edge of the pool deck. Mia scooted her chair out from under the large, buff-colored market umbrella so the late-afternoon sun could warm her. Looking around, she asked in a quiet voice, "Isn't that Steven Spielberg?" pointing discreetly at the next table.

Jordan sighed and said, "Yeah, as a matter of fact it is. That's Jeffrey Katzenberg with him. I'd better go say hello. Want to come?"

Mia stared at her, nonplussed, sure that Jordan was toying with her. When she didn't answer, Jordan shrugged and pushed her chair back. She approached the two men with her confident, smooth gait, looking like she was completely used to rubbing elbows with the power brokers of Hollywood.

Gaping openly, Mia watched in amazement as Jordan conversed cordially for a few minutes then tilted her head in Mia's direction and said goodbye. Both men stood and kissed her cheek, offering a wave to Mia when Jordan sat back down.

It took Mia a moment to collect herself enough to ask, "You know them?"

"Yeah. I told you that my dad's in development at Paramount. He's worked with both of them—Steven more so than Jeffrey, since Jeffrey was with Disney doing animated features for so many years. I've been to Steven's house on a couple of occasions—I actually like the house he and Amy Irving had better than the one he lives in now." She was being remarkably casual about the whole thing, and Mia struggled to take it all in.

"I guess I've never thought of you as being a Hollywood kid."

"Well, I'm not really. You've got to be in the biz to know my dad. His connections are more to producers and directors than to actors. We were just another family making a living in Hollywood rather anonymously."

Their server arrived, and after Mia ordered a chicken Caesar salad, Jordan asked for something not on the menu, much to Mia's surprise. "I'd like a vegetable salad," she said. "Blanched or steamed, no oil, no butter. Green or yellow vegetables only. No carrots or cauliflower."

"Would you like a dressing for that?"

"No, thank you. And an iced tea."

Mia pondered her order for a moment as the waiter scribbled a note. Jordan was usually the type who would gratefully take whatever was placed in front of her. In their time together, Mia had never seen her put much thought into what she ate, as long as it filled her up—not always an easy task. She must have looked a little puzzled, because Jordan gave her a shrug and said, "My belly has to be flat for the shoot."

Mia had seen every delicious inch of Jordan's body, and the perfectly smooth abdomen she loved didn't have a spare cell. "Honey, you're practically concave as it is," she reminded her.

"Yeah. It's the practically part that I'm worried about. This is an ad for Polo sportswear. I'll be showing a lot of skin."

"Ooo, I'm glad I came. The more the merrier."

"Mark my words," Jordan said, nodding to the server as he placed their drinks on the table, "there's nothing less sexy than a photo shoot."

"We'll see about that," Mia said. "You've never had my perspective."

During their late lunch, Jordan was much quieter than normal, finally compelling Mia to ask what was on her mind. "I think I'd better let my dad know I'm here. Do you mind if I try to find some time to see him?"

Mia took notice of the "I" and tried to hide her hurt. "Of course not. You do what you have to do."

Jordan took out her phone and spent a few minutes trying to get past his secretary, then was put through. "Hi, Dad, it's Jordan. I'm in LA for the weekend, and I thought you might have a few minutes to get together."

"What are you doing in town? Aren't they keeping you busy enough in Colorado?"

"Oh, yeah, I'm busy, but I got a shoot for Ralph Lauren, and I couldn't turn it down. I'll be working all day, but it's an outdoor set, so I'll have my evenings free."

Mia didn't like the sound of Jordan offering up one of their precious evenings, but she tried to concentrate on her salad, rather than her growing pique.

"Hmm…this isn't the best weekend for me, honey," he said. Jordan could hear him flipping through his omnipresent calendar. "I have a premiere to go to tonight, and we're having a dinner party tomorrow night. I promised Candy that I'd reserve all day for her on Saturday. We see so little of each other. Damn," he mumbled, "this is two times in a row that I can't swing it. I'm really sorry about that, Jor."

"That's okay. I'm gonna be wiped anyway."

Even though Mia didn't like to be ignored, she was even more insulted by the fact that Jordan's dad wouldn't go out of his way to see her. She knew that she couldn't say what was on her mind, since Jordan was unable to see her father in a less-than-positive light, but it incensed her nonetheless.

"I think your mother's in town," Jorgen Ericsson said. "Maybe you could drop by and see her."

"Well, that wasn't on my 'to do' list. You know we don't have much in common, Dad."

"Count your blessings," he said. "I uhm…hoped you might go to bat for me a little bit."

"What do you need?" She straightened in her chair, looking like a guard dog who'd heard a hint of a noise.

"Well, since you're out of school now, I was going to try to petition the court to reduce the total amount I pay her. For Christ's sake, Jordan, do you know that woman gets eight thousand a month in alimony and three thousand a month for your support?"

She knew full well what her mother received on a monthly basis, and she kept to herself the fact that she hadn't seen a penny of it since she left for Berkeley.

"How can I help?"

"I'm not sure you can, but I want to propose that she receive no more than five thousand a month. It's going to be a fight, of course, and I'd appreciate anything you can do to ease the way."

She rolled her eyes, already able to picture the pathetic moaning she would be subjected to. "I'll think about it, and see what I can do. I uhm…can't make any promises, though."

"That's fine, honey. No promises needed. I know you'll come through for me—you always do."

A wan smile lit her face as she wracked her brain to think of a way to reach her mother. "Do my best. See you next time I'm in town, Dad."

"How about a little notice next time? My calendar for June is almost filled and it's only February."

"Will do. See you."

She placed the phone down, and picked up her fork, lackadaisically picking at her salad. "He wants me to go pave the way so my mother doesn't stroke out when he tries to cut her alimony."

Mia had gathered as much from Jordan's side of the conversation. She held her tongue, since the only thing she could think of was how cruel it was to place your child in the middle of money arguments. "You gonna do it?" she asked gently.

Placing the fork down, Jordan cocked her head and said, "I have to. He's counting on me."

Counting to ten, Mia wondered why the words "have to" were always mentioned when either of Jordan's parents was discussed. "Want me to go with you?"

Jordan had picked up her fork and was angrily spearing each defenseless vegetable in turn, oblivious to Mia's question.

That same afternoon, the softball team was lounging around the gate at the America West terminal, killing time until they were allowed to board. They were finally called, and the group got in line. As usual, Ryan stayed right where she was, her intrinsic hatred of waiting in line compelling her to be the last one to board every flight.

When the last person was nearly at the door, she stood and slung her carryon over her shoulder. She was almost at the door when the person behind her tapped her on the shoulder. "Hey, good lookin', wanna sit next to me?"

Whirling around, Ryan's eyes bugged out when she saw her brother, Rory, grinning at her. "What are you doing here?"

"I've never been to New Mexico, and this seemed like the ideal weekend to go. I haven't been to any of your games yet, you know."

She tossed her arms around him, hugging him so tightly that he could barely move. "Oh, Rory, you're the sweetest guy in the world." Pulling back, she gave him a fond smile and said, "You don't have to do this, though. I know Jamie's worried about me, but I'll be all right."

"I know you will, sis, but I want to go. I didn't have a thing planned for the weekend, and this will give me a chance to spend some time with my favorite sister."

Shaking her head, Ryan hugged him again, saying, "Let's go, favorite brother. The flight attendant is giving us the evil eye."

As soon as her test was over, Jamie called her mother. "Hey, Mom, how would you like a guest for a few nights?"

"Oh, honey, you don't have to call to ask that. Nothing would make me happier than to see you. Has Ryan left for her trip?"

"Yeah, and I miss her already. You don't mind me sitting around and moping all night, do you?"

"You come right down here, sweetheart. We'll have a nice dinner, and then you can get on the phone and talk to Ryan all evening."

"Sounds great, Mom. I'll be there within an hour or two."

Marta pulled out all of the stops, making her famous arroz con pollo, one of Jamie's favorites. After dinner the Evans women went out to the spa to relax and chat. Catherine gave her daughter a warm smile and asked, "You've been here for over an hour and haven't called Ryan once. Are you two having a tiff?"

"No, not at all. Ryan's plane didn't leave until late afternoon, and she has a layover in Phoenix. She could call when she gets to El Paso, but I told her to wait until she arrived in Las Cruces so we could talk longer."

"How do you think she'll handle being away?"

Jamie got an impish smile on her face and said, "I meddled a little. She was very anxious and sad last night, so I got on the phone and called around until I found someone to go with her. Rory was only too happy to fill in for me." She chuckled and said, "I was prepared to start hitting the cousins, but luckily, I didn't have to."

"You, young lady, are a very, very good partner. I don't know where you got your skills, but I'm very glad that you have them."

Jamie was about to reply when her cell phone rang. She hopped out of the spa and reached for the little phone, hitting the talk button. "Hello?"

"Do you know who I love more than anyone on earth?" a deep, sexy, voice asked.

"Mmm…with a voice like that, I hope the answer is me," Jamie said, giggling.

"Oh, it's you all right. I love you with all of my heart and soul, Jamie Dunlop Smith Evans. The day I met you was the luckiest day of my whole life."

"Aww, you're making me blush."

"Well, you made me cry, so we're even. Seeing Rory at the gate was about the nicest surprise I've ever had. Thank you, Jamie. Thank you for loving me so much."

"I do love you, Ryan, and I couldn't bear to have you be alone for five days. Rory was actually excited about going. I didn't have to coerce him."

"Yeah, he loves to travel, and he's never been to New Mexico. He's going to rent a car and drive around tomorrow. He's pretty jazzed."

"Did you get any comments from your teammates? I know how they like to tease you."

"No, surprisingly, I didn't. I don't think they believed he was my brother, to tell you the truth. They seem worried that I'm cheating on you," she said, chuckling softly.

"Oh, God! What will they think when you share a room?"

There was a short silence, then Ryan said, "Uhm…Jamie? I'm twenty-four-years-old, and Rory's twenty-eight. That's a long time past cuddling in bed together. I'm bunking with Jackie, same as usual."

"But what if you wake up and need to talk to someone? That's why I sent Rory."

"If I wake up and get freaked out, I'll sneak out of my room and go talk to him. He already promised that he wouldn't mind if I woke him. Don't worry, babe. I've got it covered."

"Are you sure?"

"Yes, love. I'm a little shaky, but I'd be a lot shakier if my teammates knew I brought my brother on road trips, and then slept with him."

After chatting for a long while, Jamie hung up, giggling to herself. "You know, sometimes I'm a little goofy."

"How's that?"

"Well, I thought Ryan would sleep in Rory's room over the weekend, so he could comfort her if she was upset during the night. It didn't dawn on me how that would look to her teammates. I mean, Ryan's odd enough without sleeping with her twenty-eight-year-old brother!"

Catherine laughed heartily at that, shaking her head. "That's more than a little funny."

"I don't often think of the boys as boys—do you know what I mean? It doesn't occur to me that they're different from Ryan…even though they clearly are."

"Clearly," Catherine agreed. "I've seen all of them in bathing suits, and the differences are quite stark."

"You're telling me," Jamie said. "I much prefer the distaff version of the

O'Flaherty model."

"To each her own," Catherine said, smiling wryly. "If I were twenty years younger, I'd make a play for any one of the boys."

"They are a fine bunch," Jamie agreed. Glancing at her watch, she said, "I guess we might as well go to bed. It's getting late, and I want to go on your morning walk with you."

"Oh, that'll be fun!" Catherine emerged from the pool and dried off quickly. When they went inside, she asked, "Do you need anything before bed? Some warm milk, maybe?"

"No." Jamie hesitated for a moment, then summoned the nerve to ask, "Uhm…would you rub my head for a few minutes? That really relaxes me."

"Of course." Catherine beamed a smile at her daughter that made Jamie's heart swell with love. Taking her mother's hand, they walked up the stairs together. "I'll go rinse off, and be back in a minute."

Jamie nodded, and did the same. She was lying in bed, waiting patiently, when her mother knocked a few minutes later. "Come on in."

"Hi." Catherine sat down on the edge of the bed and patted her child's back. Jamie was wearing a thin, cropped, cotton tank top, and Catherine slipped her fingers under the material. "When you were a tiny baby, you liked to have your back scratched exactly like this." Catherine ran her short, perfectly manicured nails across Jamie's shoulders, then moved down her back, making her daughter giggle.

"I didn't know that," Jamie murmured. "I…I didn't think you…did things like that when I was little."

Her hand stilling, Catherine said, "Elizabeth didn't like it, because she said it agitated you. She believed in putting a baby into her crib and then leaving her to cry herself to sleep. But when I heard her close her door, I'd sneak into your room and rub and tickle you until you were sound asleep." She laughed softly and said, "She thought her methods were the most sound in the world, since you never cried when she put you in your crib. Little did she know that I was subverting her rules—God only knows what kind of scene it would have created if she'd ever caught me."

"How long did you do that?" Jamie asked, amazed that her mother would risk Elizabeth's wrath.

There was a long pause, and then Catherine said, "Until you didn't want me to do it any longer."

Jamie flipped over onto her back, staring, wide eyed at her mother. "Why wouldn't I want you to do that?"

Catherine wiped at a tear and said, "It was after I went to Europe for two weeks. You never…you never seemed to feel the same about me after that. You were very angry that I'd left you, sweetheart, and I think you stopped trusting me."

"Oh, Mom." Jamie wrapped her arms around her mother and they both cried for a long while. "I'm sorry I hurt you like that."

"I'm the one who should be sorry. I was so hurt that I pulled back from you. It was honestly the worst time of my life. I felt so unnecessary." Sniffling a little she added, "But there's never a valid reason to distance yourself from your child. I let my hurt affect our relationship, and that's unforgivable."

"No, it's not. I forgive you, Mom. I swear I do. You did your best with a job you weren't prepared for."

"That's an understatement. I wasn't mature enough to have a cat, much less a child. But, that's my fault, too. Having unprotected sex was merely one more indication of my immaturity."

"Daddy was in law school, Mom, he should have known better than to risk it."

"I know, honey, but you know how men are. They expect the woman to take care of birth control. I…I didn't know the rules."

"Well, even though it's been painful for both of us, I'm glad you had me when you did. If you'd waited until you were older, I'd never have met Ryan. And, believe me, she's a once in a lifetime woman."

"I believe that, dear. I know you're right for each other."

"Now, let's stop thinking about the tough times, and start creating some good memories." She rolled over onto her belly and put her arms over her head, saying, "Work your magic, Mom. Elizabeth is thousands of miles away."

Chapter Sixteen

"**F**uck," Jordan growled as she punched her pillow forcefully and tried to find a comfortable spot in the big bed.

"What's wrong, sweetheart?" It was mere moments after they'd finished making love, and even though Jordan had been a little distracted, and not as emotionally available as normal, it had still been very satisfying for Mia. Her body felt heavy and slow as she tried to gather enough brain cells to pay attention to her lover's response.

"I can't get comfortable," she groused, twitching her long body into a few different poses. "I've got to get to sleep! There's nothing worse than looking like shit for a big shoot like this. I'll get ragged at by everyone from the make-up artist up to the photographer."

Shaking her head to clear the cobwebs, Mia pushed her partner onto her stomach and reached for the bottle of moisture lotion on the bedside table. Squirting a stream of it down Jordan's back, she started to give her a soothing massage, half-listening to her mumbled grousing. It took a long while, but Jordan finally calmed and quieted down, and soon afterwards she was asleep. Mia pulled the sheet over their bodies and cuddled up close against Jordan's side. "Rest, sweetheart," she soothed, running her fingers over the soft skin of her cheek. "It'll all be fine. Don't worry about a thing."

It was pitch black when the insistent buzz of the alarm woke her. Mia blinked in annoyance, unable to reconcile the sound with her normal alarm. But the warm body she was draped over was a very welcome surprise, and her mouth slowly twitched into a grin as she woke fully. "I've got to get ready," Jordan's wide-awake voice announced. "The car's coming at five."

"What do you have to do?" Mia mumbled. "Don't they get you ready?"

"They don't shave my legs," she said, rolling out of bed. The water was running before Mia could get her mouth to reply, and she was asleep again in moments. Her little respite didn't last long, though. A damp foot was placed upon her belly, Jordan's toes twitching insistently. "How do they feel?" she asked in all seriousness.

Mia wasn't sure where she was or why Jordan's foot was lightly resting on her gut, but she finally started tracking. Struggling to sit up, she gave the long leg a quick inspection. "Looks fine."

"I can take a quick peek. I need you to look carefully." She stuck her leg out, and added, "Use your tongue if you have to—but, please make sure I didn't miss a spot."

Mia dutifully focused her attention, and covered every micrometer of the long legs, finding one tiny spot on the back of Jordan's thigh that had escaped attention. Rolling out of bed, she took her partner's hand and took her back into the shower, letting the warm spray simultaneously wake her. "Let me do it for you," she offered, and bent to her task. She wanted to spend a few minutes stopping in for a visit since she was in such a nice neighborhood, but it was clear that Jordan's mind was on business.

As soon as Mia finished, Jordan hopped out of the shower and blew her hair dry. "How do you know what to do with your hair?" Mia asked.

"Oh, this is a clean/clean shoot. I only have to wash it."

"Clean/clean?"

"Yeah, that's when you have to shave your legs perfectly and wash your hair. They assume you've had a recent bikini wax."

"What are the other options?" Mia asked. "Stubbly/dirty?"

"No," Jordan said, chuckling softly. "But sometimes they only want your hair clean. That's the easiest of all. I thank God this wasn't a clean/clean/clean shoot."

Mia's brows twitched together as she considered what else would have to be clean. Her eyes widened and she looked at the neatly trimmed patch of white blonde hair above the apex of Jordan's thighs.

"Yep," Jordan nodded. "I can't tell you how much I hate that. It takes a week for it to stop itching."

"What on earth have you modeled that required you to shave?"

"Panties, thongs, lace bikinis. If the material is thin you can sometimes see a little bump if a woman has a lot of hair."

"But, you don't."

"I know that, sweetheart, but I don't want to have to go a day early to prove to the art director that I'm well groomed. The last thing I want to do is have to take my panties off in front of one of those guys."

"Well, you're beautifully groomed," Mia said, giving her well-tended hair a little tickle. "Tell them to call me and I'll vouch for you."

"Will do," Jordan said, smirking at her partner through the shower door.

"Will they leave your hair down?" Mia asked.

"Mmm…they'll have it ten different ways before they decide on what they want. But I can tell you right now what it'll be."

"What's that?"

"If the clothes are semi-casual they'll leave it straight, probably parted down the middle. If the clothes are super-casual they'll twist it up on top of my head—and make it look kinda haphazard. It's always the same," she said, going back to drying her long tresses.

Turning off the water, Mia wrapped herself in the towel Jordan handed her. "Is there any part of this that you like?"

"Mmm…I like the money. That's it. Oh—and the free product I usually get. That's sweet."

"But nothing about the process? Nothing at all?"

"Nope," she said firmly. "I hate it, to be honest. It's prostitution with my clothes on."

She turned and went into the bedroom to put on a pair of baggy sweatpants, a Cal volleyball T-shirt, and a Polo sweatshirt. A pair of shower sandals finished her very casual attire, surprising Mia a little.

"Trying to keep potential suitors at bay?"

Chuckling mildly, Jordan said, "We're gonna be on the beach, so I want to make sure I have something to keep me warm. They always have robes, but I prefer to have my own clothes."

"I'm learning a lot so far," Mia said, giving her a kiss. "I guess I'd better get my fill of kisses now, huh?" she asked, leaning in for another one for the road.

Jordan cocked her head, then nodded. "Yeah. It's no big deal if you're a lesbian model, but smudging lipstick is a capital crime."

The sun was still a promise when the limo picked them up at five a.m. The kitchen wasn't open yet, and Mia's stomach was growling furiously, making Jordan laugh in the otherwise quiet car. "Driver, could you stop at the Starbucks down on Montana? We're in desperate need of a pick-me-up."

"I'd be happy to," he said, "but they don't open until six. I need a boost myself."

"Well, maybe there will be one near the shoot."

"There's one in Manhattan Beach," he said, obviously an animated Starbuck's locator. "It'll be open by the time we get there."

Jordan settled down into the cushy seat and extended her arm, pleased when Mia snuggled up against her. The driver looked in the rear-view mirror and caught her eye, giving her a tiny grin. Maybe a fantasy about us together will give him that little boost he's looking for, she said to herself and kissed

Monogamy

Mia gently, with the limo streaking towards Manhattan Beach.

After two hours of wandering around the deserted streets of Manhattan Beach, Mia wanted nothing more than a beach towel and a quiet patch of sand. Regrettably, the day was crisp, cold and windy, the brisk breeze blowing sand everywhere.

Jordan was dressed and in make-up when Mia returned, another giant latté in her chilled hands. Mia shivered when she saw her partner, clad in a tiny pair of white jeans shorts, a bright pink bandeau top, and a golden tan. They had spent the better part of the evening applying some very effective sunless tanning lotion to every part of the long body, and Mia had used Jordan's immobility while it dried to good advantage, making love to her while she braced herself against the marble walls of the sumptuous bath.

Mia caught her lover's eye and motioned to her to step away from the cadre of people who were huddled together deciding how to conduct the shoot. "You're going to freeze to death! Go put your clothes on!"

"Can't," she said, shivering fiercely. "The costumer just got the clothes where she wants them. I don't want to screw up the seams."

"Do you want my coffee? I can go get more."

"Can't. It might mess up my lipstick."

"Then go back in the trailer. Right now!" Mia scowled, seeing that Jordan's lips were almost blue.

"I wanted to see you," she said, her teeth chattering loudly.

"I want to see you, too, but not in the hospital. Now scoot!"

Blowing a kiss to avoid smearing her make-up, Jordan made a run for it, covering the short distance in a nanosecond. *I thought Ryan was bad*, Mia groused, rolling her eyes. *What is it with jocks?*

By eleven, Mia fully agreed with Jordan's earlier assessment. Watching a photo shoot was one of the least erotic things she had ever witnessed. She'd spent most of her time shivering in a director's chair at the edge of the crowd, covered with a spare space blanket, which did a good job of absorbing the sun. Regrettably, she had not thought to bring her sunglasses, and her head was throbbing from the bright glare off the water and the blanket. But no matter how cold or miserable she was, she knew it was nothing compared to what Jordan was going through.

Her lover was modeling with a fantastic-looking blonde guy, who was artlessly strumming a guitar. Jordan's job was to straddle his leg, while bending over far enough to merely suggest the line of her thong. It amazed Mia how much time the various professionals spent making sure that the shorts were stretched tight enough across Jordan's lovely ass to show that line—but it was obviously critical that they did so. At one point, they made her take off her shorts and try on a smaller size—right in front of two dozen people. Jordan didn't even seem to notice the crowd, however. She stood there like a beautiful mannequin, letting several strangers try to zip her into the tiny shorts. Jordan's earlier words came back to Mia, and she began to see what her partner meant about prostitution. This was clearly not an attempt to show off the shorts or the top. The whole game was to imply that this gorgeous woman could be astride your leg if you would only buy the Polo jeans that the guy had on, or that you could be a gorgeous woman if you would only drop forty bucks on a pair of Jordan's shorts. They were selling sex—pure and simple. The clothes were incidental.

The hard part of Jordan's job was to look hot—temperature wise as well as sexually. The shoot was meant to inspire mental images of a hot day, a hot woman and a hot guy—who were going to go do something even hotter as soon as the guy finished playing his song. Jordan wasn't merely supposed to straddle him, she was supposed to look like she was gliding against his leg for obvious reasons. Her head was thrown back slightly, her mouth open just enough to show the tip of her pink tongue. Full, sensual lips were wet and glossy, and she was supposed to look like she wanted to take a very sensitive part of the guy's anatomy into her mouth at the first opportunity.

Mia actually could have gotten hot from the look on Jordan's face, but they kept spritzing her bare back with a fine sheen of glycerin to replicate the glow of arousal, and Mia was positive that the cold liquid was pure torture in the brisk, cold wind. She couldn't bring herself to enjoy the show when Jordan was uncomfortable, even though Jordan's nipples were as hard as she'd ever seen them; so she concentrated on watching the various professionals scampering around with lights, bounce umbrellas, and translucent shields of plastic to keep the wind from ruffling the models' carefully arranged casual hairdos.

Mia smirked as she remembered that Jordan had correctly predicted the style her hair would be in. She wore a casual little twist, held in place with a tortoiseshell clip, long strands intentionally loose to give her that just-got-out-of-bed look.

Her stomach began to rumble, and Mia sauntered over to the craft services table and spent a few minutes chatting with the catering staff. They were having quite a time of it, trying to keep everything secured in the heavy wind, not to mention trying to keep sand out of the food. They finally gave up, and had some of the staff help them move the tables over to the paved strand. That, of course, took quite a while, since there was a small argument about which of the union workers was responsible for helping an independent catering service. Luckily, hunger prevailed over contracts, and the food was finally set in place.

Mia dug in immediately, joined by a few drivers and carpenters. The talent, as Jordan and the guy were called, were still working away, and to Mia's surprise they didn't get a significant break until two o'clock. By that time the food looked like it had been picked over by ravenous vultures, and the lanky blonde turned up her nose at it. Mia was certain that all she had in her stomach was about a gallon of hot tea, but Jordan claimed she was fine. Before she went back she grabbed an apple, then asked the caterers to cut it into small wedges. She ate it delicately, barely moving her mouth, and managing not to allow her lips to touch it.

They kept at it until four o'clock, when the sun began to fade. Jordan had been draped across the young man's body in more positions than Mia had known were possible, and Mia was no novice in the draping-one's-body-over-a-guy competition. After immodestly doffing her clothes and taking the clip out of her hair, Jordan slid back into her own roomy sweats and met up with Mia for the walk to the parking lot. She grasped her hand, but didn't say a word, nodding to the driver as they slid into the leather seat.

He had obviously driven enough actresses and models to know when to keep his mouth shut, and he did so on the long, congested drive up the 405 freeway. Traffic opened up a bit once they passed LAX, but Jordan was sound asleep by that time, her head softly bouncing against Mia's none-too-soft shoulder. Scooting to the other side of the car, Mia urged the still-sleeping Jordan onto her lap, where she gently played with her hair all the way to Bel Air, soothing her in her sleep.

The next morning was much the same as Friday had been, although Jordan was even more sedate. More painstaking leg and armpit shaving, more blow drying, and they were off again. This time Mia brought her sunglasses, as well as one of her textbooks. After an hour of walking around and drinking coffee, she climbed back into the limo and spent the better part of the day studying and napping, in equal proportions. She felt guilty about leaving Jordan alone, but they had interacted so little on the previous day that she was certain that her lover wouldn't mind.

At four o'clock, a light knock on the window woke Mia from the latest nap, and she sat up groggily, rubbing her eyes. "So, this is how you spent your day," Jordan said tiredly. "I thought you took up with a surfer and ditched me."

"No way," Mia said. "You're the only game in town. Now let's go home and get you some food and some sleep—in that order."

"No complaints," Jordan said as she curled up against Mia. "I do have one piece of good news," she yawned. "I might not have to work tomorrow. My agent was on the phone for an hour, insisting that I be paid for the day, even if it's cancelled."

"Why are they canceling? Is everything okay?"

"Yeah. My belly wasn't pooching out or anything," she said. "The weather was great, and the sky was great, and the models were great, so they think they've got what they need. They're rushing to develop the film tonight, and if they're satisfied, I'm off. Cool, huh?"

"Very," Mia said. "We can stay in bed and eat."

Nuzzling her ear, Jordan purred, "Don't you mean, make love?"

"We can do that, too, but I'm gonna get some calories into you, sweetie. You're emaciated!"

"Two and a half days of barely eating makes a difference," Jordan said. "But the photographer was pleased. He said my cheekbones really stood out." She smirked wryly at Mia and said, "Makes you proud, doesn't it?"

Mia patted her leg, not wanting to add her voice to the chorus of people who had been directing Jordan's every move for two solid days. But she privately hoped that this was the last time her lover had to spend her day doing something that she got so little pleasure from.

They slept from six until eight, the phone waking them when Jordan got the call that the assignment was indeed, complete. Jordan had steadfastly refused to eat until she heard from her agent, despite Mia's begging, and now she was ravenous—and could eat whatever she wanted. "Let's call room service," she said as soon as her eyes were fully open.

"Okay," Mia yawned loudly. "What do you want?"

"Something full of calories and saturated fat and carbohydrates and… what else is bad for you?"

"I get the picture," Mia said as she scanned the menu. "How about fettuccine Alfredo, a Caesar salad, and some tiramisu for dessert."

"You know me well," Jordan said. "Add some lamb chops, and I'm set!"

They got up and dressed just in time, since a friendly employee showed up moments later to light the fire in their fireplace. Jordan took a half-bottle of white wine from the mini bar and poured two glasses of the crisp Chablis. They shared one of the sumptuous overstuffed chairs, cuddling together in companionable silence while they waited for their dinner.

"This is pretty nice, isn't it?" Mia sighed, snuggling a little tighter.

"Yeah, it's nice to have money, isn't it?"

"Oh, I wasn't referring to the room, I was talking about how it feels to be on your lap. It's my favorite place, you know."

Jordan's warm laugh made Mia burrow even closer. "I didn't know it was your favorite place, but I'm glad it is." She grasped her chin and turned her head to place tender kisses on her entire face. "I love you," she whispered. "God, I love saying that."

"I love you, too," Mia sighed. "Nothing feels so right to me as our being together. Even today, sitting in a car on a freezing beach—I was as happy as a clam because I knew you were there, too."

"I'm sorry it wasn't more fun for you," Jordan began to apologize, but Mia silenced her immediately.

"I'm very, very glad that I came. This makes up for any minor inconveniences," she insisted, taking a delicate nibble of Jordan's neck. They cuddled for a while longer, with Mia trying to think of a way to bring up the topic of school. Finally decided to get it out of the way, she said, "Uhm…honey? I've made a decision about school."

"Huh?" Jordan asked slowly, neck nibbling always serving to both relax and distract her.

"I've decided to postpone school for a year. I cleared it with Stanford, and I've already told my parents. Now, all we have to do is figure out what I can do in Colorado for a year."

Jordan pulled back as far as she could and stared up at Mia with a stunned look. "You're doing this for me?"

"Well, yeah," she purred, playing with her hair. "For you and me."

"Oh, Mia, I don't know what I've done to deserve you, but I'm so glad that you're mine."

"You don't have to earn my love. I give it to you freely. And the day after I graduate, I'm gonna be on your doorstep."

"That's a day that will live on in my memory," Jordan sighed, holding Mia in a bone-bruising hug.

🐎

When dinner arrived, they extracted themselves from their loving embrace and directed the server to set up outdoors. Even though they were relatively close to the ocean, there was no wind in their protected enclave, and the private patio was surprisingly warm. Mia hadn't been quite so immoderate in her menu choices, sticking to some grilled salmon, new potatoes and a field greens salad. They shared a little, but Mia had to act fast to snare a bit of the pasta over Jordan's low growl. "Oh…territorial, are we?" she said seductively. "I want to hear that growl later."

"Fill my tummy up, and I'll growl at you all night long," Jordan boasted. "No problem."

Mia scoffed at her bravado. "You'll be asleep while you're still twitching from your climax."

"Mmm…I like the sound of that," Jordan said. "You make even the word climax sound sexy."

Tossing her curly locks, Mia grinned. "I do what I can."

"You do a lot for…and to…me," Jordan said, leaning in close for a kiss. She was obviously still very hungry, since she pulled away after only one and dove back into her dinner. Mia was finished, so she leaned back in her chair and gazed at her partner lovingly, never taking her eyes off of her until Jordan's head lifted and she leaned back in her chair, finally sated. "Damn, that was fine."

"It's even fascinating to watch you eat," Mia said, reaching across the table to grip her hand. "I love every little thing about you."

Suddenly serious, Jordan gazed at her intently and said, "I feel the same way about you." She dropped her head slightly and admitted, "It feels wrong to hide how I feel about you. While I stood around yesterday and today, I…uhm…had some time to think, and I decided that I'm going to tell my parents about us."

Mia nearly slid from her chair at this news. Jordan had never given the slightest hint that she was considering this, and she was frankly amazed. "Is that wise, baby? I mean, have you thought about this carefully?"

"Of course," she said quietly. "What do you think those two weekly 45 minute calls to my therapist are all about? We've talked about this until I'm sick of it!" She got up and fluffed her hair a bit, tossing it over her shoulders. "How can I tell you how much you mean to me when I'm afraid to talk to my parents about you?" She approached Mia's chair and placed her hands on the arms, tugging at the piece until they were facing each other. Squatting down she gazed at her with an earnest expression and said, "You mean so much more to me than anyone in my family. Denying my love for you is wrong, Mia. I can't do it any more. Yours is the only opinion that matters. I love you with all my heart, and I want everyone to know it."

"Oh, Jordan, that's the sweetest thing anyone's ever said to me." She wrapped her arms around her neck and held on tight, rising with the taller woman as she got to her feet. Jordan swooped her up in her arms and carried her to the canopy bed, settled her gently, and then climbed in next to her.

"Let me show you how much I love you," she whispered. "Let me worship you."

Mia answered by grasping her firmly and pulling her atop her body, nearly smothering her with kisses that grew in intensity and passion until they were lost to the love that burned in both of their souls.

🐎

Even though she was fully awake, Mia tried hard not to move a muscle. She was lying on her left side, and Jordan was pressed up against her back. One long arm was tucked across her chest, and Jordan's long, delicate hand gently held her left breast. The thought occurred to Mia that she could contentedly stay in this position for the better part of the day. She knew that Jordan could feel her steady pulse beating against her palm, and she thought, with a small amount of satisfaction, that the rhythmic beat was likely serving to allow her to relax enough to stay asleep long past her normal waking time. *Of course, I might just have sapped all of her energy last night,* she chuckled to herself.

Considering the evening, she had to admit that something had changed between them. Some hard-to-define barrier had been breached—freeing them to be more open with each other than ever before.

Mia had greatly enjoyed their physical connection from the start, and she was pleased to acknowledge that they seemed to get a little closer with each coupling. But the previous night was qualitatively different from any other time. She shifted a little and placed a gentle kiss on Jordan's hand, unable to resist tasting her skin. *Last night we became partners. It's not her and me any longer; it's us.*

This realization made her feel nearly giddy, and she snuggled down even deeper into Jordan's loose embrace. It was scary and puzzling, and actually made her stomach hurt a little when she considered all of the complications their relationship would bring to their lives. But to her amazement, the practical, problematic issues paled in comparison to the utter joy she felt to love and be loved by Jordan. *Being with her is worth anything we have to face.* Lying in that elegant bed, in that luxurious room, she knew that they had turned a corner—and she hoped with everything that she had that there was no turning back.

After spending two restful days with her mother, Jamie woke up early on Sunday and got in the shower. When she emerged, her mom popped her head into the bedroom and said, "Going to church, honey?"

"Yeah, I told Annie earlier in the week that I'd take Cait. Would you like to go with me?"

"Sure. That'd be fun. Are we taking her to Ryan's church?"

"Let's be bold," Jamie said. "The Episcopal service starts an hour after the Catholic one. We can take our time and see Poppa in the bargain." Jamie put in a call to Annie to tell her of her plans, and the good-natured woman gave her permission to take Caitlin to whichever church she chose, she merely requested that Jamie not shave her head or dress her in a saffron robe.

Jamie was chuckling at Caitlin's incessant babbling while she parked the car in the driveway of her grandfather's small house, one more perk of being related to the priest. "Have you been coming to church again, Mom?"

"No, actually this is my first time in years. I need all of the centering I can get my hands on these days, and I thought this might help."

Jamie nodded sympathetically, and watched as her mother unbuckled the toddler from the car seat. "I'm not sure how much focus you can maintain with your biggest fan hanging off of you, though."

Catherine gave the child a kiss on the crown of her head and said, "Having a sweet soul like this on my lap gives me more evidence of the presence of God than any part of the service."

They went into the church and found seats in a pew on the far side of the church—hoping to disturb as few of the parishioners as possible. Scooting close, Jamie rested her head on her mother's shoulder and let her mere presence soothe her. Caitlin flopped down on Catherine's lap, then slid off—wedging her small body between the two women. The child pressed her head against Catherine's breast, grasping Jamie's hand as she did so. Mother and daughter exchanged warm looks, and Jamie noticed a few tears slipping down Catherine's cheek. "You're gonna be the world's best grandmother," Jamie said. "Not a doubt in my or Cait's mind."

They decided to all have lunch together, and after Charles finished chatting with his parishioners, they set off for brunch at the Mark Hopkins Hotel, Caitlin happily in tow.

"So tell me how the training for your big walk is going?" Charles asked Catherine as they climbed one of the steep streets of Nob hill.

"Well, given that I can make it up these hills with no problem, I'd say it's going well. I'm honestly in better shape than I was when I was Jamie's age, and it feels marvelous."

Charles spared a glance at his daughter-in-law and decided that Catherine looked happier than he had seen her since Jamie was a baby. "I think it's a grand thing that you're all doing," he said. "And it will be a nice way to spend some time together."

"Yes, I figure that we'll chatter away the whole time," Catherine said. "None of us are tight-lipped, as you know."

"That was the worst thing about the AIDS Ride," Jamie said. "There were hours a day when I was too winded to speak. It was torture!"

"The pace I'm going to keep will allow you to have a running dialogue—if you choose to hang back with Maeve and me."

"That's our whole purpose in doing this, Mom. It's a bonding experience for both of us and our moms, as well as a way to make a statement about how breast cancer has affected all of us."

Catherine reached down and grasped her daughter's hand, giving it a gentle squeeze. "I'm really looking forward to this. I think it will be a wonderful experience for all of us. I only wish Caitlin could go."

"I pray that there's no need for the walk by the time she's old enough to join us," Jamie said. "It would be so wonderful if the babies being born now would never have to worry about breast cancer."

"Wonderful indeed," Catherine said, sighing wistfully.

Over brunch, Charles asked, "So, tell us about this golf trip, Jamie."

"It's our first spring tournament, Poppa, and it's being held over in Vallejo. Normally, we'd drive up for the day, but our coach decided this would be a good opportunity to do a little team building, so we're staying overnight. We're meeting over at Cal at two, and heading up."

"Do you like the girls on your team, honey?"

"Yeah, I like them well enough—what I know of them, that is. They're a very serious, non-chatty group. Most of them live for golf, and, as you know, that's never been my attitude."

"Well, if anyone can liven things up a little, you're the woman for the job," Charlie said, giving his granddaughter a fond smile.

Jordan was more nervous than Mia had ever seen her, and she desperately wished she could help calm her down. But there was little she could do. Jordan was not in the mood to talk; her responses almost monosyllabic since her conversation with her mother. Jordan's mom had nixed the idea of their coming to her house, insisting she'd rather visit them at the hotel. Jordan had muttered something about "sponging a free meal" when she'd hung up, and that was all that had been said since.

Their guest was expected at any moment, and Mia caught Jordan in a loose embrace, stopping her as she went to change her clothes for the third time. "Honey, you look wonderful. Please don't spend the rest of our alone time running around like a mad woman."

"I'm not…" She stopped in her tracks, took a breath and nodded. "Okay." It was a small concession, but one that Mia was very thankful for.

"No matter what happens, nothing will be different at the end of the day," she soothed. "You don't rely on your mother for any type of support—physical, emotional or monetary. She can't take anything away from you, because she doesn't give you anything." Mia knew that her words were harsh, but they were true; and she wanted Jordan to be able to look at the reality of the situation.

To her surprise, Jordan nodded her head firmly. "I know that," she said, her voice filled with emotion. The bright blue eyes were clouded with pain as she whispered, "But she still hurts me. She hurts me so much that sometimes it feels like I'll die."

Mia wrapped her arms tightly around her shaking body and hugged with all of her might. This was the most revealing thing Jordan had ever said about her relationship with her mother, and a large part of Mia wished she hadn't revealed her pain. But knowing and loving Jordan meant understanding her most broken self—no matter how hard these things were to hear. "I know it's hard," Mia whispered, "but I'm here for you, sweetheart. We'll get through this together."

A light knock on the door made her stomach flip, and she felt Jordan's entire body go rigid. "It will be all right," Mia said, her voice reflecting a confidence she didn't feel.

Jordan nodded briefly, squeezed her hand, and strode across the room to open the door. A tall, thin, elegant-looking woman breezed in, giving Mia a raised eyebrow as she entered.

"Mom, this is Mia Christopher. Mia, this is my mother, Daniella."

Daniella turned to her daughter and grasped her lightly by the shoulders. She gazed at her for a moment, then pulled her close and placed a kiss on both of her cheeks. Releasing her, she turned to Mia and graced her with a wide, confident smile. "It's good to meet you, Mia. Are you…here for the modeling assignment?" It was fairly clear that Mia wasn't a model, even though she was attractive. But Danielle knew the business well enough to realize women under 5'8" did not appear in Ralph Lauren ads.

"No, no," she replied, trying to make her smile appear genuine. "I'm here with Jordan. We're friends from Berkeley."

"Oh! Well that's very thoughtful of you to come down only to see Jordan."

What an odd thing to say.

"Are you ready to eat, Mom?" Jordan asked. "I've made reservations on the terrace."

"Yes, I'm famished. Shall we?"

Daniella led the way, her determined stride indicating her familiarity with the property. Mia hung back a bit and watched her walk, seeing so many similarities to Jordan that she was a bit stunned. Their gait was identical—smooth, long strides that ate up space, but gave the illusion that they were gliding, rather than walking. Their hips twitched in exactly the same way—barely enough to hint at the curves hidden beneath their clothes. The thought flashed through Mia's head that if Jordan looked exactly like her mother in twenty-five years she wouldn't have a complaint in the world. *She can look just like you, Daniella, but if she starts acting like you, I'll have to kill her to put her out of her misery.*

They were seated at a table under a wisteria-covered pergola, with discreetly hidden heat lamps providing enough warmth to take the chill off. They ordered their meal, with Daniella making noises about how nice it was to be young and able to eat whatever one wished. Mia tried to act friendly and show some of her natural warmth, but she dampened her affect to let Jordan take the lead.

The older woman unobtrusively eyed every other table on the terrace, and Mia let her eyes wander too. "Jordan," she whispered excitedly, after spying one of the stars of her favorite show, "isn't that Sara Michelle Gellar?"

"Yeah, it is," Jordan said, a fond look settling onto her face at Mia's excitement.

Daniella turned and gave the young woman at the distant table a long look, then raised an eyebrow at her daughter. "She's nobody," Jordan said, indicating that Sara was no one that her mother should know. Gazing again at Mia, she added, "But, we like her."

They passed an hour chatting about nothing in particular while they ate their meal. Daniella seemed polite and pleasant enough, but she didn't have one question for Mia, and didn't seem curious about her in the least. When Jordan and her mother were engaged in conversation, Mia took every opportunity to observe how they interacted, and it wasn't good. Jordan was as guarded and wary around her mother as Mia had ever seen her. She was able to carry on her half of the conversation, but there was no spark at all, not even a hint of a familial relationship between these two remarkably similar-looking women. It reminded Mia of how Jordan would be during a job interview—for a job that she wasn't that interested in and knew she was not going to get.

The longer Mia stared at the pair the more she realized that there were a few very small differences that played a very large role in differentiating the pair. They had similar coloring, their hair was the same shade and their eyes were carbon copies of each other. Jordan definitely had her mother's nose, and their high, distinct cheekbones were the same, too. But Jordan was blessed with full, rose-colored lips, one of her most sensually appealing qualities to Mia's appreciative eyes. Daniella, on the other hand, had thin lips that she tried to make appear fuller via a careful application of lip liner and gloss. And even though their eyes were the same color, there was a warmth and a playfulness behind Jordan's that Mia was always cognizant of—even when others couldn't see it. In contrast, Daniella's eyes went from disinterested to frosty to ice cold; with no indication of any warmth or compassion hidden within.

As Mia continued to avail herself of every opportunity to study the woman, she also noticed that Daniella's smile appeared composed and studied, whereas Jordan's burst onto her face like a bright light being switched on in a dim room. Even though the smile was absent today, Mia reflected that she saw that fantastic smile more and more these days, as Jordan grew more comfortable sharing her inner self.

She was so lost in her musings that she was startled when she felt a warm hand moving about in her lap. Catching Jordan's hand in her own, she gave it a squeeze and waited expectantly when she saw Jordan gather herself and clear her throat.

"Mom," she began, her voice steady, but higher than normal, "I wanted to do more than introduce you to Mia today." Her hand began to grip tighter, and Mia held on tight, waiting for the bomb to drop. Daniella inclined her head, her short, layered blonde hair moving gently with the gesture. "I want you to know what she means to me."

"Pardon?" the older woman asked, those penetrating blue eyes shifting from Jordan to Mia and back again.

"Mia's more than my friend," Jordan said. "She's my lover." The grenade was lying right there on the table, and Mia braced herself, waiting for the inevitable explosion...that never came.

"Oh! Well...that's nice," she said, giving each of them a guarded smile. She seemed at a loss for words, and Mia assumed that she was too surprised to comment. It took a moment, but as the time ticked by she realized with a start that Daniella wasn't stunned—she was truly uninterested in the announcement.

"Don't you have a reaction to that, Mom?" Jordan asked tentatively.

Jesus, Jordy! Don't go looking for trouble!

A small scowl formed on the older woman's face and she said, "You're not the first people in the world to discover lesbianism. It's a phase many girls go through. My God, the stories I could tell you about the women I worked with in the seventies. Some of the best-known models of that time slept with far more women than men. It was quite common—but not permanent." She shrugged her shoulders and gave Mia a small smile. "Not to imply anything about the quality of your relationship, of course." Another shrug and she said, "You might feel this way for the rest of your life I suppose, but only time will tell." She craned her neck, looking for their server and said, "I'd love an espresso. Anyone else?"

Jordan appeared unnerved by the conversation, and she got up to use the rest room. Mia looked up at her to see if she wanted company, but she shook her head slightly and strode off.

Daniella watched her walk away, and turned her gaze to Mia. "She's an odd girl, isn't she?"

Mia's eyes widened and she found her head shaking. "No, not at all."

The small, slightly annoyed frown returned, and Daniella said, "Oh, I didn't mean anything by that. I only meant that I can never read her. I've never been able to. She's so different from Gunnar. You know that he and I are so alike it's quite astonishing."

"That must be...nice," Mia said, not having any idea how to respond.

"Oh, it is. But, frankly, I'm at a loss with Jordan. I never know what she wants from me."

"That's not been my experience. I find her to be very open and easy to read," *once she trusts you*, she didn't add.

"Well, I suppose a parent only gets a small part of the picture, doesn't she?" She seemed perfectly comfortable with this excuse, and Mia was the last person who was going to try to dissuade her from her opinion.

"I suppose so." She took in a breath and tried to think of something to say, but she was at a loss. They sat at the table in silence, neither even making an attempt at conversation. Strangely, Mia didn't feel uncomfortable—perhaps because Daniella seemed perfectly at ease. It was almost as if they were at two separate tables, and Mia wondered if this was what it was like for Jordan when she was growing up. *My God, she makes you feel like you don't even exist!*

Jordan finally returned, and she got the conversation going again by mentioning the Olympics. "I've made the reservations for you and Grandmom and Gunnar."

"That's wonderful. We're all looking forward to it." She was smiling warmly when a concerned frown suddenly stole over her features. "Is there any chance you'll get any individual publicity? Like one of those features that NBC does?"

Shifting uncomfortably in her seat, Jordan shrugged and said, "I haven't been approached, but I guess it's possible. Why?"

"Well, I hope that you don't plan on telling them about this...lesbian thing if they do interview you. That's not the kind of thing that people need to know, Jordan."

Giving her a surprisingly forthright stare, Jordan narrowed her eyes and said, "It's not a thing. Mia and I are in love. We're going to do our best to be together for the rest of our lives, Mother."

"Oh, of course you think that," she said, smiling at them like they were slow-witted. "Every woman thinks her relationship will last forever." She laughed derisively, shaking her head. "I don't think there are five good relationships in the whole country, but more power to you."

"That's not true," Jordan said. "Just because you don't know people who are happily married, doesn't mean they don't exist."

"Now, don't get all huffy with me, Jordan," Daniella said, rather dismissively. "I know you think you're special—but humans aren't made to be monogamous. Neither your father nor I could ever manage it."

Mia watched as Jordan's jaw nearly hit the table at that revelation.

According to Jordan, her mother had played the martyr for more than ten years—repeatedly moaning about her former husband's infidelity. It was clear that Jordan had assumed that her mother had been betrayed, not that the infidelity had been mutual. Daniella continued on, not noticing Jordan's stunned look. "Now, I know you're only able to think about how in love you are, but there are many, many people who don't want to hear about that type of thing."

Looking at her for longer than was polite, Jordan cocked her head and asked her mother, "Do you wish that I hadn't told you, either?"

The older woman cleared her throat and gave Mia a pointed look. "Could we have a moment alone? We won't be a second."

"No problem," she said with false brightness, giving Jordan a quick glance. "I'll go wash my hands."

As Daniella watched her walk away, she turned back to her daughter and snapped, "Look, whom you sleep with isn't any of my business. You're a very pretty, very talented girl, and I'm sure that you could have your choice of men or women. But I don't want this to get out. It doesn't look right, and it could hamper your future opportunities." Her brow tensed appreciably as she cocked her head and asked, "What does your father think about this bit of news?"

"I haven't told him yet," Jordan said. Lying blatantly she added, "I thought you'd be more supportive, since I know how worldly you are."

That kind of false compliment usually served to please her mother, and it was clear it was working. Daniella smiled broadly. "Well, I think a mother is always concerned for her child's happiness. That's all I care about, Jordan. I only want you to be happy."

Narrowing her eyes, Jordan said, "Mia makes me happier than I have ever been. My life didn't begin until the day I met her. Now I know what it's like to be loved."

A tiny frown greeted that statement, but Mia returned and the three of them sat there with tense smiles, waiting for the check. Once Jordan had signed for it, they started to walk back to the room. Daniella linked her arm around Jordan's and said, "Walk me to my car?"

"Sure. Here's the room key, Mia," Jordan said. "I'll be back in a minute."

Mia extended her hand. "It was good to meet you, Daniella. I hope we get the opportunity to see each other again before the Olympics."

The older woman attached her warmest smile onto her face and nodded, "I hope so, too. Take care, now."

Mother and daughter walked out towards the small line of people waiting for the valets to bring their cars up to the main entrance, more than one passer-by staring at the pair in obvious appreciation. Jordan glanced at her mother and said, "Thanks for…coming. I know this wasn't what you wanted to hear, but…" With a sharp glance, Daniella cut her off.

"Not in public," she whispered. "Someone might recognize us."

Having nothing else to say, they stood in the cool breeze, waiting patiently. When the car was delivered, Daniella asked the attendant to pull it off to the side, and she motioned for Jordan to join her so they could talk privately. "Your little friend is going to the Olympics, too?"

"Of course she is," Jordan said. "She's my lover…my partner, Mom. We're not casually dating."

"Right," she sniffed. "You're going to be together until the end of time." Taking in a frustrated sigh, Daniella asked, "How will you ever afford to pay for her? You told me that money was tight."

"She's paying her own way. We're lovers, but I don't support her."

That seemed to brighten her spirits, and she smiled once again. "You're really growing up," she reflected. "I think being in love will be good for you." She opened the door to her pale green Jaguar and slid into the creamy, buff-colored leather interior. "Just remember, you have to be a little suspicious of people who want to get close to you when you start to develop some fame." At Jordan's wide-eyed expression, her mother added, "I don't want you to get hurt, or be taken advantage of. You're not very good at protecting yourself."

Yeah, that's obvious. I'm voluntarily having lunch with you! "I trust Mia. She's in love with me for me—not my small amount of fame."

"Oh, now, I meant nothing by that. I'm not talking about her specifically, anyway. She seems very sweet. Not quite the type of person I pictured you with, but very sweet." Giving her child a thoughtful look, Daniella said, "I could see you being attracted to a fellow model. You'd look so elegant with someone your height. Someone who was as pretty as you are."

Eyes darkening with anger, Jordan snapped, "Just for the record, I've never seen a woman more beautiful than Mia. And she's the most loving woman I've ever met. She cares about me—not just herself."

Now Daniella's blue eyes darkened in almost the same fashion. The two women stood, rooted in position for several seconds. Finally, Daniella blinked, ending the standoff. "Well, good for you. I suppose the next time we'll meet is in September."

"Uhm…don't leave yet, Mom."

"Why?"

"I ahh…think we need to have a little discussion about money."

"Money? Whose money?"

"Well…mine; or at least the money that should be mine."

"What do you mean by that?" Daniella's eyes were like two shards of light blue glass, and Jordan could feel them cutting into her soul. But, she was determined to get this out—no matter what.

"You haven't given me one dollar of support since I left for Berkeley. I've never told Dad that, because I knew it would cause a huge fight and I didn't want to be put in the middle…"

"Wait a minute!" Daniella leaned closer and said, "I provide a lovely home for you, and it's available to you at any time! How much do you think a home North of Montana costs to keep up, young lady?"

"I don't live there, Mom," she said quietly. "I never will, and you know that. You've kept one hundred and twenty-six thousand dollars that's rightfully mine, and I've never said one word about it."

"You're saying plenty of words now," Daniella snapped. "What are you angling for, Jordan?"

Deciding to lay her cards on the table, Jordan said, "Dad is going to petition the court for a reduction in the alimony he pays you."

"Over my dead body," Daniella said, an unattractive sneer settling on her face.

"I'm asking you to be reasonable. That's all—just be reasonable."

"Your father made over one and a quarter million dollars last year. If you think I'm going to allow him to pay me one dime less than one hundred thirty-one thousand, you're out of your mind."

"Well, thirty-six thousand will automatically go away when Dad tells the court that I'm not a student any longer."

"You haven't graduated!"

"That doesn't matter, Mother. The decree says he has to pay child support until I turn twenty-one, unless I'm a full-time student."

"But, you'll go back! He has to keep paying until you go back!"

"No, he doesn't," Jordan said, shaking her head slowly. "His obligation is over."

"How can I possibly live on ninety-six thousand a year?" she gasped.

"Dad's going to propose less than that, Mom, and if you don't want me to send an affidavit to the judge about you withholding my child support, I think you should try to think of a way to live on less."

"You wouldn't!"

Jordan sucked in a breath while she tried to keep her breakfast in her stomach. Summoning every bit of courage that she had, she said, in a calm, even voice, "Yes…I…would."

Remarkably, Daniella's eyes grew even colder, her lips pressed into a tight line. "Well, someone is going to have to pick up the slack, Jordan. You'd better hope that you continue to book some lucrative ads—because you're going to need them."

Jordan stepped back a bit, overwhelmingly intimidated by the tone and passion in her mother's voice. She felt she could incinerate on the spot, but she didn't back down. Standing as tall as she could, she said, "I'm not going to model any longer—unless I have to. I don't enjoy it."

"You'd better learn to enjoy it," Daniella snapped.

"I'm not going to do it any more. Gunnar can get a real job and help you out if you need it."

"Don't be ridiculous! I have to give him two or three thousand dollars a month so he can keep up on his car payment."

"Then you're both going to have some adjustments to make," Jordan said. She held her pose for a moment, then turned and walked into the hotel, her legs feeling as rubbery as they had the first time Mia kissed her. *Just get to the room and it'll be all right. Mia's here...my Mia's here.*

🐎

When Jordan entered the room the look on her face brought Mia to her feet. "Honey! What's wrong?"

"I can't," Jordan mumbled. "I can't." She fell onto the bed, fully clothed, staring up at the ceiling, her eyes never blinking.

"Jordan, please! Tell me what's wrong!"

"Please, Mia, just hold me. Please...hold me."

Sighing, Mia sat down by her lover. "Let me undress you, baby, then we'll go back to bed and cuddle, okay?"

"Yeah...yeah."

Quickly undressing them both Mia slid into bed. She knew that Jordan dealt with things better when she vented her feelings, but it was clear that wasn't going to happen today. As soon as Mia pulled the covers up, Jordan turned onto her side.

Mia wrapped an arm around her waist, placed a few gentle kisses on her back and whispered, "I love you."

Jordan silently lifted her hand and kissed it. "God, I hope you do." Placing the hand on her chest, she sighed, and was asleep before Mia could count to ten.

🐎

When Mia woke, Jordan was facing her, gazing intently through wide-awake eyes. "I'm gonna call my father."

"Now?" Mia gasped.

"Right now." Getting to her feet, she crossed to the phone and dialed the number, pacing across the room while the phone rang. "Hi, Candy," she said, with a look of distaste. "Is my father home?" She paused a moment and rolled her eyes. "It's Jordan...his daughter." While she waited, she quietly grumbled, "Do the fucking math, dumbshit! Who else would call the house and ask for her father?"

"Jordan?" Jorgen Ericsson said when he came on the line.

"Yeah, it's me again, Dad. I uhm…have something to tell you, and I hoped you could spare a few minutes."

"You need to see me…in person?" he asked.

"Well, that would be ideal. Can you swing it?"

"Oh, gee, Jordan, our masseuse will be here soon. We like to have a massage on Sunday evening to make Monday a little more bearable."

Oh, that makes sense. Going to yoga class and out to lunch is pretty debilitating. Candy must be beat by the end of the week. "I can be there in forty-five minutes, Dad. I want to talk to you about this, because if I don't, Mother will."

He checked his watch and sighed. "Can't we talk on the phone, honey? I tend to go to sleep as soon as my massage is over. You don't technically have to see me, do you?"

"No, I guess I don't," she said softly. "It would have been nice…but, it's not required." Swallowing the lump in her throat, she began, "I've fallen in love."

"That's great!" He paused for a moment, then added, "This is your first time, isn't it?"

"Yep. It's my first time." She turned and gave Mia a smile warm enough to melt a block of ice. "If I'm lucky it will be the last time."

Unable to resist her smile, Mia got out of bed and walked across the room, urging Jordan into one of the upholstered chairs. She climbed onto her lap and cuddled close, trying to re-assure her with her touch.

"Damn!" Jorgen said, pulling Jordan from focusing on her lover. "You probably wanted to bring this fellow over to meet me, didn't you?"

"In a way, yes," she said. "Only thing is that it's not a fellow, Dad. She's a woman." She decided to say as little as possible at this point, allowing him to process the information as he saw fit.

"Wow," he finally said, his voice softening. "That's quite a surprise." The seconds ticked by, with Jordan's stomach doing continual flips. "Does this woman make you happy?"

"Yes," she nodded soberly. "She makes me very happy, Dad. She's a great person, and I know you'll love her."

"It doesn't matter if I do or not," he said. "It only matters that you do, Jor. So, tell me about her."

"Well, she's a senior at Berkeley," she said, grinning shyly at Mia who grinned back. "She's absolutely gorgeous, she has a wonderful sense of humor, and she loves me as much as I love her."

"I guess that covers all of the important things," Jorgen said, laughing. "Is she an athlete, too?"

"No, not really. She plays golf, though. Maybe I'll try to learn and we can all play together some day."

"That would be great. Oh, what is this gorgeous creature's name?"

"Mia. Mia Christopher," she sighed, loving the way the name rolled off her tongue.

"I'm looking forward to meeting Mia," he said. "I'm sure I'll be favorably impressed."

She was quiet for a moment, then asked, "You're really okay with this, Dad?"

He let out a long breath. "I said this was a shock, honey, but in a way it isn't. You're too pretty a girl not to have had any serious boyfriends. I thought it was a pretty good possibility that you preferred women."

"Huh…I guess that makes sense. Well, it feels like more than a preference, but no matter what it is, I'm happy."

"Then I'm happy for you," he said. "Did you recently figure out that you liked women? Or have you been hiding your…desires?"

"Mmm…a little of both, Dad. But, to be honest, I'm glad that I waited for Mia. I want her to be the only lover I ever have."

Jorgen started to laugh, unable to control himself. "Oh, Jor, that's such an adorable wish. Sometimes I forget how young and earnest you truly are. It's delightful."

Sighing, she said, "Dad, I know that you haven't had very good luck at having a long-lasting relationship, but that doesn't mean that I can't."

"No, of course it doesn't, honey. I wish we could get together, but I promise that next time will be different. Tell Mia that I extend my warm welcome into the family."

"I will, Dad. Thanks," she said. "Thanks a lot."

"No problem. Say, did you get a chance to talk to your mother about that little issue we discussed?"

"Yeah…yeah, I did. I can't guarantee anything, but I think there's a chance she'll be a little more reasonable this time, Dad."

"Really?" he asked, his voice filled with glee. "Thanks so much, Jor. You don't know how much it means to me to always be able to rely on you."

"I can only imagine," she said, her voice breaking on the last word.

"Hey, now, don't get all sentimental on me," he said, chuckling softly. "Go give your girl a big kiss for me, okay? I can't wait to meet her."

"I will," she said, the tears flowing down her cheeks. "Bye."

Placing the receiver back into its cradle, Jordan gently patted Mia's butt. They both stood and Mia automatically wrapped her arms around her partner and held her as tightly as she could. Leading Jordan back to the bed, they lay together with the shaking woman sobbing as though she'd lost something vital to her existence. Jordan didn't say a word, and Mia knew it was futile to ask her to talk. So she held her and rocked her and soothed her as best she could, until it was time to leave for the airport.

⚜

They were halfway down the 405 before Mia brought it up. "Is there any chance you can tell me about your discussions with either of your parents?"

"Not really," she replied, continuing to look out the window. "I need to let it settle."

"Okay. I understand," Mia said, even though she didn't. She was the type of person who understood her feelings by talking about them—at length—to nearly anyone. But she had quickly learned that Jordan was her exact opposite in the sharing department. It sometimes drove her crazy—like today—but she knew she couldn't drag it out of her, so she contented herself with being as close physically as they could manage. As her speech decreased, Jordan's displays of affection grew, until on a day like this, she was nearly molded to Mia's body. Mia had been driving without her right hand since they'd left the hotel, and Jordan showed no signs of letting go soon. A warm hand rested on her thigh, and Jordan occasionally gave her a squeeze, to remind her that she was there. *It's not what I want, but at least she can stand to touch when she's like this,* she mused. *I don't feel nearly as shut out when we're close.*

Dreading the sight, Mia noticed the first exit for the airport. Even though they hadn't been together all that much during the weekend, and they hadn't spoken much when they were together, Mia felt incredibly connected, and knew it would be painful to let her go. They had no firm plans to see each other again, and the time they would have to be apart seemed to stretch into infinity.

When they got to the point of choosing Departures or Arrivals, Jordan directed her to the Arrivals level, saying, "This level's faster. I want you to get going. I worry about you driving all the way back to Berkeley tonight."

"But you've got another hour until your flight," Mia pouted. "I want to be with you as long as I can."

Jordan gave her a fond smile and said, "Come on, baby, give in for a change. If you get going now, you'll be home by the time I am, and I won't have to stay up waiting for your call."

Mia hated it when Jordan used concern to get her way, but it really did work. She had to give her credit. "Okay. I don't like it, though."

"I don't like it either," Jordan said quietly, sounding like she was about to cry.

Mia clasped the hand that held her tightly and said, "If you cry, I'm gonna park. You don't want that, do you?"

Her gentle attempt at humor brought Jordan partially out of her lachrymose mood and brought a wan smile. "I'm okay. Promise," she added for good measure. Mia pulled up in front of the terminal, and gazed at her partner longingly.

"How can I miss you already?" she sighed.

"I don't know, but I miss you, too, so let me know when you figure it out."

Even though her tone was light, the sadness in the clear blue eyes was too much for Mia to take. "You'd better scoot," she said. "The police are moving people along."

Jordan leaned in and kissed her firmly, squeezing her tight as she tried to stave off the tears that were desperately trying to escape. "I love you. Thanks…for everything."

"No big deal. I just loved you. That's always a pleasure."

With a sigh, Jordan got out and tugged her bag out of the back seat. She stood up, bag in hand, looking more like a lost child than an adult. "I wish that were true," she said, so softly that Mia almost didn't hear her.

Fighting to control her emotions, Mia blew her a kiss and waved, then veered her car into the heavy Sunday evening traffic for the long drive home.

Chapter Seventeen

Jamie leaned back in the bus seat, watching the scenery breeze by. She was sitting alone, as was every other player on the team. Having been on Ryan's team bus, she knew that not all of the athletes on Cal's teams were so reserved, but she had to admit that golf at the college level was a funny sport. Despite being one of the most individually focused sports, their collective success or failure depended on team results. During a tournament, each individual score was added together, giving the team a score for the day. At the end of the three-day match, their cumulative scores were added up to create huge numbers. But even with totals of over 900, the difference between first and second place was usually only a few points. So a poor round—a single missed putt—by one individual, could drop a team from first to second or even third place.

In Jamie's opinion, most golfers put a lot of pressure on themselves, and to have your entire team counting on you to hit a fairway or make a chip was often more than an inexperienced young woman could handle.

Scott Godfrey, the head coach, came down the aisle and sank into the seat beside Jamie. Leaning over so only she could hear, he asked, "How do you feel about doing a little mentoring?"

"Mentoring?"

"Yeah. We normally assign rooms at random, but I'm having second thoughts about doing that. I thought that I could assign an upperclassman to a room with each of the two freshmen to give them a little support. Lauren and Samantha both seem freaked out, and I thought it might help."

"I'm happy to help if I can, Scott," she said. "Do you mind a suggestion?"

"No, not at all."

"Don't ask Juliet to do this. I know she's the only other senior, but she's so focused on her own game that I don't think she'd be any help at all."

"Yeah," Scott nodded, "that would be like having one of the freshmen in a single room, wouldn't it?"

"Just about. How about Margo? She'd loosen one of them up."

"That's a good idea," he said. "Margo doesn't let anything bother her—and that's the attitude I want the freshmen to develop."

"Well, I volunteer to room with Lauren," Jamie said. "She's clearly the more nervous of the two."

"Good deal," Scott said. "Thanks for helping out."

"My pleasure. I'm very excited about the season. I think we're gonna surprise some people."

After settling into their rooms, the golfers gathered in a good-sized banquet room. Scott and his assistant coaches stood in the center of a circle of chairs, and all of the girls chose a seat. Jamie looked across the room at Juliet, regretting that they'd barely spoken since the incident at Juliet's home. But even though Jamie felt bad about the chilly reception she got, she wasn't about to go too far out of her way to reassure her. From her perspective, Juliet had issues far too complex for Jamie to understand; and given that she was loath to discuss them, there weren't many options.

Waiting until everyone was settled, Scott said, "Since we start our spring schedule tomorrow, this seemed like a good time to get to know each other. We're going to have to be each other's cheerleaders, since we don't have a home course, and most of our matches are played pretty far from Berkeley. So, what we'd like to do today is spend some time learning the basics about everyone.

"I'd like each of you to interview every other player." The girls all gave each other puzzled looks, while Scott continued. "Ask your teammates any questions about themselves, their families, their golfing careers…anything that you think is important to know about a teammate. When we're all done, I'll ask some questions to see who did the best job. We have a very nice prize for the winner—so do your best."

He passed out pencils and notepads to all of the players, then said, "Let's go! We'll be back in an hour to see who the best interviewer is."

To Jamie's surprise, she won the competition hands-down; beating her closest competitor by nine points. "Excellent job, Jamie," Scott said. "I hope you're planning on going to law school, because you'd be a great trial lawyer."

"I have no plans to do that. Maybe I'll become a journalist, instead."

Scott signaled one of his assistants, and to Jamie's surprise, he came back in with a beautiful, new golf bag. "One of our alums is working at Titleist, selling golf equipment," he said. "She generously donated this beautiful bag that we'll have your name put on."

"Wow," Jamie said, genuinely impressed. The big, navy blue bag had a large gold, embroidered logo of the university on the side, as well as room for Jamie's name. "This is so cool!"

"I hope you enjoy it. And, for the record," he turned to the assembled group, "we have one more. We're going to award that one to the low scorer for the tournament."

After a break for snacks, Scott introduced the next event. "Now, I'd like each of you to talk about your ultimate goal in golf. Don't be afraid to be immodest," he warned. "Jamie, since you were the winner in the last contest, you can start out."

She collected her thoughts and said, "As you all know from the interviews, I played on my high school team. But, I didn't think I had the game to play at the collegiate level, so I didn't even try to get a golf scholarship. I made some changes last year that allowed me to play more of a power game, and that's what gave me the nerve to try out for the team this year.

"I've found that I really love it, and I don't want to give it up just because I'm graduating. I know I'm not good enough to play on the pro tour, and I wouldn't want to live that life even if I were good enough—but I don't want to stop competing.

"So, I'd say I have two goals. One, is to play as well as I possibly can this spring, and help take us to the NCAA tournament; the other is to continue to play as an amateur, and eventually be able to compete in the U.S. Amateur tournament."

"Thanks, Jamie," Scott said. "I think that both of those goals are attainable. Now, who wants to go next?"

By the time they were all finished, it was time for dinner. The dining room was set up with a number of small tables, each one for four players. Jamie intentionally sat with the sophomores, since she knew those players less well than any of the others. They had an enjoyable meal, talking about golf, as usual, but Jamie enjoyed herself, nonetheless.

After the meal, Scott said, "As our last planned activity, I'd like each of you to choose one person who you trust, and talk about your life goals. I know it's easy to let golf take over your lives, but I want you to think beyond that. What would you do if you couldn't play any longer? Do you plan on having a family? What kind of career would you like to pursue? These are questions that many of us don't stop to think about until our golf careers come to a halt—sometimes involuntarily. So, I'd like you to think about them now, and discuss your thoughts with a teammate. I won't make assignments, since I want you to be able to open up, and I know that's not easy to do with a stranger. So, pick your partners, and have a good evening. We won't meet up again after this, so I'll see you all at breakfast tomorrow."

The girls all sat around looking at each other nervously for a moment, then sought out their best friend on the team and took off. Not surprisingly, the only two left were Jamie and Juliet. Most of the girls were completely intimidated by Juliet, so it made sense that no one chose her, but Jamie had to admit that she had no more real friends than Juliet did.

Standing, she walked slowly over, shrugged her shoulders, and said, "Where would you like to go to talk?"

"Uhm…we don't have to tell Scott what we talk about, do we?"

"No, I think he made it clear that this is private. Don't worry, Juliet, this is only between you and me."

"Oh…uhm…I uhm…thought that if we weren't gonna have to tell him what happened, we could go to our rooms and skip the whole thing. I don't really have anything to say."

Jamie stood a little closer and adopted one of her most serious looks. "Get up."

"What?"

"You heard me. Get…up…now."

Eyes wide, Juliet did so, stumbling a little as she pushed her chair back.

"Look, you've been acting like an idiot. You made a pass at me, and I told you no. Leave it behind you, for God's sake! You didn't stab me, Juliet—you showed me that you found me attractive. You might be willing to have this level of distance for three and a half months, but I'm not. I want this team to win, and the only way to do that is if we play as a team. Now, get over yourself."

Juliet nodded, looking mortally embarrassed. "I…I'm sorry, Jamie. I don't know what else to say. I'm very, very sorry."

"That's over, Juliet. I've let it go. Now you have to."

"I don't know if I can," she said softly.

"Let's go somewhere and talk this out," Jamie said. "Do you want to go to the bar?"

"No, no, I couldn't talk about this in a public place. Someone might hear."

Blowing out a frustrated breath that fluttered her bangs, Jamie said, "Fine. Who are you rooming with."

"No one. I've got the single."

"Come on," Jamie said, heading purposefully for the elevator.

Annoyingly jingling a pair of coins in her pocket, Juliet asked, "Are you sure you're willing to come to my room? I mean…after what happened…"

"Do you have a hearing problem?" Jamie asked, nearly ready to resort to violence. "I told you that I have completely put that behind us. I meant that."

"I haven't had a thing to drink," Juliet promised. "Actually, I haven't had a drink since that night. I don't think I'll ever drink again."

"Thanks for the reassurance," Jamie said, giving her a scowl. "Now, I don't mean to insult you, but if you tried anything again, I'd knock your block off. I'm meaner than I look, and after warning you once, I wouldn't have a problem in the world with popping you one."

"Jamie, I swear I won't…"

Jamie grabbed her teammate by the shoulders and gave her a rough shake. "Shut up! I'll also pop you one if you apologize again. Jesus Christ!"

Not another word was spoken as the elevator doors opened to take them up to the third floor. Juliet's hands were shaking noticeably as she slipped her key card into the lock, and Jamie felt a stab of regret for being so harsh with her. They entered the room, and Jamie sat down at the table, with Juliet choosing the most distant bed.

"Okay," Jamie said, trying to smile. "I guess I'll start." At Juliet's puzzled look, she said, "We have an assignment to complete…remember?"

"Oh! Right…go right ahead."

"Well, my goals for the future are to continue to work on my relationship with Ryan," Jamie began. "We've only been together since June, and we still have a lot to learn about each other. Actually," she said, smiling more genuinely, "I hope we're always learning things about each other."

"That must be nice," Juliet said, trying to match Jamie's smile.

"It is. And, since we love each other so much, we want to share our love with at least one child. Ryan hints at having a house full of kids, but I think we'll be able to work out an accommodation."

Juliet looked at her with longing in her eyes. "God, I can't imagine doing that."

"Having children?"

"Uhm…yeah. I ahh…don't think I'll ever do that."

"Why not? A lot of women on the LPGA tour have kids."

Juliet shrugged. "I don't think I will."

"Okay," Jamie said, getting the message that Juliet didn't want to reveal her reasons. "Well, even though Ryan will always be my top priority, both of us plan on having careers. I'm not at all sure what I want to do, but, luckily, I'm not under pressure to make a decision quickly. We're going to take next year off and spend the time making some long-term decisions." Jamie looked thoughtful for a moment, then said, "I used to think that the most important thing was what you accomplished in life. But, I've changed my thinking on that completely. For me, I'll have lived a good life if Ryan and I have a loving, caring relationship; and our children grow up to be good people. Accomplishments are so hollow if you don't have someone who loves you and can't wait to see you at the end of the day."

Jamie had been so focused on her thoughts that she hadn't looked at Juliet for a while. When she turned, she saw her bent at the waist, arms wrapped around herself, crying soundlessly. Jamie got up and went over, sitting next to her on the bed and gently touching her back. "Juliet, it's obvious that you're deeply troubled by something. I don't want to intrude, but I'd like to help you if I can. I'm a very good listener, and I promise that I'll never tell anyone anything that you tell me."

"You'll tell Ryan," Juliet sobbed. "You told her that I tried to kiss you."

"No, I won't," Jamie said. "I only told Ryan about what happened at your house because it affected both of us. We both try to be honest about things that happen to us—because keeping secrets can harm any relationship. But, this is about you, and it's none of Ryan's business." Continuing to stroke Juliet's back, she said, "I promise that I won't reveal anything you tell me—to anyone."

"I can't…" Juliet sobbed. "I can't…"

"That's okay," Jamie said. "You don't have to talk to me. But I want you to know that I'm willing…"

Juliet got up and walked to the window, staring out at the parking lot. "I can't ever have what you have. I can't ever have that."

"What?" Jamie asked, perplexed.

Juliet turned and faced her, tears streaming down her flushed cheeks. "I can't ever have a lover who I can be proud of. I won't be able to have children…I will always have to hide…always!"

Looking at her with compassion, Jamie asked, "Are you a lesbian?"

She nodded, eyes closing in pain.

"Why does that mean that you can't ever be open?" Jamie asked. "You make it sound like you're going into the military."

"It's almost the same. You can't survive on the LPGA tour without sponsors, and sponsors run for the hills if there's even a hint of lesbianism. The Tour is trying to focus on the pretty, straight girls to increase viewership and attendance, and they think they have to appeal to straight men to do that."

"So, you plan on what—dating guys, getting married?"

"I will if I have to," Juliet said, her normal determination back in place. "I've worked too hard to give up my dream."

"But you have other dreams. I can see that."

"Yeah, of course I do, but those dreams are going to have to wait. My life is golf, and I can't let myself get sidetracked. Being around you and Ryan and Mia made me start wishing for things I can't have. For a short time, I let myself have the fantasy that I could live like you guys do—but I can't. Not now."

"It doesn't have to be like this," Jamie insisted. "You could live a quiet, private life as a lesbian. I'm sure dozens of players do so."

"Yes, you can," Juliet admitted. "But, I don't want to merely get by. I want to have endorsements, and opportunities to do other things in golf when my productive years are over. The only women who get endorsements now are the straight ones. That's not my imagination, Jamie. It's the truth."

"Only you know what's most important to you. That's not the path I'd choose, but I'm not in your shoes. I uhm…guess this means that you can't afford to be friends with me."

Giving her a wistful look, Juliet said, "I wish I could, but it's too hard for me. I do better when I stick to golf and school. I can't stand the temptation."

"I understand," Jamie said. She got up and walked to the door. "If you ever need to talk, I hope you know you can count on me."

"I do," Juliet said, nodding. "I want to normalize things on the course, but I can't see you socially. Is that okay?"

"Sure. I'd like to keep playing golf with you. I've learned a lot from you during the times we've played, and I'd like to keep that going."

"I would, too." Giving Jamie a smile, Juliet said, "Thanks for everything. I've…uhm…never come out to anyone before. It feels…weird." Her head cocked and she added, "Good, but weird."

"I know. Believe me, I know."

When Jamie's cell phone finally rang late that night, she grasped for the little device and croaked, "Hi."

"Oh, damn. Were you asleep?"

"Yeah." She got up and went into the bathroom, so she didn't disturb her roommate. "That's okay. I wanted to wait up for your call, but I crashed. Did you just get home?"

"Yeah. Bad weather. We sat on the runway for three hours while a big weather front was stalled over New Mexico. Eight beautiful hours banging around in a storm to get to San Francisco."

"Poor baby. You get to sleep now. You've got an early class."

"I will. Did you have a good day? I feel out of the loop after not talking to you."

"Yeah, I had a good day. Mom and I took Caitlin to church at Poppa's. It was pretty funny, Ryan. Cait got to go to communion, and she decided that she rather likes red wine. Her face scrunched up a little, but then she started looking for more."

"That's my girl," Ryan said. "Never met a meal she didn't like."

"I'll let you go now, so you can get to sleep."

"Okay," Ryan sighed. "Love you."

"I love you, too, sweetheart. See you soon."

After she hung up, Jamie stumbled back into bed, mentally slapping herself when she realized she hadn't even asked whether Cal had won. *Get your priorities straight, girl! You're married to a jock!*

❧

Ryan was standing in the kitchen, getting a cold drink before she went to bed, when Mia got in. When she heard the noise, Ryan poked her head out, and was startled to see her roommate looking pale, tired and red-eyed. "Welcome home," Ryan said, padding across the floor in her bare feet to offer a hug.

Mia let out a sigh, unable to even summon the strength to respond with a smile. She wrapped her arms around Ryan, letting her cheek rest against the strongly beating heart she could feel beneath the ribbed undershirt. "She came out to her parents," she finally got out in a near monotone.

Ryan moved back and grasped Mia by the shoulders, holding her at arm's length to get a good look at her. "How badly did it go?" she asked in alarm.

Realizing why Ryan looked so frightened, Mia hastened to reassure her. "It didn't go badly—I guess. I...I don't know, Ryan. I feel so sad for her, that I'm sick to my stomach."

"Let me make you a warm drink. You go upstairs and put your jammies on."

"But what about Jamie? Isn't she waiting for you?"

"She's over in Vallejo, remember?"

"Oh, right. Where were you again?"

"Las Cruces, New Mexico. Luckily, we're almost through with our nationwide tour. PAC-10 play can't start soon enough for me. Now you go get ready for bed, and I'll bring you some Sleepytime tea."

Five minutes later, Ryan arrived with a warm mug and a warmer smile. Mia was still on the phone, but she got off quickly, relaying Ryan's blown kiss to her lover. "She said she loves you, too," Mia said, trying to, but not matching Ryan's smile.

"Here you go," Ryan said, handing her the mug. "Come sit on the bed, and I'll rub your shoulders. Your back must be stiff from all of that driving."

"Yeah," she said. "That and spending all of yesterday in a limo. I guess that's as comfortable a car as you can have, but it still sucks as a bed."

"Wanna elaborate on that?" Ryan asked as she started to massage Mia's tense shoulders.

"Oh, it's nothing very interesting. The photo shoot was on the beach, and it was cold. So, while my sweetie had to pose on the sand all day in a tiny pair of shorts, I slept in the back seat of a limo. I got the better end of the deal."

"Tough weekend, huh?"

"In a way. But being with her is worth anything, Ryan. She's so…I don't know," she said, shaking her head. "I've never felt like this about anyone. She means so much to me." She glanced over her shoulder and mused, "It's odd. You're the one who lost her mom, but Jordan seems like the motherless child. Do you know what I mean?"

Ryan nodded slowly. "Yeah, I do. She's very fragile—she seems so lost sometimes."

"You should have met the mother," Mia said, all traces of warmth gone from her voice. "She seemed okay at first, and if I didn't know how Jordan felt, it would have been a decent visit. But I do know, and by the end of it, I felt like her mom had carved a hole in my soul and was slowly sucking it out." Her whole body shivered and she said, "She made me feel so inconsequential—so unnecessary. I got a taste of how Jordan feels—and it sucks."

"Was she mean or bitchy?"

"No, no, just the opposite. She was very cordial…but they acted like people who barely knew one another. They were polite—and that's it! We were together for about an hour and a half, and she didn't ask Jordan one question about herself. She didn't ask how things were going in Colorado; she didn't ask if she was getting any playing time—nothing! Her only concern was about herself—and how things were going to be for her when she got to Sydney."

"Brutal," Ryan murmured.

"It *was* brutal. Her mom didn't give a good goddamn about us being lovers. I mean, it's not like she approved or anything—she didn't care enough to disapprove!"

"That's the first time I've heard that reaction," Ryan shuddered, "and I thought I'd heard them all."

"Something else happened, but I don't know what," Mia said. "She and her mom were alone together for about twenty minutes, and when she got back to the room she looked like she'd been beaten."

"And you don't know what happened?"

"Not a clue. She clammed up and didn't say a word about it—but she cried for nearly two hours after she talked to her father—so I'm guessing that the whole day finally caught up with her."

"Damn," Ryan said, shaking her head. "How was her dad?"

"Better. He seems to at least care for her—not enough to cross the street to see her, mind you, but he does seem to care in the abstract."

"She didn't get to tell him in person?" Ryan gasped.

"Of course not. His masseuse was coming."

"Fuck," Ryan muttered. "Some people shouldn't be allowed to have an aquarium—much less a child."

"They're the poster parents for vasectomy and tubal ligation," Mia said. "I hope to God that Jordan doesn't take after them if we decide to have kids."

Ryan's hands stilled and she leaned over Mia's shoulder to stare at her upside down. "Kids? You're thinking of having kids together?"

Mia batted at her weakly, and Ryan went back to her previous position. "Yes, Ryan. I'm thinking of spending the rest of my life with her. That is what you do with people you love more than anything on earth, isn't it?"

Ryan sank down to sit behind Mia, and enveloped her in a warm hug. "Yes. That's exactly what you do," she whispered. "I'm so glad she has you."

"I'm glad I have her," Mia sighed. "I only wish her parents loved her half as much as I do."

On Monday morning, Jamie woke slowly, the annoying buzz of an alarm barely penetrating her foggy brain. "Jamie…Jamie…" A soft voice insistently called her name, but she didn't recognize the tone, and decided that she must be dreaming. "Jamie!" Now a hand grasped her shoulder and gave her a shake.

"Huh?"

"Time to get up. We're leaving in a half hour."

Forcing her eyes open, she regarded her teammate, who was gazing at her with concern. "Oh!" She sat up rather abruptly and ran a hand through her hair. "Wow, I was really out."

"You're very hard to wake up," Lauren Takuta said. "It's a good thing we don't have single rooms. I'm afraid you'd sleep all day."

"No," Jamie replied, stretching thoroughly. "I eventually hear the alarm. How much time do we have?"

The young woman looked at the clock again. "Twenty five minutes. You'd better hurry." She was giving Jamie such a concerned look, that Jamie didn't have the heart to delay another moment. Slipping out of bed, she got up and gathered her shower things, noting that Lauren was completely dressed.

"I assume you're finished in the bathroom?" Jamie asked over her shoulder.

"Yes. I've been ready for a long while now."

Finally opening her eyes wide enough to see the look of stark anxiety on her face, Jamie smiled and said, "We're gonna be fine today, Lauren. It's only another round."

"Not for me," she said. "My parents will be here."

"Do they put a lot of pressure on you?" Jamie asked gently.

"No, but it's very important that I do well. I have to keep my scholarship."

Jamie crossed over and put her hand on her shoulder, feeling the slight tremor that shook her body. "Lauren, you won't lose your scholarship. Scott would never do that—even if you played horribly all season—which you won't!"

Lauren nodded, but she didn't look at all convinced. Glancing at the clock again she said, "You have to hurry. We'll be late."

"Go on down to the restaurant," Jamie insisted. "I'll be on time, I guarantee it."

"Okay," Lauren said hesitantly.

Jamie stood in the shower, trying to wake up. She considered the dynamics of the young team, deciding that they had the nucleus of a very good squad. The only problem was going to be convincing the less experienced women to believe that they were as good as they actually were.

When Jamie emerged from the shower, she shook her head when she saw that Lauren had neatly laid her uniform out on the bed. *Who's mentoring whom?*

🐎

After Jamie made sure that Lauren ate some of the food that sat on her plate, the team hopped in the shuttle bus for the short ride to the course. They had an eight a.m. shotgun start—so every player teed off at the same time, albeit from different holes. This type of start was used often in tournaments, allowing every hole to be in use throughout the round. Jamie was scheduled to start on eighteen, and after warming up thoroughly, she headed on over to the tee.

A long-legged, raven-haired, beauty stood right next to the tee-box, dark sunglasses covering eyes that Jamie was quite sure were the color of the Aegean. She held two cups in her hands, and was sipping on the larger one when Jamie sidled up to her. "Come here often, good lookin'?"

"Every time I hear that there's going to be a fantastic looking blonde playing golf here. I brought you a latte."

Jamie took the cup and stood on her tiptoes for a quick kiss, which Ryan gladly delivered. Taking a big sip of the still-warm liquid, she smiled broadly. "What a nice way to start the day." Giving her partner an impish look, Jamie said, "I can't tell you how hard it is not to wrap my lips and my arms and my legs around you, and kiss you until your knees turn to jelly."

"Same here, hot stuff, but I don't think that's how you want to start your spring season. You golf-types are supposed to be stoic, you know. Besides, your opponent looks nervous enough to faint, even without us groping each other."

"Ooh, I hope she's as nervous as she looks," Jamie said. "I'll take every edge I can get." She took another big sip and hummed with pleasure. "This is so good, babe. It'll start me off right."

"I know you don't like plain coffee, and I figured that you hadn't yet wound your coach around your little finger, and that he probably wouldn't run to Starbucks for you. Only doing what I can to aid in the cause."

Jamie wrinkled her nose and said, "I appreciate the coffee, but what I'm really pleased with is that you're here. Don't you have somewhere you should be, though?"

"I'm not going to grad school next year. So what if I flunk a class or two?"

Jamie knew the odds of that happening were exactly zero, but she played along. "You can always go to summer school," she offered. "Those classes are filled with you jock types."

"No way," Ryan said. "I'm gonna be way too busy this summer to waste my time in school. I'm spending the summer with an absolutely gorgeous woman. We're gonna lie in bed and peel grapes for each other all day long."

"Sounds divine," Jamie said. "She's a lucky woman."

"I hope she's lucky today," Ryan said. "I wanna see some red numbers on that scoreboard, since I'm mortgaging my future to be here."

"Do my best," Jamie promised. "Help me put my ring on this necklace, okay?" she asked tugging at the thick gold chain she wore.

"How...?"

"Just unclasp the necklace and slip the ring through it," Jamie instructed. "I'd do it myself, but I don't want to run the risk of not clasping it properly."

"Do you always do this?"

"Yeah. I tried to do what you do and tie it in my shoelace, but I don't want to drag it through the sand. I think this works better for me."

"That's a pretty substantial ring to wear on a chain," Ryan said.

"I know," she said. "But I'll gladly look like a rap star to protect it. Now, kiss me goodbye and keep sending good vibes, babe, 'cause I'm not going to look at you again until I finish up on seventeen."

"I look forward to being ignored." She gave her partner a chaste kiss and then accepted her empty cup. "Go get 'em, bulldog."

"Grrrrrr."

Catherine didn't show up until the twosome was on the fourth hole, and she was panting heavily when she came up alongside Ryan. "I got so confused!" she said, moaning dramatically. "I had no idea that Jamie wouldn't start on the first hole. I've walked this entire course!"

"Aw...you poor thing," Ryan sympathized. "Want me to carry you for a while?"

Catherine gently slapped at her and said, "I can handle it, wise guy. I've been walking so much getting ready for the Three-Day that my neighbor's dogs don't even bark when I walk by any longer. I can easily walk this course twice."

"Not a doubt in my mind," Ryan said. "Jamie's doing well," she indicated, pointing at the tote board that an affable-looking senior citizen carried.

"Red numbers are good, right?" Catherine asked.

"Right. Jamie's one under par, so she has a red negative one by her name."

Catherine reached into her purse, took out her camera, and took a photo of the board, showing EVANS -1. "This is so much fun," she said, giggling girlishly. "She looks cute, doesn't she?"

Ryan reached up and pulled her sunglasses up so that Catherine could see her eyes. "Was that a serious question?"

Swatting her again, the older woman said, "You're very impish today, aren't you?"

"A little. And yes, I agree that Jamie looks adorable. She looks good in those colors. Makes her hair look even blonder."

The Cal uniform consisted of a navy blue visor with "Cal" in bright gold script, a white polo shirt with a golden bear paw on the left sleeve, a navy blue sleeveless sweater with the "Cal" logo on the breast, and unadorned navy blue shorts. Ryan noted that under her white and navy saddle-style golf shoes, Jamie wore short socks with a bit of gold on the cuff.

"She really enjoys this, doesn't she?" Catherine asked quietly, so as not to be heard by the players.

"Yeah. It's been good for her. I had the feeling at first that she tried out for the team to make her father proud, but over time she seems to have changed her focus. I think she's doing this only for herself."

Catherine reached down and grasped her daughter-in-law's hand. "She needs to do something that she's better at than you, too. You're a tough person to compete against, Ryan O'Flaherty."

Ryan nodded, acknowledging the truth to Catherine's statement, even though it embarrassed her to do so. "I think she's far superior to me in dozens of ways, but I realize that she doesn't always see that. I get a lot of acclaim for the things that I do, and Jamie deserves some of that, too."

"She does," Catherine said. "I'm glad that she's got this. And I'm glad that you've encouraged her to play—even though it takes away from your time together."

"If everything goes according to plan, we're in year one of a minimum seventy-five year plan. I can bear having her gone for a day or two."

"I hope your plans all come true," Catherine said, squeezing the hand that she still held.

🐴

Jamie finished her round with a very respectable seventy-three, and she seemed pleased with herself when she emerged from her tunnel-visioned state. After greeting her mother, the three of them walked back two holes to find Lauren's group. The freshman was not having a very good day, and she looked downhearted as she finished with a seventy-seven. Her parents were there to greet her when she holed out, and Jamie was pleased to see that they met her with smiles and encouraging hugs. "Who's up for lunch?" she asked, now that she felt able to leave the course.

"I could be persuaded," Ryan said. "Wanna go to the clubhouse?"

"No way," Jamie said. "I have to eat dinner there tonight. The food's not bad, but it's not very inventive. I need something spicy."

As usual, Catherine knew of a place, even though they were many miles away from her usual stomping grounds. They drove in Ryan's car to a very tasty sushi bar, where Jamie's spicy craving was well satisfied. At the end of the meal, she admonished Ryan to stay in Berkeley the next day. "I'll see you when you get home from softball practice," she insisted. "You need to go to your classes tomorrow."

"All right," Ryan said, her blue eyes peeking out of her bangs while she pouted. "But only if you're going to be here to watch," she said, looking to Catherine.

"I wouldn't miss it. And I promise to call you when she finishes her first nine holes for an update."

"Now, that I can live with," Ryan said.

Chapter Eighteen

Later that afternoon, Ryan spent some time trying to track down one of her classmates to see what had gone on in class while she was playing hooky at the golf course. She was cutting across campus when she spotted Franny Sumitomo from the basketball team. "Hey, Franny! Wait up!"

The shy freshman stopped immediately, then turned and smiled when she saw Ryan. "Hi. How are you? Feeling better?"

"Yeah, yeah, things are going pretty well. I'm with the softball team now, you know. Not to dis' you guys, but the atmosphere is a heck of a lot better."

"You don't have to tell me," Franny said. She looked around rather furtively, then said in a quiet voice, "I've been talking to the coaches at Oregon and Washington State about transferring. I don't think I can stand another year here."

"Really? That surprises me," Ryan said. "I know it's important for you to be close to home—and I know that your parents enjoy watching you play. They came to every home game, didn't they?"

"Yes, they did," she said, "but Stanford isn't interested in me. Their point guard is a freshman, too, and there's no way I'm a better player than she is. Oregon and Washington State could both use me, and sitting out a year wouldn't be too horrible. I mean, it's not what I want—but I haven't had any fun this year at all, and it seems silly to work this hard if it's not enjoyable."

"Well, the two people I had the most trouble with will be gone next year," Ryan said. "Won't that help?"

"Yes, I suppose so. But, to be honest, I don't trust Coach Hayes. She's let Janet and Wendy ruin this year for all of us. I think she lets her personal feelings for people get in the way of making the proper coaching decisions. I don't even know if she cares anymore, Ryan. We've got six games left and the team is sleep-walking during practice. I'd quit now if it wouldn't look so bad to the coaches at Oregon and WSU."

"Look, Franny, I know this year has been hard for you, but give it a couple of weeks before you make a decision about transferring. I also think you should talk to the coach about how you feel. She can be surprisingly empathetic if you catch her on a good day."

"Maybe I'll talk to Lynette," Franny decided. "I don't know if I have time to wait for a good mood to overtake Coach Hayes."

When she got home from school, Ryan called the private investigator that Jim had arranged for her to work with. "Hi, Mr. Williams, it's Ryan O'Flaherty."

"Hi, Ryan. I was just about to wrap up our little matter. I've got some interesting things for you."

"Could I add one little bit, Mr. Williams? I know I wanted you to focus on Cassie Martin, but there are two more people who might have had a hand in this, and in a way, they're nearly as culpable as Cassie is."

"Sure, Ryan. Give me their names, and I'll get right on it."

On Tuesday morning, Ryan brought the papers in before she took off for school. As was her habit, she unfolded them and placed then on the kitchen table so that her partner had them waiting for her. Even though Jamie wouldn't be home until late afternoon, Ryan wanted to maintain their normal routine to welcome her partner home. The New York Times was first, since Jamie said she had to read a real paper before she could stomach the Comical, as she called it. As Ryan set the Chronicle into place, she stopped abruptly when she spied the story on the bottom corner of the front page. "Sen. Evans fully backs Admin on gay policies."

This should be good, she said, rolling her eyes in reaction. She scanned the article, then went back and re-read it, shaking her head. *What in the holy hell is wrong with that guy? It's like he can't stand to have things go well for any length of time.*

Picking up the phone, Ryan dialed Jamie's cell, smiling gently when her lover picked up on the first ring. "This had better be my father, saying that he was maliciously misquoted," Jamie said.

"No, it's just me, offering sympathy."

"Well, that wasn't the best headline for me to see first thing this morning," Jamie said. "Poor Lauren nearly fainted at the string of profanities that I let out. I think she's down talking with Scott right now about changing roommates."

"Hey, you're understandably upset."

"Yeah, upset about covers it. My stupid father got cornered and declared that he supported 'don't ask, don't tell', and the congressional 'defense of marriage' bill."

"I can't understand why he'd do that," Ryan said. "He's already said he's against Proposition 22. Isn't the defense of marriage bill the same thing?"

"It is to me," Jamie said. "In fact, the defense of marriage bill is worse in my opinion. It not only prohibits the federal government from recognizing gay marriage, it forbids the government from honoring marriages that individual states sanction. That's far worse than Prop 22. He's like a friggin' pendulum. Every bit of progress is met by an equal amount of backsliding."

"It does seem that way, doesn't it," Ryan sympathized. "I'm pissed at him as your father, and I'm pissed at him as my senator. This sucks."

"It does," Jamie agreed, "and now I've got to call and scream at him before I go play tournament golf."

"I've gotta run, babe. I've got my cell phone on. If you need to call me—please do."

"Thanks. Have a good day. I'll give Daddy your disgust."

Jamie waited patiently while her father's secretary searched for him. He was in the Senate chambers, but he stepped outside and placed a return call on his cell phone. "Hi, Jamie, what's up?" he asked, oblivious to her pique.

"I was more than a little upset to see your comments on those ridiculous policies the administration is backing, Dad."

"Huh…oh! Uhm…why would my comments upset you, honey? Those policies aren't new."

"Why on earth would you stand up against Prop 22, and yet say that you're in favor of the defense of marriage bill?" she nearly screamed. "That's so inconsistent."

"Yeah, it probably is…a little bit," he agreed, "but the administration didn't feel they could take the risk of going against the defense of marriage bill. It's only politics, honey."

Sighing heavily, she said, "It might be politics to you, but it's my life and my civil rights you idiots in Washington are playing with!"

"Hey!" he snapped, "I can hear that you're angry, but I don't appreciate being called an idiot!"

"Supporting the defense of marriage bill, while decrying the politics behind Prop 22 is idiotic," she said, enunciating each word.

"That's your opinion, Jamie, but I would think you'd have some sympathy for the position we're in here. It doesn't do much good to take the kind of stand you advocate if you're then voted out of office. You have to compromise, and take it slow."

She paused for a moment and quietly asked, "Dad, I have a question for you, and I'd appreciate a straight answer."

"Okay," he said hesitantly.

"How do you personally feel about those two issues? I don't want the administration's position. I want yours."

"Well," he said, seeming to delay his answer as long as possible, "I uhm… guess that I tend to agree with the 'don't ask, don't tell' policy. I mean, I know it's not the best solution, but the leaders of the military are clear that it can't work to allow gay people to serve alongside straight ones. I think we have to defer to their expertise."

"Uh-huh. We have to defer to their sweeping prejudices about gay people, about women serving in a combat role, etcetera, etcetera. Those are the people who you want to make social policy, right, Dad?"

"I know it's not perfect, Jamie, I've already said that. But we have to have some policy, and this is the one that seems to be working."

She tried to control the steam that threatened to whistle from her ears, and asked her follow up question. "What about gay marriage? Where… do…you…stand?"

"I uhm…I think that gay people can definitely form loving unions that are as valid as a nor…uhm…regular…couple can have. You and Ryan are good examples of that."

"Uh-huh. Go on."

"But I'm not sure it's a good idea to give state sanction to those unions. I think it sets a bad example for kids."

"What? What?"

"Now, don't get defensive," he said sharply. "You wanted to know my position, and I'm telling you."

"Fine. Tell me how it sets a bad example."

"Well, if someone is having a hard time deciding if they're gay or straight, having the option of full acceptance might push him or her over the edge. If we retain some social disapproval, that person might stay straight. I honestly think it's best to urge people to be straight if they can be."

Ignoring the idiocy of his answer, she posed her second question. "What about having children, Dad? What about adopting?"

"Uhm…I'm sure that you and Ryan would be fine parents, Jamie, but again, I don't think the state should place children in a gay home. It gives the child an impression that can be dangerous."

She was quiet for a minute, her roiling stomach urging her to spit out some of the venom that was coursing through her gut. "And yet, you've agreed to participate in our wedding. Are you going to make a little speech about how our union sets a bad example? For God's sake, at least have the courage of your convictions! If you think our union is wrong, I don't want you there! And if you think our children will be raised in a dangerous environment I don't want you to have anything to do with them!"

"Jamie, please, don't go off the deep end."

"Look, Dad, I knew that you were having trouble with this, but I can't have you participate in my marriage if you think it's morally wrong. That's not going to happen. I'm marrying Ryan in August, whether or not you're there. Think about it and let me know if you'll be part of our celebration." With that, she hung up, and pushed the off button on her phone. *Thank God he's four thousand miles away. I might actually strangle him if I could get my hands around his neck!*

Ryan called about an hour later, inquiring after Jamie's mental health. "It didn't go well," Jamie said. She proceeded to give her partner the low points, then added, "Right now I'm trying to think of how to get a blood sample from him to do some DNA testing. I'm absolutely sure he's not related to my grandfather, or to me!" She let out a deep sigh, then said, "Wish me luck. I tee off in ten minutes. I'm going to picture my father's face on the golf ball—that should improve the length of my drives."

Knowing they would have a fiery, emotion-filled evening, Ryan poked her head in the front door after softball, slightly afraid that Jamie would be hurling breakables at the walls. But the house was completely quiet, save for some soft music coming from the second floor.

Immensely pleased at the encouraging sign, Ryan nearly skipped up the stairs. She was more excited about seeing Jamie than she could convey, and her skin was tingling when she tossed open the door to their bedroom. "Where's the most beautiful woman in the world?" she called out.

"She'd better be opening the bathroom door to give me a proper welcome home," Jamie replied.

Ryan pushed the door open a crack to find Jamie neck deep in a fragrant bubble bath. A tray filled with every possible type of sushi and sashimi was resting on the counter, along with a massive bottle of Kirin beer nestled in an ice bucket, alongside two plastic glasses. Placing her hands on her hips, Ryan shook her head and said, "You never cease to amaze me."

"Don't stand there gaping at me," the low voice purred. "Drop those sweaty clothes and get in here."

Ryan did so, pausing to brush her teeth first. "I want to make a good impression," she winked.

She knew she'd have trouble kissing her partner once she got in, so Ryan knelt on the floor and spent a few minutes showing Jamie how lonely her lips had been. She did such a good job that Jamie considered ditching the dinner and the bath, but thought better of it when she realized she was starving. "Come on in, love. Bring the tray with you."

Ryan did so, securing the legs of the bed-tray as she placed it right next to the tub. It took a few minutes of fitting the human puzzle-pieces together, but she was soon nestled between Jamie's thighs—her most favorite place on earth. "Could I be happier than this?" she asked rhetorically. "I think not."

"I'm pretty high on the happiness scale, too," Jamie murmured, leaning forward for a few nibbles of salty skin.

"How can that be?" Ryan wondered. "I thought you'd be foaming at the mouth about your dad."

"No, I unloaded on my father, but I'm pretty calm now." She shook her head and said, "Damn, Ryan, he and I sure set each other off."

"I know. Did you talk to your mom about what happened?"

"Yeah," Jamie replied glumly. "I talked to Poppa, too. Neither one of them seemed surprised by his position, and they each think that he'll slowly alter his view." She shrugged and said, "Maybe I'm too impatient."

"You're hurt," Ryan said, resting her head on her lover's chest. After a moment, she felt Jamie start to relax, and soon their bodies were molded together. "I'm hurt, too," Ryan added.

"I guess that's it," Jamie said softly. "It's stunningly hurtful to have your father tell you that he thinks you'd be a bad influence on a child." She leaned forward to look at her partner, pain filling in her eyes. "How could he think that?"

"Easy. He's letting his deeply held prejudices color his actions. It would be bad enough if he was only a parent, but he's a senator, too. His actions affect millions and millions of people."

"It is just prejudice, isn't it."

"Yep. It's taking something that bothers you on a visceral level, and then intellectualizing a way to rationalize discrimination. For what it's worth, it's usually not done with malevolence. I'm sure your father believes what he said. He's got so many negative images of gay people burned into his brain that he can't let the positive images overcome them."

"But what do we do, honey? How do we reach him?"

"One thing is for sure. We don't cut off contact with him. He needs to be around people who see us as complete human beings. Being around my family can only help."

Jamie nodded slowly. "You're right of course, but I can't bear the thought of seeing him right now." She shuddered and said, "He sent me an e-mail this afternoon where he justified discriminating against us with the analogy that it's the same as discriminating against blind people who want a driver's license. Just because you can't let them drive doesn't mean you think they're bad or wrong for being blind. You're only trying to protect society at large."

"Ouch!" Ryan said, making a face. "So being gay is a disability, or a birth defect, huh? Nice."

Jamie colored a little and revealed, "I shot back an e-mail that I'm not proud of. If he were President, the Secret Service would be over here by now."

Ryan nuzzled against her and said, "He's hitting your hot buttons with this, honey. I know it's hard, but I think you'll feel better if you try not to hurt him as much as he's hurt you."

"Yeah, yeah," she said in a mechanical voice. "Do unto others, and all that crap. I'm sick of thinking about it. Let's talk about us."

They spent nearly an hour filling each other in on their weekends, then Jamie gave her partner an in-depth assessment of the golf team's victory in Vallejo. "Wish I could have been there today," Ryan sighed. "When I play it's so reassuring to look up into the stands and see your face, and I know that's true for you. I've enjoyed my sports so much more this year than I have in the past. It's been great, and I regret that I won't be able to go to any of your away matches."

"You can make some of the local ones. And I don't think we react the same to having an audience. I don't play off the crowd the way you do. I honestly try not to notice anyone in the gallery."

"Mmm…I guess that's true. I still hate it, though."

"You'll get your chance. I want to keep playing in amateur events once I graduate. I think the competition has been good for me. Maybe someday you can be in the gallery when I'm competing in the U.S. Amateur."

Ryan turned around as much as she could to gaze into her partner's eyes. "The hell you say! I'll be your caddie!"

Giving her a firm hug, Jamie pressed her cheek against her partner's warm, wet, back. "You'd be the cutest caddie on legs," she murmured.

"That's nice to think of," Ryan sighed. "I love to dream about our future."

"I do, too. And tonight, I want our immediate future to include lots of remarkably scandalous dancing. I want to be around gay people tonight. I want to act like the lesbian that I am, and not be belittled because of it. I want to be with my own kind!"

They dressed in their separate rooms, and when Ryan came out she smiled at her partner. "I haven't seen that outfit since the Dyke March. You look adorable."

Jamie pirouetted, bowing at the compliment. She wore a green ribbed tank top, green Army fatigues, and shin-height Doc Marten's, with her pants tucked into the boots. She returned to the mirror and fussed with her hair, commenting, "I want my hair to stick up, but it's a little too long."

"I like it this length," Ryan said, "but it would look cute shorter, too. Get it cut if you want."

Jamie smiled and said, "I only want it to stick up tonight. I'm sure I'll want it longer by tomorrow, so I'd better leave it alone."

"That would be the wiser course," Ryan said.

"Besides, I've been thinking about growing it out again. Would you like it long?"

With images of long, golden blonde hair trailing down Jamie's bare back, Ryan found her head nodding mechanically. "Nice," she said rather vacantly.

"You sound like Homer Simpson," Jamie said, chuckling heartily. "I enjoy your long hair so much, that I thought you should see which way you prefer mine. I'll grow it out and then let you choose how I wear it. Deal?"

"Long. I like it long," Ryan said, grinning like she'd been struck with a heavy object.

When they returned from the local lesbian watering hole, Ryan sorted through the mail that Jamie had brought upstairs earlier in the evening. She opened a small, square envelope, pursed her lips as she read the card, then threw the card and envelope away.

"What was that?" Jamie asked.

"What?"

"What did you throw away? It looked like an invitation."

"Oh. It was just some of my old buds from the gym. They have a big party every year to celebrate a couple of birthdays. Two of the women share a birthday and they always have a big blowout—a real wild one."

"Uhm…any particular reason that you threw it out without even mentioning it?"

"Oh! I assumed you wouldn't be interested. Are you?"

"Well, gee, Ryan, when we met, you had dozens of friends. I remember you always talking about hanging out with your buddies. But now you don't see any of them. Is that because of me?"

"Uh-huh," Ryan said, nodding.

"But why? I certainly don't want you to stop seeing your friends. Don't you…think they'd like me?"

"Aww…Jamie," Ryan said, tucking her arms around her partner and smiling when she heard her sigh heavily. "Of course they'd like you. I guess I assumed you wouldn't like them."

Giving her a semi-perturbed look, Jamie asked, "And why is that? Am I too straight-laced for your friends?"

"Heck, no," Ryan said, trying to think of a reason that wouldn't irritate her partner. "Well…uhm…you're not straight-laced…you're…"

"You think I'm straight-laced!" Jamie cried.

"No, no, I don't. I think they're wilder than you are. Big, big difference."

Pouting, Jamie walked over to shut down her computer. "Is not," she grumbled.

"Yes, it is," Ryan said, coming up behind her and turning her around. "They're more...I don't know," she said, "they're just kinda wild."

"I can keep up, Ryan," Jamie said, narrowing her eyes. "I think we should go, if you don't have a softball game, that is."

"No, the party's Saturday night, and my game is at home in the afternoon. I could be up for a party."

Smiling broadly, Jamie said, "Cool. Call them and accept."

Chuckling, Ryan said, "No need. They won't have any food, and they'll buy a couple of kegs of beer and make everyone pay five bucks to get in. The more the merrier."

Jamie's eyebrows rose again. "No food? Like, none at all?"

"Hmm...if anyone remembers they might have a cake, but it'll be from a grocery store. One year they were all jazzed 'cause they got one half price since it was made up for someone's anniversary."

"Well," Jamie said, her eyes widening. "This sounds like it will be interesting. Maybe we should drag Mia along with us. She always does well at parties."

"Sure, that'd be fine. But, she'll attract a lot of attention in this crowd. The drunker they get, the cooler they think they are."

"She seems so down, honey, I think we should do whatever we can to cheer her up. Having a bunch of women flirt with her is a sure-fire picker-upper."

🐴

Once she was dressed in her warmest pajamas, Jamie said, "I think I heard Mia come in a few minutes ago. I'm gonna go see how she's doing."

"Okay. I've got some work to do for class tomorrow. I'll be in my room."

"I hope you don't plan on working late, sweet cheeks. I'm gonna have my way with you tonight—and I don't want to get started at midnight."

Giving her a very sexy grin, Ryan said, "I'll gladly fit you into my schedule. I missed you something fierce."

"I'll be back in a few. Work fast."

Walking down the hall, Jamie cocked her head as she tried to discern what the odd sound coming from Mia's room was. Poking her head in, she saw her roommate lying on her stomach, head buried in her pillow. Her body was shaking roughly, and she was obviously crying, but the sound was muffled and distorted by the pillow.

Approaching the bed, Jamie sat down quietly. "Mia, baby, what's wrong?" She ran her hand up and down her back, feeling the heat that radiated off her body.

Rolling over, Mia looked up at her with swollen eyes and said, "I'm scared shitless, but I'm gonna tell my parents about Jordan."

"That's why you're crying?" Jamie asked, confused.

"No," Mia sniffed. "I'm crying because I just talked to Jordan. I'm so worried about her, James. Did Ryan tell you that she came out to her parents?"

"Yeah, she did. It didn't sound like it went very well."

"I have a feeling that not many things go well with those two. Her mom was the most self-involved person I've ever met, and even talking to her seems to wear Jordan down. I don't know what the deal is with her father," she sighed. "Jordy idolizes him, but he gives her that Hollywood bullshit that everyone seems to thrive on in L.A. Do you know what I mean?"

"No, not really. What does Hollywood have to do with it?"

"I saw this constantly when I was working in the film industry last summer. Everybody acts like they like you, and that they'd give anything to spend some quality time with you, but something desperately urgent keeps them from doing so. They have no interest at all in this other thing—but they absolutely can't get out of it."

"And Jordan's dad uses that excuse with her?"

"James, as far as I know, she's asked to see him twice this year. The first time was when we were in L.A. for the volleyball games, and this was the second. Both times he blew her off without a minute's hesitation. She asked to see him to tell him about me, but he wouldn't cancel a massage! She hasn't seen him since summer—and she was thirty minutes from his house and he couldn't squeeze her in."

"Brutal," Jamie murmured.

"She seemed to take the whole weekend in stride, but since then, she's been more and more depressed. It hurts her so much, James, but it's like she can't express how she feels about it. Talking about her father in anything less than a positive light is strictly forbidden!"

"Damn, that must be hard for her," Jamie said, shaking her head. "But what does this have to do with telling your parents?"

"I want to show her how proud I am to love her," Mia said, her eyes filling with tears once again. "Her own parents don't give a crap about her, but I love her, James. I love her with all my heart."

"Oh, Mia," Jamie said, hugging her tight. "I know you love her, but are you ready to do this? I hate to see you rush into it only to make Jordan feel better."

Mia sat up and shrugged. "When will I ever be ready? My parents will go ballistic for a while, then things will calm down. What's more important to me is that Jordan knows how much I love her, and that I'll always be proud of our love."

"I'm proud of you," Jamie said, giving her another hug. "I know you're worried about this, and I'll support you in any way that I can."

"I know you will," Mia said, smiling wanly. "But I don't think there's much you can do other than pray that my mother doesn't strangle me with her bare hands."

Chapter Nineteen

Bright and early on Wednesday morning, Ryan was sitting on the stairs leading up to Haas Auditorium, having checked to see when the basketball team was scheduled to use the weight room. She knew the work-avoiding seniors would be the first to leave, and her guess was absolutely correct—the two women looking like they'd barely broken a sweat. "Good morning, girls," she said when she spotted her prey.

Janet gave her a look of complete disdain, stepping over Ryan's sprawled-out body. But that tactic wasn't going to work. The quarry would not escape. Ryan grabbed onto the cuff of Janet's jeans, holding on tightly—nearly causing her to fall down the stairs headfirst.

Whirling, she launched a kick at Ryan's head, but didn't count on Ryan's reflexes. Quick hands grabbed the flailing foot and held it, refusing to let go. "What the fuck is wrong with you?" Janet yelled. "Did you finally lose your mind?"

"Nope," Ryan said, looking calm and collected. "The three of us are going to move over there and have a little chat." She twitched her head towards a bench in front of Zellerbach Hall.

"Fuck off, O'Flaherty," Wendy said, her voice rising. "We're not gonna spend one second with you. We have reputations to protect." She began to snicker, causing a nasty smile to bloom on Ryan's face.

"If either of you want to be on the basketball team by the end of the day, I suggest you risk your sterling reputations to spend a few minutes with me. Of course, if you don't—I'll tell Coach Hayes what I know, and let her sort things out—makes no difference to me."

Wendy cracked first, giving her friend a slightly panicked look. But Janet was cool, calm and collected, making Ryan wonder if only one of them was involved. Ryan let go of Janet's foot, making a dismissive gesture. "Go on," she said. "I'm sure you'll be hearing from Coach Hayes before practice."

"What do you want?" Wendy asked, looking to Janet once again for support.

"I want to go over there," Ryan said, pointing, "and talk to both of you. If we don't all talk, I'm going directly to Coach Hayes' office. Your choice."

"Oh, for God's sake, let's go," Janet said. "I can't imagine what we have to talk about, but given that you've killed one person this year, I suppose I can't afford to make you mad." She strode off, leaving Ryan to grip the metal handrail with enough force to leave her fingerprints.

Reminding herself that violence wasn't the answer—when there were so many witnesses—Ryan walked behind Wendy, remaining standing while the other two sat. "Here's what I want to know. Either one, or both of you, supplied Cassie Martin with the information about my uhm…"

"Nervous breakdown? Mental collapse? Acute psychosis?" Janet supplied helpfully.

"Whatever," Ryan said. "Cassie wasn't there, so one or both of you told her about it."

"There are a lot of people on the team," Wendy said. "Any one of them could have done that."

"Logically, that's true. But you two are the only ones Cassie knows. Besides, you're the only two with the required amount of…nastiness…to do something that cruel."

Janet gave her a bored look and said, "You can't prove anything, and if you could, you'd be ratting us out right now. You don't wanna spend your time talking to us, any more than we wanna talk to you. Now, get your sorry ass out of here and do what you want."

"No!" Wendy said, her voice rising in indignation. "I don't want Coach Hayes to think I did that."

"Shut up, you idiot," Janet hissed. "She's got nothing!"

"Oh, but I do," Ryan said, smiling at the rift that she could see forming right before her eyes. "I know that one of you was involved, but I can't prove which one. Coach will probably suspend both of you pending an investigation."

"I'm trying to get into law school!" Wendy cried. "I don't want this to show up on my record!"

"Lots of people get accused of a lot of things," Janet said, unconcerned with her friend's plight. "Chill."

"Fuck you, Janet," Wendy snapped. "All I did was tell you about Ryan's meltdown. What you did with the information was something I had nothing—nothing to do with."

Laughing softly, Janet said, "You knew exactly what I was going to do when you told me what happened. If I recall, you're the one who suggested that Cassie might be the best person to tell."

"I did not!"

Shrugging, Janet said, "Let's see if Coach believes you. You look just as guilty as I do. You'd better hope she doesn't have the guts to kick us off the team. Jesus, at this point we only have ten players. If she went to eight one bout of the flu would make her forfeit games."

"I didn't do anything!" Wendy repeated. "Why would you try to drag me down with you?"

"Like I said before, you're just as guilty as I am. At least—Coach will think so," Janet said, a sickeningly sweet smile on her face.

Ryan saw her opening, and smiled at Wendy. "If you're just as guilty, that must mean that you got a third of the money. Did you?"

"Money? What money?"

"Someone got a sizable amount of money for publicly humiliating me," Ryan said, maintaining her cool gaze. "I'm sure Coach can sort it all out by demanding that you provide copies of your bank statements."

"Fuck you, O'Flaherty," Janet said, venom oozing from her voice. "It's obvious what you want. How much will it take to buy you off?"

Ryan shook her head slowly. She knew they were scum, but hadn't guessed how little regard they had for each other. "Wow, you took the money and didn't even try to give your good friend a cut. Pretty nasty trick."

"How much?" Janet seethed.

"I'm not like you are," Ryan said calmly. "I can't be bought for twenty-five thousand dollars."

The woman barked out a wry laugh. "I should have known you were guessing. I didn't get anything near that amount."

"Well, you should have," Ryan said, tossing her dark hair over her shoulder. "'Cause your good friend and partner, Cassie, got fifty thousand. I've got a copy of the draft the National Inquisitor wired to her. I've also got the check she wrote to cash for ten thousand. I assume that went to you," she said, staring at Janet. "I know your scholarship is worth more than that. You should've struck a better deal. Pity," she added, striding away to her first class.

As soon as her class was over, Ryan jogged back over to Haas to talk to Coach Hayes. Knocking on the coach's door, Ryan popped her head in when she heard an invitation to come in. "Hi, Coach, got a few minutes?"

The older woman was sitting at her desk, the surface clear of papers. Her feet were up on the pulled-out bottom drawer of the desk, and she was gazing out of the window with her hands wrapped around one knee. Turning her head to meet Ryan's eyes, she said, "Sure. Come on in. You're a little late, though. One rat tried to save her skin by turning on the other."

"No honor among thieves, huh?" Ryan entered the room and took a seat.

"Apparently not." She rocked in her chair, letting her head drop back against the leather. "I thought I was ready to learn the truth, Ryan, but I wasn't. How could I be so wrong about so many people?" Wiping at her eyes, she said, "Maybe I don't have what it takes to coach at this level."

"Any interest in hearing my opinion?"

"Sure. You're one of the few people around here who has been consistently honest with me."

"Well, I think you have the talent and the smarts to coach at this level, or even in the WNBA. But, in my opinion, there's something that's prevented you from succeeding here—and it's not talent."

"What is it?" she asked, a small smirk twitching her lips. "Give it to me."

"It's the way you interact with the players. I don't know why you made this choice, but focusing only on game strategy, while leaving all of the interpersonal stuff to your assistants is not working—and I don't believe it ever will."

The coach crossed her arms over her chest, scowling slightly. "Why can't it work to have specific roles? Each of us has certain skills. Doesn't it make sense to do what we're best at?"

"Sure, it makes sense. But it doesn't work. No matter what, you're the head coach—and if players don't feel they can talk to you, you'll never know what's going on with the team. Some of the things that have happened this year have seriously harmed your credibility, Coach. Those issues eventually show up on the court—and then it's too late to do anything about them."

"For example?"

"Well, I don't want to reveal any confidences, but someone that you're relying on is thinking of transferring. She hasn't talked to you about how unhappy she is—because she doesn't think you have any interest in talking to the players. Given the reception you gave me the few times I tried to talk to you, I don't blame her a bit."

Mary shook her head, looking tired and frustrated. "I'm not good at getting into the little things that bother players. I've never liked it, and I've never been good at it. That's why I've enjoyed working on the college level. I can concentrate on the game and leave the other things to my assistants."

"Then you'd better make that perfectly clear to the team. Give your assistants full authority over those matters—or you're not gonna have enough players here to field a table tennis team. If I'd thought that Lynette had real authority, I would have felt much better about things. As it was, I talked to her without knowing if you'd ever hear my complaints."

"I can understand that," Mary said, nodding slowly. "I guess you're right. I've got to figure out how to make the environment more hospitable." She stared up at the ceiling and said, "I've shown such poor judgment at assessing girls' personalities, that I think I should avoid it as much as possible and leave those things to the assistants. I'll try to make that clear next year."

"Well, that's one way to look at it. Of course, you could try to challenge yourself to get closer to the players. A little effort would go a long way."

Giving the younger woman a warm smile, Coach Hayes nodded slowly. "I would guess you'd recommend doing it the hard way."

"That's my nature," Ryan said, grinning.

"Well, I can't say I've enjoyed our little chat, but maybe a few changes are in order."

"What changes are you going to make on this year's team? I assume it was Wendy who paid you a visit this morning."

"Yeah, it was," Mary said. "Should I believe what she told me?"

"Well, I don't think she got any money. But she admitted that she's the one who told Janet about the uhm…incident. I'm not sure she knew that Janet was going to sell the info, but once she saw it in the tabloid, she couldn't have had any doubts about who did it."

"That's what I think, too," Mary said. "I don't think I have the evidence to throw her off the team, but she's not gonna set foot on the court during a game for the rest of the year. I don't care if I have to put an ad in the *Daily Californian* for warm bodies—she's gone."

"I assume Janet will be dealt with even more harshly?"

"Definitely. I'm talking to the Chancellor's office this afternoon to see how much of her scholarship we can force her to pay back. We're throwing her out of the dorm—so she's gonna have to find a place to live for the rest of the term."

"You know," Ryan said thoughtfully, "I wish I could have kept my mouth shut and let this blow over; but in a way, I think this could be one of the best things that could have happened to the team. Knowing that you won't put up with this kind of crap might give the other players an infusion of confidence."

"I hope so, but I'm not counting on it. I've never had such a dreadful year in coaching. I guess the good news is that we have nowhere to go but up."

"That's the way to think, Coach. You're at the start of a new regime."

Mary shook her head, unable to keep from giving Ryan a warm smile. "Such an optimist. Maybe you should come back next year and be my personnel director."

"Oh, no can do, Coach. I'm under strict orders to kept my schedule open next year. I'm gonna learn how to relax." She smiled and walked towards the door. "I don't know which of us has the bigger task ahead of us."

It had taken her several days of stewing, planning, and worrying, but once she was sure of her plan, Mia called Jordan to clue her in. "Hi," Mia said when she reached her lover that evening.

"Hi, honey," Jordan replied, still not sounding like herself.

"I've got some news. I've decided that I'm going down to Hillsborough this weekend to tell my parents about us."

"What?"

"You heard me, sweetie. I've decided that there's no reason to wait. They're not going to be happy about it, so why not let them start getting over it now, rather than later?"

"Oh, Mia, I hate to see you bring this up now. Why not wait until you graduate, honey? Then they won't have as much power over you."

"Jordan," Mia said, in a tone that got Jordan's attention, "you're the most important person in my life. It's not fair to you or me or them to keep this a secret. Besides, I promised my mother that I'd tell her what's going on as soon as we had things resolved. I think we do," she said softly. "I think we've decided to love each other as well as we can—for the rest of our lives."

"God, I love you," Jordan choked out before dissolving into tears. "You make me feel so special."

"You are," Mia insisted. "You're the love of my life. Don't ever forget that."

Early the next morning, Ryan stood astride her bike, watching an apartment building near campus. It was just after seven a.m., and she mused that weeks of planning and scheming were about to come to fruition.

The moment she saw a gangly, dark-haired man get into his car and drive off, she hopped off her bike. *That's my cue*, she said to herself as a giggle escaped. Striding up to the front buzzer, she found the name and gave the bell a long, irritating ring. When a very perturbed female voice snapped, "What!" her grin increased and she dropped her voice an octave to say, "Special delivery for Cassandra Martin. I need a signature."

The next sound was the release for the door, and Ryan bounded up the stairs three at a time, trying to get to the third floor apartment before her arch-nemesis could get the door open. She managed to make it in the nick of time, and held up an official looking envelope, hiding her face from the peephole.

The door flew open, and a very unpleasant voice muttered, "Where do I sign?"

Ryan dropped the envelope to her side and stuck her steel-toed work boot into the doorway, smiling serenely when Cassie tried to slam the door onto it. "Temper, temper, temper," she said. "You don't want to throw me out

before you hear my offer, do you?"

Cassie backed up, frantically looking around the entryway, probably something to defend herself with. "Wha…wha…what do you want?"

"I want to cut your tongue out with a dull, rusty, razor blade, but settle for sharing my latest creation with you." Ryan shook the envel and dropped a CD into her hand, which she then waved in front of frightened blonde. "I think you'll want to see what's on this."

It must have dawned on her that Ryan wasn't intending to hurt her, becau Cassie regained her usual bravado. "Why in the fuck would I be interested anything you have to say, you bitch."

Ryan surveyed her outfit, noticing the black T-shirt with a red and whit faux name-tag that read, "Queen Of The Fucking Universe", and commented "Like the shirt. But there's one little corner of the universe that you don't reign over." Her eyes grew dark, and a nearly palpable menace oozed from her coiled body. "When my partner is involved."

Fixing Ryan with her own steely glare, Cassie snapped, "Wish I could stay and chat, but I don't have all day to waste listening to you. Either leave now, or leave when the cops get here." She turned and made for the phone in the hallway and began to dial.

Ryan followed right behind her and placed a photocopy of two wire transfers in front of her. "Look familiar?"

Cassie gazed at the drafts deposited to her account, each in the amount of fifty thousand dollars—each dated a short time after the tabloid stories had hit the newsstands. Dick Williams had assured Ryan that only ten thousand had been withdrawn in a single personal check—and Ryan now knew where that money had gone. "So what?" Cassie asked, but put the phone down before her call was completed.

"So…I would really like it if you'd write a new check, in the amount of ninety thousand dollars, made out to 'Safe Haven.' I wish I'd gotten here before you spent ten thousand, but it took me a while to get my facts straight." Ryan could have told Cassie about her encounter with Janet and Wendy, but she thought it would be more fun to let them blindside their former friend.

Ryan said this in such a matter-of-fact way that Cassie stared at her for several seconds, looking almost confused. But she had clearly heard her and responded with her usual charm. "Fuck off, get out, and drop dead, you bitch. Who the fuck do you think you are?"

"I," Ryan said dramatically, waving the disk again, "am the creator of the new video game that will soon sweep the Berkeley campus. And that's just the start," she said, her excitement growing. "I have contacts all over the world through a math bulletin board I'm on. People in universities all across the planet will soon be playing my game, and laughing their asses off." She

shrugged and said, "Bad choice of words, but you'll get the picture."

"You came over here at seven a.m. to tell me about a fucking video game?"

"Well, yeah," Ryan drawled innocently, "after all, you're the star of the game."

Cassie grabbed two handfuls of her long blonde hair and pulled at it in frustration. "What are you talking about?"

Looking across the room, Ryan was pleased to see that Cassie's computer was not only up and running, it was also a Mac. She strode across the room, turned briefly and asked, "May I?" then inserted the disk before the frazzled woman had the opportunity to reply. "Now, this won't give you the full effect," Ryan said conversationally, "since I could only get the streamlined version onto a disk. The version that I'll be sending out has a lot more action, more color—it's a far superior product." Ryan looked completely relaxed while she waited for the program to load. Her arms were crossed over her chest, and her foot tapped rhythmically as she hummed a song to herself. "Ahh, here it is," she said. "Wanna look?"

Cassie gave her a look that questioned her sanity, so Ryan merely shrugged. "Suit yourself. Now we're still in the beta testing phase, so we can make some modifications. You might want to be wearing a different outfit, but I think this bikini is absolutely perfect."

Unable to contain her curiosity, Cassie inched forward, slowly enabling herself to get a good look. Displayed on the screen was a picture of herself, clad in a red bikini—a picture from a pool party about two years earlier at her parents' house.

Ryan made a few keystrokes, and suddenly a wide variety of foods started to float around the screen. She started to grab one at a time, drag it over to the picture, and insert it into the now-gaping mouth. The cyber-Cassie started to chew noisily, the sounds crass and vulgar. "You won't see much yet," Ryan said, "but by the fifth or sixth hot dog, your belly will start to grow. Ahh...there it goes," she said with satisfaction.

Cassie was too stunned to even comment. All of the color drained from her face as Ryan continued to shove food into the cyber-mouth, the image of the svelte body starting to distort. Her worst nightmare, the secret she'd once shared with Jamie, was coming true right before her eyes.

"Now, I have this set up with the summer outfit, but I have a nice winter look with a ski jacket and pants, and a formal version with you in a long black dress. Okay...here's my favorite view," Ryan said, using the mouse to turn the image. "I think it's gonna blow," she said with delight as an obscene ripping sound accompanied the image of the tiny bikini beginning to break apart at the seams. "That hot fudge sundae did the trick," Ryan said idly.

"Works every time."

Suddenly, Ryan felt a pair of hands grasping at her shirt. She managed to turn and pry the clutching fingers off and grab Cassie's wrists. Looking up, she saw the mask of outrage and hatred coloring her face. "What's wrong?" Ryan asked, while Cassie tried to yank her hands away from Ryan's iron grip. "Don't you like to be embarrassed and held up to ridicule? I assumed that people who liked to dish it out, would also like to take it."

Cassie was really struggling, but Ryan was not about to let her get in a clear shot, so she kept a tight hold on her. As expected, Cassie fought dirty, and she tried to get in a knee to the groin, but Ryan managed to twist her body to frustrate Cassie's aim. "I'll kill you!" Cassie cried, tears of rage and frustration rolling down her cheeks.

"You'll do no such thing," Ryan growled. "You don't have the guts." Ryan pushed her hard, sending her sprawling into an upholstered chair. "Not only aren't you going to kill me, you're going to give me ninety thousand dollars."

"I'd rather die!" she sputtered.

"You'll die, all right. You'll die of embarrassment." Ryan pulled out one of the flyers she had designed and flung it at Cassie. A four-color photo of Cassie at her normal weight morphed into the 400-pound woman whose clothing exploded from the stress. "I'm still debating about what to call it," Ryan mused. "I'm thinking of 'Gobble'. Do you like it?"

"You can't get away with this!"

"Oh, sure I can. I'm distributing this for free. You could probably hire a lawyer and sue me for invasion of privacy, or something like that, but it would be very tough to find anyone who wanted to take the case. I'm sure it would cost you more than you'd ever be able to make back. Besides," she shrugged, "my goal will be met as soon as this hits the Internet. I honestly think this will be bigger than the 'Dancing Baby' thing from a few years ago. Once it's out there, you can never pull it back. The damage is done." An evil grin settled onto Ryan's face and she said, "Kinda like the damage that the tabloids do. See the connection?"

"This is blackmail!"

"Kinda," Ryan said, grinning. "You wanna go to the DA? That's fine, too, since the game will be entered into evidence. That would be cool, since it would be covered by the legitimate press then."

With a massive cry of frustration, Cassie screamed, "Why are you doing this to me?"

"Is that a rhetorical question, or do you have some serious long-term memory impairment?"

"Fuck you," Cassie growled, getting up to move to the desk. "Just fuck yourself."

"You can make that comment in the memo line on the check," Ryan said. "Just remember that placing a stop on a check of this size is a felony, and the DA loves to prosecute those cases."

Cassie sat down and started to write out the check. "How do I know you're not going to distribute the game anyway?"

"Well, this is an alien concept to you, but I give you my word," Ryan said. "My word actually means something. As long as you keep your evil self away from Jamie, this will never get out."

Cassie wrote out the check and signed it, leaving the payee line blank. "You can fill it in, asshole." She shoved it towards Ryan, who took it from her with two fingers to avoid touching her. "You and that bitch Jamie deserve each other."

"Huh," Ryan said thoughtfully. "Who knew you were so perceptive?" Without another word, Ryan left the apartment, once again humming a happy tune.

Later that night, Jamie stood in front of Ryan's computer, her mouth agape, eyes wide. "You created a game based on my old pictures of Cassie?"

"Yep. Pretty sweet, huh?"

Jamie sat down heavily on the bed, totally astounded. "But, Ryan, what if she sues us? You know how vindictive she is!"

"Yes, she is, but I convinced her that no matter what avenue she used to get back at me, I'd release the game. She's far too vain to ever let that happen—no matter what." She cocked her head and said, "You've always said that nothing mattered more to her than how she looks. You were dead on, babe."

Jamie looked at her partner, her eyes scanning her face. "Do you feel better for having done this? Did it give you some satisfaction?"

A vaguely guilty grin crossed Ryan's face. "Yeah. I feel a lot better, as a matter of fact. It's bad enough that she betrayed you, but for her to profit from it drove me absolutely nuts. I was having a hell of a time letting it go, so I started plotting ways to get revenge. I wasn't gonna tell you this last part, but I know we don't do well when we keep secrets."

"What weren't you gonna tell me?"

"Uhm…I went to your dad for advice on how to get revenge. He helped me think it through. I was gonna do the game and put up signs advertising it all over campus. Your dad is the one who showed me that we could use the game to blackmail her." Ryan looked supremely satisfied with herself. "He's got some damned good ideas."

"Unbelievable," Jamie said, shaking her head. "I…I'm speechless."

"Well, I knew he had the contacts—why not let him use his God given talents?"

"I don't think God had anything to do with those talents, Ryan, but if the two of you can bond by thinking up ways to blackmail people, far be it from me to discourage you."

"I think I'm finished with blackmail. Once was fun, but it was enough."

Jamie picked up the cashier's check that lay on the desk. "Did you make her go to the bank with you?"

"God no! I couldn't have been in her company that long. She gave me a personal check and I immediately went to the bank and converted it to a cashier's check—in case she tried to put a stop payment on it."

"What do you think Sandy will do with the money?"

Ryan gave her a wide grin and said, "I stopped by before softball practice and told her about the 'donation.' She nearly hyperventilated. I think she's going to buy a van so she can take the girls places as a group."

Pushing Ryan's chair back, Jamie climbed astride her lap and gave her a hug. "You did this for me, didn't you?"

Ryan nodded, but added, "Only partially. Yes, it drove me insane that she was so cruel to you after you were such a good friend to her. But part of the reason she was so mean was because you were different from her. It bugged the shit out of her that you could be gay—that you weren't who she believed you were. I decided that I had to take that money and make a positive impact on the lives of girls who are tortured because they're different. It's vigilante justice, I admit, but it's still justice."

"I'm proud of you," Jamie murmured. "I'm proud of you for taking something that was driving you nuts, and figuring out a way to make a positive statement with the whole mess."

"It was worth it to see the look on her face," Ryan said. "It gives me great pleasure to see a bully humbled."

Jamie slapped her lightly on the shoulder and said, "That's the only thing I'm mad at you about. I wish you would have told me so that I could have gone, too!"

Ryan leaned back so that she could look her in the eyes. "No. I never want you to share air space with her. You're too precious to me to ever allow scum like her to befoul you."

Jamie hugged her tight, so very grateful to have a partner who felt like that about her. Unexpectedly, she began to giggle and picked up her head to look at Ryan. "Can we play the game?"

"Your wish is my command," Ryan said, grinning while wheeling the chair back to the computer. "Go for the hot fudge sundaes," she instructed. "They have a rather explosive effect on her."

Later that evening, Ryan was working in her room when she heard Jamie's voice call to her. "Honey? Can you come in here for a minute?"

"Sure." She walked into their bedroom to find her partner sorting through their monthly bills. "This looks like fun."

"It's not," Jamie said, grinning up at her. "But it's nice to know what we have and where our money goes."

Ryan started to massage her shoulders and asked, "What did you want?"

"The cut off date for your American Express card was Monday, but I don't see an entry for my ring. You used the card, didn't you?"

Ryan's fingers stilled and she moved to the side to crouch down next to Jamie. "No, I didn't."

"Then how…?"

"I used my savings," she said, her blue eyes fixed upon Jamie's.

Turning quickly in her chair, both of her hands landed on Ryan's chest, nearly sending her sprawling. "Honey! Why did you do that? This ring must have taken everything you had!"

Ryan smiled gently. "Not quite." She leaned over to sort through the statements and found the one from their bank. "See this deposit?"

Jamie nodded, noting the twelve hundred dollars that she hadn't been able to account for.

"That's the balance. I closed the account and merged what I had left into our joint account. I'm officially broke."

"Ryan, why did you do that? I know it's important to you to have your own money."

Ryan grasped Jamie's hands and pulled her to her feet. She laced her hands behind her back, letting them rest on the gentle swell of hips. "It's not important any more. What's important now is merging—not staying separate. This is a leap of faith for me, Jamie. I'm investing everything that I am and everything that I have in the belief that we'll be together for the rest of our lives." She picked up Jamie's hand and brought it to her mouth, gently kissing the ring. "This ring represents nine years of my efforts. Every spare dime I had went into this account. I'm giving it all to you," she whispered. "I trust you with my money, with my hopes, with my dreams, and with my very soul. We're in this together—as a couple." Dipping her head, she placed a gentle, emotion-filled kiss onto her partner's trembling lips. They shared kiss after kiss, each one becoming more tender and more loving.

When they finally broke apart, Jamie added one more, unable to resist the warm, moist lips. "I love you so much, it sometimes feels like it's too much to fathom," she whispered. "Every time I think I've reached my limit, you do something that knocks me off my feet again." She chuckled gently and said,

"I'm beginning to think you'll always keep filling me up with your love."

"I like the way you think," Ryan's deep voice burred. "I think this is a perfect time to top off your tank, don't you?"

With a sexy grin, Jamie's head began to nod. "As usual, you read my cue."

Ryan's hands were busy unbuttoning the tiny buttons of her partner's shirt. "Not to denigrate my skills, but your cues are pretty obvious."

"Do tell?"

"Well, your eyelids start to get heavy," she said, "so heavy that your eyes are half-hooded when you look up at me." She slipped Jamie's shirt off, giving it a little tug to pull it from her jeans. Her hands slid down her back and started to play with the soft skin there, as a precursor to moving on with the slow unveiling of her beautiful body.

"What else?" Mist green eyes batted seductively.

"Well, there's that," Ryan said, tapping each of her eyelids. "You bat your eyes better than anyone I've ever met. Each little blink makes my heart race."

Jamie leaned in close and nuzzled her ear against the cotton fabric that covered Ryan's chest. "I see what you mean," she purred. "You're off to the races."

The clasp to Jamie's bra was unhooked and Ryan's hands began to roam at will, sending chills up both spines. "When you're seducing me, you also turn your head just enough so that you're looking at me out of the corners of your eyes. I don't know why, but you never look at me head-on. It's very sexy," she added.

"You're too gorgeous to take in all in at once," Jamie teased. "I don't want to burn out my retinas."

Ryan chuckled while her hands dropped onto Jamie's butt, her fingers exploring for panty lines. "I love to feel your underwear through your jeans," Ryan whispered, her head dropping onto her partner's shoulder. "Don't know why, but it's very exciting for me to guess what type you have on."

Jamie's butt twitched while determined fingers roamed all over her. "How are you doing?"

"Mmm...I can't feel a thing." Ryan's head lifted, and her eyes reflected her bafflement. "Commando?"

"Never with jeans. I only go commando when I'm wearing a short dress—and that's solely to drive you nuts," she pronounced, touching Ryan's chest as she said each word.

"It works," Ryan gasped, wide eyed, "and you're not even doing it today."

"Nope. I'm wearing underwear. Guess again."

Ryan's fingers covered every inch of her hips and ass, to no avail. Conceding defeat, she hooked her thumbs into the waistband of her lover's jeans and fished around briefly. A moment later, a serene smile covered her face. "G-string," she sighed, as if speaking of something divine.

"G-string," Jamie said, reaching up to nibble on an ear. "I had a feeling we'd get in a little loving tonight."

"If I'd known you had this on, we would have gotten a little loving in before school," Ryan purred.

"Why do you think I get dressed in the bathroom? It didn't take me long to figure out that I had to have some privacy if I ever wanted to leave the house."

"Good point," Ryan said, grinning sexily. The strong hands dropped to Jamie's curvaceous cheeks, and her own hips started to sway as she cupped them. "Ooh…this is nice."

"I swear that you didn't reveal what an ass-woman you were," Jamie said, giggling. "I distinctly recall asking you what part of a woman you were most attracted to, and you told me you didn't have a favorite."

"I didn't, until I got to experience yours. I'm as surprised as you are." She gave her another squeeze and said, "I'm afraid it's become a fixation. You don't mind, do you?"

While Ryan's hands were squeezing, Jamie's pelvis was skimming against her partner's thighs. "Do my responses give off a disinterested impression?"

"No…" Ryan's left hand was popping open the buttons on Jamie's shrink-to-fits, while her right hand slid down inside. She felt her heart skip a beat and forced herself to take in a deep breath. "Your body makes me throb," she purred roughly.

Jamie's hand reached behind to grasp Ryan's ass through the jeans. "Mmm…I love it when you grab me hard—exactly like that. I love to feel how much you want me."

"Un-unh," Ryan gasped out. "If I really showed you how much I want you, you'd be covered in bruises. I'm controlling myself as best I can."

"Let go," Jamie said, her eyes fiery. "Let go for a minute, baby. Show me how you feel." She reached up and bit down softly on Ryan's sensitive ear lobe. "Show me your need."

With a hungry growl, both hands slid into the half-open jeans and grasped as much of the smooth flesh as they could hold. Ryan's mouth claimed Jamie's while her hands possessed her cheeks, kneading them with a pressure that danced along the line between pleasure and pain.

"Oh!" Jamie gasped when Ryan's strong hands gripped even harder.

The dark head lifted immediately, concerned blue eyes trying to focus. "Did I hurt you?"

Jamie nodded her head gently. "Yeah." Her eyes fluttered seductively and she murmured, "It was a good hurt."

"Kiss it and make it better?" Ryan offered with as innocent a look as she could muster.

"Does anybody fall for that devastatingly sexy, innocent expression?"

"Not for a few months," Ryan said. "Somebody's on to me."

Jamie stepped back a few inches and started to twitch her hips. The jeans began to slide down her legs, but Ryan was completely distracted by the gentle sway of her breasts. "How is an ass-woman supposed to concentrate when those beauties are dancing in her face?"

"Sometimes you've gotta choose," Jamie said. Her jeans were around her ankles, a tiny white triangle of shimmery fabric showing between her legs. Her breasts stood up high, nipples erect and pink, calling to Ryan like the siren's song.

Realizing that her brain was quickly becoming overloaded with stimuli, Ryan grasped Jamie by the hips and tossed her over her shoulder. She deposited her onto the bed and began to yank her own clothing off in a mad rush. "Too many choices," she mumbled, kicking off her sweats and crawling onto the bed to lie atop her lover's luscious form. "I want it all—and I want it now."

"It's all yours, baby," Jamie husked. "And it always will be."

Her jeans had fallen off during her impromptu ride, but the G-string remained in place and was now the focus of Ryan's fascination. She traced the outline of the tiny strip of material, wondering, "I can wear one of these for a while, but it would drive me mad if I kept it on all day. Doesn't it bug you?"

"Mmm…I notice it, but that's not necessarily a bad thing. I honestly put this on this morning because I was feeling a little…"

"Horny?" Ryan supplied, grinning widely.

"Desirous," Jamie corrected. "Much nicer word."

"So you were feeling desirous, and wearing a G-string…?"

"Made me think of having sex with you every time I noticed it." She placed a few kisses along Ryan's neck and added, "I noticed it a lot."

"You've been simmering all day, huh?" Ryan asked, her darkening eyes revealing her rapidly escalating desire.

"Uh-huh," Jamie purred. "I've been on a slow burn since we got up."

"Your patience continually astounds me. If I'd been aroused all morning, I would have convinced you to come home for lunch and party. And if I couldn't arrange that, I would have gotten busy before dinner. Yet, you blithely go about your normal day, never giving me the slightest indication that you're in the mood for love. How do you do that?"

"It's not hard," Jamie said, smiling serenely. "I like to be turned on. When I feel like this, everything feels more intense. I liked the way my jeans felt against my bare skin all day; every time my nipples got hard, it reminded me of having your mouth on them; seeing how excited you were about getting back at Cassie was very close to how excited you get during sex—so it was like a little preview. I relish all of the little reminders and the sensations, and let them slowly turn up the heat. It feels divine," she purred. "And now that I'm with you, and I can feel you and smell you and taste you—it's so deliciously satisfying. Like I've just sat down at a table filled with my favorite foods after being ravenously hungry all day."

"You're a better woman than I, Gunga Din. I'd be grouchy and out of sorts by noon. My jeans would irritate the hell out of me, and I wouldn't have gotten any enjoyment at all from talking about Cassie. It would have pissed me off that we were doing that rather than having sex."

"Your fuse is about this long," Jamie said, holding her thumb and forefinger an inch apart. "Mine is like this." She stretched her fingers as far apart as she could, with Ryan nodding her agreement.

"That looks about right. Actually, I'm starting to get a little irritated now. I was on the verge of diving right between your legs when I tossed you into bed, but for some reason we've been talking for a ridiculously long time."

"You started it," Jamie teased. "But I can stop it." She pushed her partner onto her back and straddled her, shifting her hips up and down and letting her vulva skim across Ryan's belly. "Oh, yeah," Jamie growled. "The first time I feel your skin press against me is absolutely exquisite. The wait was worth it."

Ryan watched, fascinated, as goose bumps broke out all over her partner's body, and she shivered roughly. Her nipples grew so hard they looked painful, but there was a deeply satisfied look on her lovely features that spoke of pure delight. She gripped Ryan's shoulder for stability and pushed a little harder against the solid flesh, gasping a bit in reaction. "God, that feels good."

"I'm about to come from watching you," Ryan moaned. "It's so incredibly hot to watch you claim your pleasure."

"It turns me on so much to let myself go while you watch me," Jamie murmured. "It's so freeing."

"Show me more," Ryan urged, her eyes now like two blue lasers.

Jamie gave her a wickedly erotic smile and brought her hands to her breasts. Hefting the twin mounds in her hands, she arched her back and grasped them roughly. Watching the compressed flesh spill through her lover's fingers made Ryan ache with desire, but the experience was so satisfying that she reveled in the sensation of her clitoris hardening painfully between her legs.

`Now Jamie's hips started to gyrate in a slow circle, her eyes closed, head tossed back, as she squeezed her breasts in rhythm with her hips. Ryan detected the first faint scent of her partner's arousal, and her mouth started to water in response. She so desperately wanted to taste Jamie, to let the myriad of sensations burst upon her tongue; but it was utterly fascinating to watch her partner love herself, and she couldn't bear to ask for what she needed.

Jamie licked the tips of her fingers and painted her rock-hard nipples with the moisture. Impossibly, the pebbled flesh hardened even more, the nipples nearly turning purple from the blood pounding through them. Ryan heard a strangled moan, realizing after a moment that it had come from her own mouth. She squeezed her thighs together as tightly as possible to get some pressure against her clitoris, growling with satisfaction when she did.

Jamie's determined fingers continued to play with her nipples, now pinching them roughly and moaning lustily with each stab of sensation.

Ryan had been valiantly trying to let her partner display her desire without interference, but she lost the battle when Jamie cried out after one particularly painful pinch. Her hands flew to the bare cheeks and latched on, compressing and gripping the smoothly muscled flesh with gusto.

"My, lord!" Jamie cried out, her control at its limit. Her right hand slipped from her breast, making its way slowly down her body. As her fingers slid under the small swatch of fabric, her eyes met Ryan's in a smolderingly hot gaze. "Ooo," she moaned throatily when her fingers found her clitoris and gave it a lusty pinch.

The hands gripping her ass were nearly bruising her, but the passionate groping only served to excite her even more. Once again, she held onto Ryan's shoulder for stability and allowed her hand to dip lower, coating her fingers thoroughly. To her surprise, she felt another pair of fingers touch her own, Ryan having snuck in without her noticing it. She smiled at the face that gazed up at her with such desire, and moved her fingers up slightly to slather the moisture all over her clitoris.

Surprising her once again, Ryan slipped back a little, and deftly moved the sliver of material out of the way. Then her teasing fingers started to press gently, massaging the spot right behind Jamie's opening. Green eyes widened, Jamie reacting to the unaccustomed touch. "Like that?" Ryan asked, her voice low and sexy.

Jamie forced herself to experience the sensation, rather than just her emotional reaction to it. Pushing against Ryan's fingers she was forced to admit that the pressure felt fantastic. "You know I do, you persistent little devil." She closed her eyes and twitched her hips in an even wider circle, her breathing growing rough and labored as her fingers trailed gently across her sensitive clit.

"How 'bout this?" Ryan asked, beginning to circle Jamie's smaller opening. Jamie's eyes opened wide, then started to narrow into a warning look. "I'm only playing outside," Ryan insisted, her innocent look appearing anything but. "I won't come inside without an express invitation."

"Don't hold your breath," Jamie said, but Ryan's assurance allowed her to relax, and after a moment she began to enjoy the teasing touch. "That's kinda nice," she purred throatily, her fingers dancing across her own heated flesh, keeping pace with Ryan's gentle stroking.

"I know," Ryan murmured. "Believe me, I know."

"Ungh! I'm getting close," Jamie gasped out.

"Keep going," Ryan urged. "Keep touching yourself, baby. It's so damn hot to watch your fingers working away beneath that tiny G-string. I have to watch you finish." Even though Ryan was speaking in complete sentences, it was obvious that it was a struggle for her. So many sensations were buffeting her that she felt completely overwhelmed, but she remained focused on her goal of watching Jamie bring herself off. Replenishing her supply of moisture, she continued to stroke and tease her partner's most guarded spot, feeling chills race down her spine as she did so.

Moaning deeply, Jamie gripped her lover's shoulder painfully as every nerve in her pelvis begin to fire off a burst of sensation. Ryan couldn't resist slipping her other hand around and entering her partner deeply, thrilling to the pulsing that gripped and released around her fingers.

Her body still wracked with spasms, Jamie's world suddenly spun 180 degrees. She found herself on her back with Ryan scrambling to move down the bed and place her mouth upon the thrumming flesh. "I'll go mad if I can't taste you," she growled, pushing the G-string aside while she pressed her tongue into her partner.

Eyes wide with surprise, Jamie placed her hand upon the dark head, soothing her. "Slow and gentle, baby," she begged. "Let me catch my breath."

Grunting with frustration, Ryan nuzzled against her, forcing herself to stay away from the bundle of nerves that still sang with sensation. She filled her lungs with her partner's deliciously complex scent and nibbled at her thighs, sucking the damp flesh into her mouth. Murmuring softly, she pressed kisses against her, letting the salty sweet notes of her lover's passion fill her soul.

Through her sensual haze, Ryan heard her partner's voice, and she forced herself to concentrate on her words. "I need to touch you, baby," Jamie pled. "Don't make me wait."

Ryan's passion-filled eyes shifted to meet Jamie's, and she saw the deep longing reflected in them. She was so thoroughly turned on that she ached, but she had such a need to savor Jamie's very essence that she didn't see how she'd be able to forsake her position.

But her partner was insistent. "Please, Ryan, let me love you."

Seeing only one solution to her dilemma, Ryan climbed over Jamie's body, turning around completely. Rising to her knees, she lowered her head once again and lapped at Jamie's wetness while her hips twitched in invitation.

"Oh, yeah," Jamie sighed, mesmerized by the combination of Ryan's hot tongue and the voluptuous display. Ryan's entire vulva glistened with an abundant coating of lubrication, and Jamie licked her lips at the sight. She desperately wanted to taste the passion that flowed from the depths of her lover, but Ryan was already deeply focused on her task, and Jamie's self-interest prevented her from forcing the issue. Deciding to make the best of a good situation, she opened her legs a little further and let herself absorb how fantastic Ryan's gifted tongue felt against her heated flesh. Sighing deeply, she distracted herself from the orgasm that she could already feel building by focusing on the twitching vulva that vied for her attention.

She spread her hands across the expanse of Ryan's toned cheeks and delved into her shimmering wetness with her thumbs, shivering from the burst of air that Ryan blew across her clitoris at the touch. "God, you feel divine," she sighed, reveling in the sensation of possessing Ryan so totally.

A muffled moan was Ryan's only response, her tongue once again blissfully occupied. Her ministrations were so intense, so focused, that Jamie quickly climbed to another plateau, unable to even warn her partner before she convulsed into another climax, her body shaking and shivering with delight. "Stop, stop," she gasped, unable to catch her breath.

Ryan did so, but she kept her face less than an inch from Jamie's throbbing flesh, ready to dive in again as soon as she was allowed. After a minute or two, Jamie was able to function again, but she knew that she needed some time to recuperate. "Rest your head on my thigh," she urged. "Come on, baby, relax for a minute and let me love you."

"But I want more," Ryan growled, her lust for Jamie's body unquenchable.

"Just let me rest for a minute, love," she soothed. "Relax and let me satisfy you, then you can have as much of me as you want."

"That's a dangerous offer," Ryan murmured, but compliantly rested her cheek upon her lover's thigh and allowed herself to be touched once again.

Jamie slipped her fingers into her, smiling serenely as Ryan gasped at the touch. She touched her everywhere, using her thumbs and the tips of her fingers to tease every bit of flesh at once, intentionally trying to overwhelm her with the overabundance of sensation. Ryan bucked and gyrated against the pressure, her body torn between wanting as much as Jamie could give her, and being engulfed by the touch.

Jamie felt her partner's entire body stiffen, and she pulled her hands away from the wetness and gripped her about the hips, pulling hard until her mouth pressed into Ryan's drenched sex. She laved the glistening flesh thoroughly, Ryan's moans music to her ears. To her regret, the feast lasted only a few moments, then Ryan cried out throatily, her climax hitting her hard. She maintained her position for just a second, then slowly collapsed, all of her weight pinning Jamie hard to the bed.

Jamie wrapped her arms around the firm globes of Ryan's ass, hugging her tight. But after a moment to recuperate, the determined brunette slid back down her partner's body and dipped her head once again, slipping her tongue into Jamie's still-swollen folds. "Oh, lord," Jamie cried. "I don't know what I've done to deserve such an insatiable lover, but whatever it was, I'm eternally grateful!"

Ryan chuckled lightly, her attention already given over to the sensations that surrounded her. Even if she hadn't been so blissfully occupied, she wouldn't have been able to come up with a response to her partner's statement. She had no idea what caused her to be so insatiable when their bodies merged. All she knew was that Jamie spoke to her mind, her body and her heart in a way that no other woman ever had or ever would. She was so thoroughly bewitched, that she knew her appetite would last a lifetime; and she smiled to herself as she considered the never-ending quest to slake her rapacious thirst for her charms.

Chapter Twenty

The next morning, Catherine called her daughter just as Jamie was walking in the door from golf practice. "Hi, Mom," Jamie said, her mood bright and cheerful.

"What's on the agenda for today, honey? I'm coming to Berkeley for a haircut, and I thought you might be able to have lunch with me."

"Well, I could, but I won't be available until about two. I'm playing golf at ten o'clock and it always takes four hours to get around."

"Oh, that's all right. I'm sure I'll see you at some point this weekend."

"Hey, why don't you come with me? It would be a good excuse to take a nice walk, and we'd have lots of time to chat."

"Would that be fun for you? I don't want to interfere with your concentration."

"I'd really like for you to come, Mom. Most of my teammates don't speak in complete sentences, and I don't have a soul to chatter with. That's why I play better when we're allowed to have caddies—I've got someone to talk to."

"Well, I don't think I can carry that big bag of yours, but I'm very good at chattering. What time should I be there?"

Jamie was standing in the parking lot of the golf course when her mother pulled up. It was a marvel that her mother looked more like a golfer than anyone on the course, but she'd probably never swung a club. Catherine merely had the perfect outfit for any endeavor—and she looked particularly lovely in her gold turtleneck, Kelly green cable knit cardigan, and navy blue, pleated slacks. To Jamie's amazement, her mother was pulling a pair of golf shoes from the trunk of her car. "You own spikes?"

"Sure." She laced them up, and stood tall, smiling when she and Jamie were the same height. "I might wear these more often. I like being as tall as you are, for a change."

"You know, one of the most exciting days of my life was when I looked in a mirror and saw that I was as tall as you. Why is that such an accomplishment for a kid?"

"I'm not sure," Catherine said. "Maybe it makes you feel like you're close to being an adult." Smiling at Jamie she said, "I remember how excited you were. But I had very mixed feelings. It struck me that you were leaving your childhood behind, and I would never have an opportunity to be the mother I wanted to be."

Sliding an arm around her mother's waist, Jamie said, "Just shows how things can change if you give them a chance. You're the mom I've always wanted."

The Tilden course didn't allow spectators, nor did they allow caddies; but the combined charm of the Evans women prevailed, and soon Catherine watched as Jamie and the three juniors teed off. Things had normalized a little with Juliet, but the senior managed to always be in the other foursome during these outings.

Play was slow on this particular Friday—likely because the morning was warm and dry—and the weather report for the weekend was a poor one. It looked like everyone who could get away had headed out to the always-crowded public course to beat the predicted rain.

During their first substantial break, Jamie and Catherine sat on a bench on the third tee, waiting for the two groups in front of them to tee off. "Wanna hear a tale of intrigue, revenge, odd alliances and restitution?" Jamie asked.

"Well, it sounds like a Victorian novel, but knowing how exciting your life can be, I'm going to guess it's a factual tale."

"You know me too well, Mom," Jamie said, smiling brightly. "My beloved partner plays a starring role in this one, and I think you'll be surprised by her accomplice."

"Do tell," Catherine said, settling down to hear the saga.

Fifteen minutes later, Catherine sat staring at her daughter. "You can't be serious, Jamie. That detestable girl could not have received that kind of money for sharing your and Ryan's struggles with the newspapers."

"Oh, yes, she could," Jamie assured her. "They pay pretty well, as a matter of fact. But thanks to Ryan's agile mind, Cassie wasn't able to keep one dime of her ill-gotten gains. I told Ryan I was miffed that I didn't get to see the look on Cassie's face when she realized she'd have to give all of the money away—but my mental image is so colorful that I doubt the reality could have been as good."

"And this was all because of a computer game of some sort?"

"Well, that was the kicker, but Daddy was very helpful. He helped Ryan track down the money, and that was what allowed her to go to Coach Hayes and get Janet thrown off the team."

"I hate to think that Ryan has the same kind of devious mind that your father was blessed with—but I suppose it comes in handy occasionally."

"Mmm…Ryan's not devious. She's just very logical and thorough. She can't stand to have things fail to make sense—so she stayed at it until she was sure that she understood where all of the pieces in the puzzle fit."

"However she did it, I'm immensely grateful to her. It would have stuck in my craw to think of Cassie living it up on one hundred thousand dollars— received at your and Ryan's expense. I have such a hard time understanding how someone can derive pleasure from causing someone else pain."

"I'll never understand Cassie," Jamie said. "She's pure evil. There's a sadistic streak in that woman that's been there since she was a kid. I remember her making fun of other kids for having the wrong clothes or the wrong shoes when we were in first grade. I've decided that she's Satan's child."

"No, she's not Satan's child," Catherine said, a furrow forming between her brows. "But she's close."

Catherine hadn't been home for five minutes when she found herself completely unable to resist the urge to call Laura Martin. The women had run into each other on at least a dozen occasions since Jamie and Cassie's original falling out—but neither had mentioned the incident. Laura and Catherine were no longer friends—neither had called the other since Cassie moved out of Jamie's house—but they were unfailingly civil to one another when they were in public.

Not even sure of what she was trying to accomplish, Catherine dialed the long-familiar number and swallowed hard when Laura picked up. "Hello, Laura, it's Catherine."

"Catherine…Evans?"

Knowing that Laura was being intentionally obtuse, Catherine played it straight. "Yes, it's Catherine Evans. I have a question for you."

"Really? What could you possibly have to ask me?"

"I'd like to know whether or not you're aware of the fact that Cassie was the person who sold those nasty stories about Jamie to the tabloids?"

"Well, of course I don't read tabloids, but from what I heard, the more interesting elements were about Jamie's…whatever do you call that woman, anyway?"

"I call her the best thing that ever happened to our family, Laura. Her name is Ryan, and she's Jamie's partner."

"How quaint," Laura said, laughing softly. "When can we expect a wedding?"

"It's in August," Catherine replied, her voice full of pride, "but don't expect an invitation."

"Oh, Catherine, you could always put a positive gloss on anything. That must be helpful."

Taking a deep breath to calm her nerves, Catherine said, "Yes, my life *is* going well. But again, that's not why I called. I called because I'd like to know if Cassie struck this evil deal on her own—or if you assisted her."

"Look, I understand that Jamie's behavior in the past year has been abysmal—no matter how much you try to dissemble—but it's ridiculous to assume that Cassie has turned out as poorly as your own child has."

Swallowing a livid retort, Catherine said, "I have no interest in debating which of our children has turned out better. I think the answer is obvious to anyone who looks at the situation with any level of objectivity. My question is whether you knew of Cassie's actions."

"Whatever you're accusing her of, Cassie is blameless. I know that for a fact. My daughter would never consort with the types of people who run those disgusting magazines."

"She may not consort with them—but that didn't stop her from accepting two large bank drafts from them."

"Nonsense! How bad has your drinking gotten, Catherine? Are you often delusional?"

"I think we've gone about as far as we're going to go here. I'll fax you copies of the bank drafts. Bye, now."

With a satisfied smile, Catherine called her daughter, asking Jamie to send her the copies as soon as she had a moment.

❧

Just before Ryan was due home, the land line rang, and Jamie dashed to pick up. "Hello?"

"Hi, Jamie, it's Jordan."

"Hey! How're you doin'?"

"I'm all right. Is Mia home?"

"No, she left for Hillsborough right after her last class. You can call her on her cell, though."

"Actually, I only wanted to make sure you guys were going to be around. I decided to come to town for the weekend in case she needs me."

"Oh, what a good girlfriend you are," Jamie said, smiling. "Well, we were going to go to Noe, but we can easily change our plans. When are you coming in?"

"My plane's supposed to get in at seven. So, I should get to your house by eight-thirty or so. Are you sure you don't mind? I hate to have you change your plans."

Jamie laughed and said, "No, we don't mind, you goof. And if you honestly think Ryan would let you take a cab, you don't know her very well. We'll come pick you up, and then we'll go out to dinner. And don't bother arguing with me, Jordan, I'm just as bull-headed as Ryan is."

"Hi, Mom, I'm home," Mia called out when she entered the family home.

"Come in here and give me a kiss," Anna Lisa replied from the kitchen. "I'm making your favorite dinner."

"Chicken and dumplings?"

"Do you have a new favorite that I don't know about?" When Mia entered the kitchen, her mother was busily rolling out dough with a well-worn rolling pin, and she looked up from her work to give her daughter a warm, welcoming smile. "I don't know how you manage it, but I swear you're prettier every time I see you."

"You're not so bad yourself," Mia teased, giving her mother a kiss. She picked up a triangle of the dough and popped it into her mouth.

"I'll never understand how you can eat raw dough," Anna Lisa said, laughing.

"I prefer raw pie dough, but any kind will do," Mia said. "I must have a vitamin deficiency."

"You certainly look healthy enough." She gave her child her usual visual scrutiny and added, "But you look like something's bothering you. What is it?"

"Gee, Mom, can I take my coat off before you start to grill me?" She shrugged out of her jacket, then went to the refrigerator. "Got any Diet Coke?"

"Yes, I bought some this morning. Now, get your Coke and tell me what's going on with you. Are you having trouble with this mystery boyfriend?"

Sighing, Mia reached into the refrigerator, then walked back over to her mother. She jumped up onto the counter and said, "I don't have a mystery boyfriend."

"He might not be a mystery to you, but he is to me," the older woman said, her feelings obviously still bruised from Mia's reticence to reveal much about her private life.

"Well, that's why I came down this weekend," Mia said, opening her soda and taking a long gulp. "We've settled all of the things that were going on, and like I promised, I want to tell you everything."

Anna Lisa put the rolling pin down, then dusted her hands off. She looked at Mia for a long moment, her dark eyes penetrating the younger woman's defenses. "Something isn't right here. You don't look happy." Approaching her child, Anna Lisa stood between Mia's knees and placed her hand on her cheek. "Are you pregnant, sweetheart? Is that it?"

"No! There's no chance of that, Mom. Trust me."

"There's always a chance," Anna Lisa insisted. "Birth control isn't always effective."

"I'm well aware of that," Mia replied, thinking of her close call with Conor. "But I assure you that I'm not pregnant."

"Then what is it?"

"Uhm…" Mia cleared her throat and tried to get it out, but found herself struggling. "Uhm…you've always told me that I could tell you anything, right?"

"Yes, of course. You can tell me anything."

"I've always assumed that meant that you'd listen to me and not judge me before you heard me out, right?"

"For the love of God, what is it?" Anna Lisa cried, grasping her child by the shoulders and holding on a little too tight.

"It's not that big a deal, Mom," Mia said, wincing as she pried her mother's hands from her body. "But I think you might be a little upset by my choice of partner."

"Is he a drug dealer? A child molester? What?"

"He's…not a he. He's a she, Mom. I'm in love with a woman."

Anna Lisa's face froze in surprise and she took a step backwards, stumbling a little as she did. Grabbing onto the counter, she shook her head violently, then said, "You're what?"

Mia looked her right in the eye and said, "I'm in love with a woman. I love her with all my heart, Mom."

"You can't be serious!"

"I'm deadly serious," Mia said, her expression reflecting her feelings. "I'm serious enough to tell you the truth—even though I know this will upset you."

"Upset? Upset? You've never seen upset!"

"Mom, please don't yell at me," Mia begged. "You said we could discuss this."

"What is there to discuss? My only daughter comes home to tell me she's a lesbian? What can you say to that?"

Swallowing, Mia decided to tell the whole truth. "I didn't say that I was a lesbian. I guess I'm bisexual, because I'm still attracted to men. But I love Jordan, Mom, and she's the person I want to be with—she means everything to me."

"You're in love with a woman, but you're not a lesbian." Anna Lisa said this slowly, giving her daughter a look that bespoke her incredulity.

"What I call myself doesn't matter. What's important is that I've found the person I love. Why does it have to be such a big deal that she's a woman?"

"I knew I shouldn't have let you live with that girl," Anna Lisa said, fuming. "With that alcoholic mother and that cheating father, she couldn't possibly be a good influence on you. She's obviously convinced you that this is a perfectly acceptable choice. Well, it's not!"

"Mom, Jamie had nothing to do with this! You can't convince someone to sleep with a woman if she doesn't want to!"

"WANT TO!" Anna Lisa yelled. "You admit that this is something you want to do! Well, you can change your mind right back, young lady. If you can want it, then you can stop wanting it just as easily!"

"Will you listen to yourself? You can't order me to stop loving someone!"

"I most certainly can!" Anna Lisa said, her voice rising over her daughter's.

Mia jumped down from the counter, standing toe to toe with her mother. "You can't have it both ways, Mom. Either you have a rational discussion with me, or I hide things from you. I will not tell you something that means so much to me, only to have you treat me like a two-year-old!"

"You're acting like a two-year-old! You see someone else do something, and you have to jump right in and do it yourself! This isn't who you are, Mia! You're not like Jamie and her..."

"Lover," Mia growled. "Ryan's her lover. Jordan's my lover. And there's nothing you can do to stop me from loving her. Nothing!"

Grabbing her jacket, Mia stormed outside, heading up the curvy, narrow road, determined to keep walking until she felt calm enough to start round two of the encounter.

🐉

It was fully dark, and the cars barreling around the curvy streets would have frightened Mia if she hadn't been so angry. But she was so steamed that all she could think of was exactly how to tell her mother off when she returned to the house. She was so engrossed in her plans that she failed to see the British-racing-green-Jaguar slow, and then pull into the driveway in front of her. "Mia!" her father called out.

Looking up, she approached the car tentatively. "Are you armed?"

"Get in, you lunatic," Adam said, chuckling softly.

Mia did, leaning against the door, in case her father took a swing at her. "Do you curse the day I was born? Or is that only mom's wish?"

"Oh, honey, she didn't say that, did she?"

"No," Mia admitted, "but it was implied."

Adam put his hand on his daughter's knee and gave it a squeeze. "You know her temper gets the best of her, honey, but she loves you very, very much. You caught her by surprise with this one." He smiled and added, "You caught me, too."

"What were my options, Dad? It's not like I could have worked up to this slowly. I mean, I guess I could have started dating effeminate men, but that probably wouldn't have given you a big enough clue."

"No, I don't think there's a baby step for this kind of thing. I'm sorry that Mom hurt your feelings so badly. Would you like to go have some coffee or a drink and let her calm down a little?"

"A drink," Mia decided. "A nice, stiff drink."

They found a nearby restaurant with a comfortable bar, and father and daughter sat next to one another, sipping at their drinks for a few minutes before either one spoke. "Are you disappointed in me, Dad?"

"No, Mia," he said softly. "You've never disappointed me, baby." She raised an eyebrow and he smiled. "Okay, I've been disappointed a few times, but only when you've done something that's dangerous or harmful. This isn't one of those kinds of things."

"What kind of thing is it?"

"Well," he said, "I've always thought you'd find a nice guy and settle down. It never dawned on me that you might see a different future for yourself. It's gonna take some time to get used to this."

"But…you'll try?" she asked tentatively.

"Of course I will," Adam said. "I love you, Mia, and I'd never let something like this make me stop loving you." He put his arm around her and gave her a squeeze. "You haven't been the easiest child in the world to raise, but I wouldn't trade you for anything. We'll get through this, but we have to weather the storm first."

Finishing her drink with one big gulp, Mia stood and said, "We might as well head into the tempest, Dad. I think it's gonna be a rough night."

The pair went into the house through the back door, and Mia shook her head when she saw the uncooked dumplings lying in a congealed mass in the sink. "I guess a bisexual doesn't get to have her favorite dinner."

Adam put his arm around her shoulders and said, "Do you think it's a good idea to let her have a knife in her hands? Count your blessings."

Walking into the living room together, Anna Lisa fixed the pair with a withering glare. "Did you walk to San Mateo?"

"No, but I could have," Mia said. "We went out for a drink to give both of us time to calm down a little. I don't want us to keep yelling at each other."

"Fine," Anna Lisa said. "Come sit down by me and tell me how this happened."

Giving her a puzzled look, Mia sat down and said, "You want me to explain how I fell in love?"

"No," Anna Lisa said. "I want you to explain how you got into the position to fall in love."

Her mind came up with a dozen answers, all of them lewd, so Mia forced herself to answer seriously. "Jordan played on Ryan's volleyball team…"

"I knew that woman was involved," Anna Lisa snapped.

"Do you want me to talk, or do you want to assume whatever you want?"

"Talk! Who's stopping you?"

Rolling her eyes, Mia continued. "Jordan came over to the house every once in a while, and one night we went out together—just the two of us."

"Why did you do that? If I met a lesbian, I'd never agree to spend the evening with her."

"Well, aren't you the most open-minded person in the world." Mia's arms were crossed over her chest, and she took in a few deep breaths. "That was the night I learned that Jordan was gay, but that certainly wasn't going to stop me from going out for the evening with her."

"So you admit you accepted a date from a lesbian?"

"I didn't think of it as a date," she said thoughtfully. "At first, that is. But we had a wonderful evening together, and we stayed out until dawn, just talking. As the night went on, it became clear that we were…attracted to each other, and when we came back to the house I…I kissed her."

"You…kissed…her," Anna Lisa said.

"Yeah, that's right. I kissed her. I was very attracted to her, Mom, and she looked so pretty, sitting there in the kitchen, with the morning light hitting her hair. I had to kiss her."

Anna Lisa dropped her head into her hands, muttering, "Then what?"

"You really want to hear this?"

"Yes. I want to know how this happened," Anna Lisa insisted.

Mia looked to her father for help, but he just shrugged his shoulders, so she continued, "Jordan's painfully shy, so we took it very slow. We saw each other once or twice a week, until she started making up reasons to come home with Ryan at night. Soon we started spending our evenings together—talking and kissing—like you do with anyone you're starting to get to know."

Shaking her head, Anna Lisa blinked repeatedly, then asked, "Why did you want to kiss her? She's a woman!"

"I was attracted to her, Mom, it's as simple as that. I kissed her for the same reason I've kissed every boy I've ever dated—I did it because I was very attracted to her and I wanted to touch her."

"Go on," Anna Lisa growled.

"Fine," Mia said, deciding to give her mother exactly what she was asking for. "I got tired of waiting for her to make the first move, so one night I convinced her to let me give her a massage. She agreed, and I finally relaxed her enough that she could accept my touch. We made love that night, Mom." The young woman shrugged her shoulders and said, "As soon as I touched her, I knew I loved her. It's magical to be with her."

Anna Lisa scowled at her. "What are you saying? That she has you under some kind of spell?"

"We're not in the Old Country, Mom. She didn't put the evil eye on me. Jesus!"

"This doesn't make any sense. Why would you want to touch a woman—like that? What on earth has gotten into you?"

Mia looked at her father and asked, "Does any of this amaze you, Dad? I mean, come on, look at my history!"

Adam looked at his daughter for a moment, then said, "No, I suppose this isn't a great shock. You've always been one to try something new."

"Fine! So you tried it," Anna Lisa said, brushing her hands together in a dismissive gesture. "Now, you're finished with it!"

"No, I'm not," Mia said firmly. "This wasn't the first time I've been with a woman. This is not out of the ordinary for me."

"What? You're lying! You're only saying that to make this sound more normal."

"I am not! I've been sleeping with men since I was sixteen, and with women since I was seventeen."

"How can you say that?" the older woman cried. "I know that's not true!"

"I had sex with Melissa Johnston right upstairs in my room—for almost a year. Every time she stayed over here, or I stayed at her house, we had sex. She fell in love with me, Mom, and if I hadn't been so afraid of your reaction, I might have let myself fall in love with her, too."

"You were going steady then! I was so worried about you getting pregnant by Mark! Now you tell me you were only putting on a front so you could be with Melissa?"

Mia looked down, feeling guiltier about her two-timing Mark than she ever had over anything she'd ever done. "No, I wasn't putting on a front. I was sleeping with Mark while I was sleeping with Melissa."

"Adam! Do you believe this?" Anna Lisa demanded.

"Why would Mia lie about this?" he asked. "This is obviously something that she's been dealing with for quite a while."

"You had sex with a girl…right in my house?" Anna Lisa cried.

"Yep. Sure did. I had sex with Mark here, too, just for the record. When you and Dad were going to be out for the night, Melissa and Trey would have sex in Peter's room, while Mark and I would be in my room. After the boys left Melissa and I made love, and it was always—always better with Melissa."

"Damn it, Mia!" Her mother paced back and forth in front of the sofa. "How could you do something like that?"

"Mom, you know I've always had a…wild streak. I've done a lot of things that I'm not very proud of. But loving Jordan isn't one of them. She's a wonderful woman, and I'm proud of our love."

"Proud! You're proud of this!"

"I am," Mia said, standing to glare right back at her mother. "Now, I'm gonna go get something to eat. Since my 'favorite daughter' dinner was thrown away, I'm going to go get carry-outs. Dad, do you want anything?"

"I could use a bite," he admitted.

"I assume you're too angry to even think about eating," Mia said to her mother.

With a withering look, the older woman turned her back and stomped away, heading upstairs.

"Let's go out for a decent meal," Adam said. "I've had enough yelling for one evening."

"That goes double for me," Mia agreed. "Too bad there's no place around here to get chicken and dumplings," she groused. "I had my mouth set to dig into those babies."

After dinner, Jordan paced across the living room, while Jamie and Ryan tried to get her to relax a little bit. "Mia will be fine, Jordan," Jamie assured her. "Her mom is very volatile, but Mia doesn't take much abuse. They're pretty well matched, to be honest."

"I can't stand the thought of her being yelled at or having her feelings hurt," Jordan said.

"I understand that, but you've got to understand how the Christophers' interact. Mia and her mom are either kissing each other and complimenting the hell out of each other; or they're yelling their heads off. They've always been that way, and they always will be. My guess is that they're yelling now—and before the night's over, they'll be kissing."

"What about her dad?" Jordan asked. "Can she count on him?"

"He's a funny guy," Jamie said. "He lets Mrs. Christopher run the house and make most of the decisions regarding the kids. In a way, he kinda acts like one of the kids. I think he'll be on Mia's side—he usually is—but that still won't stop her mom from giving her a hard time."

"She'll call if things get bad, won't she?" Jordan asked, her face lined with worry.

"No. She'll storm out of there and come home. She'll be able to handle this, Jordan. I promise you that she will."

⚜

Over dinner, Adam leaned back in his chair and said, "Tell me a little more about this woman. All I know is her first name."

"Her name's Jordan Ericsson," Mia said, smiling from the mere recital of her name. "She's from L.A,. and her dad is a bigwig in development at Paramount. Her parents are divorced, and her mom is a psycho, and she has one older brother. He's close to Peter's age—but he's a loser."

"Doesn't sound like a very happy family," Adam said.

"No, it's not a happy family. Jordan practically raised herself, and if she hadn't had volleyball to give her some focus, I don't know what would have happened to her."

"She must be a pretty good player to make Cal's team," Adam said.

Giving him a proud smile, Mia said, "She's fabulous, Dad. She's on the Olympic team. That's why we can't be together right now—she's in Colorado Springs at the Olympic training facility."

"Damn! She must be great!"

"She is," Mia said. "And she works her butt off—she's very, very disciplined." Cocking her head, she asked, "Wanna see a picture?"

"Sure."

She dug into her wallet and pulled out a photo of the two of them taken in the Bahamas. They were lying together on a chaise on the deck of their villa, and Mia was sound asleep. Jordan had her arms around her waist, cuddling Mia to her chest. When Ryan had come out with the camera that day, Jordan had dipped her head, closed her eyes, and kissed the top of Mia's head. Adam gazed at the print for a long time, then looked at his daughter and smiled. "You look like you're in love."

"I am, Dad," she said earnestly. "For the first time in my life. I want you and Mom to like her—but whether or not you do—I'm going to continue to love her."

"I thought you were in love with Jason. You said you were at the time."

"I thought I knew what love was, Dad, but I didn't. I cared for Jason more than I ever had any other guy—and I thought that's what love was supposed to feel like. But I never felt like Jason was a part of me—I never felt that his needs were as important as mine. I didn't fully trust him, Dad. But I trust Jordan with my life. I know she'd never hurt me—no matter what."

He looked at the picture again, smiling as he said, "You *do* know how good looking she is, don't you?"

"Yeah, that hasn't escaped my attention. But that's not her biggest appeal, Dad. I'll admit that her looks were the first thing I noticed, but it's her heart that I love." She took out another couple of photos—including one of Jordan in her thong bikini, lying on the beach—striking an intentionally sexy pose. "But I'll admit that her body takes my breath away."

Adam looked at them quickly, then handed them back. "Well," he said, showing a mildly embarrassed smile, "I thought it was bad enough when Peter started bringing girls home—now I have to try to ignore the fact that my daughter's girlfriend is a knockout! I think I'd prefer to see some nice, fully clothed pictures of the two of you, honey."

"Sorry," she said, giggling. "I guess I forget sometimes that you're a guy."

"Only when your mother's not around," Adam said, laughing along with his daughter.

When they returned home, Anna Lisa was not much calmer. Adam tried to intercede, and they went upstairs to their room to talk privately for a while. Mia took the opportunity to go into the kitchen and put in a call to Jamie. "Hey," she said, when her friend answered.

"How's it going?" Jamie asked. "We're worried about you."

"Well, my mom's actually a little worse than I thought she'd be. She thinks she can order me to stop loving Jordan." Laughing softly, she added, "She seems to forget that she's never effectively ordered me to stop doing anything."

"I can attest to that," Jamie said. "Have you spoken to Jordan?"

"Huh-uh. My parents are upstairs and I think they'll be coming back down any minute. I don't want to call her until the dust has settled."

"Are you gonna stay overnight?" Jamie asked, honoring Jordan's wishes that Mia not know she was in town.

"I guess I should. I kinda hate to drop a bomb on them and then take off. My mom might be calmer in the morning, after she's vented a little."

"Well, call me before you go to bed, okay? I'm worried about you."

"Will do. Wish me luck, James."

Anna Lisa and Adam came back downstairs minutes after Mia hung up. She was in the middle of cleaning up the kitchen—the remnants of the ill-fated chicken and dumplings making her so grumpy that she had to dispose of them.

Busying herself by making a cup of tea, Anna Lisa spoke in a calm voice. "Your father tells me that your friend is on the Olympic team."

"Yeah, she is," Mia said. "I'm very proud of her."

"How long will she be where she is?"

"She's in Colorado," Mia said. "That's been one of the things we've been trying to work out. The Olympics are in September, and after that—it's still up in the air if she'll stay with the team or come home to Berkeley."

"And if she stays there?" Anna Lisa asked, still using her conversational tone.

"Then I'll be there with her." Mia turned and looked her mother directly in the eye. "We'll make the decision together, based on what's best for each of us."

"Have you forgotten that you're going to law school in the fall of 2001?"

"No, of course I haven't forgotten. That'll be one of the major things we consider. We won't do anything rash."

"You've already done something rash, Mia. Something very rash."

"Look. It's getting late. Do you want me to go home? Or can we talk about this calmly tomorrow?"

"I want you to stay," Anna Lisa said. She walked up to her daughter and hugged her tight. "I love you, Mia, and I always will. I'm upset about this, but I still love you."

"I know, Mom. I don't ever doubt that you love me. Although, sometimes I think you wish you'd stopped after one child."

Anna Lisa grasped Mia's chin in her hand and shook it, making her curls fly. "Don't you ever even think something like that! I thank God every day that he gave me such a wonderful child! And I'll thank him tonight, Mia—just like always."

"I love you, too, Mom," Mia sighed as she rested her head on her mother's shoulder. "I hate it when we yell at each other. I'll make an effort to be calm tomorrow. Will you?"

"Yes, baby, I'll try. Sleep well." She kissed Mia and gave her another healthy squeeze, then Adam came over and did the same.

"Do you need anything, honey?" he asked.

"No, I'm gonna head up to bed. Wake me when you get up, okay?"

"Okay," Adam said, ruffling her hair as he left the room. "See you tomorrow."

As soon as her parents left the room, Mia took her cell phone and dialed Jordan's apartment, frowning when the answering machine picked up. "Hi, honey. It's me. Call me when you get home, okay? Love you."

Going up to her room, she got undressed and put on one of Jordan's Olympic team T-shirts that she'd lifted when they were in Las Vegas. Falling into her bed, she dialed her house, and once again spoke with Jamie. "Hey. What's going on?"

"Not much. How's it going?"

"About what you'd expect. Things are a little better than they were earlier.

I'm gonna go to bed and wait for Jordy to call me back."

"Okay, honey. You let us know if you need anything."

"I need my Jordan," Mia sighed. "I miss her."

"I know she misses you, too. But you'll see her soon."

"We haven't made any specific plans about when we'll see each other again. I don't know how long it'll be."

"Think good thoughts. It might be sooner than you think."

Hanging up, Jamie smiled at the tall, blonde woman who paced in front of her. "She misses you."

"I miss her, too," Jordan said. "I think I'll go up to her room and call her."

"We might be in bed when you're finished," Ryan said. "It's been a long week."

"No problem. I know my way around." A charming grin transformed her previously worried countenance.

"G'night, buddy." Ryan gave her friend a kiss and Jamie followed suit.

"See you guys tomorrow," Jordan said.

As soon as she got to Mia's room, Jordan dialed the number and lay down on the bed. "Hi, sweetheart," she said when Mia answered.

"Hi. Where were you when I called?"

"Uhm...I was talking with some friends. How are you?"

"I'm all right, but I miss you so much I ache, Jordy. I don't know why it's so bad tonight, but I'd give anything to see you."

"I miss you, too. I guess it was because I knew you were doing something difficult today—but I wasn't able to stop thinking about you all day. I got hit right in the face with a ball in practice—I couldn't concentrate a bit."

"You didn't get hurt, did you?"

"Nah. It just woke me up a little bit. The teasing I had to take was more painful than being hit with the ball." Her voice grew gentler, and she asked, "Tell me how it's going."

"Uhm...it's not great, but it's also not horrible. Mom's pretty upset, and she was being fairly irrational earlier, but right before she went to bed she told me she loved me, and that we could try to be calmer tomorrow. It's been a big shock for her."

"Is your dad okay?"

"He's handling it better," Mia said, "but I assumed he would. He never gets very upset about things that I do. He was very wild when he was a kid, and I think he understands that I'm a free spirit like he was."

"You are that," Jordan said fondly. "That's part of what I love about you."

"I feel so unsettled," Mia said. "I know they love me, and I know they want only the best for me—but it's hard, Jordy. It's so hard to have to defend myself and my choices and my feelings. It makes me feel…lonely."

"I wish I were with you right now," Jordan said, sighing deeply.

"I do, too. I'd give anything to feel your arms around me. You make me feel so safe and secure and loved. I know you'll always support me." She paused, and Jordan could hear her struggle to maintain her composure. "I wish I felt the same way about my mom." Mia started to cry softly, finally saying, "I hate it when she yells at me. It makes me feel so defensive…like I'm a little kid who doesn't have any sense."

"She yelled at you?" Jordan asked, trying to control the anger she felt welling up.

"We yell at each other, honey. We always have. I can remember being a tiny little kid, standing in the kitchen and us yelling at each other at full volume. It's a stupid way to communicate, but it's what we do."

"You never yell at me," Jordan said. "Do you ever feel like yelling?"

"No, it's just my mom that gets to me this way. I never yell at my dad, or my brother. She just makes me crazy."

"Damn, you sound so sad," Jordan said. "I wish I could make you feel better."

"I feel better when I talk to you. I can lie here and imagine that you're holding me."

"I can't do that," Jordan said. "I miss you more when we talk on the phone." She sighed and said, "I miss you so much that all I think about is when I'll be able to talk to you—but when I do, it reminds me of how far away you are, and how much I miss holding you and kissing you. I…I never feel settled."

"I know, honey. I know exactly what you mean." Mia sniffed a few times, wiping at her tears. "Let's go to sleep now. I'm getting more depressed talking about it."

"Oh, baby, I'm sorry if I upset you."

"No, you didn't upset me, Jordy. The situation upsets me—having you a thousand miles away upsets me. But not you, sweetheart. You're my girl."

"I'll always be your girl," Jordan said softly. "Always."

"G'night, Jordy. I'll try to dream about how wonderful it feels to lie in your arms."

"I love you, Mia. I love you with all my heart."

Chapter Twenty-One

The chirp of her cell phone woke Mia from a troubled sleep. "H'lo?"

"Open your bedroom door," Jordan's soft voice said.

Half asleep, Mia got to her feet and opened the door, staring into the empty hallway.

"The other door," Jordan said, snickering.

"Jordy!" Now fully awake, Mia closed and locked the door to the hall, frantically keyed in the code for the alarm, then scampered across the room to throw open the French door that led to a small deck. A grinning Jordan stood right before her eyes, and Mia threw her arms around her and hugged her so tightly that she couldn't take a breath. But she didn't mind a bit—gladly willing to forsake breathing to be held in Mia's fevered embrace.

"Let's go inside," Jordan murmured. "I don't want your parents to hear us. Their lights are still on."

Mia tugged her inside, then spent a minute running her hands up and down Jordan's long body—trying to convince herself that her lover was really with her. "How did you manage this?" she asked, completely amazed.

"When I finished practice today, I decided I couldn't stand the thought of you having to do this all alone. I called Jamie, and she and Ryan came to get me from the airport. I was at your house when we talked earlier."

"Are you shitting me?" Mia asked, her tone a little loud for the setting.

"Shh! They'll hear you!"

"Why didn't you tell me you were here?"

"Because I didn't want to put any more pressure on you. I knew you'd want to come home if you knew I was there—but I wanted you to stay here if you needed to."

"Damn, it feels wonderful to be in love with someone who cares for me so much," Mia murmured, wrapping her arms around Jordan's neck.

"I do, I care for you more than anything else in the world."

Releasing her, Mia stood back and ran her hands over her lover's body once again. "You look very cute in your USA warm-ups, but you'd look even cuter out of them. Can I?" she asked, her hands on the jacket's zipper.

"Of course. There's no one I'd rather be undressed by."

Mia made short work of the clothes, getting her down to her T-shirt and bikinis. "You're still overdressed, but it's pretty chilly in here. Let's get into bed, and you can tell me how you managed to find your way down here." They climbed into the single bed, shifting around a bit to be able to fit. Suddenly, Mia sat up, and said, "Shit! If you parked on the street they'll tow you!"

"I didn't," Jordan assured her. "Jamie told me the whole drill. We called her mom, and I parked over there. I didn't realize you guys lived so close to one another."

"And she told you which room was mine?"

"Yep. As well as how easy it is to scale the trellis by the garage. You know, I don't feel very good about you sleeping in a room that's so easy to get into."

"Well, if it wasn't easy to get into, you wouldn't be here now, so let's be thankful for small favors." Mia cuddled up against her partner and said, "I can't believe this, but I haven't even kissed you."

"Let's make up for lost time," Jordan said, grinning widely.

Mia laced a hand through her hair and pulled Jordan's lips close. "I love you so much," she whispered. Pressing her lips gently against Jordan's, she let the familiar sensations wash over her body. Mia greedily delighted in the exquisite smoothness of her lover's skin; the way their bodies molded so perfectly against each other; the firmness of Jordan's supple muscles; the soft resiliency of her breasts; the minty taste of her freshly brushed teeth. Each kiss made her hunger for more—her need to merge with Jordan growing so powerful that she was unable to resist.

Jordan's hand slipped under Mia's long T-shirt and rhythmically squeezed her ass, her kisses growing more passionate as her hands continued to explore.

Without even being aware that she had moved, Mia found her hands happily filled with the warm, supple flesh of Jordan's breasts. Her tongue darted into the receptive mouth as her fingers gently pinched the firming nipples.

"Oh, God," Jordan sighed, rolling onto her back and spreading her legs apart. She maneuvered Mia into position and wrapped her legs around her, pressing her lover against her need. Her powerful thighs flexed, and Mia growled when her mound ground against Jordan's heat.

"I've missed you so much," Mia murmured, kissing down Jordan's neck and sinking her teeth into the delicate skin in the hollow of her shoulder.

Suddenly, Jordan held her tight, her eyes wide with alarm. She placed a finger to her lips, then pointed at the door. Sharpening her senses, Mia heard something creak, then heard the knob on her door turn. Her eyes nearly popped from her head, but then she remembered that she'd locked the door. To her dismay, there was a very gentle knock, and she rolled her eyes at Jordan, shrugged her shoulders, then got up and went to the door. "Who is it?" she asked.

"It's me," her father said. "Are you all right?"

"Uhm...yeah. Why wouldn't I be?"

"Well, we thought we heard something, then your mother noticed that the alarm wasn't on, and that your door to the deck was open. Are you sure you're all right, honey?"

She unlocked the door and opened it a crack. "I'm fine, Dad. I couldn't sleep, so I went out onto the deck for a minute to watch the stars."

"Do you want to talk some more?"

"No, no, really, I'm okay. I only have a T-shirt on, Dad, and I'd like to get back into bed so I can warm up."

"Oh! Well, go do that, baby. I just wanted to check to make sure you were all right."

"I'm fine. I'll see you in the morning—and I'll lock the door and turn the alarm back on, too."

"G'night, honey."

"G'night, Dad. Thanks for checking on me."

She closed the door and leaned against it, holding her hand over her heart and beating lightly on her chest to show how hard it was fluttering. Jordan looked absolutely panic-stricken, and Mia quickly locked up and crawled back into bed. "Well, I'm still excited, but it's a whole other kind of excitement. Now, where were we?"

Jordan grasped her shoulders to prevent her from leaning in for another kiss. "Are you crazy? We can't have sex with them both awake!"

"I've had sex in here dozens of time," Mia said. "They only saw the patio door open—they didn't hear us."

"No, no, no," Jordan said, her blonde hair bouncing. "There's no way I could relax enough." She looked into Mia's eyes for a moment, saying, "It's enough for me to hold you. Isn't that enough for you?"

Swallowing her disappointment, Mia nodded. "It is. Holding you is all I need to be happy."

"Just cuddle up against me and tell me everything that happened today," Jordan said. "I want to know every single thing."

Placing a quick kiss on her cheek, Mia did as she was asked, starting, "Well, I got home at about four, and my mom was making my favorite dinner..."

"Is she all right?" Anna Lisa asked, a little anxiety in her voice.

"She's fine." Adam took off his robe and tossed it onto a chair. He slid into bed and wrapped his arm around his wife, cuddling her close to his chest. "She said she couldn't sleep, so she went onto her deck to watch the stars."

"Well, at least she didn't sneak out by climbing down the trellis like she used to."

"Whose idea was it to give her the room with the escape route?" Adam asked, chuckling.

"That was poor planning on my part," Anna Lisa admitted. "I was silly enough to think that our son would be the one we'd have to keep a close watch on."

"It certainly didn't work out that way."

"No, but at least we didn't have two like Mia. I don't think I could have taken that."

"Mia's one of a kind, honey. She's truly unique."

"Oh, Adam, what are we going to do with her?"

"There's not much we can do, Anna. She's twenty-one now, and she'll graduate in just a couple of months. We've done our best raising her, now we have to let her make her own choices."

"I can't do that, Adam, I can't. You're right when you say we don't have much control—that's why we have to use what we have while we still have it."

"I don't see what that's going to buy us, Anna. I think we should let her do what she wants. What's the chance of this lasting long, anyway? She's never had a boyfriend for longer than a year or a year and a half. Why will this be any different?"

"This isn't what I want for her! I can't let her do what she wants this time. We have to show her how much we disapprove."

"But, I don't disapprove as much as you do. I don't think Mia's a lesbian, either, but I know her well enough to know that the best way to make her dig her heels in is to say no."

"You might be right, but this time I feel like we have to make a point. I know we can't force her to do what we want, but we can make her have to endure a little hardship to support her choices."

"I don't think it will work."

"It might not," she conceded. "But we have to be united on this, Adam. I truly think this is the way to go."

"All right," he sighed. "We'll try it your way—and see what happens." He stroked his wife's back for a few moments, then said, "Can we try to have a nice morning? I don't want the whole day to be filled with tension."

"I'll do my best, honey," Anna Lisa said. "I love Mia so much, Adam. I hate to yell at her, but she makes me see red!"

"Try to mend fences a little. Let her see how much you love her—try to get her to talk about Jordan, so she feels you've at least heard her side."

"I don't want to know anything about her," Anna Lisa sniffed.

"Then put on an act. You always act interested when my mother talks about her golf game—if you can do that, you can do this."

Anna Lisa chuckled softly and snuggled closer to her husband. "You're right. If I can sit through dinner with your mother, I can do anything."

🐎

"I'm getting stiff," Mia murmured. "Can we switch sides?"

"Mmm…my shoulder's asleep," Jordan said. "Are you sure you used to sleep with people in this little bed?"

"Well," Mia drawled, "there wasn't much sleeping going on, but I've had several overnight guests."

"Oh, so that's what we're doing wrong. This bed works better when your guest is on top of you, rather than next to you."

Mia shifted around and pushed Jordan onto her back, then climbed on top of her. "Does it bother you, honey?"

"What?"

"Does it bother you that I've had other people sleep with me here?"

"I uhm…I don't spend my time thinking about things like that. I…I try to focus on what I have—rather than what I wish I had."

"That wasn't a very forthright answer, Jordy." Mia rose up and rested her weight on one arm, stroking her lover's cheek with the tips of her fingers. "Does it bother you?"

"Look," Jordan said, gazing into Mia's eyes. "Here's what I wish for. I wish that I had grown up in Hillsborough, and had met you in high school. I wish that you were the first person I ever kissed; the first person who ever touched my body; the first person that I ever desired. And I wish that the same had been true for you. I wish we'd been together for four or five years by now, and that our parents were totally cool with our relationship. That's my ideal. Everything else leaves something to be desired."

"So, it does bother you—a tiny little bit?"

"It doesn't bother me because I honestly don't think about it—unless a cute little brown eyed girl forces me to," she added, straining to reach Mia's lips for a kiss. "I like to look at it positively. If you'd been as inexperienced as I was, we still wouldn't have kissed. We'd be sitting up all night, talking and talking until we both had laryngitis."

Chuckling, Mia settled back down on top of her partner. "I guess you have a point. Boy, I'm glad we started kissing." With a contented purr, Mia started to kiss Jordan's soft lips, once again finding her hands snaking up under the T-shirt to cup her breasts. "I can't resist," Mia murmured, pushing the shirt up as she scooted down the bed and captured a pert nipple in her mouth.

"Oh, baby," Jordan murmured, her eyes closing while her hands went to Mia's shoulders. She had every intention of pushing the determined mouth away, but Mia's touch was so delightful, and her mouth was so warm, that she found herself urging her on. "Oh, that's the way…just how I like it. Ooo…that feels so fine."

Mia lifted up enough to pull her shirt over her head, then she tugged Jordan's off as well, Jordan not protesting a bit. Sliding off the athletic body and lying on her side, Mia started to gently lick the soft, pink flesh—starting at the very base of each breast and moving up until she sucked the firming nipple into her mouth. She was determinedly working her way around the entire mound when she heard her lover's voice.

"Mia," Jordan moaned, "honey, you know that makes me lose my mind."

"I want you to lose your mind," Mia insisted, maneuvering Jordan onto her side and slipping a leg between her thighs. "I want to make you absolutely crazy."

"But your parents…"

"It's four a.m., Jordy. They're asleep—I'm sure of it."

"But what if they're not? We can't risk it."

"Wasn't it a risk when you climbed the trellis? Isn't it a risk to be in my bed?"

"Yes, of course it is, but you know how we get. Neither one of us is very careful…or very quiet."

"Mmm…don't you want me to touch you?" Mia asked, her voice soft and sweet and so very persuasive. She rocked her hips, sliding her thigh against Jordan's vulva, smiling to herself when her lover's eyes closed and she bit her lower lip.

"Of…of course I do," Jordan gasped, "but we shouldn't."

"We'll be quiet," Mia promised. "We don't have to rock the house. I'll just hold you and love you—quietly."

"We shouldn't, Mia. We should…wait." Mia felt her lover's whole body shake, and knew she was close to giving in.

"Make you a deal," Mia said. "You seem a little confused, so I think we should let your body decide. Let's take a little peek and see how she votes." Before Jordan could react, Mia slid a hand down her belly and snuck under her waistband. Determined fingers parted her gently, and Mia growled into Jordan's ear when her fingers were immediately coated with her essence. "That's an unequivocal yes."

"I…I can't be quiet when you touch me," Jordan groaned. "I just can't."

"We'll be quieter if we keep our mouths busy." She started to slide down Jordan's long body, a lascivious leer on her face. By the time she had snuck under the covers, she was surprised by Jordan's long, elegant fingers preventing her from reaching her goal. Popping her head out of the covers, Mia said, "Hey! That's my spot!"

"No way," Jordan said, smiling warmly. "You put your head right back down there and give me a little help. I can only be quiet if I have some control."

Eyes twinkling, Mia slipped back under the covers, saying, "I've never watched you touch yourself. This is cool!"

"Now remember, we have to be as quiet as little mice," Jordan said. She reached down and started to pull her panties down, starting when Mia latched onto them with her teeth and playfully removed them.

"You're good at that," Jordan whispered, lifting the covers to gaze into Mia's warm, brown eyes.

"Shh, we're being quiet," Mia reminded her. She spread Jordan's legs and rested her head on a muscular thigh, waiting patiently until the knowing fingers began to move.

Unable to resist the urge, Mia slipped a finger into Jordan as soon as Jordan began to touch herself. "Ooo, you're so hot and wet," she moaned, her words muffled by the heavy blanket. Jordan's scent was always alluring, but being under the blanket intensified the experience, making her mouth water. Needing as much of the long-legged beauty as she could get, Mia started to kiss and suck the smooth skin of her lover's perfect thighs. As Jordan's fingers sped across her shimmering wetness, Mia bit and licked the pale skin, groaning right along with her excited partner.

After a few minutes, Jordan began to gasp for breath, her climax rapidly approaching. Mia slipped another finger into her, then started to lick all around Jordan's fingers, competing for precious space.

Jordan clapped her free hand over her own mouth, stifling the cry that desperately wanted to emerge. Mia heard the strangled moaning, and she climbed up her lover quickly, pulling Jordan's hand away—only to replace it with her mouth. Kissing her rabidly while Jordan's body still bucked and shook, Mia finally pulled away—both of them panting and gasping for air.

Holding her lover in her arms until Jordan had recovered, Mia teased her, "Such a bad little girl. If I hadn't covered your mouth, my dad would have been down here with his shotgun."

"Your dad has a shotgun?"

"No, silly, my mom's the enforcer around here. And she's harmless as long as she can't get to the butcher knives."

"Maybe I should leave now," Jordan said, only partly kidding.

"If you try to leave now, I'm the one you have to fear," Mia warned. "I'm so hot, I'm smoking!"

"Let me help you put out the fire." Jordan started to scoot down the bed.

"No, no, no," Mia said, grasping Jordan's shoulders and pulling her back up. "If you go down there, I have no ability to control myself. Let's keep it nice and simple and safe, babe."

Blinking up at her with guileless blue eyes, Jordan asked, "Just a tiny taste? I promise I won't stay long."

"Uh-uh," Mia said, unyielding. "Your talented mouth is too much to resist. If I feel that fabulous tongue on me, you're in for the duration—and that could have disastrous results."

"You're no fun," Jordan said, grinning at the compliment.

"We'll see how much fun you have when my mom's chasing you down the street with a butcher knife," Mia warned, taking her lover's hand and guiding it home.

⁂

At seven a.m., a tall, blonde woman rolled over and reached blindly for the ringing phone. Unsure of the time, or even the day, she knocked the receiver to the floor, cursing softly while she fumbled for the instrument. "H'llo?" she muttered.

"It's Mother."

Blinking the sleep from her eyes, she disentangled herself from the body of her lover, trying to figure out what was going on. "Why…what…what time is it?"

"It's seven a.m."

"Did somebody die? Why are you calling so early?"

"Because I spent most of the night tossing and turning—getting almost no sleep. I want answers, Cassie, and I want them now."

"Answers? What answers?"

"I want to know why you stooped to the depths of selling a bit of nasty gossip to a tabloid! We're not the type of people who do that kind of thing!"

Her brain started firing, and Cassie slipped out of bed, pulling on her robe as she left the bedroom. Her boyfriend knew nothing of her association with the tabloids, nor with the money she had received. Speaking quietly, she sat in the living room and said, "I don't know what you're talking about. I don't read those things."

"I didn't ask if you read them, Cassie. I asked why you sold two stories to them!"

"I didn't!" she said. "How can you even think I'd do that?"

"Cassandra Leighton Martin, I'm going to ask you this just once. Did you, or did you not sell stories to the National Inquisitor?"

"I did not," the younger woman said, sounding absolutely guileless.

There was a short period of silence, then Laura said, "If I didn't hate her so much, I'd call Catherine Evans and apologize."

"Huh?"

"I told her yesterday that I was very proud of the way you'd turned out. Now, I'm not so sure. I don't appreciate being lied to, Cassie, and this makes me wonder about many choices you've made this year."

"Oh, God, here comes the lecture about Nick again, right?"

"You know I don't like that boy, and neither does your father. I see no potential in him at all, and he might as well be an orphan for all the good his family will do for him."

"His parents are very nice," the young woman insisted. "His father makes a very good living selling cars."

"Selling cars," Laura sniffed. "Will you listen to yourself? You're twenty-two years old, and the contacts you make now are vital. Most women marry someone they meet in college—you can't afford to waste you time on this boy."

"We're just dating, Mom, we're certainly not engaged."

"Well, given that you've proven that you feel perfectly comfortable lying to me, I see no reason to believe what you have to say about this topic."

"I'm not lying." Yawning, she asked, "Can I go back to bed, now?"

"Certainly. I hate to keep you from your pressing business. Oh, one last thing. Don't expect any more deposits to your checking account. You've gotten your last dime from your father and me."

"What?"

"You heard me. I know you got a hundred thousand dollars from the National Inquisitor. You can run through that until you graduate."

"But...but...I..."

"Yes?" Laura asked. "You had something to say?"

"You can't do that to me! I don't have any money!"

"You can lie all you want, Cassie. I saw the drafts that went into your account."

"But...but...I had to give the money away."

"Pardon me?"

"Jamie's big dyke girlfriend showed up here and made me write her a check for every dime I had!"

"She threatened you?" Laura asked.

"Yes...yes, she did!"

"My God! What kind of a brute is Jamie tangled up with?"

"She's horrible, Mom, really horrible. I think she's been following me around school, too. She caught me alone in the bathroom the other day and I thought she was going to molest me!"

Totally shocked, Laura said, "Did you call the campus police?"

"No…uhm…I'm afraid of what she'll do to me if I report her. Don't forget she killed a man."

Laura took a breath, then said, "Well, then you'd better call the police. As much as I disapprove of what you did, that woman shouldn't be allowed to get away with harassing and robbing you."

"Uhm…I can't do that. She…she blackmailed me."

"First it was force, and now it's blackmail? Get your story straight, Cassie. This is getting ridiculous."

"She…she created a video game that showed me getting fat," Cassie said, her reason for giving away ninety thousand dollars sounding less catastrophic now that she was recounting it. "She was going to show it to everyone if I didn't give her the money."

Once again, silence reigned for long moments. "I can't guess which of the tales you've told are true. All I know is that you aren't going to receive any more money from your father and me. You have a lot of growing up to do, Cassie. I suggest you get busy."

🐉

"Mia, breakfast is almost ready," Adam said as he knocked lightly on her door at eight.

"Be right down, Dad."

As they heard Adam's footsteps retreat down the hall, the young lovers continued the bout of frenzied kissing they'd been engaged in when he'd knocked. Jordan had her hand on the door to the deck, but Mia was holding on to her so tightly that she couldn't move an inch. "I've got to go," Jordan murmured between kisses. "Even if your parents don't see me, the neighbors will."

"You can't see the house from the street. I'll go downstairs in my usual noisy fashion—and my parents won't hear a thing. The kitchen's at the other end of the house, and my mom always has music on in the morning."

"I could hide out here all day," Jordan said. "I'd like to keep an eye on you, and be here if you need me."

"I need you every minute," Mia said, kissing her again. "But you should go back to Berkeley and go to bed. You didn't have a minute's sleep, and I know how you need your rest."

"Will you call me?"

"Yes, of course I will. I'll call before I come home—but it might be late afternoon or early evening. Is that okay?"

"You stay as long as you need to. This is important. I want your parents to be on our side—and the chances of that are much higher if you spend some time explaining this to them."

"I'll do my best. Now, go home and sleep! I won't call before four—so you go crawl into my bed and dream of me."

"I will. I'm sure I'll fall asleep immediately since I'll be able to smell your scent on your pillow."

"If you need to relax, just open the bottom drawer of my bedside table," Mia said, grinning impishly. "My Jordy substitutes are all in there."

Chuckling, Jordan shook her head. "I want to wait for the real Mia. There is no substitute." She clutched Mia to her chest and said, "And tonight, I get to savor every inch of you. We can rock the house, baby."

To Mia's complete amazement, the morning went stunningly well. Anna Lisa and Adam asked dozens of questions about Jordan and her future plans, and Mia went to her father's computer and showed her parents some PG-rated pictures of Jordan playing for Cal, and her profile and picture on the USA Volleyball website. By mid-day, Mia was feeling remarkably relaxed, and she gladly accepted her mother's offer to make her favorite dinner—and actually finish it this time. Even though she desperately wanted to be with Jordan, she knew that her lover was right—and that making peace with her parents was critical.

As the day went on, she felt practically giddy—her parent's support meant so much to her that she couldn't help but kiss and hug each of them every time she had an opportunity. Taking a break, she called Jordan at around five. "Hey, baby, how's my girl?"

"I'm good," Jordan said, stretching her muscles out. "I've been lazing around in bed all day, watching TV and napping on and off. I think I'm about ready for a big dose of my favorite woman. When will you be home?"

"Not for a while. My mom wants to make dinner for me—since she threw yesterday's out. Do you mind?"

"No, I'll see if I can find something around here to eat. No problem."

"What are Jamie and Ryan doing?"

"Oh, they're going to a party."

"Oh, right! I said I'd go with them. When are they leaving?"

"Pretty soon. Ryan says it's a 'bring your own everything' party, so they're gonna stop and get some carry outs to take for dinner."

"Why don't you go with them, honey? Then you can have dinner and socialize a little. I can come pick you up from there and take you back to Berkeley."

"Are you sure?"

"Yeah. I'd rather you went—I don't want you hanging around the house, waiting for me."

"All right. If you're positive."

"I am. Let me talk to Ryan so I can get directions, okay?"

"Okay. I'll see you when you get there. I'm counting the minutes."

"Me, too. I love you, Jordy."

"I love you, too. Remember that if things get tough tonight, okay?"

"I always do. You're never far from my thoughts, sweetheart."

After getting the details from Ryan, Mia went back downstairs to watch her mother make another attempt at chicken and dumplings. While her mother kneaded the dough, Mia gave her a shoulder massage, and the older woman purred with pleasure from the sensation. "You're so good at that," Anna Lisa murmured.

"I've gotten better since I've been with Jordan. She's gotten thousands of massages throughout her career, and she's shown me some techniques that have helped me improve."

"I'll just bet she's shown you some techniques," Anna Lisa grumbled, with her first sarcastic comment of the day.

"Mom," Mia said, turning her mother so she could see her face. "Jordan was a virgin when we made love. She's taught me a lot about love, but she didn't know squat about how to have sex. I'm telling you—once and for all—this was my idea. I'm the one who pursued her—I'm the one who made the first and the second and the third and the fourth moves. If anyone should be upset—her mother should be angry with me!"

"It doesn't sound like her mother would care if she were dating a serial killer."

"She probably wouldn't. She's a sorry excuse for a parent." She wrapped her arms around her mother and gave her a gentle hug. "You've always been a good parent, Mom, and part of the reason you're good is because you care about me, and you want to make sure I make good choices in life. I know this one is hard for you to accept, but it's the right one for me—I'm sure of that."

"I know you are," Anna Lisa said, giving her a kiss on the cheek. "I can see how determined you are about this."

"Jordan means everything to me, Mom. I'll do whatever I have to do to protect this relationship."

Mia pushed her chair away from the table, moaning, "I wish I'd worn sweats. I might be able to eat another bite or two if I had an elastic waistband."

"At least I don't have to wonder if you liked it," Anna Lisa said, smiling at her. "It's very simple to make, honey. I'd be happy to teach you."

"I wouldn't enjoy as much it if I made it for myself. I think it's so good because you make it for me."

"I'd do anything for you, my sweet girl. I hope you know that." Anna Lisa looked down at the table and ordered her thoughts, then said, "Even when I do something that hurts you, or makes you angry, I do it because I think it's the right thing for you."

The look on her mother's face and the tone of her voice set off warning bells; and Mia quickly looked to her father, seeing him staring at the table. "What's going on?"

"Your father and I have talked it over, and we've decided that we can't support your choice to be in this relationship. I know this will upset you, but I want to make it clear that we support you—we just don't think this is right for you."

"So, what does that mean?" she asked, her whole body starting to shake.

"We'll do whatever we have to do to stop you from going forward with this. You made it clear that you don't think you're a lesbian—someday, probably soon—you're going to see that this isn't right for you. We're trying to save you, and Jordan, from a lot of heartache."

"Bullshit!" she said, throwing her napkin down onto the table. "You're full of it. That's not your motivation, and you know it!"

"It is, too!" Anna Lisa shouted, her volume rising over Mia's. "What kind of man will want to marry you when you tell him you were lovers with a woman for a year or two? This is only a phase, but it will come back to haunt you!"

"What in the hell are you talking about? I'd never marry a guy who was so narrow minded that it freaked him out to learn about Jordan! Besides, I'm not gonna marry anyone but her!"

"You're being ridiculous!" Anna Lisa said. "You can't marry her—you'll never be able to marry her! There are laws against that kind of thing, and for good reason!"

"Great, just great! You're probably gonna vote for Proposition 22! My own parents!"

"We are not," Adam said, looking to his wife for the confirmation that didn't come. "Well, I'm not. I don't want you to get hurt, Mia. I don't want you to close off your options—you're too young."

"I'm old enough to know that I'm in love," the younger woman declared. "You can't change that."

"Maybe not," Anna Lisa said, "but we don't have to support it. If you continue with this, we're not going to support you next year like we said we would."

Mia shoved her chair back, knocking it to the floor as she stood. "So, this is what love is, huh? You love me, and support me as long as I'm doing what you want. But as soon as I do something that doesn't suit you—you cut me off financially. That sucks!"

"You watch your mouth, young lady, or we'll cut your support off now."

"Go right ahead," the younger woman spat. "I don't want your fucking money!"

"Don't you dare speak like that in this house!" Anna Lisa cried. "Don't you dare!"

Mia leaned over her mother, fixing her with a fierce glower. "Fuck...you," she said, enunciating each word clearly.

"Mia!" Adam shouted. "You apologize to your mother, right now!"

"I will not," she said, giving him the same look. "You're both a couple of hypocrites!"

She ran upstairs, throwing her things into her bag. Moments later, she was back downstairs, her parents still sitting at the dining table, but with Anna Lisa's face now filled with rage. "You think you can talk to me like that? I'll show you who's boss. As of today—you're cut off! Give me your car keys! You can take the bus back to Berkeley!"

"The car's in my name. It's paid off, and it's mine!"

"You don't pay the insurance!" Anna Lisa countered.

"Cancel it," Mia taunted her. "See if I care. I've got nothing, and if I get into an accident they can take me to the county hospital."

"We'll see how long you last without your charge cards or your checking account," Anna Lisa said. "You know you can't live without shopping."

"I won't have time to shop," Mia said. "I'll be working."

"You know as well as I do that you don't have the ability to get a decent job in Berkeley. What are you going to do? Make coffee at Starbuck's after class?"

"I'm not going to be in Berkeley," Mia declared. "I'm going to be in Colorado Springs. I'll send you my new address." She hoisted her bag onto her shoulder, and made for the door.

"Mia! Get back here right this instant!" her mother yelled.

"You can't make me stay and listen to this crap," she said. "You don't have any power over me, Mother. I'm going to be with Jordan—she's the only one who loves me for who I am."

"We love you, Mia," her father said. "We really do."

"You've got a damned funny way of showing it, Dad. Cutting me off financially, and making me have to get a job to support myself isn't the most loving act I've ever heard of."

"Anna, can't we talk about this?" Adam asked in a pleading tone.

"No! Mia thinks she's an adult. Let her prove it!"

Walking to the door, Mia stood with her hand on the knob for a moment, then turned and faced her mother. "I'm sorry I told you to fuck off. That was rude, and disrespectful." She reached for the door again, saying, "Goodbye," over her shoulder.

With tears streaking her face, Mia drove to the closest ATM. She took out five hundred, the maximum for a single day, then started to head towards the city. When she neared the airport, she had an idea, and took the first exit. After parking in a short-term lot, she went to Continental Airlines and found a pleasant woman at the ticket counter. "Hi," she said, sniffing a little. "I'm going to need to go to Denver on short notice. If I buy an unrestricted ticket, can I trade it in, or get a refund?"

"Yes. An unrestricted ticket is the same as cash. You can use it for any of our flights."

"Great." She looked at the receipt she'd gotten from the ATM, checking her balance. "I need a ticket that costs fifteen hundred dollars, tax included. What have you got?"

The woman looked at her confusedly. "I'm not sure I understand…"

"Look," Mia said, "It's too complicated to explain. I need to go to several different places over the next couple of months, but I'm not sure where or when. I've got fifteen hundred in my account, but I won't have it for long. So, I thought I'd better get a ticket to somewhere, and then trade it for what I need, when I need it."

The clerk looked at her for a moment, then gave her a sympathetic smile. "Divorce?"

"Something like that," Mia nodded. "Bad break-up."

Back in her car, Mia dialed her parent's home, pleased when her father picked up. "I cleared out my checking account, Dad. I'll pay you back after I get a job, but I had to have enough money to get to Denver. I assume that Mom already canceled my charge cards."

"Uhm…yeah, she did," he admitted. "She tried to contact the bank about the checking account, but they were closed."

"Well, I'd appreciate it if you don't put a stop payment on the check I wrote to Continental Airlines. I think kiting a check for that much is a felony, and a prison record would really turn off the man you two envision me marrying."

"Mia, can't we discuss this rationally?"

"I thought we had," she said. "But you know, you and Mom weren't alone at all today. You had to have made up your minds about this last night."

He was quiet for a moment, then said, "That's true."

"So, my talking about Jordan and trying to let you two see what she meant to me was a complete waste of my time. Nothing that I said mattered, Dad. Is that what you call discussing something rationally?"

"I'm sorry, honey," he said. "I swear that I am. I don't want you to quit school and move away. Please reconsider."

"No, I can't. I learned tonight that you have to have the guts to back up your choices in life. I…choose…Jordan."

🐎

The partygoers had to park so far away, that they were only four blocks from the O'Flaherty home. "Why didn't we park in the garage and walk?" Ryan asked.

"Look at the bright side," Jamie said. "If you drink too much, you don't have to worry about driving."

"The pizza's getting cold," Ryan grumbled. "I should have dropped you guys off first."

"Then the pizza would be gone," Jordan said, bumping her friend with her hip. "I didn't get lunch."

"You were asleep all day," Ryan reminded her. "I guess we could have hooked you up to an IV…"

"I didn't get any exercise today, either," Jordan said. "Maybe I should take that pizza and run the rest of the way."

"No, thanks," Ryan said, clutching the box a little tighter. "I've seen how you can chow down when you're hungry. I'm glad we bought a large."

"There's plenty here for both of you," Jamie insisted. "Now, behave or I'll have to separate you."

"Ahh…I haven't heard that threat in years," Ryan said, smiling fondly.

"Well, if our kids are anything like you, you'll be uttering that threat constantly in a few years," Jamie said, laughing at the insulted look on her lover's face.

🐎

When they reached the proper street, Ryan ran in to the corner mini-mart and bought a twelve pack of beer—knowing that at least half would be absconded with before the night was over. As usual, she bought the most offbeat brand she could find—merely so she could identify the thieves and give them a hard time.

Walking into the party, the trio was assaulted by a sea of humanity— seemingly filling every inch of the two-bedroom, second floor apartment. "Let's try the other place," Ryan said, leading the way to the third floor.

"Other place?" Jamie asked.

"The party's given by women who live on the second and third floors of this three flat. Eventually, the guy on the first floor will get sick of their parties and move out—then they can have someone they know move in down there, and they'll have the whole building."

As she had guessed, the third floor was significantly less crowded, and Ryan led the way to the kitchen, nodding and waving at people as they moved. A woman walked into the kitchen and gave Ryan a very friendly kiss, lingering longer than Jamie was comfortable with. "Bring your own, babe?" the woman asked.

"Yep," Ryan said. "Are you the enforcer, Judith?"

"Yeah. I try to catch people when they first get here and try to squeeze five bucks out of 'em. But since you brought your own, you don't have to pay."

"Oh, we can pay," Jamie offered. "Are you running short?"

Judith leaned against the counter and gave Jamie a long look. "Introductions, Rock?" she asked, her eyes never leaving Jamie.

"My fiancée," Ryan said with mock formality. "Jamie Evans, this is Judith Case."

"I never thought I'd see it," Judith said, shaking Jamie's hand. "Are you sure you know what you're getting into with this one?" She wrapped her arm around Ryan's neck and gave her a gentle rap on the head.

"I'm learning more every day," Jamie said, sticking her tongue out at her partner. "This is our friend, Jordan, Judith. She helps me keep Ryan in line."

"Oh, I always knew it would take more than one woman to tame this one," Judith said, laughing heartily.

"It takes a village," Ryan said, wrinkling her nose at her old friend. "But Jamie has primary responsibilities."

"Well, give me a buzz if you need any help. I know she can wear you out."

Jamie gave her an enigmatic smile, raising an eyebrow at her lover as Judith left the room. "Have you worn Judith out, sweetheart?"

"Uhm…wow, we'd better get these beers chilled, huh?" There were two plastic trash bins filled with ice, sitting in the middle of the kitchen, and Ryan dumped the beer into the depths, retaining three bottles for them to drink immediately. "Let me find a spot for the pizza, and we're ready to rock."

"Silence is affirmation, O'Flaherty," Jamie said, making Jordan snicker.

"I take the fifth," Ryan said. "I never kiss and tell." She added a wink, saying, "You know I have a fatal weakness for blondes."

While giving her partner a pinch, Jamie looked around at the small counters, bursting with boxes, bags and takeout containers. "Martha Stewart would throw up if she took a peek into this place," she said, chuckling softly.

"Hey, they have a few decorative touches," Ryan insisted. "See the nice plants?"

Jamie took note of the six potted marijuana plants, with a grow light hanging over them. "My mistake," she giggled. "Martha is very much in favor of edible plants."

"Sorry you came?" Ryan asked, leaning over so only Jamie could hear. "Did meeting Judith bother you?"

"No, not at all, baby. I love to see how you lived in your single days. It's like getting a glimpse into your past."

They took the pizza and tried to find a flat surface to place it on, but Ryan stopped short on the way to an empty coffee table. "What's wrong?" Jamie asked, having run into her partner's back.

"Look who's on the sofa," Ryan said, sounding very unhappy.

Jamie took a peek around her shoulder, seeing Jordan put the pizza down on a table just feet from a torrid make-out session—being conducted by Sara and Ally.

"Oops," Jamie said. "Well, not much we can do about it now. We'd better go say hello."

"In a minute," Ryan said, turning on her heel and disappearing before Jamie could say another word.

Rolling her eyes, Jamie went over to sit on the floor and dig into the pizza. Noting Ryan's absence, Jordan looked around questioningly. Jamie twitched her head in the direction of the trysting couple behind them, and Jordan nodded. Leaning in close, she asked, "What's up with that? Does she like those two, or not? She invites them to her house, and then acts like she can't wait to get away from them."

"That's about it," Jamie admitted. "You'll have to ask her if you want a more detailed answer. Sometimes the reasons behind her behavior elude me. Let's eat as much as we can before she gets back. If she's gonna pout, she's gotta suffer."

After about ten minutes, Sara broke away from Ally's fervid embrace, and ran her hands through her hair to settle it. Jamie saw the opportunity, and raised her voice above the din. "Hi, guys."

"Jamie!" Sara said, looking mortally embarrassed. Her eyes shifted to Jordan, and her head cocked a little, then she said, "Hi, Jordan. Uhm…I… uhm…"

Ally came to her rescue, saying, "Hi, Jamie, Jordan. Sorry about the blatant PDA. We haven't seen each other for a few days. Sara was on a business trip, and she just got here a few minutes ago. You know how it is."

"I do," Jamie nodded, smiling.

"Count me in," Jordan said. "Mia's supposed to be here soon, and when she gets here I want us to be doing exactly what you were doing."

"Where's Ryan?" Sara asked, looking around the room.

"Oh, she's around here somewhere. She knows an awful lot of people."

"How are things in Colorado, Jordan?" Sara asked.

"Cold...lonely," she said, smiling shyly. "But it would be perfect if Mia were with me."

"I know what you mean," Sara said, giving Ally a squeeze. "I just saw my sweetie on Tuesday night, and here I am, making a fool of myself."

"You don't look foolish," Jamie insisted. "When Ryan and I were first together, we snuck around campus, making out in every dark corner we could find."

Sara looked at her for a moment, then said, "You know, I could spend the rest of the evening being embarrassed—or I could slip my arms around this gorgeous woman and kiss her until her toes curl." Leaning so close to Ally that she could feel warm breath caress her lips, Sara added, "I'd have to be a fool not to choose to kiss her." As the pair came together again, Jamie turned her back to give them some privacy, and said to Jordan, "We've been together nine months, and I can't even get Ryan to stay in the same room with me. What am I doing wrong?"

"Want me to go find her for you?"

"Nah. She'll show up when she's good and ready. If she's not back by the time Mia gets here, I'll go find her." Her eye was caught by a curly head, and she elbowed Jordan. "I think it's your turn to start kissing, buddy."

Jordan was on her feet in less than a second, dashing across the room to throw her arms around Mia and hug her enthusiastically. "Mmm...I missed you," she sighed.

Mia held on tight, and buried her head deep into Jordan's shoulder. When she felt Mia's body begin to shake, she pulled back and stared in alarm. "Honey! You're crying...what's wrong?"

"Oh, Jordy, it was awful," she sniffed, tears slipping down her cheeks.

Jordan looked around the room, saw a deserted corner, and said, "Let's go sit over there and you can tell me all about it. Can I get you a beer?"

"Got anything stronger?" she asked, and Jordan could see that her whole body was shaking.

"I'll go to the liquor store for you. It's right on the corner. What do you want?"

"A bottle of tequila...and a lime," she said immediately.

With wide eyes, Jordan nodded and started for the door, saying, "Jamie's right over there. I'll be right back."

Mia trudged over to her friend and plopped down next to her. "I'm an orphan," she said, leaning heavily against her.

"What? Jordan said things were going okay. What happened?"

"My mother decided that she doesn't want me to be with Jordy, so she used the only tool she has—she cut me off financially. The money I have in my wallet is all I've got."

"She what?"

"You heard me. By the time I'd left Hillsborough, she'd cancelled my charge cards. If the bank had been open, I wouldn't have been able to take any money out of my checking account."

"Oh, Mia, I'm so sorry. That must have hurt you so badly."

"It did, it really did, James. I thought they loved me," she sobbed, burying her head into Jamie's neck. "I thought they loved me enough to want me to be happy."

They were still sitting on the floor, Jamie rocking and soothing Mia, when Jordan returned, breathless from her run to the mini-mart. She pulled a plastic cup out of the bag, then poured a generous portion of tequila and used the pizza knife to cut a wedge of lime. "Here, honey," she said, handing her the glass.

Mia drained the cup with one gulp, then bit into the lime, grimacing as she did so. "More," she said, extending the cup.

Without comment, Jordan complied, watching Mia carefully. After biting into the lime, she placed the cup on the table, then gave Jamie a kiss on the cheek. "We need to find a quiet place to talk."

Jordan took her partner's hand and said, "Come on, let's sit in that quiet corner. No one will bother us."

"Okay." She let Jordan pull her to her feet, already feeling the alcohol starting to hit. "See you later, James. We're gonna go get drunk."

"Go ahead," Jamie said, "Rory's out of town. You can have our room."

"Thanks, bud. We'll just have to see if Jordan can carry me that far."

Chapter Twenty-Two

Taking the pizza box with her, Jamie started to search through the apartment, finally finding her partner in the most unlikely of places—a bedroom. Ryan was sitting on the bed, with her arm around another woman, speaking softly and soothingly to her. The pair was facing the door, and when Jamie poked her head in, Ryan dropped her arm and gave her a stunned, nervous smile. "Hi! Uhm…I was uhm…kinda looking for you."

"Did you think I was under the bed?" Jamie asked, her voice its usual, conversational tone.

Ryan's smile grew even tighter, and she jumped off the bed. "Uhm… Mandy, this is my partner, Jamie. Jamie, this is my friend, Mandy."

"Pleased to meet you," Jamie said, extending her hand.

Mandy shook it, then got up in an ungainly fashion. As she did, Jamie noted that she was pregnant. Jamie must have been staring at the woman's belly, for Mandy patted it and said, "Six months. Seems longer."

Jamie stared as she walked away, then turned to her partner and raised an eyebrow. "You'd better not have had anything to do with that, Ryan O'Flaherty."

"Am I in trouble?" Ryan asked, swallowing audibly.

"That depends on if you're the father of that baby," Jamie said, giving her partner's hair an affectionate ruffle.

"Close the door and come over here, honey," Ryan said.

"Are you holding court in here? I haven't seen you in a while." Jamie closed the door and walked back over to the bed, holding the pizza box open for her lover.

"Thank you, thank you, thank you," Ryan murmured as she grabbed a piece of pizza and took a big bite. After swallowing, she said, "No, I'm not holding court. Mandy grabbed me a few minutes after I saw Sara and Ally, and we've been talking ever since. She's having some problems, and she thought I might be able to help."

"Do tell," Jamie said, leaning over to take a bite off Ryan's slice.

"Well, the details aren't important, but the person she was relying on to be her Lamaze coach backed out on her. She thought I might be able to step in."

Rolling her eyes, Jamie gave her a resigned sigh, and asked, "When do you start?"

"Not for a while," Ryan said, stifling a smile. "Not until you're pregnant."

"What?" Jamie gave her a puzzled look and asked, "You turned down a friend who asked you for a favor? You?"

"Yep. Me," Ryan said, nodding. "I thought about it while she was telling me what had happened, and I decided that helping a woman give birth is too intimate a thing to do with someone other than you. I want the first newborn I ever hold to be ours," she said, putting her pizza down and giving Jamie a tender hug. "It's too precious an experience to share with Mandy."

"Oh, Ryan, that's so sweet," Jamie sighed, giving her partner a kiss. Smoothing the hair back off her face, Jamie gave her a concerned look and asked, "Was it hard to say no?"

"Yeah, it was. I don't have a lot of practice in refusing favors. But Mandy's got some issues that I can't afford to get involved in. I don't think I'd be able to walk away after the baby was born—I think I'd feel like I had to keep an eye on her—and I can't afford to share my time like that." She gave Jamie another kiss, this one longer and filled with emotion. "I have to concentrate on you."

"Thank you," Jamie said softly, lying down on the bed and tugging Ryan down with her. "I know it must have been hard to turn down someone in need, but I would've been very jealous if you'd said yes." She kissed Ryan tenderly, and added, "But I can certainly understand why she asked you. You'd be a wonderful birth coach."

"We'll have to see about that, won't we?" Ryan asked, kissing the tip of Jamie's nose.

The door opened, and a pair of women stood in the doorway, one of them peering into the darkness and saying, "Is that you, Rock?"

"Sure is."

"You gonna be long?"

"All my life," Ryan said, kissing Jamie softly. "But you can have the room."

On the way through the apartment, they stopped repeatedly, with Ryan kissing each of her friends on the mouth, then dutifully introducing Jamie. "Uhm…you don't mind the kissing thing, do you, honey?" Ryan asked when they had a moment alone.

"Have you always kissed these people when you see them?"

"Yeah. Sure. Always."

"Then why should you stop because you're in love? I think it would be odd and a little awkward to try to avoid a kiss—it's like I own your lips or something."

"Well, you do," Ryan said, wrinkling up her nose.

"Okay, then I give your lips permission to kiss any of your old friends. But don't go out of your way to kiss people if it hasn't already been established, 'kay?"

"It's a deal." They stood in the living room, just a few yards from Sara and Ally, who were talking—rather than kissing. "I guess we have to go say hello, huh?"

"You don't have to do anything, honey. We can go down to the second floor if you want to."

"No, no, that's not necessary." She was looking around nervously, and spotted someone who caught her attention. "I have to go say hello to Marcus, an old workout buddy from the gym. I haven't seen him in over a year. Wanna come?"

Jamie looked over at a rather short man, who obviously spent all of his time working out. He was wearing a tank top and shorts, and his ample muscles were revealed upon every bit of exposed skin. He also had rather intricate tribal tattoos on his biceps, and down the backs of his arms, ending in cuffs at his wrists. "Mmm…I think I'll go talk to Sara and Ally. Marcus looks like too much of a gym rat for me."

"You might be surprised," Ryan said in a singsong fashion.

"I'll come get you if I start missing you. Go talk about pumping iron with your buff friend."

"Okay. Love you." Ryan kissed her, lingering a bit, then running the tip of her tongue all over the outline of Jamie's lips, making Jamie giggle and rub her mouth against Ryan's shirt. "Just want to make sure everyone knows you're taken," she murmured, adding one more serious kiss to be certain.

"Brat!" Jamie swatted her on the butt and sent her on her way, chuckling to herself when she approached Sara and Ally. "Hey, guys, what's going on?"

"Not much," Ally said. "Did you ever find Ryan?"

"Yeah, but she got waylaid again. She knows so many people!"

"She does," Ally agreed. "And I bet every one of them wants to ask her about the carjacking."

Jamie blinked at her, then shook her head. "That didn't even dawn on me! Damn, I must be getting better when that's not the first thing I think of when we run into someone we know."

"Are you both getting better, Jamie?" Sara asked.

"Yeah, we are. It's gonna take a long while to be completely over it, but it doesn't interfere in our daily lives much anymore. It still pops up every once in a while, of course—usually when you least expect it."

Jordan sat against the wall, with Mia sitting between her spread legs and leaning against her chest. "I can't imagine how hurt you must be," Jordan said, bending repeatedly to kiss the crown of her lover's head.

"That's it exactly," Mia said. "I'm not angry anymore—I'm deeply, deeply hurt. You know," she said thoughtfully, "it isn't even the fact that they don't approve. What hurts is that they'd made up their minds last night. They were fucking with me today. That feels like such a betrayal."

"I know it does," Jordan soothed. "I'd feel the same way."

"It's like they knew I'd be pissed, and they wanted to have a nice day—so they acted like they were interested in you, and how I feel about you, and how we came to love each other. But they didn't give a crap," she said bitterly. "They just wanted to get through the day in peace. That sucks so bad!" She took another swig off her bottle of tequila, no longer bothering to use a cup or bite the lime.

"They probably didn't want to hurt you. Maybe they wanted to work up to it, but it took 'em all day. I think they really do love you, honey."

"Maybe they do, Jordy, but they have to learn to love me as an adult. I'm not their little girl any more—they can't tell me who I'm allowed to play with."

"Give 'em time, baby, they'll probably come around."

"They'll have plenty of time. They can reconsider while I'm in Colorado."

"When are you coming to Colorado?" Jordan asked, completely puzzled.

"Tomorrow. I'm going with you."

"Mia! Are you serious? What about school?" Jordan's face was lit up with excitement, her expression alone reassuring Mia in ways that words never could.

"What's the rush? You and I can finish at the same time. It's not a big deal."

"Oh, but, honey," Jordan said, "you've only got two more months of class. Don't you want to graduate with your friends?"

"Sure, I want to graduate and be done with it all, but I want to be with you a hundred times more than I want to graduate. I can't wait any more, Jordy. And now that my parents know, there's no reason to be apart any longer. We'll both finish our last semester at some point—then I'll graduate with my best girl."

"Damn," Jordan said, wrapping her arms tightly around her. "Is it really that easy? Can you just decide to quit school and come to Colorado with me?"

"Yes, it's that easy. The hard part is trying to figure out how I'll support myself. I told my parents I'd drive my car uninsured, but I'd never do that. So, I'll have to have the money for the car and food and a little entertainment. And I want to make sure I'm home when you're home—so I have to get a day job. How will your roommates feel about having me around?"

"Huh?" Jordan shook her head. "Damn, I've got so many thoughts racing through my brain, I can hardly concentrate."

"I asked about your roommates," Mia repeated. "Will they mind having me move in?"

"Doesn't matter if they do or not, 'cause we won't be there long. I want to be alone with you, not have three other women hanging around all of the time. We'll get our own place."

"Jordy! How will we afford that? You said that apartments are very expensive."

"They are, but our relationship is worth too much to fool around with. Living in a dorm-like setting isn't right for us."

"Oh, Jordan, I feel like I'm forcing you to do things you're not ready to do. Are you sure you want me to come?"

"Turn around and look at me," Jordan said. Mia shifted around so that she was facing her lover, and gazed into her clear, blue eyes. "I love you with all of my heart. I want you as close to me as I can get you—twenty-four hours a day. I want to wake up holding you, I want to kiss your sweet lips when I get home at night, and I want to go to sleep cuddled up so close to you that you'll feel like you're covered with a Jordan blanket. Nothing on this earth would make me happier than to have you live with me—in our own apartment."

"But how will we pay for it?" Mia asked.

"I've got money," Jordan said. "I've been forcing myself to live on the stipend I get from USA Volleyball, and putting every dime of my modeling income into savings. But having you with me is worth more than having money in the bank. We can easily live for at least two years on my savings, and I'm only too happy to spend it."

"But, Jordan, that's your money for graduate school! You can't spend that!"

"Yes, I can," she said, her eyes blazing with determination. "I can't just look out for myself anymore. My decisions have to include what's best for you and for us. This is what's best for us right now. Graduate school will take care of itself when the time comes. We need a place of our own, we need to keep your car insured, and we need to get health insurance for you. I'm not going to worry about what will happen if you break a leg skiing."

"You sound like my dad," Mia said, chuckling softly.

"That's because I love you, and I want to protect you," Jordan said, bending to kiss her partner. "You're the most wonderful part of my life."

"I love you, too, Jordy," she sighed. "Two hours ago I was as depressed as I've ever been, and now I feel like everything will be all right." Hugging her partner fiercely, she asked, "How do you work that kind of magic?"

"Love," Jordan whispered. "The secret is love."

❦

Jamie went into the kitchen to fish out a beer, but when she took a look at how deep the ice water was, she thought better of it and started to leave the room. "Hey, good looking," Ryan said, filling the doorway by grabbing the top molding and stretching.

"Hi. I was gonna get a beer, but I don't want to get frostbite."

"Let me assist," Ryan said, pushing off from the door and making for the tub. She looked inside, shook her head and muttered, "Heathens." Looking around the kitchen, she spied a large, aluminum pot and started to bail the icy water from the container, not stopping until she reached ice and beer. Sticking her long arm into the tall tub, she extracted two of their beers and handed one to her partner with a flourish.

"My hero," Jamie said, batting her eyes.

"Hey, gotta make sure I get my date at least half drunk if I wanna get lucky."

"I think I'd better stick close to you for the rest of the night," Jamie said, smiling up at her. "I didn't mind letting you hang with Marcus, but he's practically the only guy here. You've probably had your way with everybody else at the party. I don't want to find you in the bedroom again."

"Fooled you. Had my way with Marcus, too," Ryan said, adding a randy wink. She started to leave the kitchen, but found that a hand reaching out to grab her waistband slowed her progress.

"Hold on there, stud. You'd better be joking."

Ryan turned to find a very stern look on her partner's face. "Uhm…yeah, I'm joking," she said.

Jamie slapped her soundly on the rump, muttering, "I can never tell whether you're joking or not."

"Well, I'm only partially joking," Ryan admitted. "I didn't have my way with him, but we did make out at a party once. I didn't want to go any further, though, so we stopped at that."

"What? You made out with a guy?"

Giving her a curious look, Ryan asked, "Why does that bother you?"

Rolling her eyes in frustration, Jamie said, "Because, you've specifically told me that you've never been attracted to a guy, you've never fooled around with a guy, and that you've never even been on a date with a guy. Now, which is it?"

"Wow," Ryan said, her brow furrowed, "you're really upset about this, aren't you."

Looking embarrassed, Jamie nodded. "Yeah, I am."

"Let's go for a little walk. I don't want to discuss this in here."

They went outside, and strolled up and down in front of the building, taking sips of their beers to cool off from the overheated apartment. "I've never lied to you about my sexual history. I'd never do that. But, I am puzzled about why it doesn't seem to bother you that I've had sex with at least ten women here, but you're pissed off to think that I kissed Marcus."

Scowling, Jamie took another pull on her beer and tried to explain herself. "This sounds stupid, but something about you kissing a guy is kinda… gross."

"Gross? You've kissed your fair share of guys. Was that gross?"

"No, it's not that guys are gross—but your kissing one is."

"I need a little more to go on," Ryan said, scratching her head, "'cause that makes no sense."

"Look," Jamie said, "it's like this. Expressing your sexuality with women is natural for you. That's who you are. But the thought of you making out with a guy at a party seems—perverted. It's like you did it because you needed someone to kiss, and he was the closest one around. There's something about it that doesn't sound like you, and that's what bothers me. I have an image of you as this super-lesbian; and to hear you say that it's 'any port in a storm' seems kinda sick. I'm sorry if that hurts your feelings, but I'm really bothered by it." She crossed her arms over her stomach, and said, "This is the first thing I've ever heard of you doing that bothers me. It seems…immoral."

Ryan took a sip of her beer and gave her partner a slow smile. "I guess I can understand that. And, no, it doesn't hurt my feelings to have you say that. Like I said, I've never lied to you about my sexual history. I've never kissed a man."

"But you said…"

"Marcus wasn't a man when I kissed him…or her."

"Huh?"

"Marcus was Marcia when we first met," Ryan said, smiling when Jamie's eyes grew round. "She was kinda cute, and I liked her when I met her, but there was something funny about kissing her. It sounds funny now, but she gave off male vibes, and I couldn't get into it."

"Male vibes?" Jamie asked, still trying to get her mind around this information.

"Yeah. She was more aggressive than I like a woman to be."

"You liked Ally," Jamie reminded her dryly, lifting one eyebrow.

"Ally wasn't aggressive," Ryan said. "To me, there's a difference between being aggressive and being dominant. Ally was definitely dominant, but in a very slow, gentle way. Ally makes you want to submit to her," she said thoughtfully, her mouth unconsciously easing into a smile. "Marcia was just plain aggressive. I didn't like that at all."

"But you stayed friends with her?"

"Oh, yeah, I like him a lot. Now that he's more comfortable with his sexuality, he seems much more laid back. I don't want to test my theory," she said, chuckling, "but I bet he's not as aggressive now that he's had the surgery. I think he had some trouble coming to terms with who he was back then."

Jamie's eyes grew even wider as she asked, "He had the surgery? He's…a…real guy now?"

"As close as medicine can make him," Ryan said. "He's still genetically a woman—still has the double X chromosome, but he had a double mastectomy a couple of years ago, and about six months ago he had the bottom half done."

Gritting her teeth, Jamie crossed her arms over her breasts. "Jesus, I can't imagine choosing to have my favorite erogenous zone removed. That's a man with convictions!"

"Having the mastectomy is one thing, but risking losing feeling down below is a hell of a lot bigger commitment in my book. Nobody's messing with my girl thang."

Jamie chuckled; giving her partner's girl parts a pinch. "I like 'em as much as you do, baby."

"I rather doubt that," Ryan said, barking out a laugh.

With a thoughtful look, Jamie said, "Damn, I can't get my mind off that surgery. I wonder what his…thing…looks like."

"His thing?" Ryan asked, chuckling. "For someone who's been well acquainted with 'things,' it's rather odd that you can't even use the word."

"Penis," Jamie said, sticking out her tongue. "I can say penis. Happy?"

Tweaking her lover's nose, Ryan said, "Delirious. Do you really wanna see? I uhm…can arrange for a peek."

"What?"

"He said he'd show me, but I said I didn't have enough knowledge of the equipment to give him an opinion. You could help him out, though."

"Help him out?"

"Yeah, he's kinda weirded out about showing it to a woman in a sexual setting. I think he wants to be reassured that it doesn't look freaky."

"Why do all of your friends feel comfortable asking you to do the most intimate things with them?" Jamie asked.

Ryan slid her arms around her partner's waist and looked down into her eyes. "Don't you feel comfortable asking me to do intimate things with you?" she asked, her voice sexy and low.

"Yes, Ryan," Jamie said, unable to hide a smile.

"I guess I give off the right vibes. But, don't worry, cupcake, I refuse all intimate invitations, unless they're issued by you."

"Let's go back in," Jamie said, taking Ryan's hand. "In only two hours, you've been asked to help someone have a baby, and check out a new penis. I can't wait to see what's next. Let's hit the second floor and see what kinda trouble you can get into."

"Have I ever told you what a good sport you are?" Ryan asked.

"Yes, you have, but I don't mind hearing it again."

After a tour of the second floor, and meeting more people than she could ever hope to remember, Jamie led her partner back upstairs. "I don't want Mia and Jordan to sneak away before I see them," she said. "Mia threatened to get drunk, and I want to make sure Jordan didn't join her."

"Jordan never gets drunk," Ryan said.

"No, but neither did Juliet before Mia got her hands on her," Jamie said, chuckling.

When they got back upstairs, Ryan briefly said hello to Ally and Sara, giving Sara a quick kiss on the cheek, then presented Ally with her lips. "Be right back," she said, before she even sat down. "I want to see how Mia's doing."

Jamie sat down on the couch next to Sara, while Ryan went over to the corner. Crouching down next to the pair, Ryan said, "Jamie told me about how it went. I'm very sorry, buddy."

"It sucked," Mia said, nodding. "I was betrayed by my family tonight, and I never thought that would happen."

Reaching for her, Ryan sank to her knees and wrapped Mia in a firm hug. "We're behind you. Whatever you need—whenever you need it. We won't let you down. We're your family, too."

Sniffling, Mia said, "I love you, Ryan."

"I love you, too. Now, I know how hurt you are, but don't forget that things will change over time. Your parents will eventually come around. Look at how nice Jamie's dad is to me now. If he could change that much, I'm sure your parents can, too."

"I know," she said quietly. "Someday we'll all get along. But we're a long way from that now."

Jordan unwrapped her long legs from around Mia and said, "I'm gonna go make a pit stop and then get a beer. Want one, Ryan?"

"Uhm…sure," she nodded. "I guess we're walking home, so I can indulge."

As Jordan walked away, Ryan cuddled Mia to her side. "How you doing? I heard you were planning on getting hammered."

"Yeah, I'm half hammered. I was shaking so badly when I got here that I looked like I'd been in the freezer." She rested her head on Ryan's shoulder and sighed deeply. Lifting her free hand, Ryan started to run her fingers through Mia's curls, soothing her. "Mmm…that makes me sleepy. Can I take a nap while Jordy's gone?"

"Of course. My shoulder's always available, buddy." She continued to stroke Mia's hair, quickly realizing that Mia was breathing heavily already.

I think half-hammered might be an under exaggeration. Looking up, Ryan caught Jamie's eye and gave her a wink. Sitting quietly, holding Mia in a loose embrace, Ryan allowed herself the rare pleasure of sitting back and watching her partner interact with people. She loved watching how open and genuine she was; how she brought a spark to every conversation, making both Sara and Ally laugh repeatedly.

Turning her attention to Ally, Ryan watched as Sara said something to her, stroking her thigh as she spoke. With her mouth twitching into a slow smile, Ally nodded, her eyes crinkling up as they did when she was particularly happy.

That's what it is, Ryan thought, trying to figure out what was different about her friend. *She's happy. Being in a relationship is really working for her.* She watched for another few moments, finally correcting herself. *Being with Sara is really working for her. I've never seen her look so completely comfortable and relaxed.*

Sara put an arm around Ally's shoulders and tugged her down in front of her, kissing the back of her neck, the larger woman giggling like a child. *Damn! After six years I wouldn't have had the nerve to push her around like that!* Watching carefully, she once again amended her thought. *Ally wouldn't have wanted me to push her around like that. That's the difference. She's let her guard down with Sara. Damn, I wonder why she never felt comfortable being that way with me?* Ryan sat pondering her question for a few minutes, watching them play gently with each other. Suddenly, it dawned on her. *She didn't let you in because she didn't feel the same way about you. You slept with her for six years and you were no closer at the end than you were after the first few months. And here's Sara, only knowing her since Thanksgiving—treating her like she's her own personal doll—and Ally's loving it. Something has clicked between these two that never clicked with you—it wasn't right, and you know it. You were sex partners— just sex partners.*

She smiled at the animated blonde who had captured both her body and her soul. *Thank God it didn't work out,* she thought, shaking her head. *As much as I was attracted to Ally, and as much fun as we had in bed, we never had the kind of chemistry that Jamie and I have. There's not a doubt in my mind that Jamie's the perfect match for every part of me—not just my libido.*

Just as she was considering this thought, Jordan returned, bearing a pair of beers. "Here you go, Boomer."

"Thanks. Here's your girl back," Ryan said, kissing Mia's head. "She's been thoroughly cuddled, and she's sound asleep. Now, don't rile her up again." She untangled herself from Mia's embrace and smiled when she immediately cuddled up to Jordan in the same way. "You guys are gonna stay with us in Noe tonight, right?"

"Yeah, I think we will," Jordan said. "Especially if you'll make us breakfast."

"It's a deal," Ryan said. She started back to her partner, but was once again waylaid. One of the birthday girls stopped her and dragged her over to the opposite corner of the room to say hello to a few old friends. Ryan went along willingly, and spent a few minutes chatting. The birthday girl, Shay, was feeling no pain, and she launched into a long, pointless story that Ryan was completely unable to follow.

As usual, when her attention wasn't otherwise required, Ryan gazed at her partner, enjoying the way she was interacting with Sara and Ally. *How lucky am I? I can bring her to a party full of ex-lovers, former sex partners, a trans-sexual, a woman who wants me to be her Lamaze coach, and God knows what else—and she's unflappable. She honestly looks like she's enjoying herself,* she marveled. *What a perfect match she is.*

And speaking of perfect matches, she thought wryly. *Who would have guessed that Ally would be the one to bring the old Sara back?* She watched her friend flirt and play with Ally, while seamlessly carrying on a civilized conversation with Jamie. *She's grown into such a woman,* she thought fondly, *so different from the girl I fell in love with. But, there's a familiar lightness to her now—that was completely absent when we met again this fall. It's like being with Ally lets her be the woman she's become; while reclaiming some of her girlish playfulness. She seems like Ally's equal.* She shook her head again, as she was forced to admit, *We were never really equals. She always looked to me for validation, for approval—I don't see that with Ally. She seems to trust herself more now.* Sparing another fond glance at her old friend, she thought, *I truly hope it works out for both of them—they both deserve to be who they really are.*

Looking at Jamie again, she considered, *That's what life is all about. Striving to be who you are—no matter how painful the journey sometimes is. I can be myself with Jamie—I don't have to be someone for Sara to look up to, or for Ally to control and drive mad in bed. We don't have roles—we're just ourselves. In good times and bad—we're just our struggling, questing selves. Damn, that feels good.*

Okay, she said to herself, *so, what are you doing standing all the way over here, listening to someone who barely knows you're there?* Giving a tiny wave to the more sober people, Ryan walked over to her partner, and asked, "Anyone need anything while I'm up?"

"I need something," Ally said, "let me go with you and see if any of the water I brought is still here."

"Oh, water tends to last," Ryan said, laughing. "It's the beer that disappears. Jamie?"

"Sure."

"Be right back."

The pair made their way into the kitchen. Ally couldn't find any of her water in the first tub so Ryan performed her bailing task again. The water was all gone, so Ally helped herself to a Pepsi. "I hate this stuff, but Sara likes it," she said, smiling at Ryan. "One of us might as well be happy."

"Speaking of happy," Ryan said, giving her friend a gentle punch in the shoulder, "you look positively blissful, bud."

Grinning shyly, Ally said, "I'm in love, Ryan, and it feels fantastic. Really fantastic."

"You look like you're in love." She wrapped one arm around Ally's shoulders, and gave her a rough hug. "I assume Sara feels the same?"

"Uhm…well…to be honest, I haven't told her yet. But, I think she does. She acts like she loves me."

"That's the important part," Ryan said. "Words are easy—it's the actions that count."

"Things have gone a lot quicker than either of us had planned, but it feels right. It's all falling into place."

"I'm very, very happy for you both," Ryan said. "I mean that, Ally."

Looking down at the floor and shifting her weight, Ally said, "I was a little concerned when you seemed to be avoiding us earlier. Are you sure you're okay with this?"

"You know," Ryan said, climbing up onto a bare space on the counter, "I've been having some trouble getting used to it. But seeing you both tonight has helped me turn the corner. You seem right for each other. You both look happier than I've seen either of you. Since I love you both and want you to be happy, I think it's time for me to let go. I honestly think I can do that now."

Standing between Ryan's spread legs, Ally tucked her arms around her waist and held her close. "Don't let go completely, sugar. I want to have you in my life for a good, long time."

"I do, too," Ryan murmured into Ally's shirt. "I was sitting over there with

Mia, looking at the three of you, and you looked like you were having such a good time. I want to start doing things together." Pulling back, she asked, "Would you like that?"

"Yeah, we both would," Ally said. "We wanted to go out dancing the other night, and we both thought it would be fun to ask you and Jamie. But we weren't sure you'd be up for it…"

"I am," Ryan said, "and Jamie likes you both. I'd really like to get together more often."

"I think we need to hang out with some other committed couples," Ally said. "Sara doesn't know any lesbian couples, and most of my friends are terminally single, so you and Jamie are our role models."

Ryan laughed softly, saying, "Those are some big shoes to fill, pal."

"You've got big feet," Ally teased. "And I should know. I've nibbled on those tasty toes many times."

"Yes, you have," Ryan said, chuckling. "And you were darned good at it."

Ally looked at her for a long minute, stroking Ryan's cheek with the tips of her fingers. "That's not enough, is it?"

"No," Ryan said softly. "It's not nearly enough. I used to think it was."

"So did I," Ally said, giving Ryan a wistful nod. "You know, I've been thinking about this a lot lately, and I think it would have been different between you and me if we'd been friends before we became lovers. I got into the same old patterns with you that I always fell into, and I never had the nerve to try to change them. Going slow with Sara has made a very big difference."

"I don't think either of us was mature enough to go slow back then. I know I wasn't."

"Yeah," she said, smiling. "I was newly sober, and the last thing I could have done is been truly vulnerable. I'm finally ready to let someone know me deep inside. And boy, that makes all the difference."

"It does. So, why don't we get back to those women we love," Ryan said, smiling warmly at her friend.

"A fine idea." Wrapping an arm around Ryan's neck, Ally gave her a hug. "Who would have thought that the two of us would both fall in love within a year?"

"Not me," Ryan said, laughing softly. "But I'm sure glad we did."

❧

"Hey," Ryan said, sinking to the floor beside her partner.

"My beer had better not be warm," Jamie said, taking the frosty brew from Ryan. "Are you avoiding me, sweet cheeks? Every time you leave, you're gone for a half hour."

"Never," Ryan said, giving her a kiss. "As a matter of fact, I plan on being within an inch or two of you for the rest of the evening."

Seeing the slightly hazy look in the pale, blue eyes, Jamie kissed her partner gently and asked, "Are you a little tipsy?"

Holding her thumb and index finger an inch apart, Ryan nodded, giving Jamie a slightly goofy grin. "It's hot in here," she said. "I have to keep drinking to stay cool."

"Shoulda worn your shorts," Jamie teased. "You're way overdressed."

"I thought jeans and a knit shirt was about right for a forty-five degree night," Ryan said, shaking her head. "I should put all of my long pants away until spring."

"You," Jamie said, tapping her partner's nose, "are a goofball."

"Yeah, but I'm your goofball, and you're stuck with me." Ryan tucked her arms around her lover and pulled her close. Several slow, sexy kisses later, Ryan let a sweet, languid smile settle on her lips.

"I think you're more than a little tipsy. How many beers have you had, baby? I can't even smell pizza on your breath. You're all hops and malt and barley."

With her mouth forming a little pout, Ryan asked, "Bad?"

"No, not at all. I just need to drink a little more to keep up."

Nuzzling her nose into her partner's neck, Ryan murmured, "You're such a good egg."

Jamie took a little nibble on a nearby earlobe. "Do you know that you lapse into your Irish accent when you're a little drunk?"

"I don't!" Ryan declared, sounding like a lass straight out of County Mayo.

"Oh, but you do," Jamie said, her own accent sounding much more English than Irish.

With a slightly lopsided grin, Ryan asked, "Do you like it, then?"

"Umm-hmm…very sexy."

"Well, not to brag, but we do have a certain charm with the ladies." She pulled back and focused her attention on Jamie's clothing. "Have I told you how juicy you look tonight, love?"

"Juicy?"

"Pretty," Ryan said. "I don't know what you call this little design on your jeans, but it's adorable. And the shirt looks so nice with them. It's almost a hippie look—very sixties."

Looking down at herself, Jamie said, "Yeah, I guess it is. The design is called batik, by the way. It's an Indian look, and that was pretty popular in the sixties. I bought it because I like the eyelet design down at the hem."

"I like this part," Ryan said, tracing the deep v-neck of the collarless shirt with the tip of her finger. "Just another inch and I could reach your bra."

"Go ahead," Jamie said, giggling softly. "I think I'm the only woman here who hasn't been felt up yet. I'm feeling like a real wallflower."

"Told you my friends are a little wild," Ryan said. "And they get a lot wilder when they're drunk."

"This is very frat partyish," Jamie decided. "I went to a few Stanford frat parties with Mia when we were in high school, and I was more than a little shocked."

"Are you shocked tonight?" Ryan asked, her finger dipping a little lower into Jamie's cleavage.

Jamie took her partner's hand and pushed it further into her blouse. "Not really," she purred, smiling at Ryan's wide eyes. "I'm a big girl, now."

"Mmm...here's one part that's exactly the right size," Ryan insisted, raking a fingernail along each crescent-shaped curve below Jamie's breasts. "Perfect."

"When you say that with your little accent, it sounds like pearfect," Jamie said. "It's terribly cute."

"Give us a kiss, then, will ya?"

"With pleasure, my wild, Irish rose."

"You can search everywhere, but none can compare..." Ryan sang softly before she took her partner in her arms and kissed her passionately. Before she knew what had happened, they were lying on the floor, enmeshed in each other's arms.

The hosts of the party had declared that the third floor was now the dance floor, and the pair barely avoided being hit with a couch as the guests busily moved all of the furniture to the walls to make some room. "Uhm...honey... we're about to get trampled."

"No matter," Ryan said, sucking lustily on Jamie's tender neck.

"Yes, honey, it matters. We're lying on the dance floor."

"They can go around."

Pushing against Ryan's chest with both hands, Jamie managed to extricate herself from her partner's feverish embrace. "Up. Now." Jamie got to her knees, then stood and offered Ryan a hand. "You need to cool off, hot stuff. Let's go outside for a bit."

"Huh-unh," Ryan said. "Let's dance."

"You're steaming hot—in every way. Won't you get overheated?"

"Not if I strip down a little."

"Uhm...what did you have in mind? I concede that most of the people here have seen you in your undies, but..."

"Just my shirt," Ryan said, wrinkling her nose. "I've got a tank top on under it." She tugged off her shirt, then ran her fingers through her hair. "Ready?"

"Mmm...you look fantastic in that," Jamie said, her eyes bright with interest. "Maybe we should find a quiet corner and do what our friends are doing."

Ryan looked around and saw Mia sitting on Jordan's lap; and Sara in the same position with Ally. Both couples were kissing passionately, and Ryan shrugged her shoulders as she turned back to Jamie. "I'm always up for that, but I'm not the most disciplined woman in the world tonight..."

"Mmm...good point. Let's dance a little and then go home. We can skip the foreplay," she said, giving Ryan a lusty wink.

Winding their way through the crowd, they found a relatively spacious spot near the kitchen, and started to dance. They'd each taken their beers with them, and Ryan continued to take generous sips from hers as they moved to the quick beat of the music. By the time the first slow number came on, both beers were empty, and she tossed them into the recycle bin in the kitchen. At Ryan's quizzical look, Jamie shook her head, so Ryan grabbed a fresh one for herself.

"Aisling and I used to call a set of slow songs the erection section," Ryan said, pulling her partner so close that Jamie's thigh slipped between the long legs.

"I can easily give you an erection." Jamie wrapped an arm around her, and took the ice cold beer from Ryan's hand. With a mischievous grin, she pressed the cold bottle right against the small of Ryan's bare back, making her jump in surprise. "Damn, that's cold!" She waited a moment, then said, "But it feels great." While they moved to the slow beat, Jamie ran the cold, sweating bottle across Ryan's shoulder blades, bronzed skin pebbling from the sensation. "Grrrrr..." Ryan murmured, her hips moving against her partner. "I love it when you tease me."

Moving a few inches away, Jamie took the bottle and slid it across Ryan's bare belly—the black, cropped, tank top exposing a surfeit of skin. Ryan shivered, and Jamie slowly ran the mouth of the bottle up along each rib, then flicked it against the remarkably rigid nipples. As Ryan shivered and squirmed, Jamie pressed the side of the bottle against first one, and then the other rock hard nub. "Mmm...that had a decidedly frigorific effect."

Blue eyes narrowed, and Ryan's nostrils flared. "If I had a dictionary, I couldn't turn the pages 'cause my hands are shaking so badly. You're gonna have to give me that one."

"Chilling effect," Jamie said. "Your nipples look like they've been in that tub of ice."

Blinking slowly, Ryan promised, "In about two minutes, we're gonna be back in that bedroom. I'm about to explode."

"Hmm?" Jamie drawled, moving the bottle again and sliding it under

Ryan's hair to chill the back of her neck. "Why's that?" With a devilish grin, Jamie slipped the bottle into the waistband of Ryan's jeans, then kept going when her path to bare skin was unencumbered. "Mmm...commando."

"Yeah," Ryan gasped. "These jeans are a little big and I didn't want my drawers sticking out of the top."

"Tonight I'm glad they're loose," Jamie said, pushing the bottle until it started to make a forward turn.

"Jesus!"

"Like that?" Jamie husked.

"Ye...yeah!" Ryan said, shivering all over. "Just don't make a mistake and lose it!"

"Ooh...I bet you have a place that I could easily insert this...given how those hips are grinding." She pulled the bottle from the back of the jeans, then immediately slipped it down Ryan's belly, watching it disappear beneath the faded denim.

Ryan's eyes grew comically wide while her legs instinctively spread, the bottle sliding down her thigh. "I...I...don't...I'm not sure..."

Chuckling evilly, Jamie said, "I'm teasing you, baby. You know I'd never risk hurting you."

"I'm not...I'm not tracking very well," Ryan admitted. "I'm half crazy for you tonight, and the drunk part of me wouldn't mind giving that bottle a try."

"I'm not nearly that drunk," Jamie said. "And no matter how turned on I was, I would never, ever put anything breakable anywhere near your girl parts."

"Thank God I'm marrying a moderate woman," Ryan sighed, resting her head on Jamie's shoulder as the bottle slid back up her belly.

"I've gotta admit that it's hard to stay grounded tonight. The estrogen is flowing through here like a river," Jamie said, "and there's enough smoke to get us all stoned."

"I'm stoned on your estrogen. Your pheromones are about to drive me mad."

"Show me," Jamie purred. "Right now."

Suddenly, Ryan fought through her fog to recognize an altitude change. Blinking, she found herself sitting in a chair in a dark corner of the room, with Jamie ensconced upon her lap, kissing her energetically. Fully giving in to the experience, she let her senses open up again and allowed Jamie to explore her body to her heart's content.

They touched each other unabashedly, kissing and moving against each other with alacrity. When Jamie's hands claimed her breasts, Ryan held on for as long as she could, finally pulling away enough to mutter, "Bedroom.

Now."

Panting, Jamie sat up and stared at her partner, her eyes glassy with desire. "God! What am I doing?"

"You're making love to me," Ryan answered thickly, looking perfectly happy with the development. "I just don't wanna to take my pants off in the living room."

"Oh, lord!" Jamie collapsed against her partner, groaning, "You make me lose my mind!"

"Who needs a mind when you have a perfectly functioning libido? Let's pull up our socks and claim that bedroom." She patted her partner on the butt, urging her to get moving.

"I don't think adults make love on top of a bunch of coats at a party," Jamie said, pushing her sweat-dampened hair from her face.

"We can throw the coats on the floor," Ryan suggested, looking hopeful.

"Wouldn't you rather go home and make love nice and slow and unhurriedly?" Jamie asked, licking all around the pink shell of Ryan's ear as she spoke. "And then, do it all over again, and again, until we collapse? Doesn't that sound better?"

"Mmm…that does sound nice," Ryan admitted. "And if we go into that bedroom and let a little pressure off first, I'm all for it."

"Make you a deal," Jamie said, smiling fondly at her over-excited lover, "I'll call a cab to get us home faster."

Ryan kissed her hungrily, nipping at her bottom lip with lascivious intent. "Charter a helicopter, and you're on."

"Ooo…I know you're serious when you're ready to spend that kind of money."

Slowly, Ryan stretched, taking in a deep, cleansing breath. "You've got me talkin' crazy," she said, smiling. "The thought of spending money snapped me right out of my lust-filled haze."

"I had a feeling that would do it," Jamie said, giggling. "Now, let's say goodbye to our friends, collect our roomies, and head home."

"Well, our roomies disappeared down the hall while we were dancing. They either went out the back door, or they had the sense to claim one of the bedrooms. And our friends are about to combust over there. If there's a spare bedroom, it's not gonna be available for long."

Twinkling green eyes looked Ryan up and down, then Jamie's voice dropped into a sexy register as she said, "Let's head home so I can get you into bed."

"We can't leave Mia and Jordan, honey. I know Mia's not able to drive, and God knows what shape Jordan's in."

"Let's put a note on Mia's purse, and take her keys so she can't drive. I'll tell her where we hide the spare key to the front door. We only have to say goodbye to Sara and Ally and the rest of your friends."

"If you think I'm gonna interrupt Ally and Sara—you've lost your mind!" Ryan said, bursting out in a laugh. "And no one else in this shower of savages will notice we've gone."

"Good point," Jamie said. She slid off Ryan's lap and pulled her to her feet. "I'll find our coats—you leave the note and get your shirt."

"Deal."

They went about their assigned tasks, and met up at the door. Ryan had put her shirt back on, and as they walked along they both began to chill. Jamie cuddled up to her partner, and Ryan tucked her arm around her waist to share her warmth. "Boy, this is one way to sober up! It must be thirty degrees!"

"Maybe we should have called that cab," Jamie said.

"Nah. I really am a little fluthered, and being outside for a while will sober me up."

"Yeah, thinking about consenting to have a beer bottle inserted in a sensitive spot is about as drunk as I've ever seen you," Jamie said, chuckling wryly.

"I swear, it was estrogen poisoning," Ryan said. "It's impossible to be around all of those writhing bodies and keep your cool."

"Well, I'm plenty cool now, and you must be freezing!"

"No, not yet, but we've got another eight blocks to go. Give me time."

By the time they reached the house, Ryan was shivering all over, and this time it wasn't from arousal. "Go on downstairs," she said, teeth chattering. "I'm gonna get something to drink."

Expecting her partner to arrive with a cup of hot tea, Jamie was puzzled to see Ryan gulping down an enormous glass of Gatorade. "You can't be thirsty."

"No, of course not," she said, shaking her head. "But if I force some of this down it'll help me not have a hangover."

"How's that?"

"Well, drinking as much as I did will make me get up to pee, and every time I do I'll drink another glass of this. By the time I get up I'll be hydrated—and since a hangover is usually because of dehydration, I shouldn't have a problem."

"You've got too much experience with this," Jamie said. "Are you sure I'm the one who should watch her drinking?"

"I'm sure I don't want to spend much more time talking about the issue," Ryan said, stripping out of her clothes. "Remind me of this conversation tomorrow, when I'm completely lucid, okay?"

"Deal. Now hop in bed and I'll warm you up."

"Mmm…shower first," Ryan decided. "I'm all sweaty."

"I'll wait for you," Jamie promised. "Don't take too long."

After a very quick shower, Ryan dashed across the floor and dove for the covers, crying, "I'm perishing!" She rolled up in a little ball while Jamie rubbed every part of her body vigorously—trying to get her blood moving. "Okay, I'm warm now," Ryan said, as her dark head popped out of the bedding. "I'm also pretty sober," she said.

"Good. I want you to be aware of everything I do to you tonight. I want your senses heightened—not dulled."

"They're getting there." She scooted up and sat against the headboard, propping herself up with a couple of pillows. "I uhm…realized a couple of things tonight, babe, and I think I should share them with you. There's a good chance they wont stick with me," she added, giving her partner a slow smile.

"I'm all ears," Jamie said, cuddling up to her lover's side. "Well, I'm all ears and sex drive, but the libido can wait for a few. You know I don't mind simmering a bit."

"That makes one of us," Ryan said, grinning. "Luckily, I've cooled down a little, so I can think straight."

"I like that T-shirt you have that says 'I can't even think straight.'"

"That is a good one. Did you have a good time tonight?"

"You know, I did. It was very…different…but I liked it. I like feeling like one of the big girls. How about you? Did you have fun?"

"Yeah, very much so," Ryan said, nodding thoughtfully. "I like seeing my old friends and thinking about the past. I almost always learn something from these experiences—it's very worthwhile for me."

"What did you learn tonight?" Jamie asked.

"Uhm…I guess what struck me tonight was how much I've changed in the last year. Before, I would have noticed every woman who came in the door, and within an hour I would have been trying to make a move. But now, I hardly notice anyone in that way, and I don't get a sexual vibe from anyone but you. Some of them might be sending a vibe my way, but I don't pick it up anymore. It's like I have a vibe-shield," she said, chuckling softly.

"You need one," Jamie said, giving her lover a tickle.

"No, not really. When I was sitting in the corner with Mia, I couldn't help watching you. Everything about you attracts me. Your body, your personality, your mind, your heart—there are so many layers of attraction that I couldn't even begin to tell you which is the most powerful. That's never happened to me before."

Jamie looked into Ryan's eyes, seeing that the hazy look was nearly gone. She lifted her hand and traced her lover's strong features with her thumb, making Ryan close her eyes in reaction. "Never?" Jamie asked, a slight hesitation in her voice.

Pulling back, Ryan looked at her, gazing deeply into her eyes. "Never."

"Not even with…"

Ryan bent to kiss her, lingering a good, long while, letting the intensity of their bond flow between them. "Never," she repeated, her eyes bright with conviction. "It's taken me a while," she said, "longer than I would have liked, but something became clear to me tonight."

Jamie cocked her head in question, and Ryan couldn't help but give her another kiss, just because of how cute the gesture was.

"Most of the women I've been with have appealed to one part of me," she said. "They turned me on because of their bodies, or their senses of humor, or their energetic personalities. I knew that there was nothing else there—it was only sexual chemistry. But there was more to it with both Sara and Ally," she said, and Jamie nodded in confirmation. "With Sara, I cared for her and loved her as well as a seventeen-year-old can love. But I was still a child then, and part of my attraction to her was childish. It was as real and as important as it could be at the time—but it was immature. I was immature, and so was she. We're women now, and we're both able to love as women. I'm ready to put my feelings for her where they belong—with my fondest memories. She'll always be my first love—but she'll never be my great love. That place is reserved for you, and you alone."

Jamie pulled her partner's head down and bestowed a kiss that made Ryan offer up a sincere 'thank you' to her creator for having been born. The sensations were overpowering, and seemed to assault each of Ryan's senses in sequence. Jamie's clean, fresh scent tickled her nose, while her lover's strong, determined hands ran up and down the muscles in her back. Soft, firm breasts pressed against Ryan's, her nipples growing hard once again. A warm, wet tongue gently explored every surface of Ryan's mouth, Jamie's sweet breath merging with her own.

"God, I love you," Ryan sighed. "You do more to me with a kiss than any other woman ever has."

Jamie settled back down and looked at Ryan carefully. "Any woman?"

Ryan nodded, looking a little confused.

"What about Ally?"

"Oh." Ryan nodded, and collected her thoughts. "I can see why you'd think that she had that effect on me. Mmm…not to denigrate my relationship with Ally, but I didn't feel nearly as close to her as I did to Sara. I think my feelings for Ally were mostly gone already."

"Really?"

"Yeah. I think so. I think what's bothered me lately is having the two of them together. It's like my feelings for each of them were magnified when I saw them. But, if I'm completely honest, I have to admit that what Ally and I had was barely a relationship. We had fun together in bed, and I liked her a lot, but that's not enough for a solid foundation. I think my attraction to her was partially because she wasn't attainable," she admitted.

"Huh. I guess that makes sense," Jamie said. "Do you honestly think you'll feel differently about them from now on? I hate to see you struggling with your discomfort."

"Yeah, I know I'll feel better about them. I mean, I didn't go out of my way to watch them make out, but I didn't feel like I had to avoid them once I got this settled in my head."

"I think they're usually pretty well behaved in public," Jamie said. "But Sara has been out of town for a few days, and they had some excess energy to burn off."

"They did a good job," Ryan said, chuckling.

"You're really okay with it?" Jamie asked once again. "It wasn't hard to see Ally all over her?"

"Well, I didn't spend a lot of time with them, but I caught a look when we were dancing." She looked at Jamie and cocked her head. "Wanna hear an embarrassing admission?"

"Sure. Hit me."

"Seeing them together that way has completely ruined Sara's allure."

"Huh? Why?"

"'Cause the thing that most attracted me to Sara was her purity, her innocence. When I fell in love with her, she'd never been kissed, or touched by another person. She was mine—alone," Ryan said softly. "I fantasized about her for years since then, Jamie, and in my mind, she was always that way—it was like having sex for the first time, every time I dreamt about her."

"That would be compelling," Jamie agreed.

"Well, I don't fantasize about her any longer—let me make that perfectly clear," she said, smiling softly. "But when I think of her, I think of her as she was when she was eighteen. I've been having a hard time seeing her as the woman she is now. I've been locked in the past—and that's never a good thing."

"But we've been with her quite a few times this year, babe. What happened tonight to change your view?"

A slow, warm smile settled on Ryan's face. "I think I've had the fantasy that Ally was the one pushing the relationship along. I think I've been feeling protective of Sara—like I subconsciously wanted to guard her innocence, but I didn't know how. Seeing them together drove me a little crazy, probably because I felt powerless."

"Okay, I think I can understand that. But my question remains, sweetie. What happened tonight?"

"I don't know if you saw this," Ryan said, "but when we were dancing, Sara climbed onto Ally's lap, straddling her."

"Oh-oh," Jamie said, her eyes widening. "She didn't have a stitch on under that cute little kilt she was wearing."

Ryan's head cocked, and she gave her lover a calm, but questioning look.

"I couldn't help it!" Jamie insisted. "I was on the floor—at the perfect height. I wasn't trying to look, but Sara crossed her legs at one point and..." She shrugged, blushing a little.

"Well, that makes the scene even more interesting," Ryan chuckled. "They were making out like mad, and Ally's hands disappeared under that tiny skirt. Sara's hips started to twitch, and it looked like they were gonna go for it." She smiled and said, "That's why I moved over near the wall when we were dancing. There was no way I was going to watch Ally..." She rolled her eyes and said, "The bottom line is that once you've been with Ally, you don't have a pure molecule left in your body. The spell has been broken, baby. Sara's a woman now—someone else's woman. I've got my own, and I'm very, very happy that things worked out like they did."

"I am, too," Jamie said, leaning in to kiss her again.

"And I'm doubly happy that I have a lover who gives me the space to figure these things out for myself. If you'd forbidden me from seeing either of them, I might have always had a little doubt."

"Huh," Jamie said, thoughtfully. "I guess that might have happened. Luckily for you, I'm not the jealous type."

"I'm lucky in so many ways," Ryan said, sighing deeply and tucking her arms even tighter around her partner. "I think I learned a lot tonight, honey. And one of the biggest lessons is something that I'm just now beginning to understand." She shook her head, her brow furrowing. "I've always known that I'd be able to be faithful once I fell in love. Honestly, that's never been a concern. I know how important it is, and I was brought up believing that being true to your spouse was absolutely vital."

Jamie nodded, knowing that Martin would have made that message come through loud and clear.

"But, I've always thought that having to give up sex with other women was a trade-off. Do you know what I mean?"

"Mmm...I'm not sure."

"Well, I knew that being faithful would ensure that I'd get love, and security, and commitment, and intimacy. But I thought I'd miss the variety and the thrill of the chase."

Giving Ryan an adorably hopeful look, Jamie asked, "And that hasn't been true?"

"No! Not in the least," Ryan insisted. "Monogamy isn't something that I have to endure in order to have a good relationship. It's something I freely and lovingly choose. It's what I want…it's what I need." She looked down at Jamie and gave her a warm, sexy smile, then reached out and touched her chest with her index finger, letting out a long, slow hiss. "Monogamy is sizzling hot."

The End

By Susan X Meagher

Novels
Arbor Vitae
All That Matters
Cherry Grove
Girl Meets Girl
The Lies That Bind
The Legacy
Doublecrossed
Smooth Sailing
How To Wrangle a Woman
Almost Heaven

Serial Novel
I Found My Heart In San Francisco
Awakenings
Beginnings
Coalescence
Disclosures
Entwined
Fidelity
Getaway
Honesty
Intentions
Journeys
Karma
Lifeline
Monogamy

Anthologies
Undercover Tales
Outsiders

To purchase these books go to
www.briskpress.com

To find out more visit Susan's website at
www.susanxmeagher.com

You'll find information about all of her books, events she'll be
attending and links to groups she participates in.

All of Susan's books are available in paperback and various e-book
formats at www.briskpress.com

Follow Susan on Facebook.
www.facebook.com/susamxmeagher